HEROES OF
EARTH

ALSO BY MARTIN BERMAN-GORVINE

Seven Against Mars
Save the Dragons

HEROES OF EARTH

TO THE PERSON SITTING IN DARKNESS

MARTIN BERMAN-GORVINE

WILDSIDE PRESS

For Christian, Kamryn and the hundreds of other children who have to live in the D.C. General homeless shelter in Washington, D.C., and other Persons Sitting in Darkness.

Published by Wildside Press LLC.
www.wildsidebooks.com

I'm the hero of this story—don't need to be saved.

—Regina Spektor, "Hero"

Shall we go on conferring our Civilization upon the peoples that sit in darkness, or shall we give those poor things a rest? Shall we bang right ahead in our old-time, loud, pious way, and commit the new century to the game; or shall we sober up and sit down and think it over first?

—Mark Twain, "To the Person Sitting in Darkness," 1901

Half-truths are more dangerous—and enduring—than are lies.

—John Lukacs

1

The door to the school library burst open, and a boy ran in, his eyes wide with terror. Voices called after him, the voices of other boys pitched high in falsetto.

"Hey Gross-fart, where you running to?"

"Hey Gross-fart, try not to stink up the library too much! Other people need to use the n-readers, you know!"

A woman stepped out from behind the counter in a swish of long skirts. She walked over to the door and stopped, her arms folded over a deep purple blouse, a patchwork quilt of a skirt, and high but ill-matched boots.

"Is there a problem, boys?" Skittering footsteps and mocking laughter answered her. She shut the door, shook her head, and turned to the boy who had run in.

He stared at her. "Th-thanks for scaring Matt and Jared off, but who are you, and where is Mrs. Wilkes?"

"She retired over Thanksgiving. I'm the new school librarian, Gloria," the woman said, extending her hand.

"Umm, hello, I guess, Miss Gloria," the boy said. "I'm Arnold—Grossbard." He said his last name hesitantly, and Gloria thought he must be waiting to see if she would laugh at it. When she didn't he slowly reached out his hand to take hers, but suddenly jerked it away. "Hey—you're hot! I mean, your hand, your hand is hot!" He stared at her as she smoothed her long red hair down around her ears. "Hey, what's the matter with your ears?" he asked. "How come they're pointy on top?"

Gloria smiled. "I'm glad to meet you, Arnold. You're the first person I've seen here who didn't come into the library just to use the neural readers." She motioned with her head toward two bulky gray machines mounted in carrels. To use one you sat in a bright orange Naugahyde® easy chair and attached electrodes to your temples. Then you more or less became a part of the furniture yourself. Gloria thought the people using the n-readers looked dead, curled up in a fetal position or sprawled all over the chairs with their eyes shut and their mouths wide open. Nevertheless the carrels were always occupied, and there was always a waiting list. There were two users now, a girl and a boy of about fifteen, probably the same age, Gloria thought, as Arnold himself. She noticed the way Arnold's gaze lingered on the girl's legs, which poked out from a red cheerleader's skirt. One of her shoes had fallen off.

"I'm not allowed on the n-readers," Arnold said, turning his attention back to Gloria and wrinkling his nose as if he smelled something bad. "Not since Mom got so sick from the Net. Though that happened back home—I mean, when we lived in Pikesville."

"You're not a 'from-here,' then." Gloria was still smiling.

"Me? Born on Chincoteague Island? Never in a million years. Not like Bill Cherricks and Hailee Pruitt, here." He gestured at the n-reader users. "Pikesville is near Baltimore, Miss Gloria," he added.

"Just Gloria, dear," the new librarian said, but Arnold wasn't looking at her. He was looking around the room, wide-eyed.

"Do you like how I've changed things?" Gloria asked.

"Where did you get those wooden shelves? Did you pay for them yourself?" Arnold replied. Gloria smiled and dipped her head, without answering. "And what's that hanging plant?" he added.

"It's called a spider plant," Gloria said. "You can re-pot those little clusters of leaves hanging over the sides and they grow into whole new plants."

"That's neat, I guess," Arnold mumbled, looking at the floor. The black-and-white tile pattern down there *was* pretty, as Gloria had found out herself once she'd ripped out the musty pea-green carpet that covered it, but Arnold obviously wasn't admiring the pattern. The tips of his ears were red. *How to get through to him*, she wondered, *past that awful shyness*?

Gloria had an idea how. "Well, now that you're here, Arnold, would you like to browse the new books I've brought?"

"Why did you move everything around?" Arnold asked, walking among the new wooden shelves. The old shelves had been horrible gray aluminum. *How could a kid ever daydream among them*? Gloria followed him.

"I like it better this way," she said.

"It seems you don't like the Dewey Decimal System, though," Arnold said.

"I never could figure it out."

She had science books mixed in with fiction and history. Sometimes she liked to group them by author. For instance, there was Rachel Zilber, who had written both a science fiction novel about a swashbuckling hero called Zap-Gun Jack Flash and beside it a nonfiction book about the geology of Mars. But she also felt, for reasons of her own, that an atlas of the currently nonexistent country of Khazaria belonged next to Charles

Dickens's *The Mystery of Edwin Drood*, which in some versions of history he had died before completing.

Arnold jumped. "Don't creep up on me like that!"

"Sorry," Gloria said, pursing her lips.

Arnold pulled the book he had been looking at off the shelf and held it out to Gloria. "I though Mark Twain was banned? Like, not just from school libraries, but from all libraries?"

"Really?" said Gloria, wide-eyed.

"My Dad has lots of his books anyway, up in the attic," Arnold said.

Gloria smiled more broadly. She had just known there was something she liked about this kid, the moment he ran in the door.

"But I never heard of this one," he added. Then he seemed to forget all about her, as he sat cross-legged on the floor, propped his chin in his right hand and started flipping through *Letters to a Woman Sitting in Darkness*. After a few minutes he looked up, his eyes narrowed. "Hey! This isn't a funny story like I expected!"

"Really?"

"Well, parts of it are funny in a sick way. But all this stuff that Private Sam Shipman is writing to his girlfriend Daisy back home about what the American Army is doing in the Philippines, back in 1902? Killing all those women and children? That not what the history textbook we use in Miss Kelley's class says."

"What does it say, Arnold?"

Arnold shut his eyes and recited from memory. "The Spanish-American War broke out when a feeble, declining Spain met the surging power of the New World. The new harmony that America imposed from Puerto Rico to the Philippines was like a faint foretaste of the greater, Cosmic Harmony to come later in the century, when the High Ones came from the stars, bringing peace to the whole world."

Gloria was impressed. "What do you think about that, Arnold?"

He shrugged. "It's just boring. No one else in class pays much attention to that stuff. But Dad says it's propaganda, and it makes him really mad." Arnold looked back down at the book, flipping through it from front to back, then more slowly, from back to front. "Hey, this is weird!" he exclaimed, pointing at the Author's Note.

"What is, dear?"

"It says here that Mark Twain meant for the book to be published 'only after my death, if ever, out of an excess of cowardice on my part. Frankly, I was afraid for my earnings. But then a certain enchanting flame-haired lady convinced me that I must not withhold my thoughts any longer, and so I dedicate this work to Gloria.' That's your name, and you have red hair!"

"That *is* a strange coincidence, dear," said Gloria, who knew perfectly well that it was not.

Arnold flipped back a bit further, to the title page. Then he whipped his head around and stared at Gloria. "Where is it?" he demanded.

"Where is what, dear?"

"Don't make like you don't know. Where's the sticker? The Society for Common Decency sticker?"

Gloria pursed her lips again. "You mean the tiny American flag with a pair of hands clasped around the letters SCOD?"

"That's the one! It's stuck to the title page of every school and library book I've ever seen."

"But I'll bet it's not in the books in your Dad's attic."

Arnold's whole body trembled. It was a little scary for Gloria to see, especially because he was as tall as she was.

"You're trying to get me in trouble!" he shouted. "It won't work! I'll, I'll tell the principal, Mr. Wright, on you!" He pushed past her and pounded out of the library, past the slumped-over forms of Hailee and Bill, just as the bell rang.

Gloria smiled to herself and hummed a little tune as she put the offending Mark Twain book in a cubbyhole below the counter. She walked toward the back, her boot heels clacking on the tiles, until she turned a dim corner and disappeared from sight. There was a scraping noise, followed by a thump. A few moments later an orange tabby cat with strangely curved ears came trotting briskly out, just as Hailee and then Bill yawned and stretched.

The girl brushed the blond hair out of her eyes, smiling when she saw the cat. "Here, kitty kitty! Such a sweet puss! Who let you in here?"

"Yeah, who?" Bill grumbled, stifling a sneeze. "I'm allergic! Come on, Hailee, let's go, we'll be late for English!"

"Don't worry, Bill, I've got your essay all written for you," Hailee said, taking his arm as they walked out.

The cat leaped up on the counter and yawned widely, showing her sharp teeth. *Nobody naps as well as a cat*, she thought happily as she settled in. It was true what she'd told Arnold about his being the only person to come to the library for any reason other than using the n-readers, so the counter promised to be a good place for a nice long rest. Foreseeing this, Gloria had brought in her favorite comfortable cushion, a wine-colored throw pillow that was a gift from her old friend Teresa in Philadelphia, and put it beside the date due stamp that was gathering dust next to the inkpad. Suitably settled, Gloria (or Tiferet as it said on the tag she wore when she chose to be a cat) dozed away the day.

Not all her dreams were sweet. Luckily everyone was at recess when she started yowling.

* * * *

Quiet returned with the afternoon, a quiet that was hardly broken by the two tenth-grade girls who came in to use the n-readers for their algebra class. Tiferet opened one green eye and watched as they signed their names in the register: Madison Marbury and Kayleigh Scott. Madison had dirty-blond hair and a scattering of acne on the right side of her face, and Kayleigh was a little plump, with chestnut hair and a shrewd twinkle in her eye. They kept on chattering as they applied the electrodes to one another.

"Didja see that spaz Arnold this morning?" Madison said.

"Yeah, he was acting weird even for him," Kayleigh said. "Like something was freaking him out."

"His own face, probably." Both girls laughed, then slumped as suddenly as if they'd been shot.

When the final bell jangled Tiferet looked up, jumped down from the counter, and trotted away into the dim back of the library. A moment later Gloria stepped out, smoothing her long red hair down over the pointy tips of her ears. As she walked up to the counter, first Kayleigh and then Madison yawned, stretched, and rubbed their eyes.

"Shh-kool'sh over already?" Kayleigh slurred. "That shucks. I was really into that massthink. Some of the guys in it were really dreamy."

"I wish they'd let us stay here all day," Madison said as she combed the electrodes out of her hair. "Even when I don't get to see Justin, I always feel like a million bucks after being in the net."

"You mean after 'virtually' making out with Justin," Kayleigh teased as she wiped the last of the electrode-gel off her temples with a tissue.

"Girls, could you hurry up please?" interrupted Miss Fredericks, the music teacher with the long brown hair. "You've already used up five minutes of my time!"

"Me, too!" said the gym teacher, Mr. Lynch, as he shifted his weight from one hairy, bare leg to another.

The girls shouldered their backpacks, giggling, and pushed past Arnold as he came slouching back in, his eyes firmly fixed on the floor. The two teachers had already wired each other up by the time Gloria said hello to Arnold again.

"Hi," Arnold said. "I—I just wanted to tell you I'm sorry."

"Sorry for what, dear?"

"For being so rude to you earlier." He turned around and watched the noisy end-of-the-day crowd in the hallway for a long moment.

"You can close the door if you want," Gloria said. The teachers slumped in their chairs. Mr. Lynch's eyes were half-open, staring at infinity.

Arnold nodded, the wrinkles on his forehead smoothing themselves out after he shut the door. "Thank you. I didn't want anyone listening. Everyone on this island is so nosy." Arnold clenched and relaxed his fists. "It just startled me, seeing a stickerless book like that."

Gloria said nothing.

"I mean, you were right, my dad has, like, *hundreds* of books without stickers in them in the attic, and he made a lock for the trap door himself."

"He must really like to read."

"Do the Assateague ponies like to poop on the dunes? Yeah, he really likes to read. And he doesn't like SCOD or anyone else telling him what to read, either."

"What do *you* like to read, Arnold?"

He acted like he hadn't heard. "I mean, you should be careful, Miss Gloria."

"It's just Gloria, Arnold."

"You should be careful, anyhow. It's not actually against the law for my dad to have all those books, though he'd probably get fired from his job if anyone found out. But if they catch you keeping stickerless books in a school library—"

Gloria smiled. "I know. They'd make me drink hemlock."

"Hemlock?"

"The poison they made Socrates drink for corrupting the youth, dear. I *told* him to watch what he said, but he wouldn't listen."

Arnold smiled uncertainly.

"But you don't need to worry about me," Gloria added. "I don't show those books to everyone."

Arnold thought for a second. "Who *do* you show them to?"

"So far? Just you."

Arnold frowned. "Why me?"

"Because I know you'll appreciate them." She held out the novel Arnold had been looking at. "Here. I saved it for you."

"Gee, thanks."

"No need for thanks, dear. And I have a present for you." She held out the potted spider plant Arnold had noticed earlier. "Just take it straight home and put it where it can get plenty of light all day."

"Thanks," Arnold said again. He touched the leaves and they crossed over themselves primly, like a woman crossing her legs under her skirt.

"You're welcome," Gloria said. "Oh, and please tell your big sister to come in and introduce herself. Alison's her name, right?"

2

While Arnold sneaked out the emergency exit in hopes of avoiding the bullies who had chased him into the library earlier in the day, Alison had to run her own gauntlet walking home from school. She didn't have to worry about the likes of Matt Walters or Jared Nichols lying in wait— they were the ones who should be worrying about her, if they laid a hand on her kid brother again—but she did have to worry about running into Barry Freed. The balding old hippie was tall and stringy and smelly, and somehow he was always in her path even if she took the long way home, around the trailer park.

Home was already in sight when he stepped out suddenly from the alley between the Value-Mart and the Church of Christ. Alison stifled a scream. It wouldn't do to let Barry know she was afraid of him, especially if the rumors were true and he really was an old pervert.

"It's all a lie, you know," he said, his wandering, cloudy right eye seeming to linger where it shouldn't, on her chest, before rolling up to the blank gray sky.

I'm annoyed, not afraid, Alison told herself, and tried to make her voice show it. "Can we talk about this some other time? I have to get home, Mr. Freed."

His good eye focused on her face and began to tear up. "That's what *they* want. For you to go home and do your homework like a good little girl, be an obedient cog in their machine."

Alison had inherited her father's sharp tongue. "A cog can't be obedient, Mr. Freed. It's just a piece of metal."

"And you might as well be just a piece of metal, if you do what they want all the time."‘

"Who are *they*, Mr. Freed?"

Alison regretted asking the question immediately, but it was too late. The old hippie leaned in and breathed sour breath in her face. The stink his clothes gave off showed why all the kids in town called him Barry Peed. "They, them. The President, the FBI, the CIA. J. Edgar Hoover—"

"Is dead, Mr. Freed. A long time ago."

"That's what *they* want you to think." There was no point arguing with him. Not when he still called the High Satrap "the president," which hadn't been his official title in, like, forty years. Dad said that poor Mr. Freed was delusional, which meant there was no talking him out of the crazy stuff he believed in. On the other hand, plenty of people believed crazy stuff, and nobody thought any worse of them as long as they didn't go to the bathroom in their clothes.

He tilted his head back, and Alison clapped her hands over her ears a moment too late—he had already started his infamous imitation of the most famous moment in history. "That's one small step for a man, one giant step for—*what in God's name is that?*" Alison unblocked her ears and tried to edge around Mr. Freed, who was talking in his normal cracked voice. "I mean, does that even sound plausible to you? The government goes to all that trouble and expense to put a man on the moon, and the High Ones choose that very moment to show up and announce their presence to the world?"

"You're spitting, Mr. Freed. And you're not making any sense." Not that that ever stopped him. "They've explained a million times how that was the best way they could be sure of reaching everyone at the same time, since, like, a billion people were watching the moon landing on TV, and what better way to show everyone they were friendly than picking up all three Apollo astronauts and putting them down on the South Lawn of the White House an hour later—"

"Ha!" They were starting to attract an audience. Alison hoped the cops would show up soon. When Mr. Freed got too worked up, a sheriff's deputy usually came to get him and let him sleep it off in a nice warm cell. But no cops were in sight.

"Tell it like it is, Barry!" someone yelled, just to rile him up.

Alison ground her teeth. That was just mean. It was really no better than that rotten Matt picking on Arnold just because he was a brainiac and had a hard time making friends.

"You bet I'll tell it like it is!" The old hippie had jumped up on the Birches' white picket fence, which teetered dangerously beneath his weight. "There ARE no High Ones! It's all a lie! There's no such thing as big blue starfish, or little green men, either! *They* faked the moon landing just to make people think there *could* be aliens, so they'd have an excuse to crush the Movement. Then *they* got everyone hooked on their mind-control devices, which they have the chutzpah to claim are 'neural readers' that are an educational gift from the imaginary aliens!"

That hit a little too close to home. Alison seized the chance to slink away. Her house was just the other side of Maddox Boulevard, the main road to the beaches on Assateague Island. In bleak autumn weather like this, of course, no one was heading out that way, and all the ice cream shops and tourist traps that gave the town a holiday feel in the summer were closed. A lot of the lifelong islanders, the "from-heres," depended on beachgoers for their living but also resented all the noise and crowding they brought. Alison didn't mind the summer crowds at all. When all those people came down from Baltimore and Washington, Chincoteague almost felt like home—her real home back in Pikesville.

Dad had fixed up their new house so it looked a lot like the old one, painted white with green trim. With the money he made at the fusion plant, he could have afforded instead to tear it down and replace it with a new house and a swimming pool in the backyard. But he wanted to keep it, because it was "historic," meaning it was over a hundred years old, with a living room ceiling that bulged downward in the middle as if it was about to collapse, though Dad's engineer buddy Bruce Nomura claimed there was no danger. This would have been more reassuring if Mr. Nomura had been a structural engineer instead of an expert on the High Ones' nuclear fusion technology. If it was so safe, Alison wondered why it was so noisy. Sometimes she'd lie awake at night wondering if there were ghosts making all those creaks and groans, even though at seventeen she was much too old to believe in such things. *Would I be happier if it was a burglar?* she sometimes wondered, by daylight.

Alison let herself in with her key. Dad wouldn't be home for another two hours at least, and it would be dark by then. She set a snack out for Arnold, who was doubtless daydreaming on his way home. Her little brother liked peanut butter sandwiches on whole wheat with sliced banana instead of jelly. She thought that was gross, but it reminded him of when Mom used to make them for him, back before she started spending the whole day in bed with her migraines. Then she tiptoed upstairs to peek into the master bedroom. Sure enough, Mom was lying in bed with the shades pulled and a damp washcloth over her eyes. *Good, she's asleep,* Alison thought, but as she turned to go that familiar cranky voice started up.

"You're not going to watch tri-vee before getting your homework done, are you, Allie?"

"Of course not, Mom."

The graying head turned from side to side but the eyes never opened. Since they'd moved to Chincoteague Mom hadn't found a hairdresser who could get her color right, or so she said, but Alison thought that since she'd gotten so much sicker over the past year she just didn't care what she looked like anymore. And she looked like hell, with her face wrinkling up and her hair going wild as weeds in an untended garden. The darkness she craved could only hide so much, and then there was her B.O. Allie didn't know how Dad could stand it. Basically it sucked having a mother with NINA—Network-Induced Neuronal Atrophy, a disease that struck fewer than one in a million n-net users. It was getting hard to remember what Mom had been like before, when she used to play her guitar and make Dad go out dancing with her. She'd taught Alison to play a little, but the guitar had sat untouched in a corner of the master bedroom ever since they'd moved to Chincoteague. Even if she'd been any good at it, Alison wouldn't have felt right playing it when Mom couldn't.

Since Mom was lying still, the rumpled bedsheets barely rising and falling over her chest, Alison thought she must have fallen back asleep. So she tiptoed out of the room, shutting the door behind her, and back downstairs to the kitchen, where she took some string cheese and diet soda out of the fridge. She ate her snack in front of the tri-vee stage, with the sound turned most of the way down. It wasn't as if she made a mess or anything. She'd get her homework done; she always did even though it was so much harder for her than for everyone else since she couldn't use the n-readers. So she hardly felt guilty at all about disobeying Mom. Anyway, it was practically a social commandment to keep up with "The Spacefarers." Even if the plots were sort of dumb, Donny Schmitz as the captain's son Brad was cute.

The show assembled itself in crisp 3-D above the half-meter-square, slightly raised black panel of the stage. Today's episode involved a water mining run the *UNSS Intrepid* was making out to Ganymede, the biggest of Jupiter's moons. It should've been an easy, two-week cruise, but the saboteur Izzy Goldstein, Captain Adams' nemesis, was plotting to sprinkle arsenic on the pure ice, and Brad and his girlfriend Janey were going to have to stop him. No one in Alison's class of seniors had honey-blond hair and perfect skin like Janey, played by Taylor Fields, though Sydney Birch came close. Alison couldn't claim to be the homecoming queen's friend, or even in an outer orbit, like Jupiter around the sun. Though she felt as big and fat as Jupiter, lately. Dad liked to say she was *zaftig*, an old Yiddish word that meant plump and cuddly. *Thanks a lot, Dad.*

The station logo came on just as the camera was zooming in for a close-up of Donny and Taylor smooching, their life-size faces floating a couple centimeters above the tri-vee stage. "We interrupt this broadcast to bring you an urgent news update." Alison groaned and reached for the remote, but was distracted by Arnold's thumping arrival. He threw his book-bag in the corner and slouched toward the kitchen for his snack. With his face turned away, Alison couldn't tell whether he'd been beaten up again.

"How was school?" she asked. He grunted something. She got up to follow him, did a double-take. "Where'd you get that plant?"

"It's a spider plant."

"Who gave it to you?" The noise of the tri-vee covered his mumbled response. They were saying something about a "terrorist bomb outrage" at the Capitol Building in Washington. Same old junk, but Alison made a mental note to set the clock ten minutes early in the morning, for the extra hassle they were bound to have getting to school.

"Sorry, what?"

"I said, the new librarian gave it to me!"

"Keep your voice down, idiot, Mom's sleeping. What new librarian?"

"Her name is Gloria. She said you should come see her. Can I go now?"

"Well, you don't have to be all sarcastic," Alison said to his back as he plodded upstairs. It was no use. *Why can't I just have a normal kid brother? It's not enough that we're "come-heres" and Jews, he has to be the little weird kid!*

Alison sighed and went back to the living room, turning off the tri-vee just as they were saying how many people had been killed and that the Patriotic Front and the Human Defense League were "issuing competing claims of responsibility." Tri-vee time might be ruined, but she really should use the extra time to get a start on her history term project. Being in the All-Planetary class wasn't as much fun as it had been back in Pikesville, not with the teacher, Miss Burbage, just expecting everyone to spout back at her whatever she told them.

Maybe I've bitten off more than I can chew. Alison gnawed on the eraser end of her pencil as she thought this, a bad habit she'd had as long as she could remember. The pencil had been new that morning, but the metal collar that held the eraser already looked like a shiny wad of used chewing gum. *What possessed me to write about "How the High Ones ended the Cold War"? It'll take me forever.*

Alison wondered if she could trust Arnold to put the tilapia fillets in the oven for dinner if she went to the town library to do some research. He slouched past where she sat at the dining room table with her books and her notes, and grunted when she asked him to get dinner started.

"Can't you keep it down? Mom has a really bad migraine," she said as he started banging around in the kitchen cabinets. "What are you doing up there anyway? The baking pans are down below."

"I need a plate to catch the water."

"The water?"

"For my plant. I have to water it or it'll shrivel up and die. Like I wish you would do."

"*So* witty. Listen, turd-breath, you think your friendly librarian would still be at the school?" The high school was two blocks closer than the town library. Alison figured she could run there in five minutes, spend a quarter hour or so talking to the librarian and checking out books, and still be back in time to make sure Arnold didn't completely wreck supper.

"Search me. She was still there when I left. That's when she gave me the plant."

"You better take good care of that plant. Remember what happened with Peeps?" She'd had to take over the care and feeding of the hamster Arnold got for his eighth birthday. It wasn't that he didn't care about the poor little beast, it was just that he was always too busy daydreaming. Well, this time it was his problem. Alison grabbed her book-bag, took out the binder and textbooks and headed out the door.

The sun was already low over the marshes to the west as she walked. A seagull soared overhead, cawing. When they first moved out here in the dead of winter last year, Alison thought living at the beach year-round sounded cool. But now most of the magic had worn off. She still missed her friends and the fun she used to have in Baltimore. It was true that the Wallops Island Interplanetary Base and the fusion plant drew people from all over the world to live and work in the area, but it still felt like a hick town to her. And Arnold was having a really rough time of it—not that things had ever been easy for him, even back home in Pikesville.

The high school was deserted as dusk closed in, but Alison saw a light was still on in the library, which had a separate emergency door. She frowned a little when she pushed and found it open—with all the yelling they did about security, how could they just leave an outside door unlocked?

"Hello?" she called as she walked in. An orange cat that had been sleeping on the counter mewed and jumped down, padding back among the dimly lit shelves. Seeing no one else around, Alison decided to follow the cat. The books weren't organized on any system she could see, and the selection seemed really strange for a school library. Plus, there didn't seem to be anything on recent history. She was just making her mind up to come back when the librarian was on duty when she saw a flickering shadow out of the corner of her eye.

"Hello?" she called. Between the shelves she saw a gap in the back wall that looked just wide enough to squeeze through.

This is stupid. There's nobody here. I need to get back home. But light was spilling out of the gap, and curiosity won out. This was the building's outer wall, so how could there be a corridor leading further back? Because that's what Alison saw, once she stepped in. A blank corridor, with gray cinderblock walls, a hard-surfaced floor painted a dark red, and a ceiling made of the same kind of acoustic tiles you saw in every classroom. There were no light fixtures that she could see, but the hallway was well lit. It had the familiar, slightly sour smell of school stairwells. There was nothing remarkable about it, except that she should be standing in the middle of Hallie Whealton Smith Drive. And she noticed as she walked that she didn't cast a shadow.

"Hello?" she called again. Her voice sounded oddly flat, as if she was walking outside. There were no doors in the walls, and when she looked over her shoulder she couldn't see where she had entered. Spinning back around she couldn't see an end to the corridor ahead of her, either. She gulped, said a bad word and began to run back the way she had come, but the corridor seemed to stretch on ahead of her endlessly and changelessly, like the exercises in drawing the "vanishing point" her old art teacher Mrs. Blum had made the class do. And then she tripped and went sprawling. The fall on the hard floor should have broken her nose, or at least bloodied it, but she landed squarely atop something warm and furry, which squealed in protest. Then things got really weird.

3

Alison's stomach heaved as her mind tried to make sense of what her eyes had just told her. Everything, including her own body, had turned inside out and exploded, but not really. She thought of a poster of an M.C. Escher painting Mrs. Blum had hanging in her classroom, of a staircase in the air that spiraled around and led nowhere.

Whatever she'd just seen was much stranger than that, but she was definitely *somewhere*. Just not anywhere familiar. And she didn't know the oddly dressed, redheaded woman standing looking at her with a slightly sheepish grin.

"Hello, Alison," she said in a low, rich voice that sounded like music—a cello, maybe, an instrument Mom had also tried and failed to teach her to play. "Sorry for the confusion, but I wasn't expecting you till tomorrow."

"Who are you, and where is this?" Alison said, gesturing at the wooden-floored room filled with high, tall bookshelves.

"I'm Gloria, the new school librarian. Didn't Arnold tell you about me?"

Alison pointed an accusing finger at the woman. "Your library is bigger on the inside than on the outside." She clutched her head, which was starting to ache in time to the beating of her heart, and groaned. "I think I need a doctor."

"You don't need a doctor, dear," Gloria said, stepping closer to her and doing something with her hands in front of Alison's face, too fast for her to see clearly. The headache receded as quickly as it had begun.

"But you haven't answered my question. Where are we?"

"Why, in Chincoteague, of course."

"That's not the point. There's no library or bookstore like this on the island. And I should know, I've been to all of them."

"Well, technically, we're sort of *alongside* Chincoteague. Your version of Chincoteague, that is."

"My *version*? Look, I came here for help finding books for my AP History paper on how the High Ones stopped the Cold War, not to listen to a lot of weird riddles." She paused, and added, half under her breath, "No wonder Arnold likes you."

"I have some history books over here, on this shelf," Gloria said, pointing with a lacquered fingernail. The nail was covered with more than just one color of polish—there was actually an intricate design of some sort on it.

How had this fruitcake ever gotten hired by that humorless old fart of a school superintendent, Mr. Wentworth? Alison remembered with a shudder the grilling she and Arnold had gotten when Dad enrolled them here in January.

"So your dad's a newspaper reporter, eh?" He had pronounced the words as if they were a synonym for terrorist.

"Not anymore," Arnold had said helpfully, while Alison tried unsuccessfully to shush him, "he got fired for writing articles disruptive to the Cosmic Harmony." Arnold was always saying stuff like that. But Mr. Wentworth had had to enroll them both anyway. It was the law.

Well, whatever weird magic this Gloria creature had worked on her, she was here now, and she had the most amazing collection of books Alison had ever seen outside her father's attic. But it didn't take long for her to see there was nothing in the "history" section she could use for her class. The word history needed quotes around it because it wasn't proper history, it was some weird kind of science fiction written straight-faced as if it were fact. In one book World War I had ended early and they still called it the Great War because there was no World War II, so the British and French Empires still existed and America kept mostly to itself, except for bombing the Japanese to smithereens when they tried to take over the Philippines. In another, which was printed on cheap paper like newsprint, the world was still recovering from a nuclear war America and the Soviet Union had fought over Cuba. In a third, America had gotten to Mars in 1976 *all by ourselves, without any help from the High Ones.* Alison gaped as she flipped the pages through gorgeous color photographs of white-suited astronauts walking through a rust-red desert, then flipped back to the title page with a sinking feeling about what she knew would be missing there.

She stood up and shook the book under Gloria's nose. "This doesn't have a SCOD sticker in it."

"Really?"

"Really. I doubt any of these books do. But this one could get you in *real trouble*, you know, for disrupting the Cosmic Harmony."

"I don't see how a wee little book like that could hurt something so grand, do you?"

"Don't give me that! You're as bad as my dad! Which reminds me, I'd better get home and put his supper on the table!" And with that,

Alison shoved the book in her book-bag and ran out the door, ignoring Gloria calling out to her to wait.

She expected to come out on Smith Drive, or maybe on Main Street. But nothing looked familiar. It was a lot darker than she expected, with a crescent moon floating behind a thin screen of clouds high in the sky. The familiar bright orange streetlights were gone, replaced by evenly spaced poles topped by pale, wavering blue flames that danced inside clear glass globes. They reminded her of the gas range they had back home in Pikesville, but since when was natural gas used for streetlights?

Alison began to walk without any idea where she was going. Was she even in Chincoteague anymore? The air smelled right, with the familiar salt tang and the faint sulfurous hint of marsh mud, and she could hear a seagull cawing just like the one that had passed overhead when she was hurrying to the middle school. But it was a lot colder than it had been when she'd left home, and how could that be?

Out of habit she was retracing her steps back home. But how could she be doing that, if these weren't the old familiar streets? The street signs looked different, too, but squinting up at one, which was cream colored with black cursive letters that looked hand-painted, Alison was surprised to find herself at the corner of Poplar Street and Pension Street, less than half a block from the house. But everything looked so different, as in a dream. She scratched her head and set off walking, eyes firmly glued to the sidewalk so she could ignore all the strangeness around her. *If I can just get home, everything will be normal again.* But she felt how ridiculous this thought was even while thinking it, not least because even the sidewalk was strange, being made of weathered wooden boards instead of normal concrete.

Suddenly she bumped right into somebody. "Hey, watch where you're going!" said a familiar voice. Alison looked up and started to stammer an apology, and relief flooded her—it was Shaniqua Thomas, the closest thing to a friend she'd made in this godforsaken town. It had helped break the ice that Shaniqua was black and also in the AP class, both things that made her an outsider even though her family had roots on the Eastern Shore going back three hundred fifty years. Of course, simply by their existence the High Ones had shown people that there was only one human race and we all had a lot more in common with each other than we did with three-meter-tall blue starfish with more useful appendages than a Swiss Army knife, but somehow not everybody had got the message yet.

"Shaniqua, hi! Am I glad to see you! Something really strange is happening and I haven't even got an outline for my history paper yet 'cause I went to the school library to get some books for it but all the freaky new librarian there had was science fiction and did you hear there was another terrorist attack at the Capitol so it'll take, like, *forever* to get into school tomorrow and what are you doing dressed like an American Heritage doll?"

Because she was. Dressed like an American Heritage doll, that is, in a long skirt that looked like it was made from a heavy green curtain, and were those actually white gloves she was wearing? And she was eyeing Alison strangely, and when she opened her mouth she was speaking in a weird accent, familiar Eastern Shore twang crossed with Beatles.

"My name is Sharon, and who are you?" Alison stared at her in shock. Shaniqua hated practical jokes and the people who played them. Her big brother Tavon was always hiding her homework, tying her shoe-laces together, and short-sheeting her bed. So Alison couldn't imagine how she could be playing a prank now. She waited for her to crack a smile, but instead she snorted and stomped away.

This must be a dream. The feeling only strengthened when she walked up to the house and saw that the picket fence was gone, replaced by a high wall of deep green shrubs. Peeking through, she saw that Arnold and Dad had repainted the outside while she was out with her favorite color, turquoise—although that was quite impossible because Dad hated that color.

"Okay, I'm dreaming," Alison said aloud, in as firm a tone as she could muster. "In that case, I'd like to fly now. Oh, and for Donny Schmitz to be flying alongside me and to give me a huge kiss on the lips!" Nothing happened. So it wasn't one of *those* dreams. Something flickered at the edge of her vision and she tilted her head up to look at the moon. There was a huge, dark silhouette flitting in front of it. "Oh, I see, it's *that* kind of dream instead," she said, and began to run and pinch herself at the same time. Pinch, pinch, pinch, ow ow ow, but she failed to wake up in bed. She braced herself for unimaginable pain when the dragon she'd just seen breathed fire all over her. But the only thing that hurt was the cold air roaring into her lungs, and then her knee as she tripped over something and pitched face forward on the impos-sible wooden sidewalk. She rolled around clutching her knee, crying and wishing she would wake up already.

Instead an unfamiliar but ordinary-looking girl about Arnold's age appeared, looking down at her with a tentative half-smile. "Alison? Ali-son Grossbard?"

"That's my name," she said, sitting up and drying her eyes with her coat sleeve. "But how can I be dreaming about you? I've never met you before."

"You're not dreaming," the stranger said, helping her to her feet. She was dressed more normally than Shaniqua had been, in jeans and a jacket. Her dirty blond hair was tied back in a ponytail and she had a friendly, mischievous gleam in her brown eyes.

"My name's Jo Purnell," she said. "Gloria sent me to find you. I had a little help from Ir'befunzu of course."

"Who?"

"The dragon," Jo said matter-of-factly. "Most people call her Ashley, though, and I suppose you can too, if it's easier. She sensed you right away, and she says to tell you that she never barbecues people. Well, hardly ever. Only if they really, really deserve it." They were walking back the way Alison had come, toward Main Street and the site where the high school should be. Instead there was a small, wood-framed building that said "GLORIA'S GATEWAY BOOKS AND RECORDS." That must have been the building Alison had walked out of. But what had happened to the high school? More important, what had happened to Shaniqua, and to her house?

"I can tell you're really confused," Jo said as they walked into the bookstore. A cowbell jangled, and Gloria looked up, a sheepish expression on her face, from the book she was reading. At least Alison recognized this one: Mark Twain's *Life on the Mississippi*, which Dad had a copy of along with the rest of his contraband books in the attic.

"Thanks, Jo," Gloria said. "Alison, are you all right?"

"Apart from a bruised knee, yeah, sure."

"Let me see that." The red-haired lady knelt down, rolled up Alison's pants leg and put a cool cloth on the knee. Alison blinked in astonishment as the ache rapidly faded.

"I always say Gloria is better than any doctor who I've ever met," Jo said.

"That's *whom*, dear," Gloria said. "Any doctor *whom* you've ever met."

Jo folded her arms and scowled. "Now you sound like Mum! I thought it was going to be fun when you came and opened your bookstore here. I don't need four parents!"

"How do you have four parents?" Alison asked.

"Besides Mum and Dad—he's the only real softie—there's Gloria here, and my big brother Tom's girlfriend Teresa. Three mothers constantly scolding and correcting me! I can't take it anymore! Hey, why are you crying? Did I say something wrong?"

"I'm not crying!" Alison said, clenching her fists. *Three mothers! I haven't even got ONE whole mother!* Aloud, she said, "I don't care if you've got a thousand mothers! Just explain to me what the hell is going on here!"

Jo puckered her lips. "Wow, you said a bad word!"

"What, 'hell'?"

"You said it again!"

"Jo, just tell her how she got here," Gloria said.

Jo folded her arms again. "Huh-uh. *You* explain to her how come she's important enough for you to transport her across the dimensions from her world to this one, even though you just met her, while I've known you for ages and you still won't let me visit any of the other worlds!"

The hairs stood up on the back of Alison's neck. "Do you mean to tell me I've traveled to another world, not on a giant spaceship powered by the High Ones' fusion drive, but using… a cat?"

Gloria ducked her head. "I'm not really a cat, dear, though I sometimes look like one. And this is your same old Earth, just with a few details of the past different."

"Yeah, like in your world Ben Franklin wasn't a little weasel who worked out a dirty deal with that slyboots William Pitt so we all still have to bow to a stupid git of a king," Jo said, "and Napoleon Bone-a-Fart got his butt kicked and had to go live on a desert island instead of conquering half the world. On the other hand, we don't have big blue slugs slithering around telling us what to do."

Alison's head was spinning. Luckily there was a comfy chair handy. "You can't say that," she whispered through a tight throat.

"Oh, so what if I insulted the king," Jo said with a dismissive wave of her hand. "They don't even put you in jail for that anymore. Besides, Gloria would never peach on me."

"No, I mean you can't talk about the High Ones that way. You can get in *really* big trouble." *Trouble so big, you might* wish *you were in jail.*

"That's what they call the echinodermoids from Gliese 581d," Gloria told Jo, who clasped her hands together and went down on one knee.

"Oh, please, please, Gloria, let me go back to Alison's world with her. I can't wait to see a real live alien!"

Gloria cleared her throat noisily.

"Apart from you, that is!"

"You're an *alien*?" Alison gasped.

"To me, *you're* the alien," Gloria said nonchalantly. "And I don't come from Gliese 581d. I've never even met a High One in person. That's not what they call themselves, by the way. 'Winged-Thinkers' is a better translation."

"You're both changing the subject," Jo accused. "Which is, how come I can't go visit with Alison in her world?"

"Because it's too dangerous, for now," Gloria said. "The time isn't yet ripe."

"Come on, it's only Chincoteague," Jo whined. Alison thought it sounded funny the way she said it, more like *Jingo Teag*. "Nothing ever happens in Chincoteague in any world, except the annual pony swim."

Gloria shook her head. "No. Not tonight, Jo. I told you I'd think about it, but it's important that Alison and Arnold visit you here first."

Jo flounced over to another easy chair and turned her back to Gloria and Alison.

"Oh, very mature. She and Arnold ought to get along just great," Alison said. "Can you please take me home now? I haven't got any of my homework done, and by now Dad's probably trying to cook dinner himself, and if he sets fire to the house again the Volunteer Fire Department might have to hold *two* pony swims to pay for all the equipment they have to use."

"Your fire department sponsors the pony swims?" Jo said. "That's funny. Here it's the Dragonfire Club. Oh, I forgot. It's dangerous for me to talk to you."

"Just ignore her," Alison suggested to Gloria as they made their way to the back. "That's what I do when Arnold gets into one of his moods."

"I'll bear it in mind, dear. Now, I'd better tell you something before I put you back in your world, because it's rather more difficult to hold a conversation when my cat aspect is showing. You know that weird, long hallway you had to walk down to get here?"

Alison nodded. She didn't think she would ever forget it.

"It's called the Gray Zone. The things you see there aren't exactly real. You might feel a little scared, which is sensible because there are unfriendly presences there. But I'll be watching and I won't let them bother you. All right?" Alison swallowed hard, but nodded. "Good girl. Just keep your head down and try to enjoy the journey, and you'll be home before you know it." Gloria squeezed Alison's hand.

Then everything turned inside out, and Alison found herself holding an orange cat's paw, in a room full of books. She let go, took a deep breath and turned to face the corridor. *I can do this.*

4

It took a while for Arnold to find out about Alison's strange adventure. First they had to help Dad put out the fire he'd started in the kitchen.

For a change, it was Arnold who first noticed what was going on, although that was only because Alison had gone out somewhere. If she'd been home making supper like she was supposed to, Dad wouldn't have had the bright idea of trying to make French fries from scratch.

"This'll be much healthier than McDonald's!" he called out enthusiastically as he banged a frying pan onto the stove and started rummaging around for the cooking oil.

"Uh-huh," said Arnold. He was in his room with the door shut and could barely hear Dad. Who'd have ever thought a spider plant could be so engrossing? Until now, he'd thought that the only plants that moved or did anything interesting were Venus fly-traps. Well, there were Mexican jumping beans too, but those didn't count because they only moved on account of the little worm inside them. He'd got a Venus fly-trap for his eighth birthday, but it never did catch a fly or anything moving, and it closed very sluggishly on the flecks of hamburger meat and tuna fish Arnold fed it.

But this spider plant waved its leaves around as if it were an undersea plant caught in a steady current. Arnold tried poking it with a pencil, and the leaves ducked and then weaved themselves around it.

"Cool!" he murmured. He let go of his end of the pencil, which must have been one of Alison's because the eraser end was all chewed up, and the plant continued to grasp onto it. Then Arnold smelled smoke. "Hey Dad, I think something's burning!" he said.

Mom chimed in from her bedroom. "Jerry, check the stove!"

Dad didn't respond to either of them. Must be absorbed in the newspaper like he was most nights. Arnold tried opening his bedroom door and repeating the warning, but Dad was busy yelling, "Can you believe what they're pulling now! SCOD goons broke up a Bob Dylan concert last night! I mean, a lot of those fans are using walkers!"

"Dad, the stove—"

The front door banged open and Alison came running in. "Not again! Dad!" They had a frenzied couple of minutes, but this time there was no need to call the Fire Department because Alison had bought a fire extinguisher after the last time.

"I'm sorry, sweetheart," Dad said as he grabbed another roll of paper towels to clean up the mess on the stove. "I wanted to give you a break. It's not fair for you to have to make dinner every night."

Shuffling footsteps announced Mom's arrival in the kitchen. "Why don't we go out to House of Siam?" she said with her best attempt at a smile.

"I'll help you get dressed, Ray," Dad said.

Mom knitted her brow. "Why can't I just go as I am?"

Arnold flicked a glance at Alison, who was looking at him. Mom was wearing nothing but a nightgown with little blue cornflowers on it. As recently as September she would have been with it enough to notice that, but now... now Dad took her arm and led her back up their bedroom.

"Do you think she's gonna have to go to a nursing home?" Arnold whispered.

Alison snapped her head back as if he'd slapped her. "No way! Dad will never let that happen!" She blinked several times and shook her finger at him. "Don't even say that word around me, turd-breath!"

Dad came down the stairs clutching Mom's elbow. She was dressed in a baggy maroon sweater and blue jeans, but at least she looked half-way normal.

"Going out on a weeknight! I bet you wish Dad burned dinner more often, don't you?" she joked. Arnold forced a chuckle.

The restaurant was close enough to walk to, but then, so was just about everything in Chincoteague. Mr. Freed spotted them walking from the other side of the street and raised a dirty hand to wave at them.

"How you doing, groovy chick?"

With a small shock Arnold realized he was talking to Mom, who flirted right back. "Just about ready for Woodstock Nation, soon as I get my time machine, Barry." He smiled vaguely and shuffled on his way. "We ought to get takeout for him. That poor man," Mom said softly.

Dad winced. "Maybe we can save him some leftovers, Ray." It was an old argument.

The mood brightened as soon as they got to the place and Dad spotted Mr. Nomura eating by himself and waved him over to join them. The guy was even shorter and older than Dad, but still had shiny black hair. Dad's hair was bushy and starting to go gray at the tips and along his sideburns. Mom liked to joke that it added at least five centimeters to his height and made him "only a short little guy instead of a dwarf."

Dad's friend had been just about done with his meal, but he hung out while everyone ordered their meals and ate. Their loud joking around helped cover how quiet everyone else was.

"You're one good worker drone, Bruce!" Dad said. "I can't believe they let you out of your cell long enough to get dinner!"

"Shuddup, you slacker!" Mr. Nomura said. They both cackled.

Pad Thai was Mom's favorite thing, but she just toyed with her food and even offered Arnold some of the shrimp.

He held up his hand. "They taste like rubber to me, Mom, remember?"

"Oh, of course, it's Alison who likes seafood. Seems like I forget everything these days," Mom rasped.

Dad and Mr. Nomura were still having a grand old time and didn't hear her, or at least they pretended not to, but Arnold looked at his plate, his enjoyment of the meal ruined. *Why can't I have a normal family, like everyone else?*

As they walked home afterwards through the early dark Mom spotted Mr. Freed again, lurking around a leafless tree in the waterside park, and offered him her doggy bag full of barely-touched food. The smelly old hippie tried to pretend he didn't want it but practically snatched the bag out of her hands. Dad opened his mouth only to shut it again when Mom elbowed him.

Arnold hung back, trying not to pay attention, but Sis was hanging back with him. *Why can't she leave me alone? Why can't EVERYONE just leave me alone?* He started to say something sarcastic but Alison talked over him. "Can you keep a secret, Arnold?"

This must be serious, if Sis was calling him by his real name and not turd-breath, stupid-head, nerd-face or one of her other usual terms of endearment. "Umm, sure," he said.

"You're gonna think I'm crazy." With a heroic effort, Arnold managed not to say that he already did and just listened to the wild tale Alison spun. Could any of it possibly be true? It wouldn't exactly be the first time she had pulled his leg. Take the time when he was seven and she was nine and she told him the word "gullible" wasn't in the dictionary. Unlike most kids his age, he knew what the word meant, but to prove her wrong about the dictionary required him to go into Dad's study to get the unabridged dictionary, which was too heavy for him to lift. When he asked Dad for help with it, Dad asked what he needed to look up, and when he told him Arnold discovered that people actually do roll around on the floor laughing. This prank had entered family legend.

So he eyed Alison warily. But she didn't have a good poker face, and there was no trace of a smile on it. Her eyes kept darting back and forth as if she was excited and a little scared, but not as if she was about to enjoy a good laugh at his expense. He studied her face for a long moment, then nodded. But then he scowled and pinched the back of her hand.

"Ow! What was that for?"

"It's no fair!"

"What's no fair, for chrissakes?"

"You always get to do *everything* first! I wanna see that dragon, right now!"

"You're the one who told me Gloria wanted to meet me, turd-breath. Anyhow, you'll have to wait till morning. The school library is closed now."

Arnold was about to say he was telling Dad, but for once his brain caught up with his mouth, and he followed her back into the house in sullen silence. Dad was already helping Mom up the stairs to their bedroom. Last month she'd had to go to the emergency room after she tripped at the top and ended up with a mild concussion.

"What was your buddy doing here in Chincoteague, anyhow?" she was asking Dad. "I thought he lived in those barracks outside the fence, over at Wallops Island."

"Man does not live on ramen noodles alone, Ray," Dad said.

Arnold had been to Mr. Nomura's place once. The barracks had been cut into individual apartments with drywall, but the living room still felt barren even with several Japanese prints on the walls and framed family pictures on the end tables he'd scavenged at a yard sale in Salisbury. After Mr. Nomura beat him in three quick games of chess Arnold lost interest and wandered around daydreaming outside in a grassy square that had obviously been used for morning line-ups when the Navy ran the place. He respected the guy for not treating him like a kid, but it sucked to lose at one of the few things besides school that he was actually good at.

Now Arnold followed his parents up the stairs and shut his bedroom door behind him. Finishing his homework didn't take long. Afterwards he played with the strangely lively spider plant and thought about Gloria. *Could Alison be telling the truth? It seemed impossible, but so did a dancing plant. Maybe it was all for real!*

* * * *

In the morning, when she shook him awake ten minutes early so he'd have extra time to get through security at school, Arnold jumped out of bed without protest.

Sis clutched her chest and staggered backward. "It—it cannot be! Stupid-head is getting up without having water poured all over him!"

Arnold aimed a kick at her and missed. She stuck her tongue out at him and ran out the door so she wouldn't have to stand in line with him, which suited him just fine. Still, she had put his bowl of oatmeal with sliced bananas and milk out on the kitchen table for him (for a while, "Banana-Man" had threatened to displace "Gross-Fart" as his nickname at school). Arnold slurped up his breakfast, dribbling oats and milk on his T-shirt in his haste, grabbed his jacket and pounded out the door, not even grunting goodbye to Dad the way he usually did.

On an ordinary morning he would have been early enough to beat the rush at the security checkpoint, but a lot of other families had had the same thought as Alison and he ended up smack in the middle of the line.

Madison was right in front of him, and she put out her hand and shoved him in the chest. "Not so close, spaz." Her sidekick Kayleigh put her hand over her mouth and giggled. In front of them, Darla Murray, who wore braces and was sometimes almost nice to him, told them to lay off.

"Gonna make us, metal-mouth?" Madison said, and Kayleigh giggled again.

God, Arnold hated them. As if that wasn't bad enough, Matt's buddy Jared Nichols was behind him and kept pinching his legs and arms while he had to pretend not to notice.

"Hey Grosssssss-fart, try not to stink up the changing room for us, okay?" he hissed. In case that wasn't humiliating enough, Madison heard and started snickering. *Just ignore them*, Arnold told himself. *I'm on my way to another planet. Another whole planet! Maybe there, being a nerd will actually be cool! Because it sure isn't here.* But ignoring was awfully hard, especially when Jared gave him a hard shove just as he reached the guards at the entrance. He fell against the huge, perspiring bulk of Mr. Ramsey, who had been fired as a deputy sheriff but found full employment in the schools.

Mr. Ramsey scowled and pushed Arnold away. "Sorry, I tripped," he muttered.

"Bubba, you can do clumsy here," Mr. Ramsey said. Arnold followed the tall, skinny guard into the boys' "changing room," a windowless box that had once been a supply closet. Everything had been removed from the room, including the dangling, bare light bulb, and fluorescents had been installed, along with a roundish, black bulge just below the ceiling that Arnold presumed was a video camera.

He undressed under the guard's bored gaze, shoving his tattered jockey shorts under his other clothes for fear Bubba would make the same kind of remarks Matt and Jared and some of the other boys did in the locker room. Bubba snapped on a pair of green rubber gloves and quickly patted Arnold down. He tried to stand still and pretend it didn't bother him. After all, little kids didn't get strip searched, so this did prove he was grown up, didn't it?

A grunt from Bubba let Arnold know he could get dressed again. He picked up his book-bag and put it through a wide slot in the wall, onto a conveyor belt for atomic analysis. This technology, a gift of the High Ones, posed no risk of radiation exposure, unlike old-fashioned human-invented X-ray machines. He wished the High Ones had some way of making the stuff in his backpack shrink temporarily so it wouldn't be such a struggle to shove it through that slot every morning. Walking out the door, he reached out his right hand to grab it by the strap, when a long-fingered, hairy-backed hand came down on his wrist.

"Not so fast, chief," Bubba said. "I got to go through your bag."

"But it was just scanned," Arnold pointed out. "That machine can pinpoint anything hazardous down to an angstrom across—one ten-billionth of a meter."

Bubba's head bobbed up and down as if his neck was loose—Arnold thought of dinosaurs. The guard sniffed and rubbed his upper lip with his forefinger. It looked like he was trying to grow a mustache. "Got to go through your bag, chief."

"But the machine is always good enough. You never go through bags by hand!"

"Come on, chief, you're holding up the line."

Arnold's knees began to tremble. Being strip searched was embarrassing and uncomfortable, but when it came right down to it he could always pretend he was somewhere else, doing something else. He despised his runty, clumsy, ears-sticking-out, pale little body that everyone else made fun of, anyway. But the stuff hidden among the chaos in his binder—that was where he really lived. Where the real Sir Arnold, Warrior Prince, lived and had adventures drawn in pencil and written down in a furtive, blocky hand. Where he rode out every day to rescue Princess Hailee from the endless series of threats she was helpless to escape from—fire-breathing dragons, bone-crushing trolls, tentacled creatures almost too terrible to draw in all their horror. And she knew how to express her gratitude to her gallant Sir Arnold, did Princess Hailee.

If anyone else got a glimpse of that, he was dead. So he stuck out his chin—his pasty, pointy, pimple-bedecked chin—and said to Bubba, "No, you can't go through my bag."

On such tiny acts of defiance, fate sometimes turns.

5

At lunchtime in the high school Alison was hanging out with Shaniqua. They were both eating their brown-bag lunches (egg salad for Alison, ham and cheese on rye for Shaniqua) when Sydney sashayed over, swinging her hips as if every boy wasn't already staring at her while pretending not to. She tossed her curly blond hair back and said to Alison, "Didja hear what your spazzo little brother did?"

The bite of sandwich Alison was working on almost went down the wrong way. She choked and took a sip of her cardboard-flavored skim milk. "No, but you're going to tell me, right?"

"He got in big trouble for flipping off Bubba Jones when he was searching his bag. They called your father over at Wallops. What did the little freak have in there anyway, weed?"

Heat flushed Alison's face and she had to force herself to speak calmly. "I seriously doubt it, Sydney."

"Huh. Maybe it was meth or acid, then. *Some*thing must explain how come Arnold don't act like a normal person." And she flounced off to join the other popular girls, leaving Alison to clench her fists under the rejects' table.

"Don't pay her no mind. That little witch just loves ruining other people's days," Shaniqua said.

Alison sighed. "You're right, of course. But it's just so weird that Arnold would mouth off to security. The poor kid's afraid of his own shadow."

Shaniqua leaned across the table and lowered her voice. "Think it might actually be true? About the drugs, I mean."

It took Alison a minute to answer. She was distracted imagining Shaniqua in her American Heritage getup. "Arnold? Never in a million years. The stuff he makes up in his head is so freaky, no way does he need drugs. Plus, no one would ever sell to him." Should she tell her friend about her double, Sharon, in the other Chincoteague? If she did, Shaniqua might think she was just as weird as Arnold. She decided not to, at least for now.

It was hard paying attention in class after lunch. When she went to get her books she discovered that someone, probably Don Peabody or one of his flunkies, Lee Parker or Tom Filkins, had spray-painted her locker with a swastika again. A swastika with a blue dot in its center. *Earth for the Earth-born,* was what the "blue-eyed swastika" meant; *and Jews like you ain't from Earth.*

The paint was still wet, and she was running late for history class, so she ran to the girls' room, wet a clump of paper towels, ran back to her locker and smudged up the hateful thing enough so no one could tell what it was supposed to be. Then she ran on to class, making it just as the bell rang, and tried to forget about her locker, which she could do a better job of cleaning off later with the bottle of turpentine she kept hidden behind her books. It wasn't that important—after all, she had Arnold and her parents to worry about.

Still, it was no wonder she didn't even hear Miss Burbage calling on her, though she suddenly became aware that everyone was looking at her. "I'm sorry, what was the question?"

"I said, what were some of the problems the world faced when the High Ones arrived? It's the subject of your term paper, Alison." There was disappointment in the teacher's voice.

"Oh, right! Of course. Well, there was the Vietnam War, which was part of the Cold War between America and the Soviet Union."

"It wasn't too cold in the jungles, though, was it?" The class snickered. Miss Burbage could be hard to take when she indulged her temptation to do stand-up comedy. *If she didn't have a face like a frog maybe she could do that for a living, instead of giving me a hard time.*

"No, I guess it was pretty hot over there," Alison said around an angry lump in her throat. There was an awkward silence, which Miss Burbage broke by pointing at Shaniqua, who said something about pollution and how the High Ones had ended it with their angstrom air-filters and controlled nuclear fusion, like at the Wallops Island plant.

"What was the matter with you in there?" Shaniqua asked as they walked out into the hallway after the bell rang.

"Can't concentrate. Do you think they might expel Arnold?"

"Depends what he actually did," Shaniqua said. Her virtues as a friend included being relentlessly truthful—like her little brother, Alison hated reassuring lies. "My brother Tavon got suspended once for grabbing his Kools back from Mr. Ramsay, the last time they were going through people's backpacks, after that big Patriotic Front jailbreak up in New York. But they let him go back to class a week later." That would have been more comforting if Tavon hadn't had such a hard time graduating and finding a job afterward. He now worked part time cleaning up litter in the National Wildlife Refuge across the bridge on Assateague Island.

Luckily there was no more class for the rest of the day. Instead there was an all-school assembly in honor of the victims at the Capitol. The bomb had gone off in the visitors' gallery overlooking the House of Lords just as an elementary school group from Montana was arriving, and a good hour and a half before the High Ones' diplomatic delegation was due to arrive. Once the identity and age of the victims was known, the Patriotic Front and the Human Defense League had quit trying to claim credit and instead began blaming each other. Alison went numb as the smiling little-kid faces appeared, ten times life size, in the stage box where they usually showed tri-dees of the Martian settlements and the Oort Cloud Observatory, or giant model molecules for chemistry class.

"James Allen Franklin, age seven," Principal Robert Wright intoned as a dark-haired kid with sticking-out ears like Arnold's appeared. Alison wondered if Arnold also saw the resemblance… if they were letting him attend the assembly. "He was in second grade and had just made his mom a card for her birthday," the principal said. "Sarah Jane Beckman, age eight, said she didn't mind being called 'Freckle-Face'…"

Principal Wright jogged down Maddox Boulevard early every morning, all the way out to the Assateague ocean beach and back, but he was still portly, with a shiny bald head now gleaming with perspiration. He lived on the mainland, just this side of the Maryland state line at Temperanceville. The rumor was his wife had left him and he was trying to lose weight to get more dates. Alison doubted he was having much luck, if he scowled half as much in private as he did at school.

There was a rustling behind Alison, who did her best to ignore it while also trying to tune out the images of the dead kids. At times like this she secretly envied Arnold his ability to disappear inside his own head. She felt all too grounded in the here and now, grinding along at one second per second, day after day, in this podunk little island town, sitting out school dances with nothing but a paper cup of punch and Shaniqua's chatter for company. No boy was ever going to ask the fat Jewish girl to dance. What would she do without Shaniqua? She'd be exposed as just as much of a social reject as Arnold.

Something wet slapped against the back of Alison's neck. She spun around in her seat and saw Don smirking while Lee and Tom tried to stifle their laughter.

"Which of you morons threw a spitball at me?" she hissed. They all threw up their hands.

Mr. Wright paused in his recitation. "Is there a problem up there?" he boomed into his microphone.

Oh, no. Poor Dad—first Arnold, and now me.

Mr. Wright was storming up the aisle toward where Alison was sitting. Shaniqua scrunched down in her seat while Alison steeled herself.

"Don threw a spitball!" she said, pointing.

"Who, me? I would never be so disrespectful, sir." Lee and Tom both held solemn faces for a moment, but then Lee doubled over, choking with laughter.

"All of you report to my office, right after the last bell!" Mr. Wright yelled, loud enough to send a squeal of feedback through his microphone. There was a rising murmur through the auditorium, and he spun on his heel. "You all need to show some respect! We may be a tiny part of the Cosmic Harmony, but this is still the good old USA, the United Satrapy of America, and we show RESPECT for innocent lives lost!" Dead silence was his reward. The principal pointed at the tri-dee image of a chubby-faced, brown haired, smiling woman. "Those Montana kids' teacher, Mrs. Violet Switzer! She was torn in two by that terrorist bomb! She could have been any of your mothers, any of you!" Someone let out a sob, or maybe it was just a hiccup. The principal let the silence stretch out, ten seconds, thirty, a full minute before dismissing the assembly.

The bell jangled as they filed out, Alison following Don, Tom, and Lee, who were right behind Mr. Wright—she wouldn't put it past them to spitball her again, while they were all on the way to the principal's office. Fortunately all she got was three days' after-school detention and a humiliating lecture on how Mr. Wright had expected better of her, "though maybe I was being naive, given your family background."

Alison clenched her fists below the lip of the principal's desk. *What the hell is that supposed to mean?* she wanted to shout, though they both knew perfectly well what he had meant. He was referring to the reason why they had to move out here to Hicksville, the reason Mom and Dad had given her and Arnold that long, long talk about how "we all have to keep our heads down" so no one would bother Dad in his new job as a technical writer at the Wallops Island Fusion Plant.

Nobody wanted to be the cause of discord that threatened the Cosmic Harmony. Even Dad hadn't wanted to do that with those articles he wrote back when he was a reporter for the *Baltimore Sun*, not really, not when the High Ones had brought peace and prosperity and cures for cancer and a bunch of other diseases and clean, cheap energy with them from Gliese 581d, twenty light-years away. Dad had just wanted to do his job, he said: making sure the Office of Interstellar Liaison within the State Department was doing *its* job right and making good use of taxpayer money. The High Ones were always saying they wanted to improve inefficient human ways of doing things, weren't they? So what could be more harmonious, and patriotic, too, than helping achieve that goal? But the newspaper's editors hadn't seen it that way. By that time Mom was already too sick to work, so they had a desperate couple of months until Dad found the tech writing job at Wallops and they moved out to Chincoteague.

The cloudy afternoon sky seemed to lower itself slowly over Alison's head as she hurried home after Mr. Wright finally dismissed her. Arnold should have been waiting for her, she was so late, but the house was empty. She ran out again, the cold air tearing at her throat as she crossed Main Street, heading back to school. But the main doors were locked and the hall lights were out. Circling around the building, she saw a light on in the library. Once again she found the emergency exit was unlocked. *Pretty ironic, considering all the trouble Arnold is in for—whatever he did at security.*

"Hello?" she called as she entered.

This time Gloria straightened up immediately from behind the counter, smiling when she saw who it was. Today she was wearing a bright orange, sequin-spangled blouse. *How on Earth does she get away with that?* But there were more important questions that needed answering.

"Where's Arnold?"

"Not here."

"I can see that. But where is he? He got in big trouble today."

A sigh. "I know."

"You do? Then you know they called my father at work."

"Yes. Poor Jerry. He's such a nice man to suffer such *tsuris*."

Alison gave her a long, hard look. She hadn't heard anyone use the Yiddish word for trouble since her grandfather died five years ago.

Could she be baiting me? Aloud, she said only, "So, where are they?"

"Isn't it obvious? They both needed a break after what they went through, so I helped them over to Jo's Chincoteague." Her green eyes were wide, innocent. "That's okay, isn't it? I just put them there now—if you hurry, you can catch up with them in time to see the dragon."

6

Arnold had never heard a girl talk so much in all his life as this Jo person, but it was sometimes a bit hard to understand her since she talked really fast and had a funny accent, a cross between British and Eastern Shore.

From the moment he and Dad had stepped out into the bookstore in this strange new version of Chincoteague, Jo had kept up a steady stream of chatter, pointing out and explaining everything they ran across, including things that needed no explaining, like seagulls and street signs.

The streets, Arnold finally interrupted her to say, mostly had the same names as back home. Some of the people looked familiar, too, though nobody seemed to recognize him or Dad. Arnold ducked behind a tree when he saw Matt Walters, but the bully wasn't with his usual gang. He was better dressed than usual and seemed absorbed in his own thoughts.

There were way more people out in the streets than there had been at home, which was odd considering that it was even colder here, but Jo explained that it was a holiday called Union Day, "when we celebrate the unification of all the colonies under the Crown."

"What does that mean?" It was the first question Dad had asked. He'd been quiet and wide-eyed the whole time, like a little kid on his first visit to Mars. Arnold's memory of that very moment in his own life was vivid in every detail—he could reproduce on paper every detail of the rusty-red planetscape wheeling by far below, and he did so often, especially when class got too boring. But this strangely altered Chincoteague was even more amazing than Mars!

"Oh, that was part of the dirty deal Sir Ben Franklin worked out with the king—actually, with William Pitt," Jo said. "They make us learn all about it in school. It's how the colonies first got representation in Parliament—lucky for Parliament and even for batty old George III, or they'd have had nowhere to go when Bone-a-fart invaded the Home Islands."

"I see," said Dad, the way people did when they meant they didn't understand at all. He shook his head. "I can't believe all those might-have-beens are real somewhere. It's like a fairy tale."

"I think it's fun!" Jo exclaimed. "I mean, travel to other worlds might seem pretty boring to you two blokes, but we just invented mechods last year."

"Mechods?" Dad said.

Jo rolled her eyes. Arnold thought they were her best feature, brown and lively, with sparkling green flecks. "Don't tell me you're another one like Mom, always correcting people when they use contractions! Fine, *mechanical dragons*, are you happy? Heavier-than-air craft. My Dad helped design the British ones," Jo said with unmistakable pride, "and he got a lot of inspiration of course from our real dragon. There he is now!"

Dad started and Arnold felt his heart speed up. "Who, the dragon?" Dad said.

"My dad, of course. Our dragon is a girl. People call her Assateague Ashley, though her real name is Ir'befunzu." She pronounced *Assateague* as if it were two words. "There's my dad, on top of the bandstand."

They had been walking down Maddox Boulevard toward Assateague Island. At the same spot where, back in the real world, a McDonald's marred the view of Assateague Lighthouse across Assateague Channel, an old-fashioned wooden bandstand had been set up and draped with patriotic red-white-and-blue-bunting (though the flags, when Arnold got a close look at them, were unfamiliar, looking like a cross between the Union Jack and the Confederate battle flag).

The man Jo had indicated stood before a bulky microphone, which he tested by rapping on it with his knuckles. He was a little above average height, with messy, sandy hair, and was wearing blue jeans and a black windbreaker. His face was ruddy and there were smile lines at the corners of his mouth.

A crowd milled around in the grassy space in front of the bandstand, talking loudly and laughing. Many of them were casually swigging from beer bottles—even middle-school-age kids, Arnold was amazed to note. Dad tapped him on the shoulder and whispered, "Don't get any ideas." The bright orange sun was still shedding plenty of light although it was nearing the western horizon, far off to the right in the direction of the mainland.

Jo's dad cleared his throat and asked for quiet. "Welcome, everyone, to the first-ever Union Day air show!" There were cheers. His voice was deep, resonant, and accented like Jo's. "As most of you know, I am Michael Purnell, the chief ranger at His Royal Majesty's Dragon Refuge on Assateague Island, home of our very own Assateague Ashley."

The applause was dying down when someone shoved Arnold so hard from behind that he almost fell onto the person in front of him. He spun around, expecting to see that even in another world, an alien version of

Matt Walters couldn't just leave him alone, but instead it was his big sister, who was panting hard.

"Sorry," Alison whispered, "I had to run to get here. What did I miss?"

"Nothing yet. That's Jo's dad on the platform," Arnold explained. So many people shushed him, it sounded like a windstorm had started.

"—the discovery that a few people have the ability to mindspeak with dragons," Mr. Purnell was saying. "Without which, of course, this air show would not be possible. I wish we could thank our village's mindspeaker, but she has asked to remain anonymous."

Out of the corner of his eye, Arnold noticed that Jo had a funny look on her face. Then her jaw went slack and she seemed to be gazing at something impossibly far away. It was a look Arnold often had himself when he was daydreaming. *I wonder if people give her a hard time about it, too.* But then she shut her mouth with an audible click and said to her visitors in a stage whisper, "Here she comes!"

A few moments later the crowd turned as one to the left, eastward toward Assateague. They ooh-ed and ah-ed like people watching fireworks, and no wonder—something enormous was soaring toward them from the direction of the ocean, something so big that when it passed over Assateague Channel it cast a shadow that easily bridged the watery gap.

Arnold shaded his eyes with his hand and looked up, and his mouth went dry. *Something* as big as an old-time fighter plane was passing overhead, and *it was alive!* The dragon was mottled green, like military jungle camouflage. Its head was as big as a house, but it came to a sharp point—*an isosceles triangle*, Arnold thought, proud of remembering the word at a moment like this. As the dragon soared directly overhead it flapped its wings once, twice, and a powerful downdraft blew people's hats off their heads. There was a gust of nervous laughter. The creature banked over the village and turned around, just as a biplane came sputtering along over Assateague Channel.

Arnold tried to remember if he'd ever seen one before outside the pages of a book. He didn't think *anyone* had ever seen one quite like this, painted mottled green in obvious imitation of the dragon, with shiny, curly struts connecting the two wings in a curvy, filigreed pattern. It was beautiful, a work of art, and *"Oh my God, it's going to crash into the dragon!"* Arnold yelled, covering his eyes. Spots danced behind his squeezed-shut eyelids and he heard the crowd let out a gasp. Then someone elbowed him.

"Ow! What did you do that for?" he said, opening his eyes and rounding on Alison.

"Because, nerd-face, you just missed the most amazing thing ever! The dragon and the biplane did a loop-de-loop around each other—I think they're going to do it again!" They did, to applause and cheers. Then another biplane joined them, and a third!

Arnold felt dizzy watching them, but it was exhilarating, too, like the time Mom and Dad had the Olympics on tri-vee two years ago and he thought it was going to be the most boring thing in the world, especially gymnastics, which held unpleasant memories for him—but watching those girls just a couple of years older than him spin and leap around the bars Arnold had felt something soar inside him. And this was on a much grander scale.

Arnold watched in awe until he felt an elbow in the ribs again. He clenched his fists to take a swing at Sis, but checked himself when he saw it wasn't her, it was Jo. "Sorry, but I just had to tell you—I'm going to ask Ashley to do a figure eight in the air," she whispered in his ear.

"Huh? How are you—" Her face went slack again for a moment, and then the dragon did just as she had said it would, drawing a perfect double loop around the biplanes. Applause again, and cheers.

"So you're the 'mindspeaker,'" Arnold whispered in Jo's ear.

She nodded. "Now you know my secret," she said quietly.

Arnold was mostly silent watching the surreal air show, though it was hard not to flinch when a plane or Ashley's tail dipped too close to the ground. It was like the way he felt about fireworks: he loved the colors but had only recently learned to control his fear of the noise they made. Dad and Alison also seemed overwhelmed, and Sis's eyes were shining with unshed tears. Was that from excitement, or sorrow that she could never be as powerful and free as the dragon soaring through the air? Arnold could empathize because he felt the same.

As if at a signal the biplanes zoomed back the way they had come and the dragon floated away toward Assateague. "She spends the night in a pond she dug herself over there," Jo said. Her voice was hushed.

"Does she sleep?" Arnold asked.

"That's a good question. No, not the way people do. But she does dream—often, about her family that was massacred by the early settlers."

"You mean she's not the only dragon?"

"Well, of course not. And since Old Carolina Joe knocked her up, she's had a brood of dragonets, six of them. People have given them boring names, but their real names all start with their noble family name, Ir. My favorite is Ir'gassaphet. I think that's a much nicer name than 'Nigel,' don't you?"

Mr. Purnell was speaking into the microphone again. "That's our show, folks! I hope you enjoyed it."

"How come Ashley didn't breathe fire, Mike?" someone yelled.

Mr. Purnell smiled the smile of someone who has heard the same dumb question a thousand times but still has to answer it politely and in detail. "She has barely started growing her beak back from the last time she had to do it. Dragons don't breathe fire for fun—they don't really breathe fire at all, of course, they mix fatty acids with hydrogen peroxide inside their beaks and—"

"Mike, stop boring everybody!" a woman called out. There were chuckles.

"That's Mum," Jo whispered, indicating a short, blond lady who was standing nearby. Standing with her was a young man who looked like a skinnier version of Mr. Purnell, and a chubby girl with curly brown hair and a mischievous gleam in her sparkling brown eyes.

"Nobody wants a chemistry lesson, love!" Mrs. Purnell added cheerfully. "What they probably do want is tea and biscuits, courtesy of the Gingo Teag Tourism Advisory Council! Come by the town hall, everybody!"

"Can we go Dad? Please?" Alison asked, beating Arnold to it.

Dad smiled. "Of course! Sounds like fun. Gloria said she could take us back home whenever we wanted."

"Back home where?" asked Mrs. Purnell. She had made her way through the crowd and was buttoning up Jo's coat for her, over her protests.

"Hmm? Oh, just over on—"

"They're from Alaska, Mum," Jo interrupted. "Like Teresa."

"Alaska, eh?" Mrs. Purnell looked Dad over more carefully, from his scuffed brown shoes to the "Russian" black hat with the dopey-looking flaps that he wore whenever the temperature dipped below fifty degrees. Then she smiled. "I am so sorry, where are my manners! Vivian Purnell, at your service." And she curtseyed to Dad!

Arnold had only ever seen anyone do that in old movies. Dad startled him even more, by bowing and taking Jo's mother's hand and kissing it.

"I'm Teresa," the curly-haired girl said in a normal American accent. She smiled and shook hands with Alison, then with Dad, and last of all with Arnold. *Why can't I ever be first?*

Teresa leaned toward them and explained quietly, "I'm from America, like you. Well, not *exactly* like you—long story. Anyway, we tell people I'm from Alaska so they don't ask too many questions, and you can do the same. In this world, it's a separate country."

Mrs. Purnell introduced the young man as "my little Tommy," although he was at least five centimeters taller than her.

"Mum, you are embarrassing me," he complained as she pulled his cap firmly down over his reddening ears.

"That is a mother's job," she said. Jo and Tom's dad joined them and there was another round of introductions before the group set off down Maddox Boulevard. A cutting wind was blowing, but before they had gone a single block Alison had linked arms with Teresa and they were chatting like old friends. Arnold shoved his hands in his coat pockets and watched them enviously.

He'd almost forgotten about Jo. She startled him by saying softly she hoped he had enjoyed the air show.

"Enjoyed it? I've never seen anything like it! I wish I lived here so I could watch Ashley—Ir'befunzu—every day."

"I love her more than anybody," Jo said. "But I can't wait to grow up and get out of Gingo Teag."

"Me too," Arnold said with feeling.

"I'd like to read astrophysics at university. Or maybe music. I can't decide which, I love them both so much!"

Like Einstein, Arnold thought. He could see this girl was really smart. "I don't know what I want to study, either," he said. "Just not journalism, like Dad did. You can get in too much trouble."

"Oh, that's right. You've got big blue slugs telling you what you can and can't write, don't you?"

Arnold could feel all the blood draining out of his face.

"Hey, don't get so upset!" Jo said. "I was only joking."

Teresa turned her head and said, "Alison's the same way! It's cool that you have aliens in your version of America, but why do you freak out when anyone asks about them? Do they use mind-control rays on you or something?"

"Of course not," Arnold said. "It's just that back home, you can get in big trouble if you say anything bad about them."

Jo was quiet as they filed in the door of a building with GINGO TEAG TOWN HALL inscribed on its handsome white marble lintel. She waited till Arnold had collected a paper cup of strong, sweet tea and two sugar cookies, then steered him into a corner.

"Really, what's the deal with your 'High Ones?'" she asked. "Are they sensitive or something? Why should they be? I make fun of everything, all the time. Especially our silly old King Charles III, and the way he goes on about how every cow shed and chicken coop is 'an inalienable part of our immortal British heritage.'" She stuck her chin up and said the last part in a half-strangled voice.

"Are you committing leez majesty again, you little brat?" an old guy with a red face said. Or tried to say. He had a mouthful of sugar cookies, and it was kind of hard to tell.

"Sorry, Mr. Greene, I didn't know you were a courtier," Jo deadpanned.

"Smart mouth! If you was my daughter, I'd paddle you till your bum was black and blue!"

"If she *were* your daughter, Dean, you would not dare," Mrs. Purnell said. "I suggest you mind your own business, you nosey parker. And as for you, missy," she said to Jo, "you had best not be giving our foreign visitors a wrong idea of the immense respect in which we Britons hold the royal family!"

"Of course not, Mum!" Jo said, waiting until her mother's back was turned to roll her eyes dramatically.

Arnold was liking this girl more and more. He couldn't decide what was weirder, to hear the High Ones talked about so casually, or to be called a foreigner.

Dad was having a lot of trouble fending off Mr. Greene, who kept yelling at him about "the nerve you Alaskans have."

"I don't know what you're talking about, sir."

"Yes, you bloody well do! You people have some nerve, after everything we've done for you, helping you get free of the Bonapartes' puppet Russia!"

"Umm…"

"I mean, is it really so much to ask that you not recognize those upstart rebels in Angler-tare?"

Leez majesty? Angler-tare? Are these people really speaking English?

Jo promptly jumped up and stuck her nose in the argument. "You're being darned rude to our guests, Mr. Greene!"

The red-faced man looked at her as if she was a seagull tearing at roadkill. "I don't want no brat's opinion!"

"Well, I'm gonna give it to you anyway! Any Englishman worth his salt ought to support the Anglay Republic! They are our brothers, and they fought long and hard against the French! Remember how happy we all were when they threw the Frogs out of London?"

"Then why don't they accept the authority of their rightful king?"

"Cause they got too much sense, is what I say!"

There were gasps around the room. "Jacobin!" someone muttered. "Paine-ist! Why donchya go to Australia, ya lousy republican?"

A white-faced Mrs. Purnell swooped in, grabbed Jo by the arm and hauled her protesting from the room. Mr. Purnell hurried after them. Tom looked at the floor, and Teresa whispered something in his ear.

"I think we had best be going, too," Dad said. "Nice, er, nice meeting everyone. Including you, Mr. Greene! Let's not talk politics in the future, all right?" Without waiting for an answer Dad hurried Arnold and Alison outside and back to the bookstore.

"What was that all about, Dad?" Arnold asked as they walked along the dingy underground passageway they had taken from the library. Alison looked all around, up and down and behind her, and brought her right hand up to her mouth.

"Allie, stop chewing your nails," Dad said. "And Arnold, I'm damned if I know. Politics is a dirty business, no matter what world you're in. We're lucky the High Ones saved us from our own stupidity."

Arnold felt disappointed in Dad for saying that. It sounded like something a teacher would say, when Dad was always telling them to think for themselves and not just accept what they learned in school. *Is he actually scared of seeing what the world is like when human beings get to run it? That's pathetic!*

But there was no more time to think about it because they had already arrived back at the bare wood-walled version of the library, and Tiferet was twining between their legs mewing, and this time Arnold kept his eyes shut during the transition because he had almost thrown up last time, but it didn't seem to help because somehow he could still see everything anyway, and then Gloria was standing there with her arms around him and Dad and Alison, and he hurriedly broke away because it was just too icky.

"Well, my dears," Gloria said, "did you enjoy the air show?"

Arnold wanted to shout that it was the most amazing thing ever, but that wouldn't be cool, would it? Cool was answering casually, "It was pretty good, I guess."

Alison didn't say anything, but her eyes were glowing. Dad said, "It was the most incredible thing I've ever seen, Gloria. Thank you."

"It is a pity the dracos all died out in the yellow-wood at your world's K-T Boundary," Gloria said. "They could have provided some needed balance between you humans and the High Ones."

Arnold had been *really* into dinosaurs when he was younger, so he knew what she was talking about, though the slight frown on Alison's face meant she probably didn't. "Gloria means the time when the asteroid killed all the dinosaurs, 65 million years ago," he told her. "Which means Jo's 'dragon' is really a highly evolved pterodactyl, isn't that right, Gloria?"

She smiled at him. "That's right."

"What's a 'yellow-wood,' though?"

"A yellow-wood is the turning point where two worlds' histories diverge," Gloria said. "You know, from the poem—"

"—by Robert Frost, yeah, I get it," Alison said. "We had to read it in English class last May. 'Two roads split in a yellow wood, and I took the less crowded one,' or something."

"So Jo's world isn't magical, then," Arnold said.

Gloria's expression turned very serious. "Magic is where you find it, Arnold. Never forget that. It's a truth that holds in all the worlds." She paused. "Well, I shouldn't keep you waiting here. You'll be wanting your dinner. I'll see you both tomorrow in school."

"Not me, you won't," Arnold said. "I'm suspended, remember?"

"I know. But I'll stop by your house and bring you some books so you won't fall behind in your classes."

"That's the reason Arnold and I came here after meeting with the principal," Dad explained to Alison. "To get some books so he wouldn't fall behind. We got more than we bargained for."

"How long did you get suspended for, Arnold?" Alison asked as the three of them turned onto Main Street. It was completely dark outside.

"Two weeks," he answered.

Sis whistled appreciatively. Then she jumped as a dark figure leapt out from behind a fence. Arnold jumped too, and even Dad looked scared for a second. But it was only crazy Barry Freed.

"Area 51," he said. He was wearing a plaid shirt that was buttoned up wrong. One side was untucked.

"Hi, Barry," Dad said calmly. "What's Area 51?"

"A secret Air Force base in Nevada. Ever hear of it?"

"Uh, no, Barry."

"Right, because *it's secret*," Mr. Freed said, as if Dad might be stupid. "And do you know why *they* want it kept secret?" Even Arnold knew who Mr. Freed meant by "they." The Establishment, the government, the men in gray suits and dark sunglasses. The High Satrap himself was just a tool of Them, if you believed Mr. Freed—not that anybody did.

"That's a rhetorical question, isn't it, Mr. Freed?" Arnold said, and was rewarded with a scowl.

"Area 51, ladies and gentlemen, is where *they* make the fake aliens."

"Fake aliens, Mr. Freed?" Alison said. She had told Arnold she felt sorry for him. Arnold didn't—he was scared of him.

"The so-called High Ones. They're a fake, I tell you, the biggest fraud in history! Don't feel too bad that you fell for those big blue sea slugs—so did everyone else! Area 51 is the key to everything, I'm telling you! It's where *They* make the phony flying saucers—"

"I've been in them myself, Mr. Freed," Alison explained patiently. "That's why you never see jets anymore—they're such a cheap, comfortable way to fly."

"—and the controlled fusion reactors, and the make-believe interstellar travel, and…"

Dad looked at Arnold and Alison and jerked his head toward home, and the three of them started walking, with Mr. Freed gradually falling behind as he trailed after them.

Once they had the front door safely shut behind them, Dad turned and said slowly to Arnold and Alison, "What do you suppose Mr. Freed would say if he knew we were just in a whole other universe?"

7

The first day Arnold spent at home was like a vacation. It was too cold to go to the beach, but he lay on the sofa reading Twain's *Letters to a Woman Sitting in Darkness* and listening to the cries of seagulls in the midday quiet. You couldn't hear the surf on the ocean beach at Assateague, not with the loblolly pine forest, the salt marsh, Assateague Channel, and half of Chincoteague between here and there, but Arnold felt the presence of the sea nonetheless. An island like Chincoteague was a boat afloat in vast waters that had covered the world for hundreds of millions of years, long before the dinosaurs had walked the earth, back before the continents had split apart and slowly assumed their current positions and shapes. You couldn't sense it if you were stuck in a classroom, but you could now in the faint salt tang of the air and the faint ringing of bells on buoys strung along the narrow channels surrounding the island. It surrounded and comforted him as he read about how Private Shipman and his companions had caught a Filipino rebel named Felix and given him "the water cure."

"He choked and sputtered and begged us by God and Mother Mary to stop. Deadeye Don snickered and flicked him with another wet towel, putting it over his face when he wouldn't shut up so he gagged and wriggled like a beached fish. Then he stopped moving. Tom said, 'I dunno, Don, I think you might have kilt him,' and Don said, 'Who cares? He ain't told us nothin' worth hearin' nohow.' And that, my darling Daisy, is how we civilized Felix."

Arnold laid the book aside, put his hands behind his head, and stared at a painted-over crack in the ceiling for a while. What he'd told Gloria wasn't 100% true; not every Twain book was banned by SCOD, and he'd actually read *Tom Sawyer* in fourth grade. But he knew *The Adventures of Huckleberry Finn* only from Dad's library, and he'd never read anything like the *Letters*. It went even further than Dad did when he got together with his buddies back in Pikesville, or now with Mr. Nomura, and complained about the government and "our big blue friends running around telling us what to do." What would Mark Twain have had to say about the High Ones? Would he have approved of the way they stopped people from fighting each other, or would he have scorned them like

Huck Finn scorned the "do-gooders" who were always trying to "sivilize" him? Arnold longed to talk about it with Mom, but it sounded like she was having one of her "bad days," tossing and turning and groaning loudly in bed, and he didn't want to disturb her.

There was a knock at the door and Arnold sat up guiltily, until he realized it was hours too early for either Alison or Dad. Though he didn't want to talk to anyone, curiosity won out, and he got off the couch and opened the door a crack, leaving the chain in place.

A green eye crinkled at him from about his own height. "Hi Arnold, can I come in for a second?"

"Sure, Gloria." Arnold slid the chain back and opened the door for the librarian. *Or is she a magician? What should I call her?* Whatever she was, today she had on a black jacket with bulked-up shoulders that looked like it had come out of a Goodwill bin that specialized in Eighties castoffs, a shimmery purple skirt, and thigh-high black suede boots that had been ruined by salt-marsh mud with that giveaway rotten-egg smell.

As she shut the door behind her Arnold studied the cardboard box she was carrying under one arm. It was about thirty centimeters on a side and ten centimeters thick, and was labeled, *THE REUNION, CENTRAL PARK, SEPTEMBER 6, 1983.* "What's in there? Records?"

"That's right. I'm giving them to you for keeps. Do you have a turntable?"

"I think we might, in the closet somewhere. No one seems to listen to anything that isn't on the n-network anymore."

"I know, but I thought you might be different."

"Because I'm a weirdo?"

"Because you're out of step with the times." Gloria smiled. Some of her teeth were crooked, but this didn't make her ugly. To the contrary.

"That's true enough," Arnold said. "Matt and his buddies tell me so all the time—usually not so nicely, though. Let me see if I can find that record player." He started to turn toward the coat closet, but paused halfway and said, "You're shivering. Are you cold?"

"N-not at all, d-dear," Gloria said, her teeth knocking together.

"Are you scared, then?"

"Only a little."

What do you do when the grown-ups around you are scared? Arnold remembered the hushed late-night conversations Mom and Dad used to have behind their closed bedroom door back in Pikesville. Occasionally Mom would raise her voice to a near-shout, or Dad would snarl something too low to make out.

Arnold was already much too old to think that Tiger was anything more than a stuffed animal so old he had lost his eyes and smelled like dust and ancient drool. But he used to hug him tighter whenever he heard his parents arguing and worrying. He'd try to imagine he was holding a real tiger with real sharp teeth who could tear to bloody shreds Dad's mean boss Mr. Armstrong and the mysterious "them" even he was scared of. Remembering, Arnold suddenly wondered whether Dad's "them" overlapped with Mr. Freed's, if that was why Mom and Dad and Alison always tried to be nice to the old hippie, and if Gloria was scared of the same shadowy conspiracy.

He wasn't really Sir Arnold the Brave, but he could give Gloria a quick, shy hug, with his head turned to the side and his eyes squeezed shut, and so he did before darting over to the closet, tossing old galoshes and scarves into a heap on the floor in search of Dad's record player. He missed seeing the single crystalline tear Gloria shed, a perfect diamond-bright globe that fell to the polished wooden floor and rolled like a miniature marble, coming to rest in a dim corner.

"Here it is!" he said triumphantly, pulling out the heavy, blocky black base of the turntable, knocking its dusty brown plastic cover loose in the process. When he turned he saw that Gloria had gone, leaving a chilly, wet November breeze blowing through the open door. Walking over to shut it, he saw she had left behind the record album she had brought him.

"No way," he said softly, studying the head shots of four middle-aged, long-haired men against the background of an enormous crowd. There were no names under the pictures, because no one could possibly mistake John Lennon in those round spectacles, black-haired Paul Mc-Cartney, mustachioed George Harrison, and bearded Ringo Starr—the Beatles together again, in the reunion concert that could never have been, not after John disappeared back in 1971, the only, mysterious clue ever found being the words "Imagine THIS!" spray-painted on the wall of his recording studio and a plumber's helper driven into the sheetrock wall handle first.

An artifact from a parallel world. How cool is that? He put the record player on the dining room table, plugged it in, and carefully took the first of the three shiny black disks in the impossible reunion album out of its paper sleeve. There was no dust on it, no hint of scratches.

How much would this be worth, if you could sell it? If the League didn't stop you. Arnold pushed the thought aside, switched on the turntable, and lowered the needle arm onto the outer rim of the first of the three LPs in the boxed set.

Most of the songs were familiar—Grandma was a self-described "Beatlemaniac," and a solid, throaty alto—although some were played in a minor key, lending a touch of sadness to tunes that had once been all bouncy youth.

Arnold was so mesmerized he didn't hear Mom creeping up on him. "What's that you're listening to?" she said suddenly.

Started, Arnold banged his right knee hard on the underside of the table, flipping the needle arm violently up. When it came down it made the record skip.

Nowhere man—nowhere man—nowhere man…

Arnold wanted to cry. *I've ruined something that can never be replaced.*

But Mom didn't seem upset at all. She stepped softly toward the table on her bare, wrinkled feet, her pale blue eyes wide. "Impossible," she whispered, picking up the box with a shaking hand. "I must be dreaming."

Arnold found his voice. "It isn't a dream, Mom. Gloria brought the album over. But I'm afraid I scratched it…"

"Hmm? Don't worry about that, we've got some fix-it spray somewhere…" Still staring at the box, she reached out with her other hand and took the needle arm gently off the record. "So it's true, what Dad told me about the tunnel between the worlds," she said. "I thought I must have dreamed that, too." Her pale, skinny knees were knocking together under her nightgown.

Arnold stood up, got a chair for her, and went into the kitchen to pour her a glass of milk. She smiled and thanked him absently when he handed it to her, but her eyes never left the picture of the concert that had never been.

"I should call your grandmother," she said. "She *has* to hear these songs. And what are these new ones?"

"New ones?" Arnold looked where Mom was pointing on the box. There were two unknown tracks on the B side of the third LP, both credited as "Lennon/McCartney."

Arnold found the right platter in its yellowed paper sleeve, put it on the turntable, and carefully lowered the needle arm into the right place in the shiny black circle before the first song. It was about courage, and John Lennon's voice was saying he had composed it "for my little daughter, Rosie."

Mom shook her head. "He never had a daughter. Only one son, I think," she said, but Arnold barely heard her; he was too busy listening to the music.

> *Courage, girl*
> *You'll need courage for the road ahead*
> *For the road full of dread*
> *I'd give you more, girl*
> *For this cold old world,*

But all I can give you, girl,
Is your heart that's oaken
Even when it's broken
You'll have your courage

The words made Arnold's heart swell until he almost believed he could be brave. The other new song had a strong beat that gave it an almost martial air:

Fight for what is right
Struggle on, through the night
Follow your own light
Whatever others might—

"I'm home!" Alison called, slamming the door, making the needle jump out of its groove. "Hey, you have the record player out? What's that you're—oh, wow!" she said, picking up the boxed set and examining it. "This must be from one of Gloria's parallel worlds!"

Arnold punched her on her left arm, the one that wasn't holding the box. "She gave it to me, not for you! You're always messing up my stuff!"

Mom rolled her eyes. "Come on, you two, you're too old to fight like that. I'm sure Gloria meant you to share. Can't you take the message of all those songs about peace and love to heart, just a little?"

She looked so frail, of course she got what she wanted, which was for everybody to sit around the table spellbound, listening to the greatest rock-and-roll concert that never was. Dad got home just when they had started again from the beginning, the part with the great old songs and the scratch Arnold had made by mistake. He just laughed when Mom mentioned the accident and asked him where the tube of spray stuff was. Instead he showed off a trick where you turned the turntable backwards by hand while bearing down gently on the needle arm to "erase" the skip.

Nowhere man, the world is at your command!

Was that the message Gloria had been trying to send him by giving him the album? That he might think he was a nowhere man, but actually great things were on the way for him? Parents and teachers, the nice ones anyway, were always trying to sell you that message, but Arnold wasn't feeling very inspired by it right now. Hell, he couldn't even keep for himself the one gift he'd gotten to make his suspension from school a little easier. Plus, nobody was even thinking about dinner, and Arnold was hungry.

He slouched off to the kitchen and began fixing himself a sloppy peanut butter and banana sandwich, but the gears of his mind were still turning. Gloria was certainly more than just an offbeat school librarian, so she had to be trying to tell him more than just "be the best you can be." She'd also given him the Twain book, after all. What had that been about? The book was about how cruel and hypocritical empires were. Like the Cosmic Harmony? Put that together with the Beatles' courage song, and the fight-for-what's-right song, and what did you have?

Gloria's an alien, no question about it, but obviously from a different planet from the High Ones. She must hate them as much as the Patriotic Front and the Human Defense League do. Maybe more!

The peanut-buttery knife in Arnold's hand clattered to the kitchen floor unnoticed. "That's why she's here," he whispered aloud. "She wants volunteers to help fight the High Ones. But everyone else is too scared to help her."

For the thousandth time since he'd been suspended he thought about his humiliating encounter with Bubba and Mr. Wright. *What if I've been looking at this all wrong? I'm the only one who has the guts to stand up to the way things are. Everyone at school complains about the strip searches, but they all meekly take their clothes off every morning. Dad's not much better. He may talk a good game about how the old constitution didn't allow unreasonable searches and seizures, but I don't remember him ever going to the school to complain, not back home in Pikesville and not here, either. And Mom... Mom's too sick to do anything, you can't blame her.*

Who was behind all the trouble? The High Ones! There hadn't even been such a thing as terrorism before they came, or anyway not much of it.

SCOD was their fault, too. It had been founded on the symbolic date of July 4, 1976, the same day the new constitution and the new name for the country went into effect, and seven years almost to the day after the Arrival. SCOD's goal, stated on a large wooden plaque mounted on the wall next to the athletic trophy case when you walked out of the strip-search changing rooms into the school, was to "return God's grace to America by stamping out the immorality that has brought down divine wrath."

"They claim to be godly patriots, but really they are an instrument of social control," was how Dad put it once, in a beer-soaked late-night conversation with Mr. Nomura. He had slurred the words "social control," and Mr. Nomura had hiccuped his agreement.

Does Dad really think I can sleep through all their loud talk, or does he just not care? Back in the Sixties, Dad liked to say, you could write or say just about anything you wanted, though Mom liked to ask how would he know, when he wasn't even born till 1970?

Suddenly Arnold was desperate to get back to school so he could ask Gloria directly what she wanted him to do. She had to be in danger every day she was here! What if she just up and disappeared, like she did earlier today after leaving the Beatles album for him—only what if this time she went away for good, or SCOD disappeared her? *Then I'll never learn how to join the Resistance. And I'll never see Assateague Ashley and Jo again!*

8

This stupid history paper is driving me crazy. What did I have to go and write about such a complicated subject for?

It was no good asking Dad, Alison knew; she'd only get a rant she could never write down and hand in for class. But it also made her sick to think about cleverly rewording the textbook the way anyone else in class would. Adventures in American History, ugh! It was the most boring textbook ever.

"You take things way too seriously," Shaniqua said with a wave of her hand when Alison brought up the problem at lunchtime. "Write whatever makes Miss Burbage happy."

"What about thinking for ourselves?"

Shaniqua snorted milk out of her nose, then delicately dabbed at it with her napkin. "In this town? Get serious, Alison honey. Just smile and tell them what they want to hear, so you can graduate and go off to college. You want to cause trouble, do it there. At least you'll have plenty of company."

"And get happy-foamed, or expelled, or disappeared? No thank you."

"Then I really don't understand what you're going on about, girl. Just hum along to that Cosmic Harmony in public and do what you want in private. Everyone else does."

"If everyone jumped off a cliff, would you do it, too?"

"Long as there was a big ol' pile of mattresses at the bottom, I would." Alison had to chuckle at that. "Really, why make a big deal out of this?" Shaniqua said. "Just book some time on the n-reader and you'll get all the material you need, if the textbook is too boring for you. But you'd better put your name on the list fast. As it is you'll have to come in on the weekend to use it."

"Can't." Alison lowered her voice. "My mom has NINA, remember?"

"But you could still go on the N-Network, Allie. Less than one in a million people gets NINA. You're more likely to win the lottery! Why make things hard on yourself?"

Alison bit her lip. "What if it's genetic? They don't know for sure it's not. I mean, what if it fries my brains?"

Shaniqua rolled her eyes. "It's not scary, Allie, I promise you. I've used the one here, like, a hundred times for school projects. It didn't fry my brains. Do I seem like a zombie to you?" She leaned over the unappetizing remains of her lunch, bugged her eyes out and wiggled her fingers. "Booga booga!"

Alison chuckled nervously. "But really, what's it like, being on the n-net?"

Shaniqua shrugged. "It's not 'like' anything else. For a sensum, which is all they let us do anyhow, it just feels like you're right there at whatever place and time you're supposed to be observing. It is a little strange for the earlier recordings because there's no smell or touch, but that just makes it like watching a tri-vee. Or maybe like being a ghost.

"For an assignment last year I got to sit right next to the High Satrap during that famous interview the British guy did with him forty years ago. You know, the one where he explained why he had to rewrite the Constitution." Shaniqua was a great mimic, and she lowered her voice and imitated the High Satrap himself. "Let me make one thing perfectly clear, David. I could have done the easy thing, the popular thing, and tried to retain the outmoded system of elections, even after our friends on high explained, with the wisdom of tens of thousands of years of civilization, how inefficient they are compared with monarchy, but…"

"Shh! We'll get in big trouble," Alison said, holding in her laughter.

Shaniqua went back to her normal voice. "I tried to touch his sleeve once and my hand passed right through his arm! That was kind of freaky, but there's nothing to it, really."

"But what about a massthink causing instant, total NINA? I heard they let a senior up in Salisbury join a massthink last year. She already had her acceptance letter from MIT, but now she's, like, a vegetable."

Shaniqua waved this off. "There's always rumors like that. I heard it that the girl was from Norfolk and was going to Caltech before she became a drooler. Like I said, you'll only be doing sensums, so there's no risk anyway. Booga booga!"

Up in her bedroom, Alison put her pencil down. Her history paper was due Monday morning, and there was only one solution she could think of: since she couldn't go on the n-net for a sensum of what it had been like during the Arrival, she'd have to talk to Grandma for a first-hand account. But that wasn't so simple, since Mom's mother, her only living grandparent, was in assisted living back in Baltimore. So she went looking for her father. Finding him in the kitchen, washing and drying the last of the supper dishes, she asked if they could all "go back home" for the weekend and explained why.

Dad sighed as he put a saucepan away. "I can't get away, Allie-bear. You know we've got the National Medical people coming this weekend to give Mom a custom wheelchair."

Alison started guiltily. How had she put that out of her mind?

"Tell you what, though," Dad added. "I think you're old enough to take the saucer to Baltimore by yourself."

"Really, Dad? That'd be great!"

He smiled. "I'll drive you to the Wallops Island Interplanetary Base early Saturday morning. Deal?" He held up his hand and she high-fived him.

* * * *

Alison hated getting up early on the weekend, but there wasn't much choice. The air was cold and bright when she and Dad set out a little after eight, and their breath puffed out in clouds. She'd left waffle batter all prepared next to the waffle iron on the kitchen table, hoping Arnold could manage to feed himself and Mom without too much trouble—though she'd put the new fire extinguisher out on the table too, just in case.

The family's battered old Chevy Ampere carried them the four miles down the causeway to the saucer field in just a few minutes; for once Dad wasn't risking a fine by trying to drive the thing manually, instead letting the global DriveNet on the High Ones' mothership do the steering.

While they sailed along, Dad gave Alison a pink knobbed whelk shell he'd found on the beach a few weeks ago, a little one just two inches long, to give to Grandma. "Tell her I'm sorry I can't come and bring Mom," he said.

"Are you sure you'll be all right getting her into the new wheel-chair?" Alison asked.

Dad ruffled her hair. "Don't worry, Allie Bear. That's what the Universal Health is for."

At the fenced-in entrance to the field she had to separate from Dad to go through the female strip-search. The guard was a roundish, middle-aged lady with a scowl and calloused hands who made Alison feel like she was doing something wrong just by breathing. Plus the guard "accidentally" jammed her rigid, rubber-gloved forefinger up Alison's butt, making her yelp.

"Don't be such a baby about it," the lady snapped.

Dad must have seen something in Alison's face because he asked her what was wrong, but she just shook her head. Luckily she didn't have to stand around waiting with him; the little intercity saucer was already parked nearby, hovering about ten feet above the field of bright green salt-marsh hay, with a gleaming metal ramp leading up to it from one of the wooden boardwalks. The thing created so little breeze Alison barely even noticed that her hair was blowing around since she'd forgotten to wear the bright pink cap Grandma had knitted her last year.

"Well, I'd better get back home," Dad said. "The Universal Health people are going to be there in less than an hour." They hugged quickly and Alison shouldered her pack.

There was plenty of room in the saucer, which had a diameter about as long as a school bus and could seat about seventy-five people in two concentric rings. The saucer was half empty, so Alison had no trouble getting a window seat. Of course, you never got to see the really cool part…

"Good morning, folks, and welcome aboard the *Hemi-Viscount Ooffffff'calalius*," the High One pilot said over the intercom, in what sounded like a down-home Southern accent. Not that long ago, he would have been out among his human passengers, pressing tentacles to hands, but the insurgency had gotten so bad they didn't dare emerge from their sealed-off pod at the top of the saucer. "We'd like to thank you for choosing Imperial Spacelines for this short hop to Proxima Centauri 5."

Alison sat bolt upright and shouted in alarm, but the intercom voice was chuckling.

"Jest kiddin' there, folks, this girl's only going to Baltimore. If your final destination is Proxima Centauri's fifth planet, you're going to need a bigger saucer and some rather elaborate breathing apparatus."

A kindly-looking middle-aged lady on Alison's right leaned over and patted her on the arm. "Sorry he gave you a fright, dear. I take this flight all the time, the pilot fancies himself quite a comedian." Alison managed a weak grin.

Meanwhile the saucer had lifted silently and without any sensation of acceleration into the stratosphere. Alison could see all of Chincoteague and the fat fishhook shape of Assateague Island's southern end out her window. But she didn't get to enjoy the view long.

The pilot was back on the intercom, his tone serious. "Passengers, please put your window shades in the full upright and locked position for bubble blowing."

Alison put her hand out obediently, but hesitated, her breath taken away by the green and tawny islands in the deep blue sea below her.

The pilot's voice sounded a sterner note. "Folks, I cannot hyperinflate the bubble universe we need to make the hop to Baltimore until you all—"

The lady to Alison's right reached over and snapped the plastic cover down, pinching Alison's right fingertips so she yelped.

"That's better, folks. Brace for bubble!"

Alison's stomach turned a sick somersault, which made her forget all about the dirty look the lady was giving her. She barely had time to wonder whether it was really true that seeing a bubble universe would make you go insane before the pilot said pleasantly that he'd like to be the first to welcome them to Baltimore and the passengers were free to watch their descent to the landing field.

The bus to Sunup Happy Life Dwellings took longer than the saucer ride had, leaving Alison too much time to fret over how Grandma would feel about her coming alone for help with a school assignment. What if she got mad? She'd been so transparently eager for everyone to stay the last time they visited, back in August. Alison bit her nails until they bled, punishing herself for having written so few letters in the three months that had passed since then. Poor Grandma! She'd had the same longevity treatments as everyone else, but since her stroke she couldn't live on her own—and yet she missed her family and especially Grandpa, who had dropped dead suddenly of a heart defect no one even knew he had.

When the bus pulled up at the glassed-in "sunroom," Grandma was there waiting for her, all but jumping up and down with excitement. "Hello, dear! How is school? How's my favorite granddaughter doing in twelfth grade?"

"Fine, Grandma." Good Lord, she'd obviously gotten her hair done for this visit. The chestnut strands were carefully piled up in the wasp's nest that had been popular fifty years ago, and she had on her best blue dress, the one with the white lacy collar. Her face was so carefully made up you could hardly even tell the left side was droopy from the stroke.

Alison was flattered and ashamed, all at once. As they walked up to Grandma's room she explained what she needed for her school assignment.

"So you need me to reminisce about the good old days?" Grandma said. "I can do that! But first, let's sit down in the kitchen and get you your milk and Oreos."

"I'm on a diet, Grandma," Alison protested, but the plate was already in front of her, the glass (which had originally been a jam jar) was full of ice-cold milk, and it was too much to resist as her grandmother started talking.

"Your grandfather and I were students at Towson State, north of town. We weren't really into our studies because we were hippies, of course. Counterculture freaks," she said.

"I don't know what a 'counterculture' is."

"Disturbers of the Cosmic Harmony, they'd call us now. They called us worse back then. The day of the moon landing, Phil and I went to a be-in on campus."

"A what?"

"A big party where people were passing around joints and dropping acid."

"Grandma!"

She shrugged her shoulders under her lace collar. "You want to know how it was, I'm telling you how it was. Somebody had set up a big color TV on a podium, with a dozen extension cords connected to each other running to the dean's office in the administration building. Which was closed, since it was summer, so somebody must've had to break in."

Alison clapped her hand over her mouth and let out a shocked giggle.

"When the great moment happened, Phil and I were in the middle of an argument."

"An argument? About what?"

"About whether the moon landing was real or the government was faking it."

"Just like Barry Freed!" Alison said, half-whispering.

"Who? Anyway, I can't even remember which side I was taking. But suddenly people were gasping, screaming, freaking out. I remember one guy said real loud, 'Worst trip ever!' Phil and me, we just looked at each other. Most everybody ran off, hoping that it really was just a bad trip and if they slept it off it would go away.

"We were part of the small group that stayed and got to see the mothership descending over the White House an hour later." Grandma chuckled. "People said afterward that the mothership looked like a giant bath toy, and that Risssss-erianus creature resembled a shower cap. But Phil always said it was the White House and that wind-up doll of a president who looked like toys, next to those huge things."

Alison stiffened instinctively. You just didn't talk about the Viceroy of Earth and the High Satrap like that. But Grandma had her own rules. *I'd better get to the point.* "Grandma, this is all really cool, but the point of my paper is how the High Ones brought world peace. What were the huge celebrations like that night, when the High Ones destroyed all the world's nuclear weapons?"

Grandma absently pulled apart an Oreo, dunked the half without the cream filling in her milk, and took a slow, meditative bite before answering. "So that's what they're teaching you kids now, huh? Huge celebrations? There were some pretty raucous parties that night, it's true. From what I heard, they made our 'be-in' look like a little kid's birthday party. End-of-the-world hysteria is what it was. People thought we were all gonna die."

"*What?* But the High Ones had just saved us from, like, extinction!"

Grandma shook her head. "We had our own little party that night, Phil and I." She winked at Alison. "That's when your mother was conceived."

"*GRANDMA!* Gross!"

"Look at your face, kid! Red as an apple!" Grandma laughed, patting Alison's hand. She took another bite of her cookie. "Yep, that was some night. You couldn't get away from the TV. Even if you didn't have yours on, you could hear everyone else's blaring. They kept broadcasting the same clip over and over again, of the mushroom cloud over that missile silo in Kansas being sucked back down into the ground like God was drinking it through a straw.

"From that moment, everybody knew that the High Ones could do whatever they wanted to us. If they wanted us to have world peace, by God, we were going to have world peace. Or our world would be in pieces." Grandma chuckled at her own pun. "More Oreos, dear? You haven't even touched yours."

Cookies were the last thing on Alison's mind. She was too excited. *This is so different from what the history textbook says! But it'll show how primitive humans were when the High Ones arrived. My paper is sure to get an A!*

9

Arnold was so excited about getting back to school so he could meet with Gloria and formally join the Resistance that he completely forgot not to cut across the parking lot of the Value-Mart in case Matt, Jared, and a bigger boy whose name Arnold couldn't remember were hanging out there. Which they were.

Matt got Arnold in a headlock. Then he snorted loudly. "Something smells like rotten eggs here... Well, if it isn't Gross-fart! Where do you think you're going, Gross-fart?"

"I was just on my way to school," Arnold said, wriggling in Matt's iron grasp. Jared and the other boy crowded in. Even if he could break free of Matt, there would be no escape.

"I was just on my way to school," Matt mimicked. "Thought they expelled you, Gross-fart, for flipping off Bubba."

"I didn't flip—ow, stop, that really hurts!" Arnold hated the whining, pleading tone of his own voice, but his neck was killing him.

"Thanks to you, you little kike, we all get our bags searched every morning now!" Matt snarled in his ear. "It was gonna be just for show for a day or two after those little kids got blown up, but they made it permanent!"

"I didn't mean for it to happen! I just didn't want Bubba going through my stuff!"

"Why, what you got in there? Something you haven't been sharing with the rest of us?" Arnold thought he could hear his vertebrae popping as Jared grabbed his book-bag off the tarmac and began to unzip it. But he didn't care about the pain. He was sunk now for sure, even though he'd carefully hidden the adventures of Sir Arnold and Princess Hailee in a plain manila envelope. That would have been enough to keep Bubba from seeing it, but it was sure to draw the bullies' attention.

Wait just a second. "You better not do that," Arnold said, his voice ringing unfamiliar in his own ears, as if he was some tri-vee tough guy— Captain Adams of the Spacefarers, maybe.

"What did you say, Aaaaarnold?" Jared sneered, tapping his face lightly with an open palm. Getting ready for the real beat-down.

"I said, you better not do that, or the Resistance will take care of you."

Jared recoiled as if Arnold had struck him, and Matt suddenly let go of Arnold's neck, took a step back and stared at Arnold through narrowed eyes.

But then Jared shook his head and shoved his face up close to Arnold's. His breath stank of cigarettes. "What's that you said, you little yid? I must've heard you wrong. Everybody knows you people and the Slugs are best friends."

"Sure, that's what we *want* you to think," Arnold said, amazed at the words falling out of his own mouth. "But anybody who really *knows* anything knows that we're tops in the Resistance."

Matt grabbed Arnold's arm and shook it. "That ain't so! The Patriotic Front says to get rid of the Jews and all the other carburetors!"

That's collaborators, you moron. Aloud, Arnold said, "Who said I'm with the Front?"

Matt's eyes narrowed still further. "You're with the Human Defense League? *You?*"

Arnold raised his chin and scowled at the bully. "Not them either, dummy! The name of the group *I'm* in is a secret! I do what I have to, to protect confidential information," he said, trying to deepen his voice so it wouldn't crack. "You'll do the same, if you're not traitors to the Earth!" And he grabbed his book-bag and marched off to school, his head held high and his heartbeat thundering in his ears.

The encounter with the bullies had delayed him so he just barely made it to school on time. As before, Mr. Ramsey and Bubba were the guards on duty, and again the tall, bobble-headed Bubba was the one who searched Arnold and his bag.

"We ain't gonna have no trouble today, are we, chief?" Bubba said.

"Of course not, sir. I understand now that the bag search is for my own safety," Arnold said, so straight-faced that Bubba narrowed his watery brown eyes and stared at him for a long moment. Then he shrugged and ran his rubber glove-clad hands over Arnold, a little more closely than he had two weeks ago. But it didn't take him any longer now than it had then, and while Arnold dressed Bubba unzipped his backpack and rummaged through it quickly before giving him a thumbs-up.

If I'd have known there was no way he would ever have found the adventures of Sir Arnold, I would never have made a fuss and I wouldn't have been suspended for two weeks, Arnold thought as he shouldered his backpack and slouched off to his locker. As he turned the corner into the hallway where the bank of lockers stood, he saw the double doors to the staircase at the far end closing and heard running footsteps. His stomach lurched as he thought about what they might have done to his stuff this time. They had broken in three times since the beginning of the year, and the last time all the notes for his science project had been ripped to shreds, *and* the door had been defaced with a blue-eyed swastika.

But when he came to good old number 407 all he saw on its gray metal front was a faint black smudge. He touched it and found it was still damp and smelled like Sis's nail polish remover. The few textbooks he'd left inside were undamaged. Strange. But he had no more time to think about it for the rest of the morning, he was too busy catching up on all the work he'd missed.

Lunchtime was weird, though. He shuffled with his tray to the re- jects' table as usual, keeping his eyes fixed on the floor, both to avoid provoking anyone and so that he could see any feet casually stretched out to trip him. None were, this time, and once he made it to his usual spot he knew he was safe.

It wasn't that he was actually friends with any of the other rejects— not Jason Trumbull, who had curly red hair, a massive overbite, and thick glasses, and was rumored to be retarded although he was in all normal track classes; not fat Greg Chandler, who picked his nose unselfcon- sciously as he ate; and not even skinny, intense James Park, who was never called Jim and who was destined, everyone knew, for a High Fel- lowship on the aliens' Homeworld, Gliese 581d itself, which meant in three or four years he would be boarding one of their faster-than-light Bubble Drive starships and might never return to Earth.

Usually Arnold would grunt a greeting at James, who would grunt back, not lifting his gaze from his High Astrophysics textbook. This time, though, when Arnold mumbled hello to the future space traveler, James turned his broad, round brown face up, looked at him wide-eyed through his round glasses and edged away.

What the hell? We Jews and Koreans, we have to stick together, don't we? He almost blurted that aloud, when he felt a heavy hand on his shoulder. The bottom dropped out of his stomach as he twisted his neck and turned around, slowly as in a nightmare, to look up. It was Matt's sidekick from this morning whose name he couldn't remember. *I knew it was too good to be true.*

Up close, the unknown bully didn't look like anybody's sidekick— he was simply too big for that, in every dimension: arms, legs, muscular torso, bulging neck, hard-edged face and squinting eyes. The alligator- sized mouth moved and made noises, but they were impossible noises and Arnold's brain refused to take them in. Anyway they were irrelevant since the hand on his shoulder, which was as big and solid as a steak, would momentarily form itself into a fist and pulverize his face.

But that did not happen, and after Arnold counted three and heard nothing but his heart playing his eardrums, he swallowed hard and said softly, "What?"

"I said I'm sorry for all that stuff we did to you," the giant said.

Gus, that was his name. Gus Benedict. Arnold stared at him, speechless. Since his mind was blank, the same devil that had got hold of his tongue in the Value-Mart parking lot this morning took over again and said smoothly, "Oh, that's all right, Gus. Now that you *know*, though, maybe we'll invite you to join us sometime. After we've checked you out, you understand."

Gus's eyes widened. The irises were light brown. "That'd be great," he said in a small voice. "But I don't know if my dad would let me."

Arnold's face shaped itself into an unfamiliar sneer. "You need your daddy's permission? That information will go into the file we've got on you. And Matt and Jared too, of course."

Gus's head bobbed up and down, and he turned and rushed off to tell Matt and Jared this incredible piece of news. When Arnold turned back to the table, he found that James had moved as far away as it was possible to move without falling off the bench bolted to the cafeteria table, and Greg was scrunched up so close to him their knees were touching, leaving only Jason to munch away obliviously to Arnold's left.

What have I done? Arnold wondered, his mind dazed. *How long can I keep up this bluff, before they figure out I'm lying and pound me?*

* * * *

The afternoon dragged on and on. As usual, gym was the worst. Arnold had hoped he'd left dodge ball behind forever when he started high school in Chincoteague, but to his utter horror the gym teacher Mr. Lynch was crazy about the game.

"Go out there and play like a man, *little girl*," the big, hairy, red-faced man had sneered at him when he tried to get out of it. Everyone else seemed to be having fun, but Arnold dreaded the stinging smash of the red rubber playground ball against his bare arms and legs that stuck out so vulnerably from the required gym uniform of blue and gold Chincoteague High T-shirt and shorts, and all through the last half of ninth grade and into the first half of tenth he had seen all his old fears confirmed.

The only way to avoid the pain was to deliberately toss the ball to someone, anyone, on the opposing side, so that he would be out that way instead and could go sit on the sidelines. But whenever he did this the jeers from both sides and from Mr. Lynch himself were deafening. So usually he tried to compromise, to tough out the pain for a while as Matt and company, who always seemed to be on the other team, purposely aimed at him, but no matter how long he let it go before finally tossing the ball in surrender, the taunting was never any less harsh.

"Hey Gross-fart, you sissy, my little sister throws harder than you!"

"Whatsa matter, Gross-fart, saved all your energy to come out your butt?"

"Kikes can't play even baby sports worth a damn!"

But it wasn't like that this time. As usual, Matt, Jared, and Gus were on the other side. But they never shot the ball his way. Instead they slammed the ball into every other kid on Arnold's side, except Hailee and Darla. The ball bounced Arnold's way and he caught it.

Okay, time to get this over with. He lobbed it gently at Matt, the taunts already ringing in his mind. But instead of reaching out to grab the ball out of the air, Matt turned and let it catch him on the arm. *He deliberately got himself out! Why?* There was no time to think, however, because Gus had grabbed the ball and lobbed it lazily over to Arnold, who caught it without thinking. Now only Jared was left on the other side! It had to be a trap. *Even if I win the game for my side, they'll pound me afterwards.*

Arnold started a slow overhand toss, but a volcano suddenly exploded inside him. After all, he was fighting for Princess Hailee and her lady-in-waiting, Mistress Darla! So he whacked the ball as hard as he could with his right hand, so hard that his palm stung as if he'd been hit in the usual way. Instead of ducking, Jared raised his right arm to protect his face. He was out! The game was over, and Arnold had won it!

"Hey, way to go, Arnold!" Darla said, touching him shyly on the shoulder. On the sidelines, Kayleigh began to clap and was joined by a few of the other kids from their side who had been knocked out of the game. Even Hailee smiled.

Arnold shook his head, expecting to wake up any second. But the dream continued down in the locker room, where he changed back into his plaid shirt and brown corduroy pants without suffering so much as a wedgie.

Dazed, he shuffled out of the locker room and over to his school locker, expecting at the very least to find a threatening note inside it. "We know you were lying about what you said. Watch your butt, Jewboy!" But no. The final bell of the day rang and the halls were suddenly full of laughing, shouting kids. Arnold pushed his way through them. No one pushed him back.

The library was the same as before, with Miss Fredericks and Mr. Lynch in their usual places at the n-readers. Her head was resting on his shoulder, which seemed somehow… wrong, to Arnold.

"Hello," said Gloria.

"Hello, Gloria," Arnold said, looking her right in the eye as he shook her hand.

"Well, this is quite a change!" Gloria laughed. "You were afraid of your own shadow before."

"Yes. But not now." He shut his right eye slowly and deliberately. "Not now that I *know who you are*."

Gloria's green eyes widened. She glanced at the comatose teachers, then out at the rapidly emptying hallway, and moved to ease the door shut.

"It's not such a secret, dear," she said in a half-whisper. "I mean, you're not the only one I've helped over the dimensional divide. Your dad and Alison came with you to Gingo Teag, remember."

If it's not such a secret, how come she's whispering? It must be too dangerous to discuss the Resistance at all in this world. Which means I have to get over to Gingo Teag to talk to her openly. He nodded slowly. "I understand. I'd like to go there now."

"Well, of course, Arnold! Jo will be delighted to see you. School ends half an hour later there, but by the time you get through the Gray Zone the bell should've already gone off. I told her you'd be back in school today and she said she'd tell her Mum to set an extra place at tea just in case you did come to pay a visit. So it's all set!"

How am I supposed to know what she means by all those code words? Arnold wondered as he followed Gloria back behind the counter and to the door in the back wall that opened into the Gray Zone corridor. *Maybe "tea" means some kind of poisonous stuff I can kill High Ones with!*

Arnold was so excited by the thought that he'd soon get a chance to fight the High Ones himself that he barely paid attention to the inside-out transition between dimensions, and as he hurried along the Gray Zone hallway he didn't notice the slick, oily patch on the tile floor until he was slipping on it, landing hard on his butt.

"Ow!" He tried to get up but slipped again, hitting his head on the floor hard enough that everything got funny and faraway, like that time he told Matt to get his own lunch money and Matt gave him a black eye.

He sat up and shook his head, trying to make the world stop turning around him. But it only seemed to spin harder, like in those tri-vids they saw in history class about the centrifuges NASA used before the Arrival to train astronauts for the primitive rockets they used back then.

The walls, floor, and ceiling dissolved into gray mist, then to a background of diamond-hard stars against a black night through which Arnold tumbled helplessly. Unlike that family trip to Mars they'd taken when he was in fourth grade, back before Mom got sick, there was no reassuring solidity of a spaceship around him, and no sign of the Sun or any planets nearby. He was falling through interstellar space!

I'm not an idiot, I know what that means. They'll never find me! Other kids might learn to write down the numbers symbolizing the vastness of the universe, but that was just to pass a test. They never thought about what those numbers really meant. How human beings, and High Ones, and even stars and galaxies, were less than a handful of sand thrown into the Grand Canyon. How behind everything was a gulf of emptiness. The universe didn't care what happened to him, or his family, or his planet. It was even worse than that: with its deadly radiation and its terrible gravity and its endless desert spaces, it wanted to kill him, it wanted to smash his face into the hard tarmac and leave him there to bleed to death, to send him tumbling forever like the man in the Ray Bradbury story, on his way to no particular night and no particular morning.

But as he fell through the silent blackness, a face floated before his dimming vision. A face with a mischievous gleam in its green-flecked brown eyes and its dirty blond hair pulled back in an untidy ponytail. *Jo. I was on the way to see Jo.* And with that thought, interstellar space vanished and a flickering blue gas flame took the place of the impossibly distant stars. And he wasn't imagining Jo's face, he was actually seeing it—seeing her kneeling down over him, saying his name.

10

"They're called the Gray Ones," Jo explained as she walked Arnold to her home. Gingo Teag was quiet on this late afternoon in early December. The few electric "carriages" on the streets purred quietly as they passed, and flecks of sleet hissed down from a darkening gray sky. Arnold shivered and huddled deeper into his coat. Chincoteague was a lot warmer than its sister island.

"Have you ever seen one?" Arnold asked.

Jo's pigtail flipped back and forth where it peeked out from under a brown cap as she shook her head. "But Tommy and Teresa told me all about them. Teresa was almost killed by one! It looked like an oil slick, they said. Gloria said that isn't their 'true form,' whatever that means, but she changed the subject when I asked her what they do look like. She really doesn't like to talk about them."

"Why not?"

Jo shrugged.

"Do you think she's afraid of them? Maybe they're allied with the High Ones!"

"I never heard Gloria mention the High Ones until the day I met you," Jo said. "And I'm not really sure the Gray Ones are a 'they' so much as an 'it.' A personification of the hostility we feel in the Gray Zone."

Arnold sniffed when Jo said "personification." It was a show-offy word that Alison might have used. "I know what you mean, but how can there be hostility if there isn't a person or at least an animal or something there to *be* hostile? I mean, space will kill you if you go for a spacewalk without a spacesuit, but that doesn't mean it actually hates you." *Though it sure FELT like it did, when I suddenly found myself drifting there!*

Jo rubbed her chin. "It does sound weird, I admit, but haven't you felt afraid when you had to walk through the Gray Zone, knowing that nothing you saw was really real?"

She'll think I'm a coward. She'll laugh at me like all the other girls do. So Arnold shook his head.

"Well, you're the first person I've met who doesn't," Jo said, shooting Arnold a sidelong glance.

Jo's house looked old-fashioned to Arnold, like his house had been before the contractors got to work on it. It stood on stilts above marshy ground toward the southern end of Main Street, below where the bridge to the mainland stood in Chincoteague—but in Gingo Teag, there was no causeway and no bridge. The only way to get to the island, Mrs. Purnell explained as she hung up his coat for him, was by ferry. "For which they charge a fare of thruppence. Highway robbery!"

"Mum's been pestering the Nanticoke House of Burgesses for years to build a causeway out here," Jo explained. When Arnold shook his head in confusion, she added, "It's like one of your state legislatures."

"We need the national parliament involved," Mrs. Purnell said. Her blond hair was neatly waved, and she was wearing a double strand of pearls over a soft-looking wine-colored sweater. Arnold thought she couldn't have reminded him less of his own messy mother if she'd tried. "Do you take jam or butter on your scones, dear?" she asked.

"What's a scone?"

"It's like a muffin, only not as sweet," Jo said, munching on one. "But even Teresa knew what a scone was. She says they're her favorite thing to get at Starbucks."

"What's Starbucks?"

"Teresa said there's one on every corner in her 'America,'" Jo said, looking puzzled.

"Gloria told you Arnold's America is different from Teresa's," Mrs. Purnell said. "Wipe your mouth, Jo, you have got raspberry preserves all over your face."

"Where are Tom and Teresa?" Arnold asked, first making sure he had swallowed everything in his mouth and that his face was clean. He had a vision of Mrs. Purnell cleaning his face with a napkin that he did not want to become reality.

"Revising for finals at Cambridge, I should think," said Mrs. Purnell. "Our British schools do not have the long holidays you rebels seem to enjoy with your liberty."

"Mum, you're always telling me to be polite. That seems awfully rude," Jo said.

Mrs. Purnell shot her a fierce look while Arnold tried to figure out what she had been talking about. *Oh, right, they never had the American Revolution here. So that makes us Americans "rebels" to her.*

Mrs. Purnell looked down. "I am afraid Jo is right, Arnold. It is not your fault that your ancestors were traitors to the Crown. Do forgive me."

"That's all right," Arnold said, though he hadn't felt insulted, only filled with wonder. A loud whistle made him jump.

"That will be the kettle. I shall not be a moment," Mrs. Purnell said, jumping up and smoothing her long skirts down as she walked to the kitchen.

Jo winked at Arnold. "You won't see that very often. Mum admitting that she's wrong, I mean."

"I heard that, Jodie Marybeth Purnell!" her mother called from the other room.

"Don't get any ideas about calling me Jodie. I shall flatten you if you do," Jo said firmly to Arnold.

"I won't," he said absently as he looked around the room. It was just an ordinary living room, although neater than most people's homes, with pretty, matching floral prints on all the sofas and easy chairs, a blinding white tablecloth covering the dark wooden coffee table where they were eating, and a bookshelf lined with books Arnold felt certain were better organized than those in Gloria's library. One important thing was missing, though.

"Where's your tri-vee stage?"

"What are you talking about?" Mrs. Purnell asked as she walked back into the room, carrying a silver tray with a large, shiny teapot and three delicate-looking mugs.

"Oh, right. The High Ones gave us tri-vee. I mean your TV."

"We haven't got that either," Jo said, reaching out for a mug.

Mrs. Purnell swatted her hand away. "Mind your manners, Jodie! Guests first. Do you take milk or sugar, Arnold?"

"I like my tea black," Arnold said, and Mrs. Purnell smiled. She could have been a tri-vee actress when she did that.

The tea was nice and strong, just the way Arnold liked it. It warmed him and woke him up, and he began to wonder why Jo and her mother were taking so long to get around to the point of his visit—fighting Earth's alien occupiers. They couldn't possibly be scared of the High Ones, could they? They'd never even seen one.

Arnold had, on that family trip to Mars. Back then, before the September 11 joint attack on the UN Building by the Front and the League, which killed or maimed most of the ambassadors and staff in the UN General Assembly but missed its intended target of the Exalted High Viceroy Risssss-erianus, the High Ones piloting spaceships would often mingle with the human passengers.

Arnold had watched the alien approach, excitement mingling with dread in his guts. Mom squeezed his hand and whispered, "There's nothing to be afraid of, honey! Just say hello like you would to anyone." But her palm was sweaty and she gripped his hand hard as the creature made its way around their ring of the saucer.

Arnold thought that the tri-vids he had seen, even the life-sized ones, didn't really do justice to the aliens' massive, three-meter-long physical presence. It was like being inside a zoo enclosure with a hippopotamus, not that a High One looked anything like a mammal—or even an insect, for that matter. Its closest Earthly analogue was a sea creature called a crown of thorns starfish, an echinoderm that feasted on corals in Australia's Great Barrier Reef by first throwing up on them and dissolving the poor corals in its stomach acid. Like them, the High Ones were radially symmetrical and had many more arms than the familiar five-armed starfish, but Earth's alien overlords were more discreet in their dining habits, and their spines weren't venomous like those of the crown of thorns. That was a good thing because the High Ones used their spines like little tentacles for grabbing food, starship controls, and people's hands when it wanted to shake them, as it was now doing to Arnold's.

"Sub-Baron Shhhh-iblius at your service. How are you, son? First time in space?" it asked. Its voice synthesizer made it sound like Arnold's math teacher, Mr. Podolski. Arnold started to relax a little—he liked Mr. Podolski—though he couldn't help thinking that the High One looked way less human than the starfish Sammy on the cartoon "Curly-Coral Swim-Trunks," a show SCOD had banned as "probably offensive to the High Ones."

Offending this creature was the last thing on Arnold's mind, even if he did have a Sammy action figure hidden at the bottom of his underwear drawer at home. The High One was so pretty, for one thing, covered with overlapping aquamarine scales that were pleasantly cool to the touch and useful for discreetly hiding the water-bottles they needed while moving about on dry land, like a human deep-sea diver's air tanks. Its ivory-colored spines and tentacles were as warm as a person's hand.

Arnold bent his trembling head. "My n-name is Master Arnold Grossbard. I am hon-honored t-to meet you, s-sir," he stammered, hoping he was remembering his Imperial Etiquette right. They taught it to you from the moment you started kindergarten, but it was so easy to mess up! "I'm d-d-doing j-just f-f-fine, s-sir. S-so c-cool to be in sp-sp-space!"

"My name is Mrs. Rachel Grossbard, and I am *deeply* honored to meet you, sir," Mom murmured, taking another of the creature's spines.

How could I have forgotten the "deeply"? Arnold thought. *He's almost a baron! I just had that on a quiz. Stupid, stupid! Maybe he'll forgive me…*

"He's so looking forward to a tour of Bradbury Colony," Mom was saying. "I haven't been back myself since my honeymoon ten years ago."

"Then you're in for a real treat," the High One informed her. "It's almost twice as big as it was back then, but of course the real difference is that there's no dome anymore, not since we got the atmosphere up almost to mountaintop pressure. It was a great achievement for Subduke F'ssss-terponicus. He's in high favor at court at the moment."

Struggling to get his stammer under control, Arnold said, "I'm really looking forward to seeing the t-two moons, sir. Phobos and D-deimos."

"Fear and panic, eh? You humans certainly are a timid lot, to be scared by a couple of little asteroids," the Arch-baron chuckled. "Though I suppose if we were to toss one of them at your world, it would cause an extinction-level event, wouldn't it?"

Mom let out a high-pitched squeal that sounded nothing like her real laugh, a deep-throated guffaw. "You do soooooo deeply honor us with your humor, Your Excellency!"

"Indeed. Now, young Arnold, since this is your first time traveling from your developing world, I have a little present for you." A spine reached into a pocket tucked between two scales and pulled out a glittering egg-shaped bauble about a centimeter long.

"A Homeworld amulet! Gee, thanks, deeply honored sir!" His gratitude was genuine, though it burned him to remember that now. Especially because some seventh graders had beaten him up and stolen the amulet, along with the silver necklace Mom had had it mounted on, barely a week after he got back to school from his Mars trip. People would kill for things from Homeworld. But Jo and her mother seemed no more than casually curious about Earth's overlords. How could that be, when they'd volunteered to help him fight them? He had to broach the subject with them somehow. *Maybe it's a test—they want to see if I'm brave enough to say how I really feel about the High Ones.*

Arnold put his empty tea cup down carefully in its saucer. "Mrs. Purnell, thank you very much for having me over," he said. "But I think we all know Gloria didn't bring me all the way here just to have tea." He felt *great* saying that, so important and grown-up, having heard somebody say something just like it on a tri-vee spy show.

"No? But I make very good tea," Mrs. Purnell said.

Jo nodded vigorously. "The best. Even I have to admit it."

"No," Arnold said, and then in a rush, "I hate the High Ones, I really hate them! I know Gloria brought me here to meet you so you can help me fight them, right?"

Mrs. Purnell raised an eyebrow at Jo, who explained, "They're the aliens who took over the Earth—Arnold and Alison's Earth, that is. I told you about them, Mum. They look like blue slugs, right, Arnold?"

"Worse. They look like giant, armored, blue starfish with tentacles."

"It's just like in Herbert Wells's book, *The War Between the Worlds*!" Jo exclaimed, her eyes gleaming.

"You know I do not approve of scientification," Mrs. Purnell said, frowning.

"You mean science fiction? But you're friends with a telepathic dragon," Arnold said.

"That is just normal, everyday reality."

"And Gloria?"

"She saved our lives, so of course I am fond of her. But she never asked us to help you fight the aliens ruling your world," Mrs. Purnell said. She frowned and pushed a stray strand of hair out of her face. "Arnold, I know what it is like to grow up under foreign occupation. Trust me when I say you do not want to get involved in the 'resistance.'"

"Mum grew up in Liverpool, before England rebelled against *l'Empire*," Jo explained, pronouncing the word French-style: *lump-ear*. "But you were thrilled when that happened, Mum! You jitterbugged with Dad around the parlor."

Mrs. Purnell colored slightly. "Yes, of course I was happy that Anglatare was free. We shall go there soon to visit, Jodie, I promise. But when I think of the danger Tom and Teresa put themselves in, sneaking over there just before the Revolution broke out, it makes me sick. If Tom were not eighteen years old, I should confine him to his room until Judgment Day."

Arnold smiled to himself. Some things were the same in all worlds.

"Mum's not telling you the whole story. My dopey big brother actually helped to start the Anglay Revolution!" Jo said. "Of course, Teresa was even more important, and her double Palermo Teresa was the most important of all!"

"I do not like that girl. She is trouble," Mrs. Purnell said, her brows knitted.

"I'm sorry, who is Palermo Teresa?" Arnold said.

"Oh, she is *wizard!*" Jo said, clapping her hands. "She's the double of Tom's Teresa, except instead of being from boring old Philadelphia, she's from Sicily, and she's tough as nails and hates the Frogs— *l'Empire*—and any kind of royalty! Which is only common sense, just like good old Tom Paine called for."

"Common sense, indeed! She is as dangerous a radical as he was. I cannot understand why the Crown let her into British territory," Mrs. Purnell said.

"That must be why Gloria brought you here!" Jo exclaimed, seizing Arnold's hand. Her hands were warm and soft, except for calluses on the fingertips. Holding them made Arnold's guts feel mushy and warm. She said, "Mum, don't you think there must be some reason that Gloria introduced us?"

"Perhaps," Mrs. Purnell said, "it is simply that you and Arnold both need a friend."

Jo tossed her head back, making her ponytail bob. Her neck was long and unexpectedly graceful. "Why, just 'cause Marcia moved away, the rotter?"

"She has been your best friend since you started primary school, Jodie-kins."

"Do NOT call me Jodie-kins!" Jo said, stamping her foot so hard Arnold's chair rattled. "She's a rotter who couldn't even remember to call me Jo and not Jodie! And she borrowed my copy of *A Wrinkle in Time* and never gave it back!"

"As I recall, it was actually Tom's copy, from Gloria's bookstore," Mrs. Purnell said drily.

Arnold kept silent. Denying that he needed a friend would have been too big of a lie.

"Well, young lady, if you are *quite* finished with your tea, you can walk your *non*-friend back to Gloria's bookstore," Mrs. Purnell said. "I believe you still have some revising to do for your calculus test."

"Mum! I don't have to revise for calculus. Even a baby could do those epsilon-delta proofs!"

"Jodie Marybeth Purnell, what have I told you about boasting!"

"But I'm not boasting, Mum!"

"Out the door with you," Mrs. Purnell said firmly, grabbing Jo with her right hand and Arnold with her left. Her grip was as strong as the clamp in metal shop. "Arnold, it was simply delightful having you to tea. Please do tell Alison and Gerald they are welcome any time." It took Arnold a moment to figure out she was talking about Dad. No one ever called him anything except Jerry.

"And remember my rule, Jodie," Mrs. Purnell added. "No visiting parallel worlds while you still have homework to do!"

"But Mum," Jo said, as the door shut in their faces.

Outside, it was as dark as midnight. Arnold could see his breath and more stars than he ever saw at home, though not as many as he'd seen in the Gray Zone. After a moment they began to walk. He longed to touch Jo's hand again, but she had jammed her hands deep in her pockets.

"Right then," she said after a moment, "I shall tell Teresa it is urgent she contact her double and tell her to come to Gingo Teag. Palermo Teresa is an experienced revolutionary and will have just *loads* of good ideas for you."

"Okay," Arnold said.

"And here are *my* rules. You are *not* my friend, you are my brother in arms. Together we shall free your Earth from alien tyranny."

"Roger that," Arnold said.

"Roger who? Oh, you mean *yes*. Very well. Rule number two, no hand holding."

"Roger that," Arnold said, hoping that Jo had not noticed his hesitation.

"Likewise, no snogging, no smooching, no disgusting stuff. I see Tom and Teresa doing that all the time. It's not for me, thank you very much."

"Roger that. No disgusting stuff."

"We are professional rebels, you and I. I am not going to walk out with you."

"What?"

"I'm not your girlfriend."

"Roger that."

"Next rule. Nobody but my Mum is allowed to call me Jodie. And as for Marybeth—instant death."

"Roger that," said Arnold, grateful that the darkness helped him hide a smile.

"What number are we up to?"

"Er, six, I think."

"Right. Rule six. There is no... uh, I guess there is no rule six."

"Roger that."

Jo gave him a hard stare, which again turned his insides into hot cream of wheat. Then she nodded and stopped walking. They were standing on a street corner down the block from Gloria's Gateway Books.

"Very well. We must take a blood oath to be faithful to the cause of Earth's freedom."

"A *what*?" Arnold started to say, but Jo had already grabbed his right hand—so much for no hand-holding—produced a safety pin from somewhere and pricked first her little finger, then his. He stifled a startled yelp as she stirred the tiny, mingled droplet of blood around with the pinpoint.

"Repeat after me. I do solemnly swear to protect, defend, and uphold the sacred cause of human freedom, even under hideous physical torture and mutilation, the threat of death, or alien brainwashing."

Arnold solemnly swore, and Jo said, "I hereby declare the Fighters for the Freedom of Earth *founded*." She grasped his hand once more, tightly, then let it go before they walked into the bookstore together.

11

Having Barry Freed suddenly step in front of her while she was trying to get home was the last thing Alison needed, after the day she'd already had.

"Interplanetary travel," he said darkly.

I'm not in the mood for this. "What about it, Mr. Freed?"

Today he was wearing a dark windbreaker, and he seemed to have made a haphazard attempt at trimming his wild gray-white beard. He didn't smell as bad as usual, either. Maybe Pastor Mills at the Union Baptist Church had let him use the shower there. How the old hippie had not been arrested or disappeared by SCOD after all these years was a mystery, but Dad pointed out that just because the man was paranoid and crazy didn't mean he wasn't smart. "The problem is, he uses all his intelligence to dream up new details of the plots he thinks are everywhere."

As if to illustrate the truth of this, Mr. Freed said, "Did you ever wonder how they make people think they're flying to other planets when they aren't going anywhere at all?"

"Mr. Freed, that isn't so. I've been to Mars myself, the summer I turned ten," Alison said.

"No you haven't, sweetheart. They just made you *think* you were there."

"I took a ride on the Martian surface in a pressurized buggy. It's all orangey-red, just like they say. And the horizon's too close because the planet is so much smaller than Earth, and the sun is too small, and you can see the two little moons high up and bright at the dark top of the daytime sky. It's really cool. You should go."

He shook his head sadly. "They do a great job making you think you're there, I have to give them that."

"But why, Mr. Freed? Why would anyone go to all the trouble of faking out millions of people like that?"

"Go back and read Ray Bradbury's short story 'The Rocket' if you want to know how it's done," he said, as if by answering *how* he could avoid the question of *why*. "Smoke and mirrors, I tell you. Smoke and mirrors. Phil Dick knew how, too, before they disappeared him back in '74."

Having a conversation with Mr. Freed was like wandering into a Halloween corn maze and losing track of the exit. The sun shone brightly, tauntingly overhead and the air was crisp and cool on your skin as you walked quicker and quicker, swallowing your panic. Until you started to run around blind corners and into one dead end after another lined with browning corn husks and nodding, mummified cobs.

"I'm sorry, Mr. Freed, I have to go," Alison said, trying to step around him.

He blocked her and she had to swallow a flutter in her stomach. "What's the matter, Allie? You look upset."

Afterwards she thought she must have been so startled to hear him say anything that didn't have to do with his obsessions that she simply blurted out what was actually on her mind. "Miss Burbage gave me an F on my history term paper. An F! And I worked so hard on it... I did everything she told us to, footnoted all my sources and everything... Do you know what a pain that is to do on our old electric typewriter? And not only *that*, Miss Burbage kept me after class and said I have to go see Mr. Wright tomorrow, with Dad!"

Mr. Freed narrowed his eyes. "What did you write about, kid? Lemme see that paper."

Which reminded Alison who she was talking to. "Uh, I don't think that would be a very good idea. No offense, Mr. Freed."

"Why not? I might have something useful to contribute—" he cackled—"being something of a historical relic myself!"

This was disarming, but Alison still didn't want to put her bookbag down on the sidewalk, unzip it, and reveal its messy insides to the cold, darkening street and this smelly, crazy guy, even if he was probably harmless. And talking to him about what she'd written about would only encourage him to start ranting. *On the other hand, what's the worst that can happen? I'm going to make him crazier than he already is?*

"Well, Mr. Freed—"

"Barry, please, miss." The "miss" was even more disarming.

"I wrote about how the High Ones brought peace," Alison said, tensing her leg muscles so she could sprint away if he started to give one of his long speeches about how the creatures who ruled the Earth didn't really exist.

Instead, he said mildly, "Why should that upset Nancy? That's exactly the sort of propaganda they pay her to ladle out to you."

How does he know her first name? Aloud, Alison said, "I know, right? And I was careful to say how many people had been killed in the Vietnam War before the peace treaty—almost 45,000 American soldiers and, like, three-quarters of a million Vietnamese—and how hundreds of millions of lives may have been saved by preventing a nuclear war, which the High Ones said had a fifty-fifty chance of happening in the twenty years after the Arrival, if things had kept going the way they were. And I said how amazed everyone was that the High Ones had not had a war in *eighteen thousand Earth years* and how U Thant begged on television for their help in bringing about peace on Earth."

"The High Satrap himself couldn't have put it better. So what was the problem?"

"I also interviewed my grandmother, who told me that everyone was scared of what the High Ones might do after they destroyed all the world's nuclear weapons without even leaving a radioactive mess. That should've been all right—Miss Burbage said we could use family members' personal memories."

The corners of Mr. Freed's beard twisted upward. "Alison, you knew you'd get in trouble for writing that, didn't you?"

Alison looked at the ground at his feet. "I thought maybe I could get away with it if I spent most of the paper writing about how great world peace is and how the High Ones deserve a lot of the credit. And I really think that, too. But I thought it would be even better to tell the whole truth. Isn't that what people swear to do in court? Tell the truth, the whole truth, and nothing but the truth?"

Mr. Freed chuckled. The sound was like an old tin can being kicked down the street. "I've been in court a few times in my life, Alison, and I can tell you that truth ain't the main concern there, no matter what you might see on a tri-vee stage. And even less so when it comes to politics. *They* can't stand people going after the truth, because sooner or later folks are bound to trip over all the big lies *they* use to run the world."

Alison looked up at Mr. Freed, noticing as if for the first time that he was a tall man, but hunched over until he was hardly any taller than Dad. She felt sorrier for him than ever. "But Mr. Freed, I told you, I've been to Mars myself, and I've talked to High Ones. Archbaron Shhhh-iblius was really nice to Arnold and me, and he gave us each a Homeworld amulet. I still have mine."

"Bread and circuses," Mr. Freed said sadly, "baubles and toys. They've bought us off so cheaply, Alison. But you—you've started down the path to truth, and there is nothing more dangerous to them than a person like that. Watch your step." He nodded gravely and stepped aside to let her pass, the first time Alison could remember him ever doing that. Somehow that made what he had just said even scarier. Dad always said that even paranoids had enemies.

She hurried home, her stomach churning at the prospect of having to tell Mom and Dad about her history paper, but Dad had left a note saying he had taken Mom to a doctor's appointment and they wouldn't be back until late. Arnold was around somewhere, though. The evidence was spread out all over the kitchen table in the form of an open jar of peanut butter, a banana peel, and a crumpled bread wrapper. At least he'd remembered to put his dishes in the sink.

She sighed as she cleaned up the mess and tried to think how she could break the bad news to Mom and Dad. *Maybe they won't be mad. After all, they didn't even punish Arnold for getting suspended.* Still, she wished there was someone she could talk to first, someone more useful than Turd-Breath.

She already knew Shaniqua had no sympathy, because she'd shaken her head when she saw the big red F on the paper. "Told you so," she said. "What did you want to go making trouble for?" There was no good answer to that.

Teresa from Gingo Teag might have understood. There was that mischievous gleam in her eye. Except, she wasn't really from the Gingo Teag world, but from Philadelphia, in the America that might have been if the High Ones had never arrived.

Wait a minute—that means they didn't stop World War III from happening after all! Teresa's world didn't get nuked! On the *third* hand, the High Ones had said there was a "fifty-fifty chance" of nuclear war breaking out, right? Which might mean there was yet *another* world where they *hadn't* arrived, and America and the Soviet Union *did* blow each other up! It was so confusing. How could Gloria keep it all straight, even if she did have eleven dimensions?

Alison had asked Teresa that very question, the night of the dragon air show, and Teresa had shaken her head with a smile. "I don't really get it, either. You should talk to my friend Susie. She used to be my physics teacher, but now she's finishing her doctorate at Caltech. Which has to be easier than trying to teach me physics."

"Do you go back and forth between your world and this one all the time?" Alison asked.

"Not all the time. I mostly live in this one. I'm going to college with Tom at Cambridge University. His dad's an Oxford man, so he's disappointed we're not going there instead. I mean the universities here in Nanticoke, of course—Delaware plus the Eastern Shore of Maryland and Virginia, to you and me—not the original ones in England, or 'Anglatare.'"

"But how did you get into a college here? I mean, you didn't go to school in this world. You weren't even *born*, in this world."

"Oh, we have our ways," Teresa said with a little smile. "And yeah, I actually was born in this world, too. I have a double here!"

"That's so cool! Do you guys, like, hang out together?"

"No, she's real busy," Teresa said, a little too quickly. That conversation had left Alison with a lot of unanswered questions. But it also made her think that Teresa—both versions of her—knew more than a little about getting into trouble, and how to get out of it, too.

* * * *

Alison was wrong about her parents' reaction to the F on her paper, though. Dad did get really mad—only at Miss Burbage, not at her. "That's an AP class you're in! All-Planetary! You're supposed to be the elite of the entire Earth! How can you be elite if they won't let you think for yourself?"

"It's not the thinking they mind so much," Alison said, "it's the saying so out loud. Please don't make it worse for me by arguing with them, Dad."

Mom leaned forward in her wheelchair, and Dad reached over to push her gently back so she didn't fall over. She wasn't having a good day, Alison could see; when she talked it came out slightly slurred. "Allie is right, honey," she said. "Don't p-pick a fight with her teacher and the principal. Not in a con-conservative town like this."

"I'm tired of kissing the butts of these drones," Dad said, grimly. "I've been doing it all my life. You'll never know how many times I swallowed my pride when I worked for the *Sun*, until I just couldn't do it and look myself in the mirror anymore. I'm not raising Allie and Arnold to be like that, Rachel."

"Dad, *please* don't make a scene when we meet with Miss Burbage and Mr. Wright tomorrow," Alison said. "Everything I do now affects my SAT score, you know that."

"We didn't even have the Social Aptitude Test when I was a kid," Dad said. "They should call it what it is, a butt-kissing test! A go-along-to-get-along test!"

"Jerry, k-keep your voice down!" Mom stuttered. "Y-you don't want Arnold to hear th-this. He has a hard enough time in school as it is."

"Maybe that's because he's smarter than the rest of us, did you ever consider that?" Dad snapped. Then he saw the look on Alison's face and tousled her hair. "I'm sorry, muffin. I didn't mean that. But it's just un-American to give people a hard time for thinking for themselves. Why shouldn't you question what happened when the High Ones came? What are they so afraid of?"

"J-jerry, d-don't make Allie f-f-f…" Mom's face got all red with frustration when she couldn't get the words out. It hardly mattered, because this was an argument they'd had before. *Don't make her fight your battles,* that's what Mom meant to say. Though neither she nor Dad would ever explain his biggest battle, the one he'd lost along with his job at the *Sun.* Was that because they wouldn't let him write the truth?

Mr. Freed had an answer to that. He thought the "powers that be" were afraid of the truth. But what was the truth? His ideas about it were crazy. How could he say flying saucers were made up, when Alison had just ridden on one to Baltimore and back? How could he say the High Ones themselves weren't real, when they had taken over the whole world and ran it mostly pretty well, better than people had ever done back in the old days? Maybe the textbooks and the tri-vee news were right when they said the terrorists were just "malcontents," people who would never be happy no matter what.

But by that logic, Mr. Freed was a malcontent too, though he never did anybody any harm worse than stealing a bit of their time for his loony rants. And he'd been nice to her when she was so upset just now. What did that mean? Could you be nuts but nice at the same time? Or did nuts mean dangerous, so you had to be locked up somewhere? Who got to decide? The High Ones and the grown-up world didn't want you to ask questions like that, which had to make Mr. Freed at least partly right. But how right was he?

People sometimes talked about half-truths, as if you could neatly split an idea into its true and false parts. But what about when they were all mixed up together, like in Mr. Freed's head? It was all so frustrating and confusing.

Thoughts like these whirled around and around in her brain that night like fall leaves trapped in the wind in a dead-end alley. Their clattering kept her awake and finally drove her from her warm bed, down the drafty hallway to the kitchen for a glass of warm milk. But as she tiptoed along a slight noise brought her up short. A scratching, or maybe a whispering. *Sounds like it's coming from Arnold's room.* She pushed aside an uneasy feeling that she shouldn't pry as she eased his door open, wincing at the soft scraping sound the wood made against the carpet.

He was sitting up in bed, with his back to her and his legs tucked under his butt, as he leaned over the headboard. He was whispering to himself as he played with something on the windowsill.

"Arnold? What are you doing up? Are you all right?"

He whirled around, anger rapidly chasing panic away from his pale face. "Don't you believe in knocking, butt-head?!"

Alison swallowed the temptation to insult him back. After all, she wanted a friend on this lonely night, not a fight. "I just heard noises. I was worried about you."

"Well, you don't have to worry. I wasn't doing anything. Just looking at this spider plant Gloria gave me."

"Can I see?" She turned on the overhead light, which was set in an old-fashioned glass fixture with a ceiling fan, like the one in her room. Dad had made sure they both had one, which had made the summer a lot easier to bear. But sometimes she'd hit the wrong button when it was cold out, and the chilly breeze didn't seem so nice then.

Arnold screwed up his mouth as if to yell at her to get out, but he didn't say anything as she walked up and bent over the plant. She recoiled when she saw its leaves waving around although the air in the room was still. "Does it always do that?"

"Almost every time I look at it, yeah," Arnold said. "Even in the middle of the night."

"I never heard of a plant doing that," Alison said, cautiously extending her right pinkie finger toward it. She giggled as the leaves tickled her. "It's probably not from Earth—at least, not *our* Earth. But I'm sure Gloria wouldn't give you anything dangerous."

"It calms me down to talk to it," Arnold said softly, glancing up at her. "That probably sounds really stupid, doesn't it?"

"No—it's making me feel a little less anxious right now. Which is good because I have to get some sleep." She yawned, covering her mouth with the back of her hand. "I got in big trouble today, Arnold, just like you. *Worse* than you, maybe—Dad has to go talk to Miss Burbage and Mr. Wright because of my history paper."

Arnold's eyes gleamed. "Why? Did you say the High Ones are yucky alien oppressors of the human race?"

"No. But I did say that part of the reason we had world peace after the Arrival was that people were scared of them."

"Oh." Arnold started to say something, stopped, shook his head.

"What is it, Arnold?"

"Nothing. Good luck tomorrow, Sis. Dad is really good. When we started out Mr. Wright wanted to suspend me for a month!"

I guess that's reassuring.

Her dreams when she went back to bed were not, though. In one she was a flying dragon dodging cannonballs shot from wooden ships far below. The air was thick with smoke, and terrible screams tore at the air around her. In another she was running through a corn maze at night, under a glowering orange moon. Something was behind her, she could hear it rustling and crashing. It was getting closer—she dared not turn around, *just looking would be enough to kill her*—and then it clamped down hard on her shoulder.

"Allie, calm down, honey!" Dad was saying, his hand still on her shoulder as she sat bolt upright. Morning sunlight made slanted yellow bars across her blankets. "I just came in to get you up for school when the alarm didn't wake you. Are you all right?"

"Fine. Sorry, Dad."

He was already dressed in a suit and tie for work. It was the lighter of the two gray suits he owned. She reminded herself she had to go pick up the other one from Park Place Cleaners on Main Street. And that tie—it was awful. How could Mom let him wear it?

He glanced down when he saw she was looking at it. "Do you like this American flag pattern? I figure Mr. Wright won't be too hard on you if I wear a nice, patriotic tie like this to our meeting this morning!" He chuckled.

"Our meeting. Right." She ran her hands through her hair, wincing at the knots she encountered. Then she glanced at the clock, which was still buzzing, and bolted out of bed. "Can you give Arnold breakfast, please, Dad, after you help Mom? He likes Wheaties—there's a box in the pantry—"

"Fine, fine. Just calm down and get ready. Your old Dad will get you out of this."

She ran to the bathroom and showered with one ear out for the smoke alarm in case Dad got any ideas about fixing a hot breakfast, but things stayed quiet. By the time she was dressed and her hair mostly untangled, Dad had set out a bowl of her own favorite cereal, Rice Krispies, and even topped it with out-of-season blueberries.

"I was saving them for next week, when it'll be Christmas and they roll up the sidewalks here in town, but, well," Dad shrugged.

Alison hugged him lightly around the neck before sitting down to eat. It was hard to get used to being taller than him.

It helped a lot knowing he was on her side as they walked into the principal's office. Miss Burbage was already there, sitting in a chair holding her grade book, her mouth a tight, narrow line. Mr. Wright stood up to shake hands with Dad, then sat back down, running his finger around his collar and glancing absently out the window.

He's as fidgety as I am! Alison thought. *What worries does he have?*

"Mr. Grossbard, I am sorry to keep you from your job. I made this meeting as early in the morning as I could," he said.

Dad waved his hand grandly, as if welcoming guests into his home. "That's quite all right, Bob. It comes with having kids."

Alison's stomach clenched at these words, and the room blurred. *Is he mad at me, too?*

"Yes," Mr. Wright said, glancing sideways at Miss Burbage. "Well. Nancy, here, has raised some serious concerns about the views Alison put forth in her history paper."

"Subversive stuff, Mr. Grossbard. Stuff that could get us all in trouble," Miss Burbage said, pinching out each word.

Dad spread his hands. "She's just a kid, Nancy! Teenagers say things just to provoke. They like to get a rise out of their parents and teachers. It doesn't mean anything."

Oh, so that's the tack he's taking. Well, I did tell him not to carry on the way he always does about freedom of speech. So why do I feel so disappointed?

It didn't work, anyway. "Some teenagers also steal cars or set fires," Miss Burbage said, leaning forward and baring her teeth at Dad. "Parents are too indulgent, these days." Alison felt all the blood rush to her head. She clenched her fists under her chair.

Mr. Wright glanced at Alison and his face darkened. "Miss Burbage is right, young lady. Everyone knows that teenagers like to stir things up, but you went much too far."

She couldn't contain herself any longer. "I did not go too far! All I did was report what my Grandma said. She was alive at the time of the Arrival, so doesn't that count as firsthand history?"

"But her views are not acceptable," Miss Burbage said. "What we have here is a family history of subversion." She turned on Dad again. "Everybody in town knows why that newspaper in Baltimore fired you, Mr. Grossbard!"

Alison's palms hurt from her nails digging into them. She tried to blink away a vivid mental image of blood gushing from Miss Burbage's fat nose.

"Nancy, thank you very much for your input. I'll take it from here," Mr. Wright said.

Miss Burbage opened her mouth, closed it, opened it again. But no sounds came out.

Ha ! She looks like a beached fish. Fish didn't stomp out of rooms or slam doors behind them, though.

"That was really uncalled for, Bob," Dad said quietly. "My family are good citizens and supporters of the Cosmic Harmony. And there's no reason why my daughter should be punished for turning in a paper that she worked on very hard, even if it does include some unpopular views." He pushed a chuckle out of his throat. It sounded like he was choking. "If you want to call anybody a provocateur, it's my poor mother-in-law. She loves shocking people."

Mr. Wright cleared his throat. "Be that as it may, Mr. Grossbard, we still have a problem on our hands. I am proud to say I have just been elected president of the local chapter of the Society for Common Decency."

Alison could see her own shock reflected in Dad's face.

Mr. Wright smiled, but his gray eyes were cold as a winter fog. "Oh, yes. Some people might think Chincoteague is a backwater, that we're a bunch of rubes here who don't know any better than to let a lot of loud-mouth troublemakers run around trying to disrupt the Cosmic Harmony. I am sure that a man as *sophisticated* as you is under no such illusions."

"Of course not," Dad murmured.

"Great. We all know about the trouble you had back in Baltimore, Mr. Grossbard, but we don't believe in holding a man's past against him."

"We" islanders, or we SCOD members? Alison wondered. She got the feeling she was supposed to wonder about that.

Mr. Wright cleared his throat again. "As I say, you and your family are welcome here in Chincoteague, Jerry. Obviously you have a security clearance, or you wouldn't have gotten the job at the fusion plant. And we all know how thorough those security guys are, right? How concerned they become if there is derogatory information about a member of the family."

Alison couldn't believe it. Dad had come to stick up for her, and now the principal was threatening his job! And there was nothing she could do about it.

Mr. Wright turned his gray eyes on her. "This is the first blemish on your record, Alison. I am sure a smart girl like you doesn't have to have everything spelled out, do you?"

"No, sir," Alison said faintly.

"Great. So this is what's going to happen. You will get an incomplete on your final paper, which means you flunk this semester of history." He grinned when Alison flinched. "Bet you never had an F before in your life, did you? *You people* always think you're so smart."

There was no doubt who he meant by *you people*. He might as well have said *kikes*. And he wasn't finished.

"I'm transferring you from the All-Planetary history class to the general class."

The freaks' and losers' class, he meant. Even worse, history was one of only two classes she shared with Shaniqua, and in math class Alison was always so busy doing her friend's homework for her they didn't have time to chat. She almost groaned aloud, but she didn't want to give Mr. Wright the satisfaction.

"I'm exercising discretion on the unavoidable reduction in your Social Aptitude Test score. I think you'll agree a penalty of only ten points is more than fair on my part."

Dad opened his mouth, then closed it. Alison was silent. Losing ten points off her SAT was a really big deal. It could make the difference between getting into Olympian University on Mars, which had an all-High Ones faculty and was her first choice, and getting into one of her safety schools like Harvard. If nothing else she couldn't wait to see with her own eyes the Martian university's main building, the brand-new, five-kilometer-tall Olympus Tower perched atop the solar system's highest mountain, Mount Olympus. Now that dream was slipping out of reach.

"Next time, the consequences will be more serious," Mr. Wright said. "So there'd better not be a next time." He stood up and extended his hand to Dad. "Mr. Grossbard, thank you for coming in to see me about this very serious matter. Alison, you can pick up your hall pass and your new class schedule from the secretary."

Alison looked at her feet, dragging them as she walked out of the principal's office into the hallway, which was just starting to fill with students who had gone through the strip search.

Dad put his hand on her shoulder, then yanked it away as if it were a hot stove. "Sorry. Don't mean to embarrass you."

Alison looked at him and managed a smile. After all, the humiliation she'd just undergone had to have been just as bad for him. "You're not embarrassing me, Dad." She paused, looked around to see if anyone was paying them any attention, lowered her voice and said, "Dad. I still don't really know why you lost your job at the *Sun*."

"What?" Dad looked at her and blinked. "Not here. Not now. Have a good day at school, sweetheart, and try not to get in any more trouble."

"I won't," she promised, but he had already turned his back and was heading for the door. She stared after him. *Why doesn't he trust me enough to tell me what happened back in Baltimore?*

12

"And what's the matter with my idea?"

Arnold found it hard to concentrate on what to say to Jo when she was standing with her hands on her hips and her face thrust so close to his that her breath tickled his cheeks and he had to lean backward, because she had backed him into a coffee table. He couldn't help noticing her skin was ruddy and healthy. She obviously spent a lot more time outdoors than he did, even though Gingo Teag's winter was turning out to be so much colder than Chincoteague's.

He was having tea in her home again, and she'd taken advantage of her mother's excusing herself to deal with an urgent "voicegram," whatever that was, to tell him she wanted to come to Chincoteague to "gather intelligence" on the High Ones.

"Um, well, when are you even going to do it? No offense, but your 'Mum' watches you like a hawk."

Jo bristled. "I do whatever I want to! I just have to sneak around sometimes. Anyway, Mum won't object if Gloria says she'll watch me."

Now THAT might be interesting. "You mean we'll take Gloria along with us to spy?"

"No. We'll do it ourselves. We're the Fighters for the Freedom of Earth, remember? We humans have got to do it ourselves."

"But we wouldn't even have met if not for Gloria."

Jo glared at him. "The Earthling is out of order! The chair says so."

"The *chair*?"

"I mean me. I'm the chair. I say so!"

Arnold decided to let this go for the moment. "But when are we supposed to do this? Don't you have school and stuff? You told me yourself you don't even get a Christmas vacation like we do."

"Don't rub it in! And we do get Christmas Day and Boxing Day off. The day after Christmas, I mean. That's one custom you Americans could stand to adopt."

"That's another thing! You're not American."

"So what?"

"So what? You have a weird accent, that's what!"

Arnold could see the little bumps on Jo's tongue when she stuck it out at him. "I think YOU have a weird accent!"

"No, really! You sound like you were born in England but moved here to Virginia when you were six, or something. People are bound to ask questions. And spies have to be inconspicuous, don't they?" Arnold was proud of using the word "inconspicuous" in conversation. It had been on last week's vocabulary quiz in Mr. Wolff's English class.

Jo's cheeks reddened. "Don't you EVER call me a Virginian! I'm from Nanticoke Colony, and proud of it! And besides, I can talk like youse guys perfectly good." That last sentence made Arnold blink. She smiled at his surprise. "I've spent enough time around Teresa to tawk like her. And she says I got the right addy-tood to be from South Philly, too." When Arnold was silent, she said, "Hearing no further objections, the chair declares the motion carried!"

"But we could get in huge trouble! It'll be dangerous!" he blurted.

Which of course was Mrs. Purnell's cue to pop her finely coiffed head into the room. "What will be dangerous?"

"The polar bear swim in Assateague Channel in January," Jo said smoothly. "Please can I go this year, Mum?"

"You absolutely *may* not, young lady. Now, I am afraid you must walk our guest back to Gloria's bookshop. There is an emergency at the Tourism Council that demands my immediate attention." She stepped into the room and Arnold saw she was wearing her sleek, black winter coat. It made her look a bit like a seal. A stylish one.

"Emergency? What kind of emergency?" Jo protested.

"Do NOT take that tone with me, Jodie Marybeth Purnell. Mean Greene called our visitor from the Republique du Louisiana a 'Froggie fop,' and Monsieur Du Sable has challenged him to a duel!"

"Wicked!" Jo said with a huge grin. "Can I be his second? Monsieur Du Sable's, I mean. I want to make sure he shoots Mean Greene dead!"

"Very funny, young lady. I shall make certain Mr. Greene apologizes. How ignorant must one be to confuse our Western friends and fellow lovers of liberty with the Bonapartist Imperials? Meanwhile, Arnold, *I* must apologize for cutting your visit short."

"It's okay, Mrs. Purnell. Thanks for having me."

"Not at all, Arnold. Jo, you could stand to learn some manners from your boyfriend, although his grammar is as appalling as Teresa's."

"He's NOT my boyfriend!" Jo yelled as Mrs. Purnell shut the front door behind her. She punched Arnold hard on the arm, just to prove it.

"Ow! Jo, that really hurt!" he said, rubbing his arm.

"Oh, don't be such a baby," Jo said absently as she took the tea things to the kitchen. "So, when I come to Chincoteague on Boxing Day, where should we go to gather intelligence on the High Ones?"

"It's not like you see them walking down the street every day, not since the terrorist attacks got really bad," Arnold said, pushing his bruised arm carefully into his coat sleeve. "The easiest thing would be if we could get Dad to take us to his job. The director of the Wallops Island Interplanetary Base is a demi-viscount. My dad has spoken to him only once, though, the day he was hired."

"Wizard! We'll think up some way to get in to see him," Jo said, pushing Arnold out the door.

"But Jo, you've got to promise not to kill him. The demi-viscount, I mean. They'd probably expel me from school for that!"

"My word of honor as a freedom fighter, Arnold. This will be an intelligence gathering mission only."

* * * *

Arnold was so anxious waiting for the day after Christmas, it made the whole vacation basically stink. Mom and Dad always used to say Hanukkah was even better than Christmas because you got eight presents, one for each night, but this year the holiday came so early it was over before vacation even began, and anyway the eight mini-gifts had been pretty lousy—on the last night he got a *scarf*, for Pete's sake.

Then Dad and Alison got into a huge fight when she watched "The Spacefarers" holiday special and he flipped out over it. "How can you watch that anti-Semitic trash?"

"It's not anti-Semitic! Mom, tell him!"

Mom frowned as she strained to sit up straight in her wheelchair. "Well, Allie honey, the bad guy *is* called Izzy Goldstein."

"So what?"

"So what?" Dad said. "So he just tied up that cute girl and threatened to suck her blood, that's what! It's straight out of the medieval blood libel against Jews, the idea that we drink blood like vampires!"

"He's not gonna actually *do* it, and you don't really think Taylor Fields is 'cute,' do you?" Alison said. "Just look how fat her lips are!"

"You're changing the subject," Dad said. "Which is that I never want you watching that trash again!"

"Why can't we be normal people!" Alison yelled, storming upstairs and slamming her bedroom door behind her.

Mom sighed and slumped back down. Dad shook his head, settled into his favorite easy chair, a battered forest-green one salvaged from the house in Pikesville, and changed the channel to the Interplanetary News Network.

Arnold sidled up to him. "I always thought that program was stupid," he said.

"Hmm? Yeah, shh, I'm trying to listen to the news."

"You know how you said that time that you'd be happy to have the Purnells over if they ever want to visit Chincoteague?"

"The SCOD broke up what it called 'an obscene performance by the notorious Jewess Sally Silverstein,'" the announcer was saying. Green-jacketed Decency Shock Troops were shown handcuffing a pretty, dark-haired, mini-skirted woman who mugged for the camera.

"What? Yes, of course. I'll cook dinner for them. Rachel, you'll really like them," he said, half-turning to face Mom. But she'd fallen asleep, her head propped on her right hand, her graying bangs plastered over her forehead.

"You won't have to do that," Arnold said. "It's just Jo who wants to come over, the day after Christmas. I'm sure she'd be fine with a pizza or anything."

"Fine, fine," Dad said. The announcer was prattling on about a dispute over water imports from Jupiter's moons: "The Martian colonies need several cubic kilometers of water if the project of making the planet earthlike is to succeed, according to Subduke F'ssss-terponicus, but the Sahel irrigation project in Africa could save millions of human lives, according to the Arch-Marquess Tse-isssh-donitian, the Under-Viceroy for the Eastern Hemisphere. Given the small difference in noble rank between these two benefactors of the human race, the outcome is as yet uncertain…"

"Huh. That'll be settled according to Imperial interests, and nothing but," Dad muttered. "What were you saying, Arnold? Of course you can order pizza for Jo. I'll leave you some money."

"Do you think they'll let us bring it on base?" Arnold asked shrewdly.

"Hmm? On base? Why not? I never heard of anyone at Wallops Island not liking pizza."

"Great! So I'll order it on Christmas Eve and put it in the fridge so it's ready to take with us when Jo gets here the morning after the holiday."

Something finally caught Dad's attention. Probably the word *us*. He turned and gave Arnold his full attention. "Wait a minute. Why would you and your friend want to waste a vacation day at Wallops Island? You've been there twice already. You yourself said it's boring."

"But Jo's never been. They just barely invented the airplane in her world! It'll be so exciting for her to see even the little intercity saucers, let alone the huge interplanetaries!"

Dad frowned. "That's true, I guess. But you know they've started strip-searching us at work too. I don't think they have that, ah, custom, in Gingo Teag."

"It's all right. She won't mind," Arnold said, mentally crossing his fingers. "And she really wants to meet your boss!"

Dad blinked. "What on earth would anyone want to meet Mr. Willoughby for? The man's got the soul of a tech manual."

"Not him. I meant the Demi-Viscount, of course."

Dad sat up straight. *Not a good sign.* "He won't have time to see a couple of kids. I've only met him once, myself, and that was just to shake hands. I mean, grip tentacles. You know what I mean."

"We'll take that chance. Please, Dad? Jo never even heard of the High Ones before we went to her world, just like we never heard of dragons being real. I have to show her something as cool as that air show, I just have to! Please, Dad? Pleeeeeeeease?"

Arnold knew Dad wasn't much good at resisting whining. The big problem was going to be convincing Jo to submit to a strip search without causing even more problems than he had with Bubba.

* * * *

But she seemed to take it in stride when the day arrived and he sneaked in the school library's side door to meet her, as Gloria kept watch to make sure they weren't spotted by Bubba, who was patrolling outside the building.

"A spy has to be ready to submit to torture," Jo said, as matter-of-factly as if she was reciting the Table of Ranks. Well, her world's table of ranks. After all, they had genuine British aristocracy, in her America. "I don't mind them going through my pockets."

"Umm, they don't just go through your pockets, Jo."

"Where else would they look? I don't carry a purse. I'm not a girly girl."

"Ummmmm…"

"What's the matter with you, soldier? Why are you humming like that?"

"Uh, uh, uh… they kind of, well, that is, they make you take off your clothes."

Jo's eyes got huge.

"Not in front of me!" Arnold said, his hands flying up to his nose of their own accord. Sure enough, Jo was balling her hands into fists.

"Nodd in frondd of any guy!" he protested, squishing his nose in his urge to protect it. "They have a lady do idd. Jusdd like add school!"

Jo's cheeks puffed out. "That's… that's disgusting! How come you don't have a revolution?"

"I thought that's what we were planning," Arnold said, cautiously lowering his hands.

"Well… fine, I'll go along with it for the sake of my oppressed human brothers and sisters!"

"Go along with what?" Gloria asked, peering over the desk. Arnold and Jo were crouched down behind it.

They looked at each other. *You explain. No, you!*

"Jo's helping me fight the High Ones," Arnold said, after a long pause.

"Fight them? You can't just fight them," Gloria said.

"Why not?" Arnold and Jo said at the same time.

She chewed her lower lip. "It's… it's kind of complicated. The first and most important thing is, I want you two to become friends."

Jo narrowed her eyes. "That's what Mum said. But we're not friends! We're not *mates*, for goodness sake!"

Arnold stared at her. Out of the corner of his eye he saw Gloria screw up her face, as if she was about to cry.

"You're not?" she said in a small voice.

Jo stood up. "No! We are brethren in the fight for freedom! We have taken a blood oath!"

"You *have*?" Gloria said, wide eyed. She stepped around the counter, leaned back against the wall and put her head in her hands. "Oh dear, oh dear, oh dear," she mumbled.

Jo folded her arms and snorted. "Don't tell me you're as big a sissy as Arnold!"

"I am NOT a sissy!" Arnold said, louder than he meant to. He stood up too. "Let's go right now! My Dad's getting ready for work. He said he'd pick us up right here, outside the school. We'll get in to see the Demi-Viscount if I have to storm his headquarters to do it!"

Gloria uncovered her face and stared at him with her bright green eyes. "You mustn't do any such thing!"

"Oh, he won't. I'll make sure of it," Jo said cheerfully. "This is just an intelligence-gathering mission. Ready, soldier?"

Arnold saluted with a hand that hardly shook at all. "Ready, chair, uh, chairwoman!" He dropped his hand to his nose again when he saw her clenching her fists. "Whadd did I say now?"

"You're making fun of me! I don't clean anyone's house, not even my own home. Especially not my room! Even Mum doesn't set foot in there!"

"*Charwoman* is a cleaning woman in British English," Gloria said faintly. "Jo, he did say *chair*woman, I heard him. But I don't like you two playing at this military stuff. Someone could get hurt."

"Yeah, someone with lots of tentacles who's got no business being on Earth," Jo said darkly. "But not today. Like I said, today we're only gathering intelligence."

"The problem I have found with intelligence," Gloria said, "is that once gathered, it is so little displayed."

Jo tossed her head so her pigtail bounced. "You're talking in riddles, Gloria. It's a really annoying habit. Like the way you dress. I mean, I'm no fashion queen, but you do know your boots don't match, right?"

Gloria reached down and hiked up her long skirts to examine the offending footwear.

Jo nudged Arnold. "C'mon, while she's distracted!" she whispered, then grabbed his hand and darted around the counter.

"Maybe you shouldn't piss off Gloria so much," Arnold panted as they ran down a dim hallway lined with lockers, "after all, you need her to get back home."

"Oh, she wouldn't leave me stranded here," Jo said as they rounded a corner. "Hey Arnold, how do we get out of this building?"

"Uh, up the stairs and—oh no, here comes Bubba! Run!" As they darted back around the corner there was a low, mechanical hum, and a patch of skin on Arnold's upper left arm went numb. "Ohmigod, he's firing his stunner!" he gasped.

Jo shot him a wide-eyed glance, then tugged him into an unlocked classroom. Lumbering footsteps sounded closer and closer.

Jo looked around the darkened classroom. "Arnold! Help me push the teachers' desk up against the door!" she whispered. He raced to comply, his heart thundering so loud he barely heard the protesting squeak of the table legs against the scuffed tile. They shoved it into place just as the door handle began to turn.

Wham! Wham! The door knocked against the desk. "I'm calling the police, you vandals!" Bubba shouted.

If Jo hadn't already opened the window and jumped out, with Arnold wriggling out behind her, he'd never have had the nerve to shout back, "What, you mean the REAL police?" There was a roar and a crash behind him, and Arnold pounded after Jo, both of them laughing hysterically as they staggered up to Dad's car.

"What's so funny?" Dad asked as they tumbled in.

"Nothing, Mr. Grossbard, sir," Jo said, straightfaced, which set Arnold off again.

Dad shook his head. "Well, we're going to have to hurry, I'm already running late," he said. "Jo, I hope you like pizza."

Arnold's mouth watered at the sight of the square box that lay between them on the back seat. It had taken all his self-control not to open it in the past thirty-six hours.

"I love it!" Jo exclaimed. "Teresa brought some once from South Philly. She said she even knows how to make it! If I didn't hate cooking, I'd 'invent' it in my world and make a million quid!"

"A million what?" Arnold asked.

"Quid is slang for pounds," Jo explained, rolling her eyes.

"Pizza can make you fat, but not that fat!" Arnold said.

"No, I mean our money. The British Pound, with Dummy Prince Charlie on it."

But Arnold wasn't listening. He was peering over the seat at the dashboard. "Dad! Did you disconnect from DriveNet again?"

"I told you, I'm running late."

"But you'll get another ticket," Arnold said.

"Don't worry about it. I know how to beat the—" Red and blue lights flashed in the rear windshield and Dad let out a snarl. He took his hands off the wheel and the car pulled itself over to the curb.

"Wow, Mum would ground for me life if she ever heard me use that word," Jo said, awe in her voice.

Dad said several other words that Mrs. Purnell would not have approved of.

Arnold slumped in his seat. "Why do you always think you can beat the cops, Dad?"

The dashboard spoke next, making Jo start. "Mister Grossbard. You have disengaged from DriveNet without authorization. This is your third violation in the past six months, please acknowledge."

"Yeah, that's right, you—"

Jo whistled on a descending note. "I don't think I ever *heard* that word before!"

"The fine is 500 solars, plus 75 solars for disrespecting the Cosmic Harmony with foul language and 60 solars, 21 lunars in court costs."

"They never fined me for cursing before. And what court costs?" Dad grumbled, once the flashing lights went off.

Jo twisted around in her seat. Her eyes widened when she saw the empty road behind them. "Where did the police carriage go?"

"Nowhere. They don't need a police car," Dad sighed, his hands in his lap as the car started itself and drove off at a sedate speed.

"Then where did those lights come from?"

Arnold turned and pointed up at a pair of red and blue reflectors embedded in the car roof. Jo blinked in amazement.

"I better not do that again," Dad said, resignation in his voice. "Next time they might take away my license, and I'd have to take the bus to work."

"What difference would that make," Jo wondered, "if the car drives itself anyway?"

"It's the freedom of the open road," Dad said, sounding bewildered. "That's one of the few freedoms we have left."

"Maybe Mum has a point. You Americans *are* crazy," Jo said. "But at least your cars are nice and quiet."

"They're all electric. The High Ones made us get rid of gasoline-burning cars years ago because of the greenhouse effect," Dad said.

"I don't know what gasoline is, or the greenhouse effect. But our carriages have been electric ever since Sir Ben Franklin invented them," Jo said. "They do clack a lot, though." Glancing out the window, she gave another start. "We're driving over the marsh!"

"Well, sure we are," Dad said. "There's been a causeway here forever."

"Not in Gingo Teag," Jo said. "We have to take a ferry to the mainland. Mum keeps saying they need to build a causeway if they ever expect tourists to come."

Dad mumbled something that sounded like "primitive," and to change the subject before Jo could blow up, Arnold said quickly, "That reminds me, what happened with that duel?"

"Oh, there was no duel, worse luck," Jo said, "Mum made Mean Greene apologize, and Monsieur du Sable said that was all right, he could see he was dealing with an illiterate bumpkin, and Mean Greene said that was the stupidest insult he ever heard, seeing as how he was neither round nor orange, which I think rather proved Monsieur du Sable's point."

"You still fight duels in your world? How barbaric!" Dad exclaimed.

"Oh, yeah? Well, at least we don't make kids strip in school so some pervert can feel them up with rubber gloves, thank you very much!"

There was a silence. "You've got us there," Dad said. "I agree that that shouldn't be happening. But Jo, if you want to visit Wallops Island, you'll have to allow yourself to be strip-searched. If you won't, you'll just have to stay in the car."

Jo crossed her arms and said, "Fine, on one condition. You can't *ever* tell my parents about it, or they'll never let me come here again."

"No problem," Dad said quickly.

"Huh? Me either! I'll never tell, I mean!" Arnold said quickly, when Jo turned and eyed him. Which was just as well, because the car was already gliding into a parking space.

Everyone got out and walked toward the checkpoint. There were two separate, slow-moving lines, one for men and one for women. Dad sighed loudly and fidgeted with his briefcase. Arnold kept glancing back nervously at Jo, who was far behind at the end of the longer women's line and didn't look very happy about it.

When he got through being strip-searched—the guard was young, clean cut, brisk and efficient, not creepy like Bubba—he grabbed the pizza box and darted over to the exit from the female side. There he had to wait, hopping from one foot to the other, until Jo finally emerged. That she came out at all was a huge relief.

"It wasn't as bad as I expected," she admitted. "Not much worse than changing for sport. Where's your dad?"

"He ran off to his office mumbling something about being late for a very important meeting."

Jo covered her mouth and giggled. "Like the White Rabbit in *Alice in Wonderland*. All he needs is a pocket watch."

Arnold scowled at her. "Very funny. What's our next move, oh mighty chair?"

She stopped giggling. "You tell me. I don't want to go watch your dad work in an office, though. *Bor*-ing."

That was true enough, although Arnold didn't want to admit it. "Well, we could go out to the landing field and watch the saucers take off."

Jo clapped her hands. "Wizard! I mean, what an excellent opportunity for espionage."

It was a busy morning in the spaceport due to all the holiday travel. They crouched behind some crates and Jo watched for a long while without saying anything, as Arnold pointed and explained. The big ones, with a diameter that made an old-time jet plane look like a sparrow, were interplanetary liners, departing for the Moon, Mars, Venus, or Ganymede. They only saw two or three of those take off, and one arrive, growing from a pinhead directly overhead in the milky-pale winter sky to a huge, featureless disc of shining metal that looked as if it was about to crush them.

"It doesn't make any noise," Jo whispered. "How can that be?"

"Sound dampening technology," Arnold said, as if he knew what he was talking about. As if any human being did.

The saucers barely kicked up a tiny breeze when they landed, or rather hovered—there was no tarmac, and the landing field was literally a field of grass. Human physicists had tied themselves in knots trying to explain how such huge machines could manage to barely stir the air at all. Whatever their size, they always stopped moving at the same height, a bit more than ten feet between the lowest point in their distinctive bottom bulges and the ground. A cozy fit, for a High One, but too high for comfort for humans; hence the ramp that extended itself now, forming a gentle incline down which a ragged line of people staggered.

"What's the matter with them?" Jo asked. "Did the High Ones torture them?"

"Nah, they're just lunatics." Jo shied away, and Arnold smiled. "Not lunatics as in crazy people. Lunatics as in Luna—they live on the Moon. Or maybe Ganymede, which is about the same size, so it has the same low gravity."

"How can you tell?"

"The Martian settlers don't have quite as much trouble walking in Earth gravity, and the Venusians hardly notice the difference. It's all relative."

"It's all relative," Jo mimicked. "Smarty pants!"

Arnold restrained an urge to punch her. She *was* a girl, after all.

They watched for a while, but after the passengers finished disembarking there wasn't much more to see. Dad said there used to be a lot more activity around jets at airports—refueling trucks, food and beverage trucks, maintenance workers wandering around checking things. The giant outer space saucer just hovered.

If there was maintenance going on, it wasn't obvious. They watched three smaller intercity saucers, with diameters not much bigger than a city bus, as they came down and hovered, disgorged and took on passengers, and took off again, one after the other, each in less than ten minutes.

Jo looked thoughtful. "Hmm. When the FFE has more members we could take over a fleet of those little lorries and use them to fight the motherships," Jo said.

"Who's Laurie?"

Jo swatted him on the arm. "Are you really as dumb as you look? A lorry is a big electric carriage." She sounded pleased to have someone to lord it over.

Arnold could sympathize, to a point; the High Ones' monster technology could make you feel very small. Still, he was tired of being everyone's punching bag, and he was starting to catch on to this parliamentary procedure stuff. "I move we adjourn to the picnic area and eat our pizza. Do I hear a second?"

"Motion is—" Jo clutched Arnold's arm so hard he could feel her nails digging into his skin. "Arnold, what in God's name is that?"

He turned and looked where she was pointing. The ramp from the interplanetary "mothership" had been retracted, and something else was emerging from the craft. Something big and spiny.

"That," he said calmly, "is a High One."

Instead of watching it as it plopped to the ground and began to make its slow, majestic, slime trail-paved way to the terminal building on the far side of the saucer field—after all, it was hardly the first time he'd seen one of these Benefactors of the Human Race—he watched Jo's face. Her eyes were as round as one of the alien craft, and all the color quickly drained from her cheeks. Her pale lips smacked together and apart, together and apart, like a fish gasping to death on the beach.

"I see what Gloria meant," she said finally, in a very small voice. "How are we going to fight those things?"

"I thought you knew. You acted like you knew all about it." He winced as the words left his mouth, expecting her to turn on him, but she didn't even seem to hear.

"Arnold, if there are all those versions of Earth, there must be just as many versions of the High Ones' homeworld."

"An infinity of Gliese 581d's?" Arnold gulped. "I, uh, I hadn't thought of that."

"They could come and take over my world just as easily as they took over yours. And Philadelphia Teresa's Earth, and every other Earth there is."

There wasn't anything to say to that. So after a few more minutes, he suggested again that they go to the picnic area and eat their pizza, and Jo agreed, all her plans to meet the demi-viscount apparently forgotten.

As they walked she pointed to a huge, doughnut-shaped building in the middle distance. It gleamed with shiny metal and was busy with a million wires and pipes. "What's that?"

"That?" Arnold glanced where she was pointing. "That's the nuclear reactor my father does the tech writing for. It supplies electricity for all of Delmarva. Uh, what you call Nanticoke."

"One building can do all that? How?"

This put Arnold on the spot. He wasn't taking physics till next year, so he covered up his ignorance with sarcasm. "It's something to do with hydrogen atoms sticking together. It's only the force that powers the sun. What, you people don't understand that?"

"Oh, yeah? If *you* people are so smart, how come the High Ones had to build it for you?"

Fortunately they arrived at the picnic area before the quarrel could get any worse. It was a warm day for early winter, and a few office workers were also eating outside, including Dad's buddy Mr. Nomura.

Arnold introduced Jo as his cousin, giving her a chance to try out her South Philly accent.

"I'm down here in Chincoteague for winter break," she said smoothly. *Chincoteague, not Gingo Teag; winter break, not Boxing Day. So far, so good,* Arnold thought, letting out a breath he didn't even realize he'd been holding.

"How are you enjoying it? It's a funny time of year to come down to the shore," Mr. Nomura said, taking a bite of his peanut butter sandwich.

"Oh, my family loves coming here all year round." Arnold tried to shoot her a warning look, but she kept on chattering. "We love the wild ponies of Assateague, especially. At least I do. My dad says they just get in the way of the drag—uh, of all the other wildlife on the island."

That was a close one, Arnold thought.

But Mr. Nomura didn't seem to notice Jo had said anything strange. He nodded in agreement. "The Wildlife Refuge staff have to keep them in check so they don't crowd out all the other species," he said. "The High Ones are particularly concerned with reviving the blue crab population. No one knows exactly why, but I think it's like how people always seem to care more about polar bears and harp seals than endangered fish or snails. It's easier to feel concern over things that look familiar." He sighed. "I used to enjoy crab sushi, but these days you can't get it anywhere. You can't get a California roll to save your life!" He chuckled a little nervously. "Nobody wants to bite the tentacle that feeds them."

"Invertebrates of the world, unite," murmured Arnold. "You have nothing to lose—not even your spines!"

Mr. Nomura gave him a strange look and a tiny thrill of triumph ripped through him—he had finally succeeded in topping Dad's friend for rude and dangerous humor. Arnold liked Mr. Nomura, but he and Dad were always hinting that "the younger generation" were too timid for their own good.

Perhaps because he felt Arnold had actually gone too far, Mr. Nomura excused himself, saying he had to get back to work. The guy was always working, even on the weekends.

Arnold opened the pizza box and found it empty except for crusts. "Hey! I barely had any!" he protested to Jo.

"Soldier, you are overruled. The chair doesn't have any access to pizza back home. Anyhow, it's time to get back to surveillance."

"Who appointed you chair, anyway?" Arnold said as they walked back to the landing field.

"It is a well-known fact that girls make better leaders," she said firmly.

Arnold wondered if that could be so, as they spent the afternoon saucer watching. Adventure stories always had the man taking the lead and saving the damsel in distress, and he was honest enough to admit to himself that the Adventures of Sir Arnold and Princess Hailee were firmly in that tradition. He also knew he enjoyed this private fantasy because in real life he felt so powerless. With Jo he had a chance to make things different, but here he was letting her take the lead.

When it began to get dark they finally stood up, stiff and sore, and began to walk back to the parking lot to meet Arnold's Dad.

It's now or never. I can't let Jo bully me, Arnold thought, and elbowed her in the ribs.

"Ow! What was that for?" Jo said, rubbing her side. She punched him in the arm before letting him answer.

"I don't like the name 'Fighters for the Freedom of Earth' for our group. It's too much of a mouthful," he said. "Isn't 'Freedom Fighters of Earth' catchier?"

Jo scowled at him, but then the left corner of her mouth turned up. "Yeah, I guess it is. Motion approved by the chair and carries." The glow that gave him was even better than hot cocoa for warming power.

13

Waking in a freezing cold bedroom in a bed-and-breakfast place so shabby even Dad would never have wanted to stay there was the most exciting adventure of Alison's life so far.

Although it was a lazy five-minute stroll from her warm, comfortable room at home, Smitty's Tea Room and Inn wasn't really in Chincoteague, it was in Gingo Teag, which meant it was in a whole other world! A version of earth that had no United Satrapy of America and no High Ones, but did have telepathic dragons! Where the ruler wasn't the boring, hundred-year-old High Satrap, whose face looked like it had been chiseled in marble by an eight-year-old, and who had been in charge since he was still called "the President," before Dad was born, but a rather bumbling, harmless-looking British prince who had only been king less than ten years. And the Prime Minister of British America had only been in office since July, or so Teresa said.

"So a monarchy is more democratic than America," Alison had said as they enjoyed Christmas dinner at the Purnells' house the night before. Mrs. Purnell, who was carving the goose, snorted, but Teresa, who was sitting to Alison's right, said, "Well, maybe more democratic than *your* America, but *my* America isn't ruled by giant starfish from outer space, and we *do* still have elections."

"Ghastly affairs. Sorry, my love," said Tom, who was seated to Teresa's right, "but you know it to be the truth. I watched some of those dreadful tee-vee advertisements during your elections last year, and it is no wonder to me that half your people do not even bother to vote."

He said "tee-vee" with exaggerated emphasis, as if it was a foreign word. Alison had noticed there was nothing like a TV set or a tri-vee stage in the Purnells' living room, but she had thought the Purnells were only oddballs. They certainly were odd in other ways.

"Oh, yeah?" Jo interrupted. "Well, at least they don't have a stupid king who meddles in party politics when he ought to be off shooting defenseless foxes or feeding the Queen Mum's stupid corgis who have even less brains than him!"

"Fewer brains," Mrs. Purnell said between clenched teeth. "If you are going to insult the Royal Family, young lady, you might at least use proper grammar!"

"After dinner, I would like to show our guests the drawings Larry Frost has made of a new type of aircraft," Mr. Purnell said, a bit too loudly. "They are quite brilliant. I'm sure they don't have anything like it in their, uh, hometowns!"

"I met the major just after you, ah, came back from Assateague that time," Teresa said, also a bit too loudly. "He was very nice to me, and he seemed really smart! What's his idea?"

"I say the king should mind his own business, if he doesn't want us going the way of the real England, as we ought to!" Jo said.

Alison watched in horror as Mrs. Purnell's pretty face flushed brick-red.

"You won't believe this, but he wants to build a kind of mechod without a fixed wing!" Mr. Purnell said loudly.

"Really?" Teresa was almost shouting.

"Young lady," Mrs. Purnell growled.

"Indeed!" Mr. Purnell yelled. "It has a rotating wing on top, believe it or not! He wants to call it a davinci, after the Italian artist who first sketched something like it, but I think calling it a whirligig would—"

"Wow! We don't have anything like that!" Teresa shouted, elbowing Alison hard.

None of it did any good, though, as Mrs. Purnell picked up the carving knife and pointed it at Jo. She didn't shout, however; she spoke so softly everyone had to lean forward to hear her, which only made what she had to say that much more menacing.

"Young lady. I have had quite enough of your trampling upon the Crown which affords you protection and liberty every day of your foolish, young life. You will proceed straight to your room, where you will remain until tomorrow morning, when you may go to Gloria's bookstore only because I have already given my word. When you return, however, your father and I will inform you of what punishment we shall have decided to mete out to you. You may take it as a given that you are to be confined to home and school until after the New Year."

"Fine! I don't like your stupid, cheapjack Tourism Council New Year parties anyhow!" Jo screamed, and stomped off upstairs to her room, slamming the door so hard Alison could have sworn she felt her chair shake.

It seemed as though the punishment was really hers and Teresa's, though, because Mr. Purnell actually did make them look at the blueprints for some sort of primitive helicopter and his own plans for dragonesque airplanes for hours until they were able to make their escape to the inn, although not without a prolonged struggle with Mrs. Purnell, who pronounced herself "mortified" that Alison insisted on staying at the inn and not in their family home.

Teresa was finally able to bring her boyfriend's mother around, and Alison was grateful—she needed an interpreter for this strange new world, and she really liked Teresa.

"I have to stay here every time Tom and I come to visit his folks," Teresa explained once they were in their cold bedroom in the inn. "At least in the winter, when nothing else in town is open. Mrs. Purnell is quite old-fashioned and would be shocked if she knew we share a flat in Cambridge."

"A 'flat?' Don't you mean an apartment?" Alison said.

Teresa chuckled. "Of course. My English is becoming Britishy from hanging out with all these sort-of Brits. I mean, they play rugby instead of football and call flashlights 'torches' and everything!"

"And you don't mind? Having to pretend about your boyfriend, I mean, when you're all grown up and away at college?" Alison asked.

Teresa shook her head. "Nah. You might think their world is backward, but it's really just different. You'll see. Now, I stay at this inn often enough that Mr. and Mrs. Smythe are almost polite to me, but you can be sure Edna'll treat you like you're planning to steal her worn-out tea towels. Don't pay her any mind, she's like that with all strangers, and she's not much nicer to people she does know."

Which turned out to be exactly right, like so much of what Teresa said, but Alison was just too excited to care. Mr. Purnell had promised to take her and Teresa on a private tour of the "Assa Teag Royal Dragon Refuge" in the morning, even though it was officially closed for Boxing Day.

So of course Alison was awake as soon as gray winter light began to seep through the dusty curtains. It was all she could do to tiptoe over to Teresa's bed instead of jumping up and down. Soft snoring turned into mumbling when Alison shook her. "Teresa! Wake up!"

"Wha—" The older girl sat bolt upright. "I'm not faking, I swear! *Da*, I really am from Alaska—Oh, it's you." She ran her hands through tangled hair as curly as Alison's and scowled. "What are you doing up so early?"

"I want to see the dragons! Especially the babies! Mr. Purnell says they're really cute!"

"They are, but Alison, it's barely six-thirty! Can't I sleep a little longer?"

"But I'm only here until four o'clock! Please, Teresa!"

"Young people these days," Teresa grumbled, swinging her legs over the side of the bed. "Oo! This floor is even colder than the last time I stayed here! I might have to get Tom to marry me just so my toes don't get frostbitten in the morning! All right, hand me that sweater, will you? Lucky for you, Mr. Purnell is an early riser."

Indeed, he was already patrolling the piney woods on "Assa Teag" when the two girls arrived after a brisk twenty-minute walk over a wooden sidewalk and bridge. He grinned and wrapped Teresa in a bear hug. "You're in luck, Assa Teag Ashley is still in her nest," he said.

Teresa's eyes got a far-away look for a moment. "She says she's looking forward to meeting you, Allie."

"Umm, great!"

"You can't hear her, can you? In your mind, I mean," Teresa said.

"Uh, no." Alison paused. "But I have this strange feeling… like the trees want to be my friends!"

Teresa and Mr. Purnell smiled at each other. "She's got the gift too, just not as strong as me," Teresa said, and then explained to Alison, "I can actually 'hear' her words in my head—thoughts as complicated as you or I think. But we think only one in a million people have that 'mind-speaking' ability. Maybe one in ten thousand are like you, and can sense the dragons' feelings."

"Can you 'mindspeak' with other telepathic human beings?" Alison asked.

"Jo and I have tried, but we haven't succeeded yet."

"Girls, how about we have a quick cup of cocoa over by the light-house?" Mr. Purnell interrupted. "If I know Edna Smythe, she didn't give you much of a breakfast, and it's cold out on the beach."

Teresa stared at nothing again for a moment. "It's okay with Ir'befunzu, I mean Ashley," she said, refocusing. "She can wait a few more minutes. The school of marlin she's going after is still miles off-shore."

"How can she tell?" Alison asked as they emerged from the trees onto a hill topped by an old lighthouse. Unlike the candy-striped one back home, it was painted solid orange.

"Dragons use sonar, like whales and dolphins," Teresa said.

"I learned that word from Teresa," Mr. Purnell said. "We don't have radar here, in our, ah, in our Earth."

"It was developed during World War II in the history you and I know," Teresa explained. "Neither of the world wars happened here!"

"History after hot cocoa," Mr. Purnell said firmly, opening the door of a little red outbuilding with a snug kitchenette inside. "Or would either of you rather have tea?"

"I love cocoa," Alison said as Mr. Purnell lit a gas burner.

"But it's really expensive here," Teresa said. "Are you sure it's all right, Mr. Purnell? I can just have tea instead."

"Nothing is too good for my guests," he said, winking. "Anyway I have a secret stash." He made it nice and thick. Alison's mouth started watering at the aroma.

"I know I've got some biscuits around here, too," he said, searching under a counter.

"Cookies," Teresa explained. "Mrs. Purnell bakes the best sugar cookies."

Alison had to agree when she bit into hers, but she was so eager to see Ashley and her babies she couldn't enjoy the snack much. Still, it was good to have something warm in her stomach as she jogged after Mr. Purnell and Teresa, over the dunes and out to the beach. A brisk wind was blowing fine grits of sand and sea spray along the shore.

"We have to move it now," Teresa explained, "Ir'befunzu says she's going out to sea in the next minute or so, and she's going to let Ir'delprina and Ir'gassaphet follow her—her first two hatchlings. It should be quite a sight!"

They panted their way to the top of a tall, wind-sculpted dune, the low orange sun over the ocean throwing stretched-out shadows behind them. Mr. Purnell was too winded to speak, so he simply handed Alison a pair of binoculars and pointed over the tops of the pine trees toward a pond that lay in the midst of the salt marsh.

Alison had visited Assateague Island often enough to notice something strange right away: there were no ducks bobbing on the dancing, choppy wave crests of the pond, which was a couple hundred meters away. Nor were there egrets or herons stepping daintily through its waters. Even the seagulls steered clear.

She tried without success to remember whether there was a pond on that spot in her world. If there was, it surely wasn't bubbling as if something big—or several somethings—were splashing around in it. Then what she had taken for a field of dark green marsh grass began to shift, and she realized with a thrill that it was Ashley, or Ir'befunzu. Like an optical illusion resolving itself into the intended shape, the roiling, varied shades of greens turned into one huge form rising slowly from the pond and plodding to the right, northward through the marsh, gathering speed as it went.

Alison made out the head, with its huge black eyes, and an enormous, blunted horn that looked melted at the tip. She watched, fascinated, as the dragon pushed against the ground with her hind legs and then vaulted over her own forearms, which were attached to her wings. Like a plane rolling down the runway, the maneuver gave the dragon enough forward speed to launch into flight, after which she glided on the fresh morning wind. Then she found a thermal updraft and used it to spiral upward, like an enormous hawk.

Behind her came the two hatchlings, or "dragonets;" Alison caught glimpses of their brood-mates in the water. The young dragons looked like miniatures of their mother, except that their underbellies and the undersides of their wings flashed bright pink, shading off into white and pale green on the sides. Only along the backs of their bodies and the tops of their wings did they show the deep green that was Ashley's main color.

They imitated their mother's motions clumsily. One clipped the top of a pine tree, which snapped off with a reverberating crack, quickly followed by a thud as the beast hit the ground headfirst. He, or she, let out a cry that sounded like a million crows cawing at the same time, but was soon airborne again, and as if to make up for the mistake rode the thermal in even tighter spirals than Ashley.

"Show-off," Teresa murmured, which made Alison jump—she'd almost forgotten there was anyone else watching with her.

Ashley turned slowly, majestically, to face the sea, and the dragonet that hadn't crashed followed her almost as gracefully. The other one kept riding the thermal higher and higher, spiraling tighter and tighter until it suddenly broke off and zoomed after the other two.

Alison lowered the binoculars and turned to ask Teresa something, but her eyes had that glazed look again that meant she was mindspeaking with Ashley. Alison shook her head and raised the binoculars again, but there was no need—all three dragons were headed right toward her! A thrill shot up her spine, strong as an electric shock, and she wondered if she was sensing Ashley's feelings again. A strong downdraft blew in her face as Ashley flapped her wings. The dragonet behind her mimicked the motion so precisely it was comical, and Alison started to laugh. The one that had crashed was out of sync, though, and it began to dip lower. Alison just had time to wonder whether it had been hurt by its fall when everything happened at once.

She noticed its beak was pointing straight at her and froze. Mr. Purnell yanked on her arm and shouted "Get down!"

But she had no time to comply because something huge clamped around her stomach, something hard and inflexible as a steel band. She tried to push against it and found her arms were pinned to her sides. She kicked and realized with a sickening lurch that her feet weren't on the ground. Something was blocking her view, something huge and pink. *Pink? Ohmigod...*

A tremendous screech split the air, then a deafening bellow so close at hand her ears rang. She began to struggle as hard as she could. *Put me down put me down putmedown putmedown!!!*

There was a blinding flash. Pain cracked through her head as if she'd been hit with a baseball bat. She heard a roar and a screech, and then she was falling freely through the air. There wasn't even time for panic before she hit something hard and almost blacked out.

Her eyes blurred and stung, and when she tried to breathe she inhaled a mouthful of seawater. The cold was a worse shock yet, surrounding her whole body, soaking through her clothes that were suddenly heavy as bags of ice. Alison was a good swimmer, when wearing a swimsuit and diving into a swimming pool with nice, neatly marked out lanes. But now she gasped and choked, breaking the surface and drawing a ragged breath while her clothes dragged her down. The cold made it hard to move, hard to think, but she felt a distant terror when it began to fade, replaced with an impossible warmth as if she was in bed at home on a weekend when she didn't have to get up for anything.

Hypothermia, she thought, trying to shake it off so she could do a dead man's float on the choppy waves while her soaked clothes tugged at her. *I'll die of the cold instead of drowning.* She tried to fight free of her jeans, jacket, and shirt, but her fingers were numb and clumsy with the cold. *Mom and Dad are going to blame themselves for letting me come here*, she thought distantly.

Her glimpses of the sky were fading, but Alison seemed to see Mr. Purnell's friendly, quizzical face floating among the high, wispy clouds. When a wave closed over her head she fought it, tried to reach for that smile, to put her arms around his thick, muscular neck. But it was so hard. She was trying to fight her way free of warm, thick syrup.

Every wave that passed seemed to cover her longer, the glimpses of the sky grew briefer and briefer… Something clamped around her waist, not nearly as hard as the dragon had, but firm and strong. There was a sense of motion, and then she was lying on the cold, hard sand, staring up at Mr. Purnell and Teresa. When they saw her blink, Teresa looked relieved, and Mr. Purnell scrunched up his face as if he was about to cry.

"I'm all right, Mr. Purnell," Alison said hoarsely, reaching up to pat him on the shoulder. The movement brought on a fit of coughing.

"Come on, love, let's get you to the lighthouse. I keep a couple changes of clothes in there," he said. "They'll be big on you, but at least they'll be dry." He and Teresa helped Alison to her feet.

She tried to speak, but ended up retching seawater, narrowly missing Teresa's shoes. "We'd better get you to Dr. Sherman," she said when Alison tried to apologize, and Mr. Purnell nodded vigorously.

They set off down the beach in the direction of the lighthouse, though Alison had to rest, leaning on Mr. Purnell, every few steps. When she doubled over coughing Mr. Purnell squatted down and picked her up. She was too exhausted and cold to protest, and the tea Teresa brewed while Mr. Purnell hurriedly got his boat ready tasted like life itself.

The rest of the day passed in an exhausting blur for Alison. The doctor's office didn't have all the shiny stainless steel that they had back home, but he was gentle and seemed to know what he was doing. After taking her temperature with an old-fashioned mercury thermometer and listening carefully to her chest with a stethoscope, he said she would be all right but should rest in bed for a few days.

Teresa walked with her to Gloria's Gateway Books (the sign in the window said "CLOSED for Christmas and Boxing Day," but the door was unlocked) and through the Gray Zone, which was mercifully quiet. Tiferet rubbed up against Alison's legs, purring, but when Alison reached down to pick her up she started coughing again, so Teresa had to bend over and do it.

As she stroked the cat she told her what had happened to Alison, and a few moments later the two girls were standing with Gloria on the Chincoteague side of the gateway.

"You poor thing!" Gloria exclaimed. "I'll fetch you a nice cup of tea."

"But I already had some," Alison said as Gloria fussed around with an electric kettle in the corner.

Teresa put her hand on Alison's arm. "Don't turn down her tea. It has magical healing powers. Really."

It tasted like ordinary black tea with honey to Alison, but she did feel stronger after drinking it. Still, she was a little unsteady on her feet, and Teresa held onto her elbow to steady her. The older girl was looking around curiously.

"So this is what an Earth conquered by aliens looks like," she mused. "Looks pretty ordinary to me." They stepped around the counter. "Those are funny-looking computers," Teresa said, pointing.

"Those are n-readers," Alison said, and tried to explain what they did.

"Oh! Cool," Teresa said, with a little frown. "An Internet of thoughts. So that's alien technology?"

"It's how we tap into the Cosmic Harmony," Alison said. "At least, that's what they tell us in school."

Gloria was staring out the window into the early night. "Looks pretty quiet out there," she said. "The school guard is probably just sitting by the front door. Teresa, would you mind walking Alison home?"

"Happy to," Teresa said with a mischievous grin. "Do I get to meet some of these cosmic starfish?"

"The High Ones don't hang out in Chincoteague," Alison said. "You have to go over to the Wallops Island Interplanetary Base for that. That's where Arnold took Jo today."

"Guess I won't see them this time, then," Teresa said with a sigh. "Tom and I are driving back to Cambridge early in the morning."

"Here's the famous picture of Ambassador Risssss-erianus with the Apollo 11 astronauts and the President on the South Lawn of the White House," Gloria said, handing Teresa an open book.

"He's now the High Viceroy," Alison added helpfully. "You can see how much Earth means to them by the fact that they sent an Archduke to govern the human race!"

"An archduke, huh?" Teresa murmured. "Like poor Franz Ferdinand." When Alison looked at her blankly she added, "The guy who started World War I by getting shot."

Alison paled. "You'd better not make jokes like that around here, Teresa. You can get in real trouble!"

"Okay, okay. I don't want to end up as starfish food."

Alison turned to Gloria. "Please tell her, Gloria."

"It's not the High Ones you have to worry about so much as SCOD—the Society for Common Decency," the cat-woman explained. "They have their own police force and secret detention camps and everything. Even the government is afraid of them!"

Teresa rolled her eyes. "I can hold my tongue, guys! I'm only walking a few blocks with Alison anyway." As soon as they stepped out through the library's back exit Teresa exclaimed over how warm the weather was compared to Gingo Teag. "I'll never get used to the difference global warming makes!"

"You mean the greenhouse effect?" Alison said. Teresa nodded. "That's one of the things the High Ones are fixing for us. They gave us controlled fusion, so we don't need to use so much oil—there's a fusion power plant right over at Wallops Island, in fact—and they also did something they haven't really explained to the atmosphere so that not as much heat from the sun gets through. But they warned us it'll take time to fix what we messed up."

"I wish they'd help out my Earth that way," Teresa said. "But then they'd be in charge there too, wouldn't they?"

Alison kept quiet. People just didn't make those kinds of remarks in her world, unless they were reckless or completely nuts, like Barry Freed.

As if the thought had summoned him, he stepped out from behind a streetlight. "Flying saucers. They aren't real, you know," he said to Alison, and then turned to Teresa and said politely, "Hello, I don't think we've met. The name's Barry Freed." He stuck out his hand.

Teresa shook his hand, seeming unfazed by the ambush, or by Mr. Freed's wild hair and beard, ragged clothes, and pungent smell. "I'm Alison's friend Teresa," she said, "and we'd love to chat, but she almost drowned today. I need to get her home."

"Oh! I'm sorry to hear that," Mr. Freed said as Teresa stepped around him, pulling Alison after her.

Alison was amazed—was it really that easy to avoid him? Maybe not, because now he was following them.

"What happened to her?" he asked.

"A dragon grabbed her and dropped her in the ocean," Teresa said, not looking back as she tugged Alison along. The footsteps behind them stopped.

"That's my house over there," Alison said, pointing. "Thanks for getting rid of Mr. Freed—he's harmless, but he can be kind of a pest." She giggled. "I think you actually freaked him out!"

"Oh, I'm used to seeing homeless people back in my Philadelphia," said Teresa. "A lot of them are mentally ill."

"Mr. Freed sure is. I mean, imagine saying flying saucers don't exist, when I've gone on rides in them, like, at least half a dozen times!"

"Um, yeah," Teresa said, shooting her a look as they walked up to the front door. There were loud voices coming from inside. The door swung open, nearly knocking Alison over.

"Oops! Sorry, Allie," Jo said. She was bundled up for Gingo Teag rather than Chincoteague, so the hand-knitted, purple scarf over her mouth muffled her voice, but her eyes narrowed when she saw Alison. She pulled the scarf down and said, "What happened to you? You look like a drowned rat."

Alison told her, with excited interruptions from Teresa.

Jo shook her head. "I'd best have a word with that lad," she said, stalking out into the night.

"I'd better follow her and make sure she goes straight home, or Mrs. Purnell will kill both of us," Teresa said. "Sorry!"

Alison had collapsed on the couch, and Dad hurried to get a blanket. "Sorry, honey, I've been upstairs with Mom ever since I got home from work. She's not having a good day. Now, *what* happened to you, again?"

Arnold was also staring at her wide-eyed.

She smiled tiredly. "It's not so much the dragons you need rescuing from," she began, "as the dragonets."

14

Arnold was using his free-writing time in English class to update the adventures of Sir Arnold and Princess Hailee, but his heart wasn't really in it. What's the point of imagining you are rescuing a damsel in distress from a dragon, when your obnoxious big sister actually *was* in peril from a dragon and was rescued by your best friend's dad? It might have been interesting if Jo had been in peril from Ir'gassaphet and Arnold had been the one to rescue her, but knowing Jo she'd have dunked him in the cold seawater by way of thanks. Anyhow, Jo was, like, best friends with the dragon mama, if you could believe her, whereas to Arnold they were just huge, majestic, impossibly evolved pterosaurs soaring with graceful ease through the skies of that other Earth. It was No Fair!

Even being in the Resistance wasn't all he had imagined it would be. It did have the advantage that Matt and his gang were still keeping their hands off him. But so far being in the Freedom Fighters of Earth involved being bossed around a lot by Jo, who ordered him to pester Dad into taking him to work on a teacher's in-service day in mid-January so he could waste his time watching the saucers take off and land with a stopwatch in his hand and a notebook by his side. Jo of course didn't have off from school the same day, so where was the fun in that? It was hardly any consolation that the stopwatch was also an old-fashioned windup pocket watch, a beautiful, handmade device of wood and glass and little metal gears from the Gingo Teag world that Jo told him he could keep when the mission was done. He'd rather have spent the day at home with Mom watching tri-vee, not freezing his butt off on the coldest day of the year.

It was a far cry from the world of his fantasy, a fantasy that it hardly seemed fair to call a daydream considering how much work he had put into it. He'd filled four composition books with stories, maps, and drawings of the Kingdom of Givrinia, and an account of Sir Arnold's quest to rescue Princess Hailee from the clutches of the evil Lord Matthew of Tingo Cheag.

        Sir Arnold sallied forth on his faithful
    horse Bufessalon, his magic lance at his side,
    ready to be drawn in deadly earnest at a moment's

notice. He rode alone always, this paladin whose sword served those who could not fight for them- selves. Those like Princess Hailee, whom the evil Lord Matthew had imprisoned in the dreaded Tower of Terror, deep in the darkness-cursed Forest of Fear. What bravery it must have taken the princess, with her hair like morning sun- light and her eyes blue as the summer sea, to write him a note in her own blood from a tiny cut she made in her perfect forefinger, entrust- ing the epistle to the enchanted parrot Tuki who was her faithful servant!

Arnold was proud of remembering the word *epistle*. And the Hebrew word for parrot.

"Fly, Tuki, fly!" she cried, letting a single pure teardrop seal the letter as she lay lan- guishing in the Dungeon of Doom, and the trusty magenta bird caught it in its beak and flew up, seeking the sole ray of sunlight to penetrate the moldy prison where

"Arnold, the bell has rung."

Arnold looked up, startled. The classroom was rapidly emptying, and Mr. Wolff was looking down at him curiously. He mumbled apolo- gies and started to gather his books.

"No, that's all right, Arnold, I was going to ask you to stay after class anyway."

Now what? "Sure, Mr. Wolff," he said aloud. "I have lunch next any- way." Lately he'd been eating at the Matt Gang's table—off in a corner of his own, to be sure, but he no longer felt welcome at the Reject Table, whereas the bullies no longer chased him away.

Mr. Wolff went over and shut the door, walked to his desk and shuf- fled through a pile of graded papers, pulled one out and walked over to the empty desk next to Arnold's, which he perched on.

Arnold looked up at his long, lean face with what he hoped was a wide-eyed gaze of innocence. *I don't have anything to feel guilty about, do I?*

Mr. Wolff had a wild, rich mop of graying hair that extended down to sideburns that curved exuberantly around his sticking-out ears, which were handy for perching his oversized glasses on. Some of the kids called him "Brillo" behind his back, because of his hair. He was tall and lean and favored brown tweed jackets with elbow patches.

"Arnold," he said, removing his glasses with his left hand while he handed him the paper with his right hand, "I've had a look at your paper on *Macbeth*."

"Yes?" Arnold said, keeping his tone as level as possible as he took the paper and noticed there was no grade on it. Not a red mark of any sort. *Am I about to get into the same kind of trouble Alison got into? There's no way Mr. Wright will let me off easy a second time!*

"Don't look so panicked, Arnold," Mr. Wolff said with a little smile. "Wolff may be at the door, but he will not tear your throat out!"

"Yes, Mr. Wolff," Arnold said uncertainly.

"Now what you wrote," the teacher said, pacing back and forth in front of Arnold's desk with his glasses dangling from his left hand, the same way he did when he was lecturing to the class, "was that Macduff's rebellion against Macbeth was not a true rebellion, which would be a disruption of the Cosmic Harmony, but rather a restoration of the Cosmic Harmony, which Macbeth and Lady Macbeth had themselves disrupted by murdering Duncan. Is that a fair summary?"

"Umm. I guess so?"

Mr. Wolff slow-clapped, the way he did when someone gave a stupid answer, like that time Bill Cherricks said that Romeo and Juliet "should of just run off together, what was the matter with them?"

Arnold was so annoyed at being classed with Princess Hailee's muscular toad of a boyfriend that he forgot to be afraid. "What's so bad about what I wrote?"

"Why, nothing. Nothing at all, Mr. Grossbard. It's so unexceptional it could have been written by Pierre LaWayne himself. Your paper displays all the marks of *common* decency." Mr. Wolff bent over and leaned so close Arnold could smell his breath, which had a metallic edge, as if the teacher had eaten raw hamburger for breakfast. "But what is it you really think, Arnold?"

"About what? About *Macbeth*?"

"Yes, about *Macbeth*. Just blurt out whatever comes into your mind. Don't let Pierre LaWayne think decent, timid thoughts for you."

Arnold wasn't in the habit of blurting out whatever came into his mind for teachers. He always thought carefully and gave them the answers he thought they wanted to hear. And it usually worked, which was why his grades were so high. Why was Mr. Wolff asking him to go against this tried-and-true method? Was he trying to get him in trouble?

It was hard to think what to say, with the teacher's hairy face so close and those steel-gray eyes boring into him. Without his really deciding that it should, his mouth began moving. "Well I don't think it's very fair what happened to Macbeth I mean the witches set him up, didn't they, and Lady Macbeth was, like, pushing him and pushing him to be king and she didn't care how it happened 'cause she wanted to be queen I mean the poor guy never had a chance and he felt really bad about all those murders she made him do and it was a lousy trick, Macduff and all those guys dressing up as trees to make the witches' prediction come true, and if rebellion is supposed to be bad and wrong it's bad and wrong *all the time*, I mean, like, Shakespeare can't have it both ways and neither can SCOD, saying how the American Revolution was really a restoration of the Cosmic Harmony just like Macduff killing Macbeth to make Malcolm king."

Mr. Wolff stared at Arnold for a long, long moment. Then he smiled, a smile that spread all across his face and into his eyes and displayed two rows of bright white teeth with sharp, pointed canines.

Arnold thought he might wet his pants. "I'm in big trouble now, aren't I?" Arnold said.

"The tree of liberty," Mr. Wolff said slowly, deliberately, "must be refreshed from time to time with the blood of patriots and tyrants. It is its natural manure." He studied Arnold's face, his gray eyes shifting restlessly, and Arnold stared back at him. "Did you ever hear that quote, Arnold?" Arnold shook his head. "Of course you didn't. SCOD would never allow it. I am amazed they haven't censored Thomas Jefferson completely from the history books." Mr. Wolff put his glasses back on, which made his eyes look even bigger. "I know you want to join the Resistance, Arnold," he said abruptly.

Arnold stopped breathing. When he tried to speak there was no air in his lungs, and he coughed and sputtered. "Wh-what are you talking about?"

Mr. Wolff smiled, showing a flash of white teeth. "I have my sources."

Arnold gaped at him. *It has to be Matt who told him. Jared and Gus wouldn't dare, unless he told them to. But does that mean Matt is actually in the Resistance? The way he looked at me…*

Aloud, he said, "You and Matt are in the League, right? I mean, it has to be the League if you're inviting me to join. The Patriotic Front wouldn't even let me in because I'm a Jew."

Mr. Wolff winked and smiled tightly. "Security, my friend. The enemy's watchword is security, so ours must be as well."

"What do I have to do to join?"

"You already have," said Mr. Wolff. "Wait for instructions. Your contact will be either myself, or Matthew Walters."

Arnold nodded so violently he was afraid his head was going to fly off his neck. Not trusting himself to speak, he grabbed his books and bolted out the door, his heart exploding in his chest.

The cafeteria was jammed and noisy when Arnold speed-walked in. He bought a hamburger, orange juice, and gooey canned peaches, and sat down in his new spot at the edge of the Matt Gang's table. He took out his biology textbook and pretended to study for the upcoming quiz while sneaking glances at Matt, who was discussing the charms of none other than Hailee with Jared.

"I think if you French kiss her she'd taste like cherry pie," Matt hypothesized.

Jared proposed something less savory. There were guffaws around the table. Arnold did his best to suppress the urge to defend the princess's honor and watched Matt carefully for signs of secret agenthood.

It was hard to detect any. No, it was impossible. He had the same dumb, self-satisfied look on his face as always. Everything about his appearance was loathsome, from his carefully gelled but greasy-looking black hair to his pudgy but muscular chest and arms to his gleaming white high-top sneakers with yellow lightning zigzags so bright they hurt your eyes. Could it be that Matt's supreme jerkiness was really an elaborate cover for being in the Resistance? Or did the League accept jerks as members?

Eventually Arnold must have pushed his luck too far, because the secret Leaguer said, "What're you staring at, retard?" But his voice was a monotone, as if he was giving an answer to a math problem—or just keeping up jerky appearances.

"Nothing," Arnold muttered, breaking eye contact. He winced, expecting a looming shadow to fall over his lunch tray and textbook, to be followed by a sharp pain in his butt as he was wedgie'd out of his seat and evicted from the gang's table once and for all. But nothing happened. Could it really be true?

He was so absorbed in this mystery that when he went to bus his lunch tray he narrowly avoided bumping into Kayleigh. "Watch where you're going, Arnold," she said. "Arnold," not "spaz." She even smiled a little.

The mystery deepened in the days that followed, and Jo had no ideas about it. "The chair commends your initiative," was all she said when he timidly told her about his recruitment into the League. She looked at his face and rolled her eyes. "It's a good idea, is all I mean, Arnold."

"So you're not mad at me?"

"Huh-uh." They were sitting on the edge of a wooden pier facing Assa Teag, sipping cocoa out of covered mugs and watching Ashley and four of her dragonets wheel around in the late afternoon sky like enormous green crows.

It was a relatively warm day for winter in Gingo Teag, and Jo had defied her "mum" and gone out without a coat and gloves. Arnold had both on and was still freezing. But he wished he could feel her warm hand against his, just once. They'd been meeting almost every day for weeks and still the only contact they had was when she pushed him or punched him on the shoulder. There definitely had not been any "disgusting snogging."

"Maybe you should join too," Arnold said, when Jo didn't say anything.

"Me? No, I don't have time." Jo shook her head and her dirty-blond braid bounced enchantingly around. "As it is, Mum is starting to grumble about all the time we spend together. She wants me to concentrate on my schoolwork, when I'm already doing university-level math. I mean, what else does she want?"

Maybe she's afraid we are snogging, Arnold thought. *Little does she know I'd never dare!*

* * * *

Back in school, Mr. Wolff was acting no differently than usual—there were no more requests to see him after class, no notes penned into the margins of Arnold's homework assignments—and Matt, Jared, and Gus seemed to totally ignore him.

What would happen if I sat right next to them at lunch? The idea was terrifying but once it had entered his head it stayed there. *What would Jo say? Do it for the Cause, for your fellow humans, that's what she would say!*

So when lunchtime oozed around again, Arnold raced to get to the cafeteria early, loaded up his tray with shriveled pizza, wilted lettuce salad, and soggy fruit cocktail, and tiptoed over to the gang's table, which was so far unoccupied.

He carefully chose his place, just to the right of where Gus usually sat—Gus, who had actually apologized to him on the fateful day he told them he was in the Resistance, never guessing it would actually come true. Then he waited, occasionally poking at his food, though if he had tried to put anything in his mouth he would have thrown up.

Matt was the first to arrive. He stared at Arnold but said nothing. The others followed right behind him, jabbering away. But they stopped talking all at once when they saw Arnold. No one looked at him; instead they all turned to Matt, who stabbed at his burrito with his fork, making it bleed gray.

"What are you morons looking at?" he demanded.

If we're all morons, I'm just the same as Gus and Jared! The thought was incredible.

"Nothing, Matt," Gus said. "I was just wondering whether Arnold, here, knows what's gonna be on the next bio test." Everyone turned and looked at him.

"Evolution," Arnold croaked. He cleared his throat and tried again. "Evolution! Uh, the theory of natural selection!"

"Natural selection?" Jared echoed.

"Yeah, you know. Survival of the fittest. Er, um, living things that are, uh, adjusted to their environment survive, and those that aren't, don't."

"My pastor says that's all a bunch of lies from the High Ones," Gus said with a frown. Arnold quailed, expecting a blow any second. "But I guess we'd better learn it for the test. What do you say, Matt?"

There was a long pause. Obviously neither Gus nor anyone else cared whether God created the universe in six days or Darwin in six billion years, they just wanted Matt's ruling on Arnold's invasion of the gang's lair. Matt gave out with a single, low grunt. And that was all it took! Arnold was accepted, a wolf among wolves.

When the bell rang at the end of lunch Arnold gathered up his books and prepared to slink off to his next class. Gus and Jared had already disappeared into the swirling mob of students when Arnold felt a hand on his arm. He turned and saw that it was Matt.

"Listen, Arnold," he said, blowing out a breath as if he'd just been running the fifty-meter dash, "lunchtime is no good for *business*, okay? Not everyone who sits at my table is *cleared.*"

"Sure," Arnold said, dropping his voice to a whisper. "Are there, um, instructions?"

"The parking lot behind the Value-Mart. Four o'clock."

So it was true! Arnold had begun to wonder if he'd somehow daydreamed the strange encounter with Mr. Wolff. Maybe the Matt Gang had only accepted him because they'd bought his line of bull about being in the Resistance. But when he got to the parking lot, where a lone orange streetlight turned the dirty slush into a giant dish of melting orange sherbet, Matt and Jared were waiting for him—and it wasn't murder in their eyes, it was fear.

"Listen, you can't tell anyone else about this. Not even Gus—his mom is a secretary at Wallops Island," Matt hissed when Arnold walked up.

"My father works there too—but he's gathering intelligence," Arnold quickly added. He glanced at Jared's slack face and thought, *which is more than some of us can say.*

Matt merely nodded. "All right. Orders have come down—"

"From the League?" Arnold asked excitedly.

"*Orders have come down*," Matt said firmly, "to deal first with the traitors who are close at hand."

"What does that mean?" Arnold asked.

"Yeah, what?" Jared said. His mouth stayed open after he stopped talking.

"Not *what*, but *who*," Matt said grimly. He glanced around to make sure they were alone, then pulled a crumpled piece of paper out of his pocket. "Get a load of this. I swiped it off Miss Patrick's desk."

"The algebra teacher is a traitor?" Arnold was dismayed. He had a bit of a crush on Miss Patrick, who was young and blonde and bubbly and never called on anyone by surprise like most of the teachers did.

"Not her, Arnold," Matt grated out. "Just read."

When Arnold did his stomach lurched. It was a blank form for a letter of recommendation for James Park for a High Youth Fellowship. Only a few hundred of those were given out every year in the whole United Satrapy. The winners got an all-expenses-paid Grand Tour of the solar system, followed by a summer-long program at Olympian University and preferential treatment when applying for a full High Fellowship a few years later.

Arnold couldn't really say that James was his friend, but then, he hadn't made any friends in Chincoteague until Jo. But last spring he and James had walked home together a few times, and he'd even been inside James's house once. It was pungent with exotic spices, but Mr. and Mrs. Park were nowhere to be seen. James said they worked long hours at Park Place Cleaners, their dry-cleaning shop on Main Street, and rarely got home before eight o'clock. He shared some chocolate chip cookies with Arnold and they watched a rerun of "Superastronauts" in which the hero, Jack McInnes, almost has his trusty saucer repossessed by the greedy banker David Cohen. The program wasn't very realistic since it had a human piloting a saucer, but it was still fun watching it.

"I don't get it," Arnold said now. "Why does the League care if somebody gets a High Youth Fellowship?"

"It's carburetion, that's why," Matt said.

"I think you mean collaboration, Matt." Before he could take offense at being corrected, Arnold added, "Why don't we hand out pamphlets against the High Ones at the entrance to the Wallops Island base?"

He'd gotten the idea from Jo, who had gotten it from Teresa, who had gotten it from the *other* Teresa. The mysterious "Palermo Teresa" hadn't been down to Gingo Teag in ages because she was very busy rabble-rousing in Boston and Philadelphia, or at least that's what Jo said her mum said.

Matt wasn't impressed by the idea. "*Duh*, are you stupid? We'll get arrested and your father'll probably lose his job!"

"Yeah, but…"

"No, we got to do something about James Park." He stopped and fixed his face in a sneer. "What kind of name is 'James Park,' anyway? It sounds like there ought to be a bunch of picnic tables on him."

Jared used his index fingers to pull up the corners of his eyes. "Me James Park! Me alien-loving Chinaman!"

"But James is Korean," Arnold said.

Matt's face darkened and he clenched his right fist.

Arnold ducked. *Oh well, I knew it was too good to last.*

But Matt didn't hit him. Instead he said, "Who cares what he is? Except a traitor to the human race! We've got to teach him a lesson!"

Do people really say that? I guess they do. "What if I can talk him into not applying?" Arnold said.

Matt eyed him. "You can do that? You're his bud?"

"I'm not his bud, but I used to sit at his table at lunch. Maybe he'll listen to me."

Matt screwed up his eyes his eyes in thought. Jared shoved his pinkie finger up his right nostril, worked it around, and examined the results with interest.

How different is that from how Greg at the Reject Table acts? Of course, Jared could beat me up and Greg can't beat up anybody…

"All right," Matt said at last, "I'm giving you till Thursday to talk him into pulling his application. Otherwise, we spray-paint his locker Friday during lunch."

Spray paint it with what, Arnold didn't have to ask: A blue-eyed swastika, just like the ones Matt and his gang had painted on *his* locker, and the senior boys had painted on Alison's, several times over the past year. Today was Tuesday. He had three days to stop that from happening.

15

Arnold gets a little girlfriend out of this "yellow-wood," parallel world deal, and all I get is dunked in freezing water and nearly drowned by an overgrown salamander. It is No Fair!

Alison had caught pneumonia and had to spend three days in the hospital in Salisbury, Maryland, followed by a whole week off school, which she didn't even get a chance to enjoy because she was too busy trying to keep up with her schoolwork.

The only consolation was that Mom let her watch the new episode of "The Spacefarers," which meant she got to see it before Shaniqua. The tri-vee people had decided that the program was a daytime soap opera and had switched showtime to noon on Thursdays, overriding the protests of the loyal fan base it had developed among teenage girls who had a crush on Donny Schmitz. If only there was some way of recording programs at home! All you could do was wait for the Sunday afternoon reruns, unless you happened to be home sick.

Mom was feeling well enough to come downstairs and watch with her, "though this Izzy Goldstein business is really disturbing." She didn't agree that Donny Schmitz was such hot stuff. "He's too much of a kid. I just want to pinch his cheeks," she said as she passed Alison the popcorn. "I like Eric Fenner better."

"The guy who plays the captain? But he's half bald and, like, fifty years old!"

"And so distinguished looking," Mom sighed. When she caught Alison eyeing her she quickly put on a stern expression. "This is a special treat because you're sick, Allie. Dad's really right about the anti-Semitism, you know."

"Of course, Mom." It was easier to agree than to argue and risk Mom changing her mind.

After the program ended Mom went to take a nap in her room, shaking off Alison's attempt to help her as she dragged herself up the staircase by clinging to the railing. She always said resting helped keep her NINA flare-ups down.

Alison left the tri-vee on for company while she tried to catch up on her physics homework. There was going to be a test on Monday about the High Ones' Bubble Drive, and as a point of pride she didn't want to have to ask for an extension. Anyway the math was pretty easy. "If the speed of light is 300,000 km/sec in the regular universe and 3×10^8 km/sec in a bubble universe created by the *HSS Hhhh-ssss-appulium* for a trip between Homeworld and Earth, what is the minimum possible time, in Earth-days, for the trip?"

Everyone knew that Homeworld was 20.5 light-years from Earth, so a ship traveling from Homeworld in the regular universe, and therefore slower than light, would take at least 21 years to reach Earth (though it would take much less time for the passengers than for planet-bound observers due to the "time dilation" effect of Einstein's Special Theory of Relativity, more properly known as Th-shhh-limalalia's Shining Insight, since she had after all discovered it first, sometime around 3700 B.C.—but whatever you called it, Alison didn't have to know it till spring semester). At 3×10^8 or 300,000,000 km/sec, light in the bubble universe would travel from Homeworld to Earth 1,000 times faster than in the regular universe, so a ship could also go 1,000 times faster, so that would be 0.21 of a year... times 365 days... umm...

A knock on the door startled Alison awake from a dream in which she had been piloting an interplanetary saucer, with Donny Schmitz by her side in the astrogator's chair, whispering sweet nothings in her ear. It was Shaniqua, and of course she wanted the latest scoop from "The Spacefarers."

"We'll have to keep it down, my mom is sleeping," Alison said. "But it was a really good one today! First Brad had to help Captain Adams when a course error sent the Intrepid hurtling toward an asteroid! Then when they stopped to refuel on Phobos, Izzy Goldstein sent his slutty daughter Portia to come on to Brad, but he—"

Shaniqua held up her right hand. "All right, all right, I get the idea. Don't spoil the whole thing for me. Anyway, they'll never get rid of that Janey. I wish she would get hit by a meteor or something. She's as bad as Sydney Birch—would you believe she dumped Steve Dawkins and started going out with Gil Devlin?"

"The starting quarterback? Really?"

"Really!" Shaniqua caught Alison up on the rest of the gossip, which didn't take long. Nothing much happened around Chincoteague High in January, except that the assistant principal had caught Don Peabody painting a blue-eyed swastika on Shaniqua's locker and made him clean it off, "which serves that dirtball right." Eventually she paused and stood there on the front step shifting her weight from one foot to the other. "How are you feeling, anyway?"

"A lot better," Alison said. "It's getting pretty boring staying home, to tell the truth. I hope I'll be back in school Monday."

"Just how did you catch cold? You've never been sick before, far as I can remember."

"I fell into the ocean at Assateague, the day after Christmas."

Shaniqua raised an eyebrow. "How did that happen? Don't tell me you went swimming!"

"Uh, no, not exactly." Alison looked at the floor. Suddenly she felt bad for having kept the whole thing secret from Shaniqua. Wouldn't she like to meet her "twin"? Teresa had told her it was fun getting to know the other Teresa, the person she could have been—would have been—if she'd been born in Bonaparte-ruled Sicily instead of Philadelphia.

Alison stood there biting her lip for a moment, thinking. "Shaniqua, can I tell you a secret? But you'll have to come inside and shut the door."

"Okay by me, long as you don't sneeze on me." She came in and sat on the saggy green sofa Dad had picked up at the local Goodwill before his first paycheck came in.

Alison switched off the news, something about a SCOD campaign to make sure school prayers were being recited sincerely, and told Shaniqua about Gloria and Gingo Teag, the Purnells, Teresa, and Assa Teag Ashley.

Shaniqua cupped her chin in her hands and listened, then shook her head. "You must be real bored at home, Allie."

"I'm not making it up! It's really real. I even met your double over there."

"My what?"

"Your double—who you would have been if you'd been born in a British-ruled America. Your name was Sharon and you were dressed like an American Heritage doll."

Shaniqua snorted and stood up. "You sound like something out of those old science fiction books my dad likes. It's a shame no one publishes that nonsense any more—you could make a fortune!"

"But it's all true! I've really been there."

"Girl, I don't have time for this. I've got to get home and try to do my homework before Tavon and his buddies show up and start drinking and breaking stuff like they always do."

"No, wait!" Alison jumped up and grabbed her arm. "What if I show you?"

"Show me what? The wardrobe with the secret tunnel to Narnia?" Shaniqua had read Alison's dad's copy of the C.S. Lewis book over the summer, since SCOD had banned it from the public library.

"It's not a wardrobe, I told you! It's just a really scary hallway under the school library!"

Shaniqua tugged her arm free. "Allie, I ain't never known you to play practical jokes, but I got to tell you I have no use for them. I get enough of that sort of foolery from Tavon and his jackass friends."

"I'm not playing a prank, Shaniqua, I swear!" Alison started to tear up. Why wouldn't her best friend believe her? She felt like Brad on "The Spacefarers" when he tried to explain to Janey how Portia's perfume-soaked bandanna came to be in his quarters. "Look, if I'm lying, I promise I'll do your math homework for a week."

Shaniqua hesitated. She loathed math, but she had to get through pre-calculus and get at least as far as basic calculus for the colleges she wanted to apply to. "But if you're lying, you could be lying about that too," she said.

"Pinky swear I'm not! But we'd better go now, so I can get back before my dad gets home." Alison grabbed her coat from the closet.

"Go where?" Alison cursed silently at the sound of wheels rolling over the wooden floor. How had Mom managed to walk all the way downstairs, gripping the railing with both hands the way she always did these days, and still sneak up on her in the wheelchair?

Alison turned around and forced a smile. "I'm just going out for a bit with Shaniqua. The doctor said I'd be well enough to go to the movies on the weekend, so I figured, why not start a little early?"

"Uh-huh. That's some movie you're going to see, with doors to parallel worlds and everything." Mom laughed at Alison's dismay. "Shaniqua, it's nice of you to stop by. I don't you blame you for being skeptical, but if anyone's a storyteller in this family, it's me. Alison hasn't got that good of an imagination."

"What!" Alison said, while Shaniqua laughed.

"I'm sorry hon, but it's true. When you made me that get-well card when I was diagnosed with this disgusting disease, you drew me a very pretty house with a very pretty daisy under a nice, bright yellow sun. This was nine years ago," she added to Shaniqua. "Arnold drew a picture of a twelve-armed octopus swimming in Lake Michigan. At least, that's what he said it was. There were so many arms, he said, to give me lots of hugs so I would get well soon. Lucky for us, it was all a big black and blue scribble to the untrained eye, or we might have got in trouble with SCOD!"

Mom wheeled closer, reached up, and touched Alison's cheek. "I don't mean to hurt your feelings, honey. You've got a good heart and a good mind, and that's what's important. So you'll understand when I say I'm coming with you if you're planning on visiting that other world Dad told me about! I'm not too sick to do whatever I want to. NINA's not stopping me!"

"But Mom, it could be a little difficult." Mom's eyebrows came together and her mouth turned down in a scowl. Alison held up a hand. "I don't mean I don't want you along! It's just that, uh, well, Gloria is the school librarian."

"So? It's just a couple of blocks away. I can wheel myself that far without help."

"Yeah, but non-students aren't allowed there without special permission, or after school hours. We were going to, um, well…"

"Yes? What kinda trouble were you gonna get us in?" Shaniqua demanded, looking up and folding her arms.

"We were just gonna sneak in the library's fire exit! It's fine with Gloria! She helped me and Teresa do it, the night I fell in the water."

"Right, the night a dragon dropped you in the ocean," Shaniqua said, rolling her eyes. "You sure about Allie's lack of imagination, Mrs. Grossbard?"

"She's like an accountant. Scout's honor, and I was a Girl Scout," Mom said, snapping off a salute. "Now, let's get going so we can be back before your father and Arnold get home. This trip will be our little secret!"

As the three of them approached the high school, Alison spotted Arnold with that Korean kid, what's-his-name, further up the block. They were so deep in conversation they didn't even look up. Alison was glad: she'd been worried that Arnold was spending so much time lately hanging out with Matt Walters and his thuggish sidekicks. The same kids who used to pick on him all the time! When she tried to ask him about it he told her to mind her own business.

It took a while to get to the school, with Mom propelling her own wheelchair and refusing all offers for help from Alison and Shaniqua. When they finally arrived, there were still stragglers coming out the front door, kids who had been in detention and teachers who had stayed late. Alison spotted Bubba driving away in a beat-up pickup truck that looked like it had been built before there even was an automated traffic network, leaving the ex-sheriff's deputy Mr. Ramsey alone on guard duty at the front door. He settled himself down on a wooden chair that creaked under his weight and covered the bare stomach protruding from under his untucked shirt with the sports section of the paper.

"Come on," said Mom, "we're going up there."

"But how? There isn't even a ramp," Alison said.

"I can walk up these steps," Mom said, eyeing them. Alison tried to see them through her eyes: they weren't that steep, but there were at least two dozen of them.

"I'm afraid you'll have to carry my wheelchair," she said. She stood up slowly, straining against the armrests till Alison thought she could see her biceps rippling.

Shaniqua rushed over to pick up the wheelchair, and Alison tried to offer her arm but was swatted away. Mom leaned against the iron railing that bisected the stairway, pulling herself along it one step at a time.

Mr. Ramsey completely ignored the struggling woman until she staggered up to the front door, sitting down heavily in the wheelchair Shaniqua rushed to put under her. Then he looked over his paper and said, "Just where do you think you're going, ma'am?"

"My name is Mrs. Rachel Grossbard. My daughter Alison, here, is a senior, so I've come to visit her classroom."

"The school day is over, ma'am. Anyway you need to call ahead for a visitor's pass."

"She's my daughter, and my son Arnold is a sophomore, and I am going to visit their school." She paused. "The school librarian, Gloria, is expecting me. Call her if you want."

Mr. Ramsey scowled. "The Resource Center ain't got a phone I can call. And even if it did, there's no way I can let you through security. I ain't even got anyone on duty to search you."

"Search me yourself, then." Mom smiled dangerously. "You can see I must be a terrorist."

"There's no need to be sarcastic. Rules is rules."

Mom said, "Come on, girls. We're going in to visit Gloria," and wheeled herself toward the door.

Alison and Shaniqua looked at each other.

Mr. Ramsey put his newspaper down, grunting with annoyance as a stray gust of wind picked it up and blew it rattling down the staircase. Puffing with effort, he managed to block the doorway before Mom could get through it. "I told you, ma'am, you ain't allowed in without no visitor's permit. If you leave now I won't have to arrest you for trespassing."

Mom shoved the wheelchair forward until her bare, skinny knees rammed into Mr. Ramsey's fat, trousered ones. She poked a finger into his untucked midriff and he grunted with surprise.

"You gonna handcuff me, tough guy? Go ahead, I dare you. I'm sure everyone on this island would just love to see a fake cop like you manhandle a lady in a wheelchair."

Alison bit her lip to keep from laughing as she watched Mr. Ramsey's piggy little eyes shift left and right, right and left, looking for someone to rescue him. At last he stood aside. "I'm gonna hafta write this up in my log!" he said, shaking his fist as Mom wheeled herself into the echoing school lobby.

"That was awesome, Mrs. Grossbard!" Shaniqua said after they turned down a corridor toward the library and were safely out of earshot. "Where did you learn to be so tough?"

"When you've got a handicap like I do, if you let idiots stop you from doing what you want to do, you might as well just dry up and blow away," Mom said. There was an awkward pause. "Well, which way is the library?"

When they got there they found Gloria talking softly to herself as she reshelved some books. She looked up and smiled broadly. "Hi, Alison! Who are your friends?"

Alison did the introductions and added, with a nervous glance at the door, "They know, that is, I told them, and they'd like to see, that is to go, uh, I hope that was all right, I'm really sorry if I..."

Gloria leaned forward. "It's all right, Alison. I trust you and your family, and anyway I've already met Sharon."

"Sharon? Who's Sharon?" Shaniqua said. "Oh, right, my so-called double! Don't tell me all this stuff is for real! Y'all are gonna lead me into a closet with a full-length mirror in it and then laugh your fool heads off at me, right?"

"Actually, no," said a new voice. Shaniqua turned and her eyes widened. Her mouth moved but no sounds came out.

"I know, it's pretty amazing," said a girl who looked just like Shaniqua, or would have, if Shaniqua would ever have been caught dead wearing a skirt so long it brushed the floor. The stranger stepped out from behind the dimly lit shelves to the left of the counter. She smiled, and it was definitely the same smile, starting on the left side of her face and spreading all over. "You look a little pale, double mine. You should sit down and have some of Gloria's tea, it works wonders."

"Wh—where'd you get that accent?" Shaniqua said faintly.

"Pshaw, it's just an ordinary Gingo Teag accent."

"Pshaw. Some girl who looks just like me actually said 'pshaw.' I think I will have some tea, Miss Gloria."

"Certainly," Gloria said. "Why don't you two get acquainted, and I'll bring tea for everyone. Then Sharon will take you all on a little tour of Gingo Teag."

Alison followed Gloria back behind the counter as she filled the electric kettle. "Umm, Gloria, I hate to bring this up, but there could be a bit of a problem."

"A problem, dear? What kind of problem?"

"Well, it's just that—the steps down to the Gray Zone. I don't think my mom can manage them."

"I heard that!" Mom called. "I can climb steps just fine, Allie! You just saw me do it!"

"Yeah, but—"

"Here, would you help me carry these cups?" Gloria said to Alison. "There's nothing to worry about. The physical set-up of the Gray Zone isn't to be taken at face value."

The back of Alison's neck prickled. "What does that mean?"

"The Gray Zone is an interdimensional location. Its appearance is reached by consensus."

"By consensus? What's that mean?" Shaniqua said with a frown as she took her tea cup from Gloria.

"It means by agreement," Alison said.

Shaniqua's eyes flashed. "I know what the word 'consensus' means, Allie! I meant who's doing the agreeing?"

"Sorry. And that's a good question," Alison said.

"I would suppose," said Mom, "it's something about the observer altering the physical characteristics of an experiment? Like quantum mechanics?"

"Something like that," Gloria agreed, handing her a cup. "This library is in a school building, so stepping down beneath it, you expect to see a cinderblock-lined hallway with awful fluorescent bulbs overhead that make everyone look dead. So, that's what you see. But there's no reason there have to be stairs going down there. There could be a ramp."

"And we have to pass through this Gray Zone to get to Sharon's world?" Mom asked.

"Yes. But there's really nothing to worry about there."

"Except that you keep telling us there's nothing to worry about," Alison muttered.

"But Rachel, my dear, why do you use a wheelchair, if you don't mind my asking?" Gloria said.

"I don't mind. I'm not ashamed of having NINA. What? Don't get that look on your face!"

Alison turned and saw with astonishment that Gloria was tearing up. A big, crystal-bright drop rolled down her cheek and hit the floor, where it rolled some more instead of spreading out on the tiles.

Alison bent over and picked it up between her thumb and forefinger—and it wasn't liquid at all! She dropped it in surprise.

Everyone else was too preoccupied by Mom's furious reaction to notice. "Don't you dare pity me, you silly girl!" she said, rising shakily from the wheelchair and wagging a finger in Gloria's face.

"Oh! I'm sorry, Rachel. This isn't pity," Gloria said.

"Why are you crying, then?"

"From anger."

Alison looked up in surprise. Gloria's delicate orange eyebrows had turned into straight lines pointing downward at the bridge of her nose, and her voice, though no louder, held an edge she'd never heard in it before.

"There's no need for this. None!" Gloria said, stepping across the room to the carrels where the n-readers sat unused for once. "Do you see these things?" She slapped the gray metal side of one of the machines with the palm of her hand.

"What are they?" Sharon asked.

"Mindspeaking devices, if you please! The Winged-Thinkers—what your world calls the 'High Ones'—adapted their own technology so humans could use it to trade thoughts."

"Why 'Winged-Thinkers?'" Alison asked. "I've never seen them fly."

"Have you ever seen them in the water? No? You'd understand, if you did. But what you'd find hard to understand—even I find it incredible—is how they were able to take a device tuned to the echinodermoid nervous system and adapt it for humans. A miracle of engineering. But do you know why they did it?"

Silence. Alison hesitantly supplied the answer that was always expected in class: "Because they are humanity's benevolent protectors? No, you're gonna tell me that's stupid, right?"

Gloria took Alison's hand. The librarian's hands were incredibly soft and incredibly hot, with a pulse beating as rapidly as a baby bird's. Alison nearly jerked away in surprise.

"No Allie, I am not going to tell you you're stupid for believing what you've been told all your life, even if it was a complete and total lie. Which it isn't. It's a half-truth."

"You mean it's partly true and partly false?"

"No, dear. The historian John Lukacs once said that half-truths aren't like math—that they're not a fifty percent truth plus a fifty percent lie, but a whole truth and a whole lie, all mixed up together. And that's what makes them so dangerous."

"I don't get it," Alison said.

"Me either," Mom said. Shaniqua and Sharon also looked puzzled.

Gloria sighed and let go of Alison's hand. "When there was a French Empire, in your world and Teresa's, people in France used to say it was because they had a mission civilisatrice."

"The Bonapartes still say that in my world—that they have to keep ruling over Europe and Africa because they're the only civilized people and everyone else is a bunch of savages," Sharon said. "That's a nice excuse for lording it over everyone!"

"But, my dear, you British said the same thing about India until Mohandas Gandhi led that rebellion back in 1930."

Sharon scowled and folded her arms. "That's different! That's ancient history. We don't lord it over anybody anymore."

"No? What about the Seminoles in West Florida?" Silence. "Look, I'm not meaning to pick on you. The point is, the Winged-Thinkers aren't really any better than humans, though they pretend they are and they have all the power. Nevertheless, they actually do believe they're uplifting and helping your world. But they're also doing it because they can also make a profit."

"A profit? How?" Alison said.

"You know how people who are plugged into the n-readers look like they could be in a coma?"

Alison winced. "That's what it looks like, yes."

"Well, what do you think the resting parts of their brains are doing while their conscious mind interacts with the network?"

"I don't know, what?" Alison said. Then it hit her. "The High Ones take over people's minds," she said in a horrified whisper. "At least while they're plugged into the n-readers, and maybe afterwards too."

She turned her head slowly, wondering if they were going to turn Shaniqua and Mom into attack robots that would kill her now that the secret was out. Instead she saw that Shaniqua's eyes had gone wide, and Mom's mouth was compressed in a thin, pale line. Sharon had plastered herself against the wall, her eyes darting left and right.

"It isn't mind control, not like you're thinking. In a way, it's actually worse than that," Gloria said. "The Winged-Thinkers only use the networked power of the resting parts of people's brains while they're plugged in. Use them for their own purposes. That doesn't affect people's conscious minds. But it does burn out neurons by the millions in people's brains. That affects everyone who has ever used the n-network—not just the unfortunate few like you, Rachel, who are extra sensitive to the damage and quickly come down with full-blown Network-Induced Neuronal Atrophy."

Mom was trembling, but not with the palsy she sometimes got. No, it looked like pure rage. "They told me cases like mine are less than one in a million," she said. Softly, but with a roar behind it.

Gloria smiled sadly. "Not true, Rachel. All n-network users suffer from NINA. The more time they've spent on the system, the greater the damage."

"I used to be on it for hours every day," said Mom, stricken.

"But if it's causing brain damage," said Shaniqua, who was gripping the back of a chair, "how come it's, like, addictive? People always be fighting over time on the n-net. I remember once I almost punched Sydney Birch when she cut ahead of me in line!"

"Addictive is the right word, Shaniqua," Gloria said. "And it's actually because of the dead neurons. The brain function that's been lost is more than made up for by the network—as long as you're on the network. That's why you feel so powerful when you're using it, am I right?"

Mom and Shaniqua nodded dumbly.

"But why do they do it? What for?" Alison asked, forcing her voice through a closed-up throat. It sounded like someone was strangling her. *Which they might do, once they find out what I know!* Suddenly Mr. Freed's kind of paranoia seemed almost naive.

Shaniqua's eyes narrowed to hard little slits. "There's only one possible answer to that," she said. "Only one thing them monsters do is complicated enough that they'd need to kidnap people's brains to make it work. They want us for calculators, don't they, Gloria?"

The look on Gloria's face was enough to confirm that Shaniqua was right.

"The Bubble Drive!" Alison gasped, covering her mouth with her hands.

To Sharon, Gloria explained, "The Winged-Thinkers have faster-than-light-speed starships. But since nothing made of matter can go faster than light, they can only work by creating temporary 'bubble' universes where the speed of light is much faster than it is in the regular universe. The ships go into these bubbles, where they can go much faster than the regular speed of light. Then they drop back into the regular universe at their destination."

"A cosmic shortcut," said Sharon, blinking. "Like when I cut through the marsh on the way home."

"That's it," said Gloria, nodding.

Shaniqua stood up straight, her hands clenched in fists at her sides. "That's all we are to them—them blue slugs? Ships' computers made of meat?"

"We need to get them to see you as what you are—human beings, fully their equals despite your distressing lack of tentacles," Gloria sighed. "It won't be easy."

"Not easy?" cried Alison. She felt as if her head would explode. "Look what they did to my mom!" she said, pointing at her wheelchair with a shaky finger. "Look what they've done to—to the whole human race! We ought to kill them all, that's what we ought to do!"

"And what," said Gloria, her eyes shining, "would that settle?"

"What would it settle? It'd settle their hash, that's what it would settle!" said Mom. It took her a full minute to get the words out, she was stuttering so badly.

Alison hugged her, and another strange tear rolled down Gloria's face.

"It didn't have to be like this," she said softly. "If only the Winged-Thinkers had dealt with you fairly. Volunteers who knew the risks could have been the ones to use the n-network. And with their knowledge of biology, the Winged-Thinkers could have worked to minimize the damage to people's brains... or even figured out how to reverse it. But this way, it's such a one-sided deal—and being eleven-dimensional, I can't abide anything one-sided."

Mom's face got even redder. "You mean to tell me those slimy bastards could cure my NINA, and they don't?"

"That's exactly what I mean! If they can adapt the n-network to use on nervous systems as alien to them as yours are, why can't they fix damage to those nervous systems? I'll tell you why—because it doesn't pay." Gloria spat the "p" in "pay."

"And you want us to talk nice to them, when they've been fooling us and hurting us for almost fifty years?" Shaniqua shouted. "When people find out about this, the League is going to have more people who want to blow stuff up than they can handle!"

"Yeah, but so will the Front. And you know what they're like. To them, blacks and Jews and Asians and a whole bunch of other people aren't really human," Alison said.

"I think I'd like to go home now," Sharon said.

16

"But why won't you join with the rest of the human race in fighting the aliens?" Arnold said. He hated the whining tone that had crept into his voice, like when he nagged Dad to take him out to the House of Siam on a weeknight. He was just trying to talk James into doing the right thing—even if he had to walk all the way down Main Street with him in the gathering darkness.

"I don't see the whole human race asking me to give up my chance to go to Mars," James pointed out. "Just you and your new, goony friends."

Arnold flinched. "They're not as bad as they seem," he said. "They're patriots who want to free America from the High Ones."

"Patriots as in Patriotic Front?"

"No! We're not the Patriotic Front. I'm with the FFE—Freedom Fighters of Earth."

"Never heard of them. Don't really care, either. Far as I can see, all these groups are just as bad. You know what Samuel Johnson said—patriotism is the last refuge of a scoundrel. All they want to do is blow stuff up and make it so nobody can go into space or use the n-network. They'd send us right back to the twentieth century."

"And what would be so bad about that? We were free then."

James gave Arnold a look. "Maybe you were, here in America. When my parents left Korea, it was a military dictatorship. Now the generals call themselves nobles, and General Song is the king. What's the difference?"

"That's not the point. At least we should have human beings ruling us, not Slugs!"

James looked all around the snowy street in alarm. "You'd better keep your voice down if you don't want to get in trouble. Me, I'm going home."

Arnold grabbed James's arm as he started to turn away. "Don't do that. Please," he added, when James stiffened. "Hear me out. It's really important that everyone do their part to get rid of the High Ones. If we would just all stick together, they wouldn't be able to give us orders anymore. Their so-called Empire would collapse."

"Let me tell you something about empires," James said, shaking Arnold off and wagging his finger in his face. It might have been funny if there wasn't a rumor that James knew tae kwon do and could break you in half just like a karate-chopped brick. "Korea was part of an empire until the end of World War II—the Japanese Empire."

"I know that," said Arnold, who had learned that fact for a history test and promptly forgotten it, until this moment. The textbook said that back then Japan had tried to impose a version of the Cosmic Harmony but was tragically stopped by America. A lot of people had been killed for no reason. Wasn't it so much better that Earth enjoyed the real Cosmic Harmony now? Give five reasons why.

"Japanese soldiers came and took my great-grandfather away from his farm. They made him work for them for nothing in New Guinea, carrying huge heavy packs and breaking rocks in the mountains so they could set up machine-gun nests. Some American soldiers took him prisoner and almost killed him because they thought *he* was Japanese. My family didn't see him for four years, and when he came home, his health was ruined because he had caught malaria."

"That's awful, but I don't see—"

"You don't see? Then you're blind," James snapped. "All the old human empires were like that. And what do the High Ones want from us, in return for stopping all our stupid wars and giving us space travel and longevity and the n-network? Nothing, except to try and be a little more like them. Sounds fair to me. Now if you'll excuse me, I have to study for my Basic Starflight test. I have a date with Olympus Tower." And he shut the door to his house in Arnold's face.

There was no dinner waiting for Arnold when he got home. In fact, the house was dark and empty. Even Mom wasn't there. Where could everybody be?

Much as Arnold disliked having to make conversation with other people, he hated being home alone even more. Especially at night, though he knew he was too old to admit this to anyone. So he decided to have his snack in front of the tri-vee stage.

First he had to go make himself the peanut butter and banana sandwich Alison was supposed to have waiting for him, but the only banana left was too mushy to open and when he tried to force it, it turned into a big gooey mess. He had to settle for plain peanut butter and a big glass of milk that slopped over as he walked to the living room with it. *Alison can clean that up. It's her fault!*

"Superastronauts" would have been fun, but the program was interrupted by a special news report, something about terrorists causing a high-speed train derailment outside Chicago. He started to change the channel when he remembered *he* was in the Resistance now, so he decided it was his duty to watch.

"...the so-called Human Defense League claimed credit in a telex," a grim-faced announcer said. A half-crumpled piece of paper covered with scrawled handwriting appeared briefly on the tri-vee stage and was quickly replaced by a helicopter shot of a collapsed bridge over a muddy river, and a broken silver train lying in the murk.

They didn't want you reading the telex the League had sent, or at least not anything more than the words HUMAN DEFENSE LEAGUE. But Arnold was a fast reader, and he'd caught the gist. That train was bound for the O'Hare Saucer Field, and the League had announced years ago that all "alien-controlled transport" was a "legitimate target." Logically, that included transport *to* the evil flying saucers, too, didn't it?

The message said the League was under no obligation to forewarn collaborators who disregarded its declared policy, but nevertheless it had informed Amtrak that there was a bomb on that train, so "any human blood is on their heads. Or would be, if they had heads."

The human blood included fifteen dead passengers, five of them kids younger than Arnold. As a member of the League, did he have to cheer their deaths? Or was there some way to protest? *Mr. Wolff will know.*

There was a knock on the door. Arnold shot to his feet guiltily, as if his thoughts had summoned the police. Instead his thoughts seemed to have summoned Matt and Jared.

"We saw you talking to James," Matt said as soon as Arnold opened the door. "Is he going to drop out of the Youth Fellowship? No, I can see from your face that he's not."

"Give me till tomorrow at least to change his mind," Arnold said.

"Tomorrow's Friday. Then you're going to want to take the whole weekend. Let's teach him a lesson *now*. We saw him go into his house, and his parents keep their dry-cleaning shop open till 8:00, so he'll be all alone there."

"They put honest hard-working people like Mr. Fielding out of business, working them crazy hours," Jared said. "Serves 'em right if we TP their house. Wanna come?"

"I can't. My dad's gonna be home any minute. I'll get in trouble," Arnold said.

"Fine," Matt said. "But you're gonna help us with his locker tomorrow at lunch. Don't try and get out of it."

"Yeah, or we might have to tell the Front on you," Jared sneered.

Arnold shut the door, his heart hammering away as if it wanted to leap out of his chest and go sliding away into a corner, like a slimy High One. He tried to calm himself by sitting back down to watch

"Superastronauts," but the leering face of the banker Mr. Cohen failed to put his mind at ease, and he switched the tri-vee off and headed to his room, leaving the half-eaten peanut butter sandwich to marinate in spilled milk.

He meant to do his homework, but he was distracted by the sight of the spider plant, which was waving its leaves around more than usual, like a person wringing his hands.

"Do you want some water?" he said. He went back down to the living room and retrieved the milk glass. There was still a little liquid left in the bottom, so he poured that over the spot where the leaves poked out of the soil. Their movements immediately slowed and for a moment Arnold was afraid he had poisoned the plant, but when he held one of the leaves between his thumb and index finger it felt soft and pleasantly plump. He rubbed the leaf, and another leaf reached down and rubbed him back. The iron hand clutching his guts seemed to loosen its grip.

"What should I do?" he whispered, squatting so his eyes were level with the plant. "What is the right thing to do?"

He wouldn't have been shocked if it had spoken to him, aloud or in his mind, but all it did was to reach over with a third leaf and stroke his palm. It tickled a little, but when he moved his hand closer the touch was soothing. Gradually the troubling thoughts in his mind faded, along with the images of the smashed train lying below the broken bridge in Indiana, Matt and Jared telling him he'd better do what he promised, and James telling him he had no problem with the way the High Ones ruled the world. When Alison came in and tapped his shoulder it took him a while to come back from wherever he had been.

"I need to talk to you," she said. Her eyes glinted.

"What?" With the return of normal feeling, the first thing he felt was irritation. "How come you weren't here when I got home? Where's dinner? Where are Dad and Mom?"

"It's Thursday. Dad's out playing cards with Mr. Nomura. We're supposed to get our own dinner with the money he left us." She didn't call him stupid-head or any other insult, which seemed odd.

"Is something the matter?"

"I took Mom and Shaniqua to meet Gloria and get a look at Gingo Teag."

"Okay." Arnold didn't really think it was okay. If he'd had his own way, nobody but him would know about Gingo Teag and the Purnells. But that didn't explain what Alison was so upset about.

She told him about the n-readers, in a near-whisper. "Mom thinks you're too young to know about it, that it'll just scare you. But I think it's more important to make sure you never use one of those things! I was so freaked out I came straight home to tell you and didn't even go over to Gingo Teag. I guess Mom and Shaniqua are still there. Shaniqua's double Sharon was going to show them around."

"Aliens invading our brains! It's a shame I didn't know about that when I talked to James."

"Who?"

Arnold looked into his sister's face. Could he trust her? Probably, but what would happen if he got caught and she got in trouble? Weren't secret agents supposed to avoid involving their families? Or what if he told her and she felt that to protect him, she had to tell on him to Dad? *Too risky, either for me or for her, or both of us.* But on the other hand, *she* had trusted *him* enough to tell him the biggest secret in the world!

This problem was too complicated. Suddenly he wanted very much to talk to Jo. Maybe she could help him decide. "I—never mind," he managed to say.

"All right. You want to order Pad Thai for dinner as usual?"

"Sure."

They ate in silence when the food came. Arnold kept glancing at Alison, wondering what she was thinking. It was a sign of how upset she must be that she didn't punch him on the arm for "giving me the evil eye." *She must be worried the enemy will find out what we know. But that can't be so, or they'd have busted down our door already.* No sooner had he thought this than he heard a knock. Arnold jumped up, spilling what was left of his rice all over the floor.

"Arnold! What's the matter with you! I already had to clean up from your snack!"

"S-sorry." But when Alison got up, Arnold grabbed her arm. "Please, don't answer it!"

"What? Why?"

Before Arnold could answer, they heard Mom's voice. "Hello-oo, anybody home?" He nearly crumpled to the floor with relief as Alison went and let her in. "It's amazing! So amazing!" Mom shouted, rolling into the room and popping a wheelie with her wheelchair. Her cheeks were red with the cold and exercise, but she was laughing like a little kid. "I saw it! I saw the dragon. Assa Teag Ashley! I actually saw a dragon!" She whooped and turned her wheelchair around and around until Arnold started to get dizzy.

"What about the dragonets?" Alison asked, smiling.

"The little ones? I saw three, no, four of them! It was the coolest thing EVER!"

"Wait'll you see them flying around with the biplanes they just invented over there," Arnold said.

"What about the Gray Zone?" Alison asked. "Didn't that scare you?"

"You mean that long, bare hallway where you get the feeling monsters are hiding just out of sight?" said Mom. Alison and Arnold nodded, and their mother smiled a little sadly. "Not so much, honey. You see, I spend so much of my life in a gray zone as it is."

Just then Dad arrived home, and once he got over his surprise that Mom had been to Gingo Teag, the rest of the evening was full of talk of how incredible and fun it was over there.

Arnold almost forgot about his troubles, though once or twice he caught Alison's eye and they nodded at each other, which only made him feel guiltier that he hadn't told her about the FFE and the League and what Matt and Jared wanted him to do.

Sleep was a long time coming that night. It felt like a string was being drawn tighter and tighter inside his guts. Fearful thoughts were rising in him like the bubbles in a can of soda, bursting on the surface of his mind and then forming all over again. Just when he was thinking he would never fall asleep he felt something brush against his forehead. It was the spider plant!

He reached out and touched its leaves. Immediately he felt calmer. Now the creaking of the old frame of the house didn't sound like the High Ones or their agents coming to take him away, but like crickets in the summer.

He woke up feeling refreshed, but then he remembered what he had to do today and his stomach clenched up again, so he skipped breakfast and started down the street to school. No use putting it off. As he expected, Matt and Jared waylaid him a block from home.

"Don't forget what we're doing at lunch," Matt said.

"Yeah. No chickening out," said Jared.

Arnold took a deep breath. "Look, guys, can we come up with some other way of getting James to quit the program?"

Matt stared at him. "Like what?"

"It's just that… the thing you guys always paint on people's lockers…"

"Oh, I get it." Matt nodded. "It's 'cause you're a kike—sorry, I mean a Jewboy. You don't like swastikas. Right?"

"Yeah. That's it. You understand." Arnold's lungs suddenly seemed able to hold twice as much air as they had a second ago.

"Weenie," said Jared.

"No, no," said Matt. "I see why it would bother him. The thing is, Arnie, the Nazis stole the swastika."

"They did?" Arnold was so delighted and confused to be called Arnie he had trouble focusing on what Matt was saying.

"Yeah! The swastika's been around, like, forever. Hitler and those guys just misused it. Anyway, I bet you never noticed the arms on *their* swastika go clockwise, which is backward. Our swastika goes the right way, and it has the blue dot for Earth in the center. It's not a Nazi thing at all!"

"I-I dunno, guys. Couldn't we just write a note and put it through those vents in the locker door?"

"How's a plain old note gonna scare him? Besides, he might recognize the handwriting. No, we'll see you there at lunch."

"But—but… how are you gonna sneak a can of spray paint through security?"

"We don't have to. I have a stash I stole from the art room. See you at lunch!" Matt turned and walked off, followed by Jared, who paused and gave Arnold a meaningful look.

"There's only one way out now," Arnold muttered to himself a few minutes later.

"What's that?" Bubba said.

"Huh? Nothing." *The last thing I need now is trouble with Bubba again,* Arnold thought as the rubber gloves danced down his back. *The only way they'll leave James alone is if Mr. Wolff tells them not to do it. They'd have to listen to him. Wouldn't they?*

"You're clear. Get dressed," said Bubba.

"Thank you," Arnold said absently. *It's a good thing he can't see what I'm thinking.*

"Look, kid, take a little advice from me."

"What?" Arnold paused in the act of putting on his belt, flustered that Bubba was speaking to him.

"Quit talking to yourself. They'll put you in the funny farm."

"But I—I…"

"Look, it ain't none of my business." Bubba's head bobbed up and down on his thin neck. "But my little brother got sent to one of them SCOD holes." That was what people called the detention camps the Society for Common Decency officially denied having, though they must exist because occasionally the people SCOD disappeared did come back, as pale and weak shadows of what they'd once been.

"Why? What did he do?" Arnold asked.

The right corner of Bubba's mouth turned up. "Hey, your knees are shakin'! Calm down, kid. You gotta do more than talkin' to yourself to get sent away. Though Junior did that, too—mostly when he was drunk. He was pretty plastered when the cops picked him up down in Accomac last year, during the High Satrap's Hundredth Birthday celebrations. Normally they'd of just tossed him in the drunk tank for the weekend and let him sleep it off, but he really let loose about the Birthday, and the High Satrap himself, and the High Ones. They couldn't just let that go."

"No, of course not," said Arnold, wide-eyed. "Gee, thanks, mister. I'll watch my tongue from now on." But he had put his shoes on the wrong feet, and when he tried to walk he tripped and fell flat on his face.

17

English class was taking *forever*. When was the bell going to ring so
Mr. Wolff could stop talking about Romantic poetry and Arnold could
ask his advice? William Wordsworth was horribly misnamed—not one
word he had written was worth reading and discussing, and yet here
they were, devoting a whole class period to a poem called, "The French
Revolution as It Appeared to Enthusiasts At Its Commencement." The
title didn't rhyme or have any music, the poem itself didn't rhyme, and
how dull it was!

"So what does Wordsworth mean, 'we who were strong in love?'
Who is the 'we?'" Mr. Wolff asked.

"What difference does it make?" demanded Helen Wright, the principal's daughter. "Everyone knows terrorists are full of hatred for the
Cosmic Harmony! That's why everything they do just results in people
getting killed."

Arnold glanced at her round, acne-flecked face and imagined punching her right in her pudgy nose.

"Who said anything about terrorists?" Mr. Wolff said mildly. "I
thought we were talking about revolutionaries."

"Same thing," Helen said.

"Is it? What about the American Revolution?"

"That's not—you're just being unpatriotic!"

"Perhaps Wordsworth was, too? After all, he was English, but he
was writing about the revolution in France, England's mortal enemy! So,
what made him say 'we' about the supporters of that revolution? Who is
the 'we?' You haven't answered the question, Helen."

And she didn't have to, either, because the bell finally, *finally* rang.
As the room rapidly emptied Arnold gathered his books and walked over
to Mr. Wolff's desk. The teacher was making a note in his gradebook;
Arnold, looking upside-down at it, was not pleased to see him giving
Helen a checkmark for class participation.

"Why are you giving that suck-up credit? All she does is parrot
whatever her father says!" he blurted.

Mr. Wolff looked up at him and smiled, showing his teeth.

Uh-oh, I shouldn't have said that.

But it seemed Mr. Wolff wasn't angry at him. "I'm not trying to get my students to agree with everything I say, Arnold. I'm only trying to get them to *think*. That's something schools these days don't do enough of. It's all about preparing for the Social Aptitude Test, not about real learning." He looked straight at Arnold with his steel-gray eyes. "But that's not what you wanted to talk to me about, I'll bet."

"No, it isn't. It's, uh, League business."

"I see. How is that going?"

Arnold told him.

"I see," Mr. Wolff said again. "And you want me to tell you whether Matt and Jared are right?"

"Yeah. Not just about *what* they want to do, but about whether it's right to go after James in the first place. I mean, he's not hurting anyone or telling anybody what to do. We should be trying to get rid of the High Ones and those who, those who, uh, directly do their bidding, right?"

"Those are good questions," Mr. Wolff said, nodding slowly, the corners of his mouth turned down. He put his hands palms down on the desk and levered himself up. "Come with me, Arnold. There's something special in the closet that might help you resolve your dilemma."

"Okay," Arnold said, following Mr. Wolff's broad back down the aisles of empty desks. The teacher opened the door of a perfectly ordinary classroom supply closet. "Here, give me a hand with these," Mr. Wolff said, grunting as he moved a cardboard box full of paperbacks of *To Kill A Mockingbird* and *Huckleberry Finn.*

The Twain book gave Arnold pause. "I thought SCOD disapproves of these."

"That's why they're in the closet. I occasionally give a copy to one of my better students. Those I know won't run straight to Mr. Wright."

Arnold winced, remembering his cowardly threat to Gloria. "I know someone else who likes Mark Twain. The new librarian," he said.

"Really? I haven't had time to talk with her yet. Just a couple more of these boxes, Arnold."

"They're really heavy."

"Better in the closet than in the bonfire, eh?" Arnold had nothing to say about that. There had been a giant *auto-da-fé* of SCOD-condemned books in Salisbury on July 4, which Dad had of course forbidden him and Alison to attend even though there was going to be free ice cream and popcorn and fireworks afterward.

A day later, the local paper said the first book thrown into the flames was Ray Bradbury's *Fahrenheit 451.* "Look at that, he even got the temperature at which paper burns wrong!" Stuart Bobson, the president of the local chapter of SCOD, was quoted as saying.

"Okay, good job," Mr. Wolff said, patting Arnold on the back after they had cleared a path to the back of the closet.

Arnold peered in, expecting to see dusty gray cinderblock, but all he saw was darkness. "What was it you wanted to show me, Mr. Wolff?"

"The future," said Mr. Wolff, and grabbed him around the midriff, lifting him off his feet. Arnold gasped in surprise, but it was a shock of recognition: everything had the same inside-out look as when Gloria carried him and Jo between Chincoteague and Gingo Teag. *Mr. Wolff must be another being like Gloria!* Suddenly the grip around his waist was released and Arnold fell to the floor, landing clumsily on his knees. He saw a flash of gray fur nearby and a triangular head with triangular ears on top. *Wolf!*

He yelped and tried to dive deeper into the closet and pull the door shut behind him. Instead he found himself in a long, featureless tunnel. *The Gray Zone! It's here, too!* But it was darker than the one under the library, and the ceiling was too close—Arnold almost hit his head on it as he inched carefully along. The light faded further as he went along. *Maybe I should turn back.* But he wanted to see where Mr. Wolff had taken him.

"The future," he had said. Gloria said that Gingo Teag was *parallel* to his own time, not ahead of or behind it. Was she also capable of time travel, or was that something only Mr. Wolff could do? And if Mr. Wolff could move people forward or backward in time, why not send trained soldiers back to 1969 to repel the High Ones before they could take over the Earth?

Maybe his time travel works only to the future. In which case, how will I get back home? The frightening thought yielded to a dismal sight. Arnold stumbled over a hidden bump and found himself in the shell of a collapsed building, in a corner where two walls came together. There was a pile of rubble in front of him, mostly broken concrete with rusty metal bars sticking out of it.

He climbed over it carefully on his hands and knees, looking where he was going and taking care not to put his feet into any holes where he might get stuck. By the time he got to the far side of the mound he was sweating, and not only from effort: the day he had left was a typical mid-January day in Chincoteague, overcast and about ten degrees Celsius, but here it was hot and humid, with a thunderstorm about to break: the sky was covered with thick, dark gray clouds and there was an expectant hush in the air.

He was congratulating himself on having gotten out of the ruined building without getting hurt when he felt a pain in his right hand. Jerking away, he saw blood welling from a gash in his palm. He pressed it against his side to stanch the bleeding and peered at the thing he'd cut himself on: the sharp edge of a metal sign. In large black letters on a yellow background it said "AIT" and below that, "CKLE." Which didn't mean anything until he suddenly remembered Greg Chandler, the nose-picker at the Reject Table, saying once that the teachers ought to cut him a break "'cause this whole stupid school is built on what used to be my dad's bait shop."

So had he gone into the past? No, Mr. Wolff had specifically said "the future." And a grim future it was, Arnold saw when he made it to the street. All the buildings he could see seemed to be damaged in some way. Across the street was an old home Arnold thought he recognized. It had those funny sharp-angled peaks above second-floor dormer windows that all the older houses on the Eastern Shore had. But it also had an enormous hole in its roof, around which broken shingles dangled like torn skin over a cut.

Arnold stepped onto the sidewalk to get a better look and his foot crunched into something. He looked down to see what it was and screamed. It was a skull—a skull with shreds of leathery skin still clinging to its outside and black mold inside it, where his shoe was resting. He shook his leg, frantically trying to get rid of the thing, and it sailed up in a clean arc and then down into the street, where it shattered with another sickening crunch.

Now that his eyes were opened to the horror he saw the street was full of what had to be human bones—and not neatly laid out skeletons, either; there were skulls lying on their own like the one he had stepped on, a complete set of arm and hand bones here, foot and leg bones there, an empty rib cage lying around someplace else. A few of them were awfully small, as if they had belonged to babies or little kids. It was as if everyone in town had been gathered here, in the middle of Main Street, and they'd all been killed at once by poison gas. And then wild animals had torn at their bodies. *Like wolves.*

Arnold staggered away, trying to avoid stepping on any more bones as he made for Maddox Boulevard, with some vague idea of following the causeway over the marshes to the mainland to see whether the catastrophe that had struck Chincoteague was confined to the island. A sick feeling in his gut whispered that it wasn't.

You know this one, Arnold. You're the Last Man on Earth. Like the guy at the end of that H.G. Wells novel, The War of the Worlds, *thought he was. Only there isn't going to be any last-minute save as the High Ones are all killed by Earthly germs. They were always too smart for that.* Because there was no doubt in his mind what kind of future Mr.

Wolff was showing him—a future where the High Ones had extermi-nated the human race.

They had finished sucking people's brains dry, and now the human race was unnecessary, a pest to be destroyed. It was boiling hot because the Slugs had given up on saving Earth from the greenhouse effect and were now altering its climate to make it more like Homeworld, which lay under a permanent cloud cover and a blanket of muggy heat, by all accounts from the few people who had visited there and returned.

Okay, okay, I get it, he thought, and turned back to the ruined bait-and-tackle shop, meaning to climb over the rubble and back into the corner where he had emerged so he could find his way back into the Gray Zone. But then he saw a flicker of motion out of the corner of his eye.

Probably a dog gone wild or something. Time to go! He disregarded the voice of reason and turned his head, trying to get a better look at what he'd glimpsed. Across the street, behind the glassless windows of the house with the giant hole in its roof, something flickered. Without really meaning to, he found himself starting across the street, weaving in and out of the piles of bones.

"Hello? Is anybody there?" *I'm going to get killed. For sure I'm go-ing to get killed. That's what happens in all the horror movies. Something heavy or sharp or slimy is going to fly out of that house and kill me.* But still he kept advancing. He couldn't understand why. When something blurry did shoot out of the hole where the ground-floor picture window had been, it shouldn't even have surprised him. But for the second time since he'd stepped into this nightmare world, he screamed. The hand on his shoulder reached down and covered his mouth.

"Quiet, you idiot!" a voice hissed. "They'll hear you!" He nodded his understanding and the hand removed itself from his lips. It was a dusty, dirty hand, and the most wonderful thing he had seen so far. He peered into the darkness of the ruined house, trying to see who the hand belonged to, but all he could make out was a silhouette.

"Sorry!" he whispered. "I wasn't expecting to find anyone alive here."

"That makes two of us. But it'll be *none* of us, if you don't get out of the open!"

The back of Arnold's head itched as he climbed carefully over the windowsill, which had sharp teeth of broken glass jutting out of it. This time he managed not to cut himself. Inside, a broken coffee table and an easy chair with soggy stuffing leaking out of it had been piled up along with some other rubbish into a makeshift barricade. He peered over it and saw someone crouching down on the other side.

Whoever it was said a bunch of bad words. "Listen, you moron, if you want to get your head blown off, you can go do it out in the street. I'm trying to stay alive back here!"

Arnold gulped and scooted around the pile of furniture, with his hands over his head as if that could stop whatever the High Ones were shooting at people.

"It has sentience! Amazing, we have found a rudimentary intelligence right here in Chincoteague!" the stranger whispered.

"There's no need to be nasty."

A pale face turned to face him. In the dim light all he could make out was the gleam of the stranger's eyes, a vague blob where the nose should be, and a hard, firm line of a mouth.

"Tell me, how did you manage to survive here so long?" *When you are such an idiot,* she didn't have to add. Because that was the only other thing Arnold could figure out about the stranger: she was a girl.

"I didn't. I just got here from… from somewhere else."

"Where?"

"You wouldn't believe me if I told you."

"Who's your clan leader? He shouldn't let you run around without a leash."

"What's a clan?"

The girl, who was squatting, rocked back on her heels. As she did, a rare, stray beam of sunlight lit up her face. Arnold gasped aloud. It was Hailee!

18

Hailee's blond hair was buzz-cut short as a Marine's, there was a long scar down the left side of her face, from just below the corner of her eye to the jawline, and she was dressed in fatigues and worn-out brown boots. But he had no trouble recognizing those blue eyes he'd written about so often. "Princess Hailee's winter-blue eyes smiled whenever Sir Arnold came to court... The princess's eyes cleared, like the light over the sea when the sun came out... Hailee's eyes were more beautiful, because purer, than the loveliest sapphire in the Dragon's Horde."

He said her name and she blinked those amazing eyes. "How do you know my name? I've never seen you before in my life!"

She never knows who I am back in school, either. Could it be the same girl? It could be her, after a couple of years filled with unimaginable suffering. He decided to test the idea. "Hailee, it's me, Arnold Grossbard. We sat next to each other in Miss Kelley's history class—well, not exactly next to each other, but near each other, well, you did sit most of the way across the classroom from me, but it *felt* near to me. You were going out with Bill Cherricks—"

Her face froze. "How do you know Bill? He was killed on that forage up in Delaware last year!" She seized his wrist and squeezed it so hard he cried out. "Let's peel this stupid fake skin off so the killer bot underneath can breathe!" With her other hand she flicked open a switchblade, a metal knife at least thirty centimeters long that gleamed wickedly in the dimness.

His guts locked up. *She's going to kill me!* He tried to say something, but as in a nightmare no sound would emerge from his throat.

But then she saw the long cut on his hand. It was still oozing blood, and her eyes narrowed at the sight. She folded the knife shut and reached into a hidden pocket of her shirt, from which she took a thin strip of paper that she rubbed against the wound and held up to the light.

"Hmm. Blood-litmus paper turns purple in the presence of hemoglobin... Congratulations, you are a genuine human fool." She let go of his wrist and he fell backward, gasping, as she reached into her pocket again and took out a cotton swab and a miniature spray bottle. "Give me your hand... come on now, don't be such a baby!"

After cleaning away the clotted blood, Hailee aimed the bottle at the cut. The mist that it made was cool and smelled faintly of crushed plants. The pain from the cut eased, but Arnold let out a startled yelp as it was replaced by a thousand tiny pinpricks. He wrenched free of Hailee and shook his hand to make it stop. The sensation faded and Arnold stared open-mouthed at the healthy, undamaged skin where the cut had just been.

"Don't gape like you've never seen heal-spray before! It was one of the first things we took from *them* on the day of the Uprising!" Hailee said.

"I've never seen it before. They never gave us anything like that, Hailee."

"Stop using my name! You don't know me!"

"Yes I do, I told you! We're in Miss Kelley's history class together at Chincoteague High School—"

"I never made it to high school, though I'm from here, all right!" She certainly was a *from-here*. Her last name of Pruitt was a giveaway that her family had lived in the area since the first English settlers arrived almost four hundred years ago.

Okay, so this isn't really the future. This is another one of those parallel worlds, like Gingo Teag. How can I get Hailee to understand that and believe me? "You may not have made it to high school in this world, but in my world—"

"In your *world?*"

Arnold did his best to explain. She didn't interrupt, but the hard line of her mouth never softened, either. "That is the craziest thing I ever heard," she said finally.

"But it's all true! Why don't you come back with me and I'll show you?"

"I ain't going nowhere with you, Arnold. My orders are to finish my patrol and report back at—" She glanced at her wrist and let loose with a torrent of bad words, words so bad they should have knocked down what remained of the house around them.

Arnold was impressed.

"You dumb ass!" she finished. "You made me miss my rendezvous."

"What does that mean?"

"What it means, doofus, is that I'll be stuck here all day. And there are Harvesters and Shredders reported in the area."

Arnold didn't know what Harvesters and Shredders were, but he suspected he would not enjoy finding out. He grabbed for Hailee's hand, but she backed away and pulled out her switchblade again.

"I'm trying to help you Hailee, really I am!" Arnold pleaded. "You can come back with me to my world and stay there until it's safe! Where I come from, the aliens still rule everything, and it sucks—I'm part of the Resistance fighting against them—"

"Ha, you?" She snickered and Arnold felt himself shrink to the size of an ant. "You couldn't fight your way out of a paper bag, puppy!"

"That's not true! I'm a member of both the Freedom Fighters of Earth and the Human Defense League!"

"The League? We got rid of those traitors and the so-called Patriotic Front first thing after the Uprising!"

"What?"

"Yeah! Didn't it seem a little suspicious to you that they—" She broke off and put her finger to her lips.

Arnold didn't hear anything at first. Then there was a distant thumping and crunching. A *whump* that sounded like a wall falling over. Arnold curled himself into a ball.

Hailee whispered in his ear, "Harvester. They go mainly for metal. We should be safe for the moment."

He lifted his head up just enough to look into her eyes. God, they were beautiful. Whatever he'd written about them so far didn't do them justice. He was going to have to learn the art of writing sonnets just to fix that. "Hailee. The gateway to my world is right across the street, in the corner of the bait-and-tackle shop," he whispered. "You've got to trust me. If we can just make it there, we'll be safe."

"You are crazy." She paused and he could see her pondering the impossibility of a babe-in-woods like him having survived for any length of time in the ruins. "We'll never last till nightfall here," she said after a long moment. "So I guess we should try to make it over there after all. At least the cover will be better."

Arnold's heart soared at those words. *Sir Arnold gets to save Princess Hailee after all!* He jumped to his feet to make a run for it, trusting Hailee to follow him.

Instead she grabbed him by the ankle and he fell, hitting his head on something hard. He lay there stunned while Hailee hissed in his ear that he was a nincompoop and a dunderhead and a dope and a dunce and that if he had any less brains, his skull would cave in from the vacuum.

"And I'm not going to have your death on my head! You wait till I tell you it's safe to go!"

"I'm sorry," he croaked.

"Never mind," she said, and applied her magic bottle of healing spray to the lump rapidly forming on his head. He sat up a few moments later, clutching his forehead—not because it hurt but out of surprise that it didn't.

"It's really true, isn't it?" Hailee asked, watching him carefully.

He nodded. "Yes, it is. In my world there was no Uprising. Or there hasn't been one *yet*. Maybe we need you to tell us what to do so that—" He broke off when he realized what he'd been about to say.

She said it for him, with a wry smile. "So that you don't end up with your Earth in ruins and the aliens hunting down the last human survivors? Maybe if I was a general I could help with you that. But I have no idea what went wrong. I was six years old when the Uprising happened. I only remember how exciting it was. How happy everyone was!

" We'd beaten them, kicked them right off the Earth, and killed all the traitors and collaborators too! My parents tried to keep me inside 'cause they didn't want me seeing the bodies of the people who'd been lynched, but I wanted to see so I climbed out a window. There was a whole row of them hanging from the trees all down Main Street. I was just a kid, I didn't find it scary or disgusting. If you didn't look at the faces it could've been just clothes hanging out there, like in a department store.

"At night they cut the bodies down and there were fireworks. The Eighth of December was gonna be the biggest holiday ever, bigger than the Fourth of July and Christmas all rolled up in one." She paused and brushed her cheek with the back of her hand. "The attack came before the fireworks ended. For a few seconds, everybody thought it was *part* of the fireworks, all those electrical transformers exploding on the light poles. But then they sent the Shredders in. It's only thanks to my dad that I survived."

"And your mom?" Hailee stared at Arnold until he turned away. "What are these clans you mentioned?" he asked after a long silence.

She blew out a puff of air and ran her hands through her hair, raising a fine dust that sifted Arnold's way and made him stifle a cough. "They're how we've organized ourselves, we survivors. Mine is the Wolf Clan. We mostly hide out in the marshes along the Wicomico River, a good eighty klicks from here, west of what used to be Salisbury. But Headman Gus says we ought to go exploring now and then, see if we can make contact with other clans. He only sends out those he can afford to sacrifice. Like me."

She spoke without bitterness; these were just the facts. So Arnold stifled the urge to touch her hand; again, he sensed she would only despise him for this show of pity. Besides, he had to know something.

"Gus… his last name isn't Benedict, is it? And is he also from Chincoteague?" Hailee's eyes widened, and he knew he'd hit the mark. "Is everyone in your clan our age, then?"

Hailee's mouth tightened. "Yes. The aliens started some kind of plague right after the Eighth of December. It killed everyone over eighteen. My Dad was tough, though; he lasted almost till spring. Some clans we've been in touch with have Headmen as young as twelve."

"And Wolf Clan… why do you call yourselves that? Is it after someone's name?"

"I don't think so. Headman Gus says we must have the courage of wolves, that we have to be fierce like wolves to hunt down and kill the aliens. Not that we've been too successful at that." She paused and laid her hand on his arm.

Her touch was cool and light, but it set off flames that raced down Arnold's arm and into his gut, and lower.

"Okay, it's been quiet for a while now," she said. "We might as well make a break for it. Stay low to the ground."

Arnold nodded. He tried to think of something to say to her… a quick word or two that would somehow include *The Adventures of Sir Arnold and Princess Hailee* and the sonnets he meant to write about her blue eyes and everything that was in his heart about her… how even back home, where she was a Popular Girl and he was a Reject, he had always known there was so much more to her and now he had learned how right he was. But all he could do was nod. She pushed against his arm, a go signal.

Arnold tensed and sprang like the jocks he'd seen at school starting a fifty-meter dash. At least, that was what he meant to do, but his legs had cramped up and he came down on the other side of the barricade at a stumble. Doing his best to ignore the pain shooting down his legs, he made for the window and jumped through it, accidentally kicking over a large, sharp triangle of broken glass.

The noise of its shattering made him freeze, but Hailee was right behind him, kicking him in the butt, screaming "Go, go, go!"

So he crouched and scuttled into the street, not even trying to avoid the scattered bones this time, just running as fast as he could, straight toward the ruins he had first found himself in, when he heard a metallic grinding chattering like hundreds of giant scissors madly slicing all at once, and Hailee screamed "SHREDDER!" and threw herself on him, so he fell flat on his stomach on the broken asphalt, and the noise was all around him, and something whizzed past his left ear, and he instinctively put his left hand up to shield his face but couldn't reach it because Hailee was pushing against him even harder, and the noise began to diminish until finally there was silence once again.

"Hailee?" Arnold said in a hoarse whisper. "Hailee, are you all right?"

When there was no answer he tried to slide out from under her and sit up. She was surprisingly heavy for someone who looked so skinny, and it took all his strength to work himself free. Then he turned his head to check on her and nearly threw up. She lay on her stomach, unmoving, with her head turned away from him and two huge red gashes seeping blood from her back through her shredded shirt.

Ohmigod she's dead, she's dead, what'll I do, what if that thing comes back what'll I do, what'll I do if she ISN'T dead, how am I supposed to save her I don't even know first aid?

The bottle! The magic healing bottle! If I can find it, maybe that would help her! Didn't she put it in the front pocket of her shirt?

He edged up to her and gingerly rolled her back onto her stomach. She moaned, and a bloody spit bubble formed at the side of her mouth.

"I'm sorry," he whispered, "Sorry! Sorry I'm such a, a, baby and an idiot!" His eyes were filling with angry tears as he fumbled through her shirt pocket, spilling out what looked like dried food and a picture of a man who had to be her father and at last the tiny spray bottle.

"All right," he said, "all right, all right!" and rolled her onto her back, or tried to—it took three tries, his hands were so slippery with sweat and blood, and he was half-blinded by tears. But he did it.

He held the bottle over one of her gaping wounds—was something *pulsing* in there?—then remembered she had cleaned his cut before spraying it. Better get her ruined shirt off her, then, but how could he do that? By grabbing at the torn edges and pulling gently until the cloth came away, that was all he could think of. The material was soaked with her blood, and he swallowed bile as he strained, trying to ignore the crazy corner of his mind cackling that he was undressing a girl, that he was undressing *Hailee Pruitt!*

When he'd pulled all the cloth away he tried to dab at the edges of her wounds with the few patches of her shirt that had remained dry, but it was no use, and swallowing hard he held the bottle up and sprayed and sprayed over the bloody mess, sprayed until there was nothing left and nothing he could do but fling it away and stare, wondering if he'd done any good at all.

It took a lot longer than it should have until it occurred to him to take off his flannel shirt and use it to wipe away the blood, so he could see if the wounds had closed up. Unbelievably, they had, though they were leaving enormous pink scars that crisscrossed at the lower right part of her back.

Still he sat there and watched, afraid to touch her and afraid it was all for nothing and she was dead anyway. But after an eternity she sighed as if waking from a deep sleep, pushed herself up off the street and stared down in disbelief as the front of her shirt fell away.

Arnold turned away and took off his undershirt, holding it out to her. "Here, put this on."

"But you don't have anything—"

"It's all right, we'll be back in my school in a minute." Continuing to dangle the undershirt, he heard Hailee gasp with pain as she reached out to take it, then gasp some more as she had to stretch to put it on. "Are you really all right?" he asked.

"Don't worry about me, just go, go, go! Another Shredder could be along any second!"

He risked a glance back and saw her eyes were bulging out and her jaw muscles were clenched, as if she could bite down on the pain and crush it. *She's suffering because of me, and there's nothing I can do about it. Except get her to safety.*

He turned around and raced toward the rubbish heap in the ruined shop, praying that the Gray Zone tunnel was still on the other side of it. He could hear her footsteps behind him as he clambered over, managing not to cut his hand on anything this time. As he came down the far side he thought he glimpsed something gray and furry slipping out of sight. "Did you see that?" he asked Hailee.

"See what?"

"Never mind. There's the tunnel," he said, relief hitting him so hard his knees buckled. "Just a few more steps and we'll be safe!"

She didn't move, didn't take his outstretched hand. "You'll be safe. I'm staying here, Arnold."

"Wha—?" His stomach lurched and her silhouette wavered in the dimness as his eyes teared up. "B-but you have to come with me! You'll be killed if you stay here."

"No, I'll be all right hiding here till my ride arrives. Shredders can't climb over so much stuff."

"But you're my prin—I mean, you have to come back with me, to warn people in my world what'll happen if they don't start to fight."

He thought he could see the corners of her mouth turn up. "That's your job, Arnold. My job is to rejoin my clan."

"But you can't, I mean, I can't, I mean, if you stay here then *I'm* going to stay here—"

"No you're not, Arnold. Now get going before I kick your ass."

It was humiliating. She didn't even want him to stay. His ears burning, he turned and slinked away into the Gray Zone. Nothing there could be half as awful as what he'd just seen, and what he'd just found out about himself. Sir Arnold was a fraud—Princess Hailee had had to save *him*, and even though he saved her right back, it couldn't make up for the fact that he was not her hero, that he was no hero at all and never would be.

When the wolf padded up to him, its teeth and eyes gleaming in the darkness, Arnold flinched, then sighed, "Go ahead and eat me, wolf. I'm better off as puppy chow."

It leaped, knocking him over, and everything turned inside out. Arnold blinked and saw he was back in Mr. Wolff's supply closet—Mr. *Wolff's* supply closet—*God,* was he slow!

The English teacher was looking at him, smiling slightly. "Well? Did I answer your question, Mr. Grossbard?"

"Yeah," he nodded slowly. "I know what I have to do, now."

"Good. Now, it's right in the middle of third period, there's no one using the gym at the moment. Go shower and find a shirt somewhere."

When Arnold came out of the locker room, wearing a stolen varsity T-shirt someone had unwisely left in an unlocked locker, the lunchtime wave of students had already seethed its way into the cafeteria, and the hallways were deserted and echoing. James's school locker was in the same row as his own, and he stood beside it, waiting patiently until Matt and Jared came around the corner, looking over their shoulders as they scuttled along.

Arnold couldn't help but laugh silently; what was the worst that could happen to them? Being caught by Mr. Wright and getting a detention? They looked like such scaredy little kids, trying to pretend they were tough. Maybe that was all they had ever been.

But Jared's face was fixed in a sneer when he walked up, with Matt right behind him. "So, you think you got the guts to do it, you little wuss?"

"Shut up, Jared," said Arnold calmly, and punched him squarely in the nose.

He never saw it coming, and both of his hands flew up to cover the trickle of bright red blood. "Ow! He punched me in da node! In DA NODE! Matt, get him!"

Matt eyed him. "Seems to me you had it coming." He held up two cans of spray paint, one black, one blue. "Ready, Arnold?"

"You bet. But I'm not painting that stupid swastika of yours." He grabbed the black paint from an astonished Matt, turned to James's locker and without hesitating made the can hiss out two words that covered almost the whole gray panel: TRAITOR BEWARE.

19

Dad didn't get what Alison was so worried about. "So Arnold's got some new friends. That's great! You always said he needed to make friends."

"Yeah, but not this kind of friend. These are the same guys who were bullying him last year, Dad."

"Even better! That shows he's really improving his social skills. I don't see what could be bad about that."

Alison paused in emptying the dishwasher and wondered whether she should tell Dad her suspicions that Arnold was now doing unto others as they'd done unto him—not an application of the Golden Rule she thought Dad or Mom would approve of. But then again, she didn't like tattling and she didn't have any real proof, just rumors she had heard.

"Nothing, I guess. I just don't like them. Especially the ringleader, Matt Walters. He thinks he's some kind of big shot, but he's just like Don Peabody and those other jerks who got me in big trouble during the school assembly."

"Allie, honey, not everyone is as mature as you. Let Arnold do his own thing. He seems happier than he's ever been since we came here."

That was certainly true. He'd been positively strutting around these late winter weeks, spending a lot less time whispering to that weirdly mobile plant Gloria had given him, and for that matter, spending a lot less time with Gloria and Jo.

Alison didn't see her brother and Jo together nearly as often as she used to, either around town or when she went to Gingo Teag with Shaniqua, which happened practically every day—her friend was fascinated by her "twin" and the feeling was mutual. The two of them were sitting in the new Taylor Family Teahouse in Gingo Teag one February day comparing notes on some obscure bit of Thomas family lore when Jo ran in and interrupted them. To tell the truth, Alison was relieved.

"—so you say your Uncle Devin, not Dennis, opened a barbershop instead of a carriage-battery dealership? That is wizard!" Sharon was saying.

"Yeah, and they're both married to a woman named Nicole, though mine is Aunt Nikki and yours goes by 'Fluff'—oh, hi Jo," Shaniqua said.

Allie turned and saw Jo struggling to catch her breath. "Here, have some tea. It's almost as good as your mother's."

"N-no thank you," Jo gasped. "Have any of you seen Arnold?"

"No, why? What's the matter?" Alison said.

"If you see him, tell him it's urgent FFE business," Jo blurted, then turned and ran out.

"Excuse me," Alison said to Shaniqua and Sharon, and ran after her. The gaslights had just been turned on, and in their now-familiar blue glow Alison easily spotted Jo darting around a corner, heading for Gateway Books. She ran after her, grabbing the shop door just as it was about to swing shut.

"I say, young lady, it's about time!" said a man wearing an oily gray raincoat and a bowler hat—a familiar combination around Gingo Teag, where many more people still relied on the sea to make their living than back home. In contrast, Alison's Chincoteague had turned into a bedroom suburb of the interplanetary base and the fusion plant, with a sideline in nature tourism.

"I wish to register a complaint!" the man said.

"I don't work here," Alison said, but the man's bushy gray mustache was quivering with outrage and he wasn't listening.

"Never mind that, my girl! I came back round this bookshop to complain and there weren't nobody here but a mangy orange cat!"

"Tiferet owns—I mean, Tiferet isn't mangy."

"Aha, so you DO work here! Well, I wish to register a complaint about this book that I bought here this afternoon!"

Alison eyed the thick, hardbacked volume the fisherman shoved at her. The title, in an old-fashioned font, was *Light Houses of the Atlantic Coast.*

"So what's wrong with it?" Alison couldn't believe she was asking, but it seemed like the fastest way to get rid of the man.

"What's WRONG with it?" The man's face turned brick red and he began dramatically waving his arms around. Alison was afraid he would have a stroke right in front of her. "Better ask, is there *anything* true in it?"

"I dunno, is there? Say, you didn't happen to notice a girl about thirteen years old run in here a minute ago, did you?"

"Yes, an annoying little brat did come barging through and nearly knocked me down! Then she grabbed that ridiculous orange feline and disappeared behind the counter with it, and good riddance I say to both of them! Now, are you going to give me satisfaction for this miserable excuse for a book?"

"But what's wrong with it? It's supposed to be a book on lighthouses, isn't it? What do you call that?" she said, opening the book at random and pointing to a picture.

"Look, my girl, when I spend my hard-earned shilling on a new lighthouse directory, I expect it to be just as reliable as *Olsen's Standard Book of British Lighthouses*, not some scientification fantasy!"

Scientification. He must mean science fiction. Alison began to suspect what was wrong. Taking a closer look at the picture, she saw at once why the man was annoyed. Instead of a tall stone structure with a bright light atop meant to warn passing ships away from dangerous shoals, the page held a three-dimensional image even crisper than a tri-vee stage could generate of a metal-banded sphere of blazing light hovering high above a wild, rocky shore, with focused laser-like beams of ruby red light extending to the horizon in three directions. There was a caption in oddly formed, barely legible letters:

```
Ye Plimouth Harbor Light House doth provide
galvanic energie for ye cittie of Greate Wam-
panoag, ye town of Plimouth Plantation, and ye
hamlet of Boston, by ye Grace of God.
```

Alison sighed. Another of Gloria's books from another of her strange, parallel worlds. She didn't have the time or the desire to try to explain that to this man, so she reached for her pocket, wondering if she had enough "British" change to make him go away.

"Is there a problem?" a woman's voice asked.

Alison turned and saw with relief that Gloria was standing behind the counter, panting slightly, her orange hair a mess. The fisherman explained sarcastically that were he to try to navigate to the Chesapeake Bay using this book as a guide, he was apt to end up on the Sea of Tranquility on the Moon, and Gloria readily agreed. "I'm so sorry, sir. Perhaps thou, I mean you, would prefer this volume on mermaids?"

"Mermaids? What good are mermaids—oh. OH. Yes, I think this will do quite nicely," he said, taking a large, coffee table-style album from Gloria and walking out the door with it.

"Pleasure doing business with you, Mr. Monteith!" Gloria called after him.

Alison had caught a glimpse of what had captivated the man and stood with her arms folded, staring narrowly at the cat-woman. "Really, Gloria, I didn't think you were THAT kind of bookseller!"

"You mean the kind who purveys psychically interactive books?"

"What?"

"The pictures the reader sees in that book depend on what is in his mind. Why, what did you see?"

"Never mind," Alison said firmly, determined not to get further sidetracked. "Did you just take Jo over to my Chincoteague?"

Gloria's pixieish smile faded. "Yes, I did. She's looking everywhere for Arnold, and something seems to be worrying her about him. I was hoping he was with you."

"I haven't seen him since this morning, and I'm worried about him too. I don't like those guys he's hanging out with. I'm sure they're up to no good. And now Jo mentioned something about an ef-ef-ee before she ran away. That sounds like code for something, but what?"

"I don't know either," Gloria confessed, "and I don't like it. I thought Jo and Arnold would be best friends by now. But he seems to be avoiding her. Why are you shaking your head?"

"Because if you can jump to any universe you like, and even travel in time—Teresa told me about that, Gloria, don't look so surprised—then how come you can't figure out what's going on with my little brother?"

Gloria took a step toward Alison and held her hands.

It's not just that they're so hot and her pulse is so fast, Alison thought, willing herself not to pull away; *her hands feel as light and fragile as baby birds, too.*

"My dear," Gloria said quietly, "the mysteries of time and multi-space are as nothing to the tangles of the human heart."

There was a long silence. Finally Alison withdrew her hands. "Speaking of 'multi-space,'" she said, "when is Mom coming back?"

"A couple more weeks," Gloria replied. "Even where I took her, they can't work miracles overnight. I hope she took it to heart when I explained to her that the Eisenstein method may not be a cure, but at least it will stop her NINA from getting worse."

"Explain to me again why even in Teresa's world, they can't fix brain damage like that?"

Gloria sighed and pulled up a chair. Suddenly she looked older than Dad, or even Grandma. "Because in both your worlds, Dr. Mordecai Eisenstein was a medical student who starved to death in the Warsaw Ghetto. In the world I took Rachel to, nobody ever heard of the Nazis."

Even though she'd just had tea, Alison stayed for a cup with Gloria, not because she wanted any but because she sensed the librarian was sad and lonely, whatever that might mean for an eleven-dimensional being. Alison tried to pump her for more secrets about the High Ones, but Gloria didn't want to talk about them.

"I didn't come here to work as a librarian for their sake, but for yours—yours and Arnold's, and Shaniqua's, and anyone else who needs books that haven't been approved by SCOD," she said.

"But aren't the High Ones responsible for SCOD?" Alison asked.

"Not unless Pierre LaWayne has lots of tentacles nobody knows about. You humans are capable of causing yourselves quite enough trouble without any outside help."

"I always learned in school that the High Ones' arrival saved us from ourselves," Alison said. "Now I know they were coming to exploit us—but they may still have saved us from a nuclear war, or environmental disaster. But Arnold and Mom seem convinced they're totally evil, and I felt that way too when you told us what the n-network is really for… but now I'm not so sure about that, either. I mean, what if they hadn't come and we'd killed each other off and trashed the planet?" She paused.

"Maybe you're right, and the thing to do is just tell everybody the truth about the n-network so we can get a better deal from the High Ones and people's brains will stop being damaged. But then I think, maybe *you* don't have all the answers either, Gloria! We could ask them nicely, and they could make us into slaves! But all this confusion must mean I don't know enough or maybe I'm not smart enough to figure things out for myself, right?"

Gloria put her tea down and took Alison's hands in both of hers again. For a confusing moment, looking into those green eyes, Alison thought she could glimpse a being older, grander, and more glorious than anyone on Earth had ever seen, and yet so sad from all the things she had seen.

"No, darling girl. It means you're discovering the answers aren't always so simple. Sometimes a problem is so hard, there *is* no right answer. Sometimes all the bravery and all the love in the world can't put everything right. But that doesn't mean we're excused from working to make things better. A very wise man named Rabbi Tarfon once said, 'It's not for you to complete all the work, but neither are you free not to try.'"

The silent seconds ticked by while Alison tried to figure out what she meant by that, and how an eleven-dimensional being could go around quoting Jewish sages.

Then Gloria said, "I think you should probably go through the Gray Zone before it gets any later. Jo would rather die than say so, but she gets nervous wandering around your world all by herself."

Gloria must be disappointed in me, Alison thought. *That's why she wouldn't answer my question.* But her embrace was as gentle yet firm as always, and Alison tried not to notice the world turning itself inside out all around her.

It didn't help to close her eyes, she had found, because closed eyelids weren't a barrier to seeing the distorted view from the higher dimensions any more than closed book covers prevented you from glimpsing their contents when you were caught in that vortex. Then everything settled down and Alison knelt down to rub Tiferet's tummy as the cat rolled on the floor.

"I should have asked you on the other side, what is this Gray Zone, anyway?" Alison murmured. Tiferet meowed, rolled over onto her paws and shook herself. "What kind of an answer is that?" Alison demanded. Tiferet followed at her heels as she walked down the dim, foreboding underground corridor. *All right, I'm safe then*, Alison thought, and a few moments later she found herself in the deserted school library with dusk falling outside. Tiferet mewed goodbye as Alison squeezed out the fire exit and scuttled away down the cold, wintry street.

She was only a block from home when she nearly ran into Mr. Freed. His clothes were torn up and he had the beginnings of a black eye. Alison's fear for herself quickly turned to concern for him. "What happened to you, Mr. Freed?"

"Your brother hit me," he answered. Alison recoiled, as much from surprise that he had given a straightforward answer to a direct question as in reaction to the unbelievable answer.

"Arnold hit you? Are you sure it was him?"

"Yeah. He was with two of his buddies, and they held my arms while he punched me right in the face."

Alison was too shocked to say anything.

"I didn't believe it either. He always seemed like such a mousy kid before, begging your pardon, Allie."

Alison opened her mouth. "I," she said. "I, uh—"

Mr. Freed smiled sadly, and she could see he was missing one of his front teeth. With a dizzy, sick feeling she wondered if her little brother was to blame for that, too.

"Don't you worry. I'm not gonna tell the pigs. They'd just as soon send me to a SCOD hole and give your brother a commendation for beating up the old psycho hippie. Oh, don't give me that look. I know what people say about me. But usually they're happy just to laugh at me. It doesn't usually make them mad when I say there's no such thing as High Ones. A little nervous, maybe, since The Man wants you to believe there are, but not angry."

"I, I'm sorry, Mr. Freed. I really don't know what to say. Arnold hasn't been himself lately."

Mr. Freed leaned uncomfortably close. She could smell something sour on his breath. "Then who has he been, Allie?"

It was a good question. Too good. Alison backed away, then turned and ran, going all the way around the block and entering her house from the back so she wouldn't have to think about it.

She could hear the tri-vee going in the living room. A news broadcast, something about a roundup of suspected terrorists at ten different colleges. It had to be Arnold in there, he'd become obsessive about watching the news lately.

She stormed in, shouting, "How could you do such a thing!" but stopped cold when she saw Jo staring back at her.

"Do what?" Jo said.

"Never mind. I was worried about you, and so was Gloria."

"You were? Why?"

Alison took a breath. "Well it's just, um, look, it's getting late for you, isn't it? And how did you get in, anyway? I don't see Arnold anywhere."

"You dad let me in. He said he had to pick up a few things at Value-Mart and he'd be right back."

"But what are you doing here?"

"Looking for Arnold. So you haven't seen him either? Your Dad said I could wait here till he got back, and he showed me how to turn on the tri-vee stage. I think it's wizard! But I don't understand the news at all. How can a bunch of college students be terrorists?"

Alison shrugged. "Probably just 'cause they think for themselves, that's what Dad would say." *And Mr. Freed, too.*

"Well, it sounds to me just like what Tom and Teresa told me the Imperial gendarmes did at Oxford University—the old, original Oxford back in England, when the revolution broke out there." Her eyes gleamed. "So that's great! History is repeating itself. Beating up on people isn't going to work any better for the Slugs than it did for the Frogs."

"I wish you wouldn't call them that," Alison said, sitting down with a sigh and propping her chin in her hands.

"Oh, don't tell me you don't approve of calling the French Imperials Frogs. It's a good name for them. You are what you eat, right?"

"Jo, that's, like, really immature. But I meant the High Ones. You can get disappeared for saying things like that."

"What on earth does that mean? It's not even good grammar."

It was so complicated trying to explain the real world to Jo, it was giving Alison a headache. She asked her to turn off the tri-vee, which was showing a frightened-looking girl not much older than her saying her boyfriend had tricked her into being a terrorist by making her read some book called *Brave New World*.

"That's better. Now, I have some questions for you, Jo. What is the FFE?"

"I—I can't tell you. Unless you take the blood oath."

"Unless I do WHAT?"

"You have to swear allegiance to the Freedom Fighters of Earth. I'll just prick your pinky finger—it won't hurt hardly at all—and—"

"Freedom Fighters? What the hell are you playing at, Jo?" She grabbed the younger girl's hands and squeezed them hard.

"Ow! I'll tell you all about if you let me prick your finger, really I will!"

"And I'll cut your throat if you don't tell me what kind of trouble you've gotten my little brother into, really I will!" Alison grabbed Jo by the shoulders, hauled her to her feet and began to shake her.

Jo was almost as tall as her and probably stronger, in her tomboyish way, but she didn't fight back at all. Instead she began to cry big sloppy tears that rolled silently down her cheeks.

"Oh, jeez! Don't cry, you silly little kid!" Alison said, letting go of her. Part of her wanted to give Jo a hug, the other part still wanted to throttle her for what she knew was coming. "You two babies decided you were going to fight the High Ones all on your own, didn't you? Well, didn't you?"

Jo confessed. It took quite a while for it all to come out, from the day she had founded the secret club to the first "intelligence gathering mission" at Wallops Island to the weird way Arnold had been acting for the past few weeks, being all rude and nasty and saying he was the one who had to live under alien domination so Jo had better just shut up and do what he told her, now that he was a real resistance fighter, to today when Jo came home to find Palermo Teresa visiting and immediately ran off all excited to find Arnold so she could tell him there was a real, experienced heroine of the resistance to the French Empire in town who had just *loads* of wizard ideas for making trouble, only now she couldn't find him anywhere.

"Well, he's here somewhere," Alison said grimly, "I mean here in *this* Chincoteague, I know because on the way back here I ran into a harmless crazy guy who likes to say there's no such thing as High Ones, and Arnold had two of these toughs he now hangs out with hold him still while he punched him in the face."

"What? How does that help fight the Slugs?"

"Stop calling them that! You're part of the problem! It's your fault he's turning into a fanatic, into a t-t-t-" She couldn't say the word *terrorist*, it was too frightening.

"That's why he has to meet Palermo Teresa! She's really *wizard*, remember that she's just another version of Teresa, only she was born in Sicily instead of Philadelphia so she wears pantyhose and smokes garlic cigarettes and she started fighting the Bone-a-farts in Italy when she was the same age as me, and then she escaped to England and was studying at Oxford and she made so much trouble she helped start the whole revolution there, *and* she saved the other Teresa from the jail the Frogs had thrown her into! And she did it all without hurting anyone except the Frogs and their hirelings."

Alison hadn't ever heard anyone say the word *hireling* or seen it anywhere but in really old books before. But she got the point. However— "Garlic cigarettes?"

"That's the one bad thing about her," Jo said, wrinkling her nose. "They really stink something awful."

Alison sat thinking. "I don't know if it's such a good idea for him to meet a professional troublemaker," she said, "when the whole idea is to get him to stop making trouble."

Jo stuck out her chin. "That may be your whole idea, but it's not mine, and I doubt he'll go along with it. Are things really so great here for you that you think everybody ought to just go along with whatever the Slugs and their lackeys say, just to avoid trouble?"

Alison didn't want to admit she didn't really know what a *lackey* was. But it was clear enough what Jo meant, and she wasn't happy about it. In fact she had to restrain herself from grabbing the younger girl and shaking her again.

"Look, Jo, for you maybe this is all a fun, exciting game. A bit of adventure just down the block! But you can always go home. We have to *live* here. And I don't like the kind of person Arnold's turning into."

"I don't either," Jo admitted, "but that's why I want him to meet Palermo Teresa—so she can show him how to fight the bad guys without hurting innocent people."

Alison bit her lip. "All right. Let's wait till he gets back and you can tell him about her," she said finally. *After all, some Italian girl can hardly make things worse.*

20

"So, bambino, I understand you want to be a revolutionary."

"Umm, I guess?" said Arnold, trying not to choke on the thick cloud of smoke wafting his way.

It was later that evening, and he was sitting uncomfortably close to Palermo Teresa while Jo sat facing them in the easy chair and Alison had brought in a kitchen chair to monitor the proceedings. Dad still wasn't back from Mr. Nomura's. Alison had tentatively asked their new guest not to smoke in the house but had given up on being met with a hard stare.

Palermo Teresa raised a carefully tweezed eyebrow. "You guess you want to be a revolutionary? This is serious business, bambino. You'd better do more than just guess."

"I'm sure. I definitely want to get rid of the High—OW!" he said as a sharp elbow rammed into his gut.

"First rule. Careful what you say. The *carabinieri*, they are always listening."

Having a good excuse for coughing, Arnold indulged freely, while trying to nod his understanding. He guessed correctly that *carabinieri* meant cops.

"Excellent. Now, bambino, tell me what revolutionary activities you have engaged in so far."

Arnold was finding it hard to concentrate. The smoke was already so thick it was making his head swim, and the shortness of Palermo Teresa's skirt, with her white pantyhose-clad knees just a few centimeters from where he was sitting, was extremely distracting. Plus there was that word she kept using.

"Could you please not call me bambino? My name is Arnold."

She smiled broadly. How could she keep her teeth so white, with all that smoking? "*Si, compagno*. But you are in fact a bambino. I do have rather more experience than you in these matters."

"Of course," said Arnold, swallowing another cough. He saw Alison exchange a glance with Jo and reddened.

It was humiliating having all these older girls stifling laughter at him—even Jo had three months on him, not to mention parallel-world

Hailee who seemed like she was twice his age. So he puffed out his chest and told all three of them everything he had done since Jo pricked his little finger, even exaggerating a little so they would respect him more. Spying on the Wallops Island Interplanetary Base. Talking James into dropping out of the scholarship program (he assumed, anyway—James hadn't been to school in weeks, and when he walked past Park Place Cleaners lately it was always shuttered and dark). Standing up to the pro-Slug propaganda his history teacher Miss Kelley was handing out (mostly in his head, though he did mumble something that got him two days' detention). Confronting some idiot who had the nerve to say the Slugs didn't even exist!

"Mr. Freed is a harmless crazy guy who nobody believes, so why did you have to hit him?" Alison interrupted.

Because he smells, he's scary, and nobody minds if I pick on him. "He might fool somebody who doesn't know better," Arnold said, hearing how lame this sounded even as he spoke the words.

There was a silence. "And that is all, bambino?" Palermo Teresa said.

No, that isn't all. I saw what the Slugs are bound to do if we don't stop them. But he didn't think he should tell everyone about that. A secret wasn't a secret if you went and told everyone, was it? He didn't want to have to share with the others the fact that Mr. Wolff had the same powers as Gloria, or they'd all be trooping over to Parallel Hailee's world too, and the next thing you knew the tourists would ruin the place. Besides, there was the humiliating fact that Sir Arnold had had to be rescued by Princess Hailee, and he didn't want *her* telling *them* that. So he nodded.

"Very well," Palermo Teresa said, leaning back and exhaling a smoke ring which everyone admired in silence for a moment. "So, the secrecy of your little *Liga* is admirable, as is your zeal. But secrecy must be balanced with publicity, eh, or how will anyone know what you stand for? As our French *compagni* say, we must to make *attentats*!"

Arnold nodded as if he understood what she was talking about, but Jo scowled and said, "What do you have Froggie mates for, Teresa?"

The rebel chuckled and pinched her cheek. *She must be the only person in* either *world who can get away with that!*

"You are so much like your brother, Jo," Palermo Teresa said, "who is a fine fellow, but a bit of a jingo! Is not the struggle for liberty the struggle of all mankind? I can name for you many, many honorable Frenchmen and women who have been made to suffer by the despicable Bone-a-fart family, and don't you ever forget it!"

"Yes, Teresa," Jo said meekly.

"*Buono.* What I was saying? Yes, it is time to put the local *carabinieri*, and their slimy overlords, in fear of the rebels. You must to print up lots of *volantini*—leaflets—and slip them under the door of every house in Gingo Teag!"

"We pronounce it 'Chincoteague,'" Alison said.

Palermo Teresa waved her off. "I can help you with the wording, bambino."

"I asked you not to call me that!"

He was ignored again. This was getting really annoying. "Go get one of your miniature babbages so you can take dictation," Palermo Teresa ordered.

"Miniature what?" Arnold and Alison said at the same time.

Jo stepped in. "She means computers. We call them babbages in our world, but Teresa, they don't have the little household ones in this world. You're thinking of the *other* Teresa's world."

The rebel scowled. "It is too confusing, all these different worlds. When I made my own *volantini* back in Sicily, I did it on my own hand press, which I built myself. I don't suppose you have one of those."

"No, and the only ditto machine in town is kept locked up in Mr. Wright's office," Alison said. "He's the high school principal, and the head of SCOD in town, *and* a major jerkwad. I always hear the teachers complaining about how even they have to get special permission just to print up class handouts. But we do have a typewriter, and lots of carbon paper."

Teresa raised an eyebrow at Jo, who said, "I think she means a scri-printer. I have no idea what carbon paper might be."

Alison got up, went to her room and came back with both items, as well as a pack of typing paper.

Teresa was delighted with the carbon paper, especially when she worked out that you could make three legible copies of anything you typed by layering two sheets of it between the typing paper.

"This will do for practice. But you must to break into this Mr. Wright's office and steal this ditto machine, so you can make enough copies for the whole town!"

"But what should we say in the pamphlet, if we do get hold of the ditto machine?" Arnold asked, trying to swallow his unease at the thought of becoming a burglar.

Teresa's dazzling smile cut through the clouds of smoke she had filled the room with. "I thought you never ask, bambino." She began pecking away furiously at the typewriter, using only the index fingers of each hand.

He'd never seen anyone do that before, and he and Alison watched, fascinated. Out of the corner of his eye he could see Jo grinning, as if she knew exactly what was coming next.

"Here!" she said, her grin showing all her teeth as she pulled out the finished copies and handed one each to Arnold, Alison, and Jo. Arnold had worried that her writing would be ungrammatical, like the way she talked, but that wasn't the problem at all.

```
Free Men and Women of Earth!
    Do not use the Slugs' neural network! It de-
stroys the brain, the precious seat of love and
art, of courage and honour, and leaves us help-
less slaves before their fiendish plots!
    When you cease to do the bidding of the slimy
oppressors of humanity, you strike a blow for
freedom. Do not fear their weapons! Against a
people united in courage and determination, they
have no hope. Their terrible reign of tyranny is
coming to an end!
    The Day of Revolution is dawning, a day of
struggle and glory! You bring it closer with
each and every heroic deed, be it great or
small! Join us, brothers and sisters, for we
are everywhere, our cause is just, and we shall
triumph!
    Human  Defense  League—Freedom  Fighters  of
Earth
```

"Wizard!" exclaimed Jo, jumping to her feet and grabbing Teresa in a bear hug. "Tom Paine himself never wrote better!"

"I don't know, Teresa," Alison said, frowning. "Some of these words are pretty fancy. I think we'd better make sure everyone can understand it."

"Pah! Does that not prove the point?" Teresa said. "They are making you stupid, these stellar starfish."

"I think she might have a point, Allie," said Arnold. "What else could explain reality tri-vee?"

"But I've never been on the n-net, and I happen to like 'The Real Goofily Giggling, Gossiping Gals of Ganymede!'" said Alison.

At that moment they heard a key scraping in the front door lock. Arnold jumped up, grabbed the typed pages from Jo and Alison and shoved them under the couch in the nick of time, just as Dad opened the door.

"Arnold, did you try to cook again?" he asked, coughing as he stepped in. He stopped when he saw Teresa and looked confused.

Jo made the introduction, without of course explaining that this version of Teresa was a professional troublemaker.

Dad looked wary anyway when he shook her hand. "Nice to meet you, Miss D'Angelo, but I wish you wouldn't smoke in my house."

"It is not *tabacco* I smoke. It is garlic leafs. Good for the digestion," said Teresa.

Dad blinked at her, then asked, "What is the typewriter doing down here?"

"I try your son to teach a little Siciliano," she said smoothly. Well, almost smoothly.

"Yeah? Good luck with that. He's getting a C in Spanish."

"Thanks a lot, Dad," Arnold said, his ears burning as Teresa laughed. It was a rich, deep, smoker's laugh.

Dad looked at his watch. "I hate to break up this party, but it's getting late. Jo, I'm sure your mother will be worried about you. Would anyone like something to drink before you go? Milk, orange juice, soda?"

"No vino, I suppose," Teresa said.

Dad shook his head with a little smile.

"You English are such puritans," Teresa sighed, earning a puzzled glance from Dad. "So then, Arnoldo, you will remember the vocabulary words I taught to you this time, si?"

"Vocabulary words? Oh, si!" He watched Teresa type out three words on a fresh sheet of paper, and he smiled.

Coraggio. Obviously courage.

La resistanza. Even more obvious.

Omertà. Not as easy, but Arnold knew this one too: "The Godfather" had made it to the big screen in the High Ones' America, although with a bit more trouble and a lot more censorship than in the other Teresa's America. *Omertà* meant the mafioso's code of silence. Or the resistance fighter's.

21

Alison studied her copy of Palermo Teresa's vocabulary lesson long after she and Jo had gone back to Gingo Teag and Dad and Arnold had gone to sleep. She wasn't at all happy about the idea of Arnold turning into a little rabble-rouser, with all the trouble that would inevitably cause. *But it's better than watching him turn into a bully. Or a terrorist.*

In fact, for the next couple of weeks things quieted down considerably as Arnold spent all his free time plotting the break-in at Mr. Wright's office. It was going to be tricky, considering that the principal kept it locked up tighter than Fort Knox. Still, Alison was happy not to blow the whistle as long as it kept him out of other trouble. Jo accompanied him on "scouting expeditions" near the high school, and the two of them became a familiar sight around town. She told everyone she was his cousin from South Philadelphia, and Alison had to admit the younger girl had the accent down cold.

Alison was not so happy to become the third member of the FFE, but it seemed the best way of keeping tabs on her little brother and his girlfriend. So she went through the whole silly finger-pricking business and promised to help out with *Operation Volantini*, hoping she would get a chance to tone down Palermo Teresa's hair-raising polemic.

"What's that weirdo little brother of yours up to, anyway?" Shaniqua asked her at lunch one day. Spring was in the air and they were eating outside.

It should have been a relief that Shaniqua wasn't complaining for once about how hard it was to finish her homework without using the n-network—but not if she was going to insult Arnold.

"Shut up, he's not a weirdo," Alison said, throwing a pebble at a seagull the size of a small chicken that was eyeing her tuna fish sandwich, but it only hopped a few feet away and kept glaring at her with its beady black eyes.

"I talked to my twin Sharon and she says that girlfriend of his is a hell-raiser. Wicked smart, though."

"Tell me something I don't know. But they both claim they're not boyfriend and girlfriend."

Shaniqua rolled her eyes. "What, they haven't kissed or nothing? It's only a matter of time."

"They're too busy with their secret club."

"Doing what?"

"I don't know, it's their secret." Alison felt ashamed of lying to Shaniqua, but it was for her own good, in case they all got in trouble later. Still, she thought she'd better change the subject. "You really feel like Sharon's your twin? What's that like?"

"Pretty cool, actually. We like a lot of the same kind of stuff, which is sort of strange considering how different things are in Gingo Teag from here. I mean, they don't even have telephones."

"I know. It makes things a lot quieter over there, don't you think?"

"Yeah. It's nice at first, but I think it would get dull after a while. Those voicegram things they have aren't quite the same as talking to someone on the phone. I mean, they have to be recorded and played back."

"Well, I think they're actually better than the tape recorders we have."

"You mean that you have. My family hasn't got one."

"We only have one since my dad used to be a reporter." Alison got defensive every time it came up how much poorer the Thomases were than her family, even when Shaniqua didn't mean to put her on the spot.

"He used that big bulky thing when he was out reporting a story?"

"Yeah. He always used to complain about the hassle of changing the reels just when a 'source' was about to say something interesting."

"Why'd they fire him, anyhow?"

"He's never told me. I get the feeling he thinks it's safer if I don't know." *Just like I'm doing, keeping things from you.*

"Well, I'm glad they did. Not 'cause he lost his job, of course—but 'cause you got to come here."

When Alison looked at Shaniqua in amazement, she quickly added, "And without your weirdo little brother, I'd have never met my twin."

* * * *

Walking home that day, Alison thought she really should try to get Dad to tell her why he'd lost his job. If it was political, as she suspected, it could make the trouble Arnold was courting even worse. It would be best at least to know how deep the water was before they all fell in.

But she forgot all about it that evening. First she was distracted by running into Mr. Freed. The black eye Arnold had given him had healed, but every line of his face drooped as he shuffled out from behind a hedge.

In her mind Alison sometimes called him "the bush man" for his habit of lurking in the shrubbery.

"The n-network," he said, as if he was talking about a large, smelly dog turd.

"What about it, Mr. Freed?" Alison said, trying to keep her tone light.

"You know it's really a mind-control device."

"Actually, you're right," Alison blurted before she could stop herself.

Mr. Freed reeled back as if she'd punched him in the stomach. "You *agree* with me?" he asked.

"Yeah, but it's not the government reading your thoughts. So you're wrong about that. The High Ones use people's brain power when they're plugged in to steer their starships. And they cause brain damage doing it. That's how my mom got NINA and ended up in a wheelchair."

Mr. Freed stared at her. "That's just nuts," he said after a moment, quickly adding, "But I'm glad you've seen the light about how evil the n-network is. What do you intend to do about it?"

Alison stared at him. "What do I intend to do about it? Who's nuts now? I'm just a kid, Mr. Freed!"

"I was younger than you when I was arrested at a protest for the first time," he said with unmistakable pride.

"Maybe so, Mr. Freed, but America was a very different place in the 1960's. You had the First Amendment—"

"—which was more honored in the breach—"

"—not the Free Speech Clause in the Bicentennial Constitution that says that you can say what you want only as long as it's 'responsible' and 'decent' and 'not a threat to public order.' And there weren't any SCOD holes they could send you to if you said something they didn't like." There was a long pause while Mr. Freed stared intently at the muddy sidewalk, before Alison half-whispered, "And besides, maybe I *am* doing something about it."

By the time Mr. Freed looked up, a question on his lips, Alison was already shutting her front door behind her.

Whereupon she completely forgot about Mr. Freed, because Mom was standing there. *Standing there*, without leaning on anything and without her wheelchair! She smiled and held her arms out for a hug, which Alison leaped into. "Mom—how…"

"Gloria was trying not to get my hopes up, honey, but they did way more than just keeping my NINA from getting worse, which she said might be all they could do. They actually cured me!"

Alison pulled away and peered intently into her mother's warm brown eyes to make sure she wasn't joking. When she decided she wasn't, her own eyes filled with tears so blinding she missed the beginning of

Mom's whirling dance around the living room. Alison wiped her eyes on her sleeve and watched in silent amazement.

"Wheee-hee-hee! I'm in love, I'm in love, I'm in love with Dr. Mordecai Eisenstein!" Mom sang. She whirled to a stop and grabbed Alison's hands again. "I actually got to meet him. He's almost one hundred, a little old stooped-over Jewish guy with a funny Polish accent, and they don't have immortality serum there, but he's my hero! My hero, my hero!" and she was twirling again, pulling Alison along with her this time, until they knocked over a lamp.

"We'd better stop now," Mom gasped, holding her sides. "He did tell me to take it easy at first, but I'm so happy! So happy, so happy!" and she skipped and stretched her right arm up as far as it would go, till it almost brushed the ceiling.

Arnold walked in at that moment and stood speechlessly staring, till Mom swept him into her wild dance too. Then they got out the record player and put on Dad's precious Beatles albums one after the other, starting with "Please Please Me."

When Dad got home he said Thai food wasn't good enough, they were going to Annapolis for a steak dinner at the fanciest restaurant in town. If it wasn't the best night of Alison's life, it was certainly the best she could remember since Dad lost his job in Baltimore and they had to come live here.

It was after midnight by the time they got back home, and Dad and Arnold went straight to bed. But Mom was still full of energy. "I keep thinking about all the things I'll be able to do now that I thought I'd never do again, like traveling. Remember when we all went to Mars?"

"I wish I could go there now," said Alison. "Anything to get away from this stinky island."

Mom gave her a sharp look. "What happened while I was gone? It's something to do with Arnold, isn't it?"

"What makes you think that?"

Mom gently elbowed her. "Come on, Allie. I may have been in a wheelchair, but I wasn't completely out of it."

Alison sighed and gave in. Mom listened carefully as she talked, interrupting with questions only once or twice. Alison told her about everything except the plan to steal the ditto machine, print up leaflets, and distribute them to every home in town.

"I'm really worried about what kinds of ideas this crazy Italian Teresa will come up with," Alison finished, "but I'm a lot more worried about what Arnold is turning into. I think something happened to him that he won't tell me about. Something at school."

Mom held Alison's hands in both of hers. "You've taken good care of him while I was sick. Which was years and years."

Alison shrugged. "He's my little brother. Dad was clueless. There wasn't anybody else."

"I should have tried harder."

"How? You were sick."

"That's true enough. You can't imagine what it means that I'm cured, Allie honey. I can't even absorb it. I worked very hard not to think of myself as a patient, but I did think I was always going to be sick. I didn't even expect to live out what we used to think was a normal human lifespan, let alone—what are they saying now? Two hundred years or more?"

Alison shrugged. The numbers didn't mean that much, when you were only fifteen years old yourself. "I'm just worried that I did the wrong thing, letting this crazy Teresa person come here and fill Arnold full of ideas that could get him disappeared. And get the rest of us in trouble, too."

Mom shook her head. "That won't happen, Allie. They don't send kids under eighteen to SCOD holes. The worst that can happen to you is, they'll put you in juvie. Which is no fun, but it's not like the holes."

"But they could send you and Dad there, right?"

Mom said nothing.

"Especially given his record, right?"

Mom looked out the window at the dark and quiet street.

"Mom, what happened to him at the newspaper? You know, don't you?"

She shook her head. "I can't tell you, Allie. It's not my business. But if you and Arnold are going to be breaking the anti-terrorism laws, I think it's only fair that you tell Dad first. And that he tell you—both of you—why the *Sun* fired him after twenty-one years on the job."

* * * *

But Alison put off talking to Dad for several more days, while the weather grew warmer and the air filled with huge flocks of birds migrating north. One thing you had to give the High Ones credit for—they had brought a lot of species back from the edge of extinction. Every puddle was filled with splashing ducks and downy ducklings.

One especially warm weekend Dad took everyone for a picnic on the beach at Assateague. The water was still too cold for swimming, but lots of people were out flying kites in the stiff offshore breeze. The wind was blowing the blankets around and getting sand in everything, and Alison braced herself for Arnold to start grumbling about it, but his gaze was fixed on something a million miles away. Mom and Dad were blissfully unaware of anything going on around them as they strolled hand in hand down the beach.

It hadn't been like this since Alison was little, and she knew she should be glad for them—she *was* glad for them—but she had nothing to do but chew on an egg salad sandwich that was crunchy with wind-blown sand and wait for them to finish what Jo would have called their "snogging," so she could get some time alone with Dad and finally worm the big secret out of him.

After what seemed like a very long while Mom and Dad came over to the blankets Alison was reluctantly sharing with Arnold. Mom sat down and stretched out, and Dad said, "Wait here, kids. I have a surprise for you in the car."

Alison managed to stop herself from saying that all she'd been doing all morning was waiting. Dad went over to the car and took a Chinese dragon kite out of the trunk.

"In honor of Assa Teag Ashley," he said, smiling, "who is probably soaring overhead right here, right now, on the other side of the dimensional divide."

"A kite? Really, Dad, do you think we're still little kids?" Arnold said, and stalked off toward the water.

There was an awkward silence until Mom, with a glance at Alison, said she'd pack up the picnic things and go check on him, so Alison and Dad could fly the kite by themselves if they liked.

"Are you sure, darling? I don't want you exerting yourself too much. You know what Dr. Eisenstein said," Dad said.

She waved him off. "It's all right, the car's really close by. Good thing I still have that handicapped sign! You and Allie have fun."

Alison and Dad looked at each and shrugged. She took the kite from him, held it and backed away as he unspooled the string. When they had put several meters between them he waved to her, her signal to start running up the beach. The wind tore the kite out of her hands, and it was airborne in no time. She put her hands on her hips and squinted into the sky, watching the kite as it rapidly shrank into the brilliant blue. She had to smile, thinking how little its gaudy colors resembled the real Ashley.

"I'm worried about Arnold."

Alison jumped, not having heard Dad approach. He was at her elbow, looking at the kite and then at her.

"I knew something was up with that Teresa girl the moment I saw her. She didn't seem like the type of girl who enjoys hanging out with kids. So when Mom told me what you'd said, I wasn't very surprised. Worried, yes, but not surprised."

"You're not mad that Arnold's mixed up in something that could be dangerous, and that he's gotten me involved too?"

"Mad? No. I'm scared, very scared, for both of you, but I'm also proud. What can I say except that you're both chips off the old block?"

But some of the things Arnold has done would make you the opposite of proud. Alison wanted to protect her little brother—though she also wanted to keep him from turning into a bully, or worse—so she didn't say that aloud. Instead she said, "Dad, what did you do that got you fired from the paper?"

"Oh, Allie, you don't want to know about that. It didn't do anybody any good, it only lost me my job and our old home, so what's the difference? I didn't change anything for the better. But any father hopes his children will do better than him, and I'm sure you and Arnold will."

That made her feel very small and scared, and it was in a small voice that Alison said, "I'd still like to know."

Dad sighed again and looked around the beach. They had wandered away from the surf line toward the dunes, the kite swooping and diving in the sky high above them. No one was nearby.

"All right, Allie. I trust you with this, but I'm not sure if Arnold is mature enough to handle it. You can decide whether to tell him or not."

Alison's shoulders suddenly weighed a million tons. But Dad wasn't looking at her. He was staring off into the distance.

"You know I had a regular 'beat,' writing about the Office of Interstellar Liaison at the State Department."

"Yes. That's why you had to drive down to Washington so often. Mom used to complain about how late you would get back. You used to bring us all those souvenirs, slow globes and brass replicas of the Capitol Building."

Dad smiled sadly. "That's right. I had some good sources, but my editors cut out almost everything interesting I wanted to write. Once I stormed into Ted Armstrong's office and asked why he bothered sending me to D.C. when he might as well just be printing the OIL's press releases? He could even put his own name on them, for all anyone cared."

"You said that? Really?"

"Yeah. Pretty dumb, but Ted calmed me down, somehow talked me into believing there was some value to my work. How he did that, I don't know, because we both knew it wasn't true. Well, word got around the office about my useless little temper tantrum, and an old guy at the sports desk took me out for a beer. Carl, I think his name was. He used to be an up-and-coming political reporter at one of the Washington papers, but he came up to Baltimore many years ago, long before my time—just before the Bicentennial, in fact, when any political reporter worth his salt was trying to get a scoop on what the new Constitution would look like.

"Well, he had a crazy story for me, but he took me into a dark booth in the bar and made damn sure the booths on either side were empty before he would talk to me. It seems that more than forty years ago, he and his partner, Bob, had reported on a burglary that turned out to have political implications. *Big* political implications. The High Satrap was running for re-election then—the only time he ever had to, of course, because this was under the old Constitution. To cut a long story short, they figured out that the burglars were working for the High Satrap—he was still called 'the President' then—and were trying to get into the other party's headquarters. Er, a political party was—"

"I know what a political party was, Dad, we learned all about them in history class. Mr. Bainbridge calls them great examples of the chaos that used to go on before the Cosmic Harmony came to Earth. They were always fighting over stuff and taking bribes. It's amazing anything ever got done."

Dad grimaced. "Yes. That's one way of looking at it. Well, the old Constitution was still in effect, like I said, but so was the National Emergency that the president, I mean the High Satrap, had declared at the time of the Arrival, and their articles never appeared in the paper. They had found out a lot of other stuff too, stuff that people working for the High Satrap did that was way illegal at the time, some of which would be illegal even now. There were other break-ins, and hush money paid, and all kinds of bad stuff. And none of it ever became public, and Carl and Bob were both encouraged to find work elsewhere."

Alison digested all this. "Okay. So what does all of this have to do with you and the OIL?"

"Well, Carl mentioned that one of the burglars—" Dad broke off and looked around again. When he resumed speaking he lowered his voice. "Don't repeat this to Arnold or anyone else, but one of the burglars was George Libby, the Deputy Secretary of State for Interstellar Liaison—the head of the OIL. Carl told me that to make me think twice about messing around anymore than I already had with the OIL, but I," Dad barked out a laugh. "I didn't take his advice. The next time Libby showed up at one of the OIL press conferences in person—it was to announce an increase in the American quota of visitors to Homeworld, I think—well, I waited till all the other reporters had left, and I asked him about Carl's story."

Alison stared at him.

"Not only did he admit it, he was proud of it!" Dad said. "He boasted about how he and the others had made sure the High Satrap would be re-elected, when there were so many others working to bring him down!

'America needed him more than ever, after the Arrival, and thanks to us he won every single state that November!' He bragged about a bunch of other illegal things they did too—everything Carl told me about and more besides. He never said it was off the record, so I drove back to Baltimore and wrote it all up in an article."

"Dad," Alison said. She couldn't think of anything else to say for a long moment. "Dad, wasn't that kind of dumb? I mean, did you really think they'd let you do that?"

"I don't know what I thought. But Ted called me in to his office the next morning, and there were two strangers there with him—they didn't identify themselves, but what difference did it make whether they were from the FBI or SCOD? I was lucky not to be arrested or disappeared. I came home and told Mom, and you know what happened then." Dad paused for a moment and gazed out to sea.

"I only got the job at Wallops because Bruce pulled strings for me," he continued in a different tone. "He and I were college roommates, remember. But someone must have decided it was safer to have me working here, where they can keep an eye on me, than causing trouble someplace else. That's the kind of country we live in now—a country that strip-searches kids going to school. So, if you and Arnold are trying to do something about it, what can I do but cheer you on?"

"All right," Alison said. "But I'm scared—not just of getting in trouble, but of some of the things Arnold might do. He's been palling around with the same kids who were beating him up last year. I don't really understand it, but…"

"I'll talk to him," Dad said. "I'll tell him the same thing I'm telling you: don't hurt anyone, and try not to break the law." He grimaced. "I can't believe what I'm saying. This is what we've come to… but I'm proud of you both."

I don't know if you should be, Alison thought, hugging Dad tightly.

22

Arnold was so busy between schoolwork and planning how to break into Mr. Wright's office that he didn't have much time to brood about how Alison had snitched on him. But he wasn't going to forget it. Not after the long, serious talk Dad had had with him as soon as they got back from the picnic, coming into his room and shutting the door behind him and telling him that he was proud of him for standing up for what was right against the government and SCOD and even the High Ones, and he wasn't going to stop him, but he should be careful, try not to break the law, and most of all not hurt anyone.

"Don't get mixed up in anything violent, Arnold. If you do that you're playing their game, and they can be much more violent than you. You'll be the one who ends up getting hurt, and you'll also play right into their hands by being a 'terrorist.'"

He paused and peered intently into Arnold's face. Arnold tried to keep his eyes and mouth as still as possible. Those tiny muscles seemed to need an awful lot of energy.

How much does he know? How much has Alison told him? He didn't want to have to try to explain to Dad why he'd spray-painted the warning on James's locker, but fortunately Dad seemed to know nothing about that.

Dad also must not know that he had punched Mr. Freed in the face, because he'd certainly have had something to say about that. *I had to do it. He was mocking what happened to Parallel Hailee, saying the High Ones don't even exist!*

How many times since Arnold was little had Dad and Mom drilled into him to "just ignore them" and "just walk away" when he was teased and bullied? What good had that advice ever done him? If you did try to ignore the bullies they'd grab you by the shirt collar and holler in your face until you took a lame-o swing at them, which gave them all the excuse they needed to punch you out. Matt and Jared had done that to him many times before they turned out to be the allies he needed to help fight the High Ones.

One lone nerd like Arnold was never going to be able to take on the Slugs on his own. He needed a posse behind him, and he would rather not have to explain that to Dad. Fortunately Dad was clueless enough to nod slowly, squeeze his shoulder and walk out of the room, leaving Arnold alone to whisper his troubles to the spider plant, which caressed his hand with its leaves.

By trial and error he had learned that while the plant could tolerate plain water, it actually preferred to drink a few teaspoons of slightly sour milk a day, which he supplied with an eye dropper he'd bought at the drugstore. This made the leaves plumper and more active.

"I can't trust Alison," he whispered as the leaves stroked his palm. "My own sister betrayed me! It can't be because she's a girl, though— Hailee from the ruined world would have understood what I have to do. She'd have backed me all the way! Jo's a little like her, but not enough— she comes from a world where they still bow down to a king! And how different is that from bowing down to the High Emperor Whissssh-igula? She might say she hates kings, but if Charles III ordered her to tell him what we're up to, she probably would, wouldn't she?"

He kept talking to the plant, and it took much longer than it usually did for its calmness to spread over his mind, like a pond gradually smoothing over after someone throws a stone in it.

He had told Gloria once that the spider plant made him feel that way, and she smiled and said, "There's an old Yiddish proverb: if a fool throws a stone in the water, a dozen wise men can't stop the ripples."

"So the spider plant is better than a dozen wise men?"

"That's why you need it."

* * * *

The next day was Monday. Most people hated going back to school after the weekend, and for Arnold it had always brought out mixed feelings; he liked school because he liked being the smartest kid in class—or at least one of the smartest two or three, knowing all the answers while the others were still struggling to catch up—but he hated being singled out as the weirdo nerd-ball, the mental freak who was also a weakling and fair game for whatever anybody wanted to do to him.

Now that was all over, and if he was never going to be a Bill Cherricks, hero to all on account of being the most promising sophomore on the Chincoteague Colts football team, at least now everyone was afraid of him. No one would dare give him a wedgie, or trip him while he was carrying a loaded lunch tray, or make fart noises and snicker behind his back, or pass notes and look significantly at him, then whisper behind their hands and crack up.

Some girls had even started to flirt with him! Not Hailee, of course, but Madison and Kayleigh.

He'd been shocked the first time it had happened. "Hey, tough guy!" Kayleigh had purred at him. He spun around, balling his fists, certain he was being mocked, but the giggles she and Madison pealed out didn't sound that way.

"Hey, uh, yourself, uh, doll-face," Arnold said, reaching back in his memory to some old movie he'd once seen. This of course led to more giggling. It felt as if he'd swallowed a ball of fire, but instead of burning him it had spread all through his body and given him super powers. He viewed everything around him from a different, higher angle and strode with more confidence from class to class. The female attention gave him something to talk about with the guys at lunch, filling the awkward silences when Gus was around.

"I think you should ask Kayleigh out," Matt said on this bright Monday. "She'd do whatever you want. Madison's a tease."

"How would you know, Matt?" Gus said. "Your old man doesn't even let you go out on dates." Matt scowled as everyone else laughed.

"Me, I'd rather ask Hailee out," Jared said, his eyes half-shut and his mouth half-open.

"Yeah, if you don't mind Bill Cherricks ramming his fist down your throat," said Gus.

"Sure, but if not for Bill? Can you imagine poor little Hailee, all alone?" His voice turned into a breathy squeak. "'Oh please, Jared, I'm so scared to walk home alone. Won't you please go with me?' You bet I would. And once we got there, I'd—"

"Don't talk about Hailee that way!" Arnold snapped. "Please," he added when everyone stared at him.

"Do you have a crush on her?" Jared said. His protruding front teeth came out and nibbled his lower lip, rabbit-like. "You do! You have a crush on Hailee Pruitt! Hey, everybody! Arnold has a crush on Hail—UH!"

Arnold had punched him in the mouth.

There was a shocked silence. Mr. Wolff, who was on lunchtime duty, hurried over to the table. "Is there a problem here?" he demanded, putting a hand on each boy's shoulder.

Jared had his hand in his mouth, testing whether a tooth was loose. "Arnold punched me!" he said. Or tried to say. It sounded more like, "Hah-hold hunch hee!"

"I'm sorry, Jared, I can't understand what you're saying," Mr. Wolff said.

Arnold watched in amazement as the teacher's knuckles turned white, and Jared stared at him with round eyes before taking his hand out of his mouth.

"Uh, n-nothing, Mr. Wolff! I just bit down on a chicken bone," he said.

"Yeah, you wanna watch out for those chicken bones," Arnold said. "Choke you to death, they will."

There was a sharp twinge in his shoulder as Mr. Wolff squeezed it in turn. "Want some of my chocolate milk, Jared?" Arnold said, his voice slightly higher pitched than usual.

"Sure," Jared said.

Mr. Wolff smiled, showing two rows of dazzling white teeth, and let go of both of them. As the noise level in the cafeteria returned to lunchtime normal he growled softly, "Remember who we're fighting, boys. Not each other." He clasped his hands behind his back and strolled back to the corner where he'd been standing, eyeing them all the way.

Jared gulped down Arnold's chocolate milk, looking dazed.

Arnold got to thinking: Should he actually ask Madison or Kayleigh out? What if they shot him down? Wouldn't his newfound reputation suffer?

Pondering, he got up to throw out the trash on his tray and bumped right into Darla. He said hi absently and she shied away. *Weird. She was always nice to me before.* It was so weird he actually said something about it when he sat back down.

Jared had recovered enough to sneer, "Who cares about that metal mouth?"

"Yeah, she'd be a dog even without braces," Matt chuckled.

Arnold thought he should stick up for Princess Hailee's lady-in-waiting, but somehow couldn't find the words.

It was almost as hard to find an opportunity to talk to Madison or Kayleigh alone. He decided that he'd ask out whichever of them he managed to catch by herself first. That turned out to be Kayleigh, who was squatting in front of her locker looking for something when Arnold walked past on the way back from the bathroom in the middle of sixth period Wednesday.

He stopped and just admired her butt for a split second, thinking that her being a little plump wasn't so bad. Then he cleared his throat. She got to her feet quickly, books spilling out of her hands, panic in her eyes until she saw who it was. She smiled and Arnold knew he'd made the right choice even before he said anything.

"Hi, Kayleigh."

"Oh, uh, hi Arnold."

"Let me help you with those," Arnold said, bending down to pick up her books for her.

She murmured thanks. When he stood up he saw he was a little closer to her than he'd meant to be and suddenly wondered if he'd remembered to brush his teeth this morning—Alison was always nagging him about that, saying she wouldn't call him "turd breath" if he'd remember to use a little damn toothpaste.

"Wanna see a movie this weekend?" he said in a rush. "'Spacefarers Epic' is playing at the Island Roxy."

"I have to go see my grandparents in Salisbury on Saturday," she said, and Arnold's stomach lurched. "But we could go see the Sunday matinee."

"Okay, that's great," he said. "We could get ice cream at Muller's afterward. It's the best in town! Where do you live?"

"Over on Taylor Street, the corner house by Deep Hole Road," she said, tucking her hair behind her ear. "It's the white clapboard house with a white picket fence, you can't miss it. Just stop by half an hour before the movie and I'll be ready."

"That's just a few blocks from my house. No problem. See ya then."

"See ya," Kayleigh said, raising her right hand and wiggling her fingers goodbye.

Arnold noticed she had scarlet nail polish on. He stuck his hands in his pockets to look extra casual as he strolled back to class.

It was only when he reached for the classroom doorknob that he remembered he was supposed to be meeting Jo on Sunday afternoon so they could finalize the burglary plot.

They'd decided to do it themselves, or as Jo liked to put it, "the Freedom Fighters of Earth will have to act on its own," because Arnold wanted to show Mr. Wolff he could act without the teacher guiding him every step of the way, while Matt and Jared seemed to be getting their ideas from Saturday morning cartoons. At a council of war in the Value-Mart parking lot one chilly evening last week, Jared had proposed smashing the window over Mr. Wright's desk with a rock in the middle of the night, and Matt had added enthusiastically that he knew a construction site where they could get some big rocks.

"But then we'll have to climb over broken glass, and won't the noise bring the bobbies?" Jo had asked.

"What are bobbies?" Matt asked.

"She means the police. That's what they call them in Philadelphia," Arnold said quickly, shooting her a look. "But Jo is right. It's too risky."

"I don't see why some girl from Philadelphia is telling us what to do," Jared sneered.

"You got a bad addy-tood, soldier," Jo said.

Jared clenched his fists, but when Jo and Arnold both clenched theirs, Matt stepped in and said with a little laugh, "Ah, what the hell. Maybe the pamphlet ain't so important anyway."

So it was up to Arnold and Jo, and what excuse could he possibly give for not meeting up with her? He wasn't going to see her before Sunday, since she had a lot of homework and had to "revise" for a biology test.

The simplest solution was to ask Gloria to tell her he couldn't make it. But he decided he couldn't risk it—she might look at him with those wide green eyes and have him blurting out his plans for *Operation Volantini*. No, it was safer not to say anything and just end the date with Kayleigh a little early—and if he was still a little late for Jo, she wouldn't mind too much, a free spirit like her. He could handle the two girls, he was sure of it.

23

After all that trouble, Arnold wondered whether Kayleigh was even going to come to the door when he knocked at her house, but he had just raised his hand when the door swung open and she was standing there holding an energetic-looking blond lady's hand.

"Hi, I'm Kayleigh's mom, Mary Lou Scott," the lady said, grabbing Arnold's hand and shaking it so vigorously it felt like it was trembling when he snatched it back.

There was something odd about her pleasant, unlined face. Arnold was so busy trying to figure out what it was he almost forgot to introduce himself.

"Um, I'm Arnold, I guess."

"You guess? You're not even sure about your own name?" Kayleigh's mom tilted her head back and laughed loudly.

When she bent her neck Arnold saw what it was that had caught his attention—she'd put lots of makeup over a faint, bluish bruise.

But then Kayleigh smiled, or at least her lips turned up slightly, and Arnold's full attention turned to her. She had glossy pink lipstick on, and was more dressed up than he had ever seen her in school. Under a light, pale-blue jacket, she wore a bright white blouse and a lavender skirt that reached down below her knees. Her shoes were shiny and black.

Mrs. Scott glanced at her. "I told her to change out of her church clothes, but she wouldn't listen to me."

"Mo-om! You're embarrassing me!"

"I'm sorry, punkin," Mrs. Scott said, ruffling her daughter's hair. She smiled at Arnold. "I don't think I've ever seen your family around Union Baptist. What church do y'all belong to?"

Kayleigh looked at the floor as Arnold stammered, "I don't, I mean, we don't, I mean, we're um, uh, we're Jewish."

"Oh! I'm sorry," Mrs. Scott said, and Arnold wondered whether she meant she was sorry she had embarrassed him, or sorry that he was Jewish. The silence that followed seemed to last a very, very long time. Arnold looked down at his jeans and sneakers and thought he really should have dressed better.

"Well. Y'all have a good time. Kayleigh, I expect you home to start setting the table for dinner at 6:00 sharp. Granny is coming."

"Yes, Mom."

Arnold wondered whether he should take Kayleigh's hand as she stepped down onto the sidewalk with him and stood to his right. He decided to move his right hand away from his side just a little, to give her the choice whether to hold it or not. It was too warm for gloves, and he was afraid his palm might be sweaty. She did grab his hand and he was surprised that hers was even slicker with sweat than his.

"This is gonna be a great movie! It's so cool they actually got Donny Schmitz to play Brad, just like in the tri-vee show," Kayleigh said, speaking in such a rush it was hard to make out what she was saying.

"Yeah. Neat," Arnold said, or thought he said. It was hard to hear over the thundering of his heart. He was staring at Kayleigh's rosy cheek, wondering if he should kiss it. *Not yet.*

"I wonder why Taylor Fields isn't playing Janey? Madison says she heard it's because she got knocked up and they're trying to keep it quiet. I think that's probably true, she is *such* a slut."

"Uh-huh," said Arnold, still staring at her cheek, and the unattainable goal of her glossy lips beyond it. It was a good thing she was looking as they crossed the street because if she'd been relying on him, they probably would have got run over.

At the Roxy, Alison's friend Shaniqua was selling tickets.

"Two for 'Spacefarers' Epic,' please," Arnold said, pushing a ten-solar bill under the window glass. Shaniqua pursed her lips and looked at Arnold and Kayleigh without touching the money, which brought fresh sweat out on his forehead. "What is it? What's the matter?" he said, willing his voice not to crack.

"The movie's rated SCOD-16 'cause of 'adult situations.' I ain't supposed to let you in unless you're both sixteen."

"I am," Kayleigh said, flashing her school ID. Her tiny three-D portrait was adorable.

Arnold wondered if he could get her to give him a copy.

"Me, too. But I left my school ID at home," he lied.

Shaniqua shook her head, but she gave him his three solars and fifty-four lunars in change, which ought to be enough to buy a big bag of popcorn, a Coke each, and a banana split sundae to share at Muller's afterward.

They separated at the door for the strip search. Arnold was not very surprised to find Mr. Ramsey in charge here too. "Don't you have any hobbies?" he asked as the rubber gloves moved briskly down his sides.

"Careful with that mouth, Jewboy. Or you might end up like Izzy Goldstein in the movie," Mr. Ramsey smirked.

"Thanks for spoiling it for me."

"Any time, Jewboy, any time."

When Kayleigh came out of the women's changing room a couple minutes later she looked upset, and her blouse was buttoned up wrong.

"What's the matter?" Arnold said.

"That old witch Mrs. Parsons smudged up my blouse!" Kayleigh said, hardly bothering to lower her voice. "My mom is going to kill me!"

Arnold gave it another look. At first he didn't see anything wrong with it, apart from the buttons, which Kayleigh noticed the same time he did and began fixing. Then he saw an oily light brown stain located, distractingly enough, right over her right breast.

"Um, I'm sure it'll come out in the wash," Arnold said, though he'd never done a load of laundry in his life.

"No, it won't! It's got to be dry cleaned."

"Just take it over to Park Place Cleaners," Arnold said, before he remembered.

"Can't. The Parks closed up their place and moved to Philadelphia. I heard it was 'cause James had a nervous breakdown after someone spray painted a death threat on his locker."

They had walked into the theater and were looking for seats while they talked. Arnold was glad Kayleigh couldn't see his face in the dim light. He didn't know how to feel about what she'd just said. If it was true, he'd succeeded beyond his wildest expectations. But it could just be an exaggerated rumor—after all, he hadn't actually threatened to kill James, had he? And what was a nervous breakdown, anyway?

He imagined James's nervous system burning out in a sudden flash, leaving him to flail around and then drop motionless to the floor. A knot formed in his stomach. James had never done him any harm. He'd almost been friends with him. The High Ones were the real enemy, weren't they? But how else were you supposed to fight them when they were so few and so well protected, and when so many people saw nothing wrong in collaborating with them?

He was afraid Kayleigh was going to ask him if he'd had anything to do with the vandalism, but her mind was already on other things. "I heard that Scarlet Fontaine, the girl they got to replace Taylor Fields in the movie, isn't nearly as pretty as her," she said with satisfaction. "I guess we'll see, won't we? Hey, pass the popcorn, will you?"

He handed it over to Kayleigh, who was sitting to his left, just as the house lights went down. The giant movie tri-vee stage lit up with the previews. Some people Dad's age or older wouldn't go to movies because they said they just couldn't get used to five-meter-tall giants stomping around the stage.

Arnold thought that was silly. Didn't old movie screens used to show two-dimensional images that were just as large? So what was the big deal if they had depth, too?

The sound was turned up a bit too high, but that was probably the fault of the Roxy's owner, Fred Boyce, who was going deaf. "From Leni Riefenstahl Studios and the pen of writer Duke Davis," a commanding masculine voice said, "comes a dark and suspenseful tale of a worldwide conspiracy."

Black-coated figures appeared on stage, huddling in a shadowy stone courtyard. Occasionally one threw a bloodshot glance over his shoulder, and it was apparent that even for five-meter-tall figures, they had over-sized noses.

"They call them the Elders of Zion," the commanding voice said in a confiding half-whisper, but Arnold had already stopped paying attention. He had a much more urgent problem to consider: where to put his left arm. At the moment it was pressed up against the armrest that divided his seat from Kayleigh's. He knew his goal should be to drape it casually around her shoulders, as if this was something he did every day. But this seemed a feat of mechanical engineering that would have stumped the builders of Olympus Tower.

His left arm seemed to weigh a ton as he fought heroically to lift it up to the armrest. He risked a glance at Kayleigh, fearing that her face would be wrinkled in disgust at his stealthy approach. But she was absorbed by what was going on onstage. Good, then, it was on to the next stage of Operation Arm-Drape, which involved reaching up to scratch his neck with his left hand, while leaving the elbow in place on the arm-rest. He had to lower his head a bit to make that work, and leave his neck bent awkwardly for several increasingly uncomfortable seconds so that he didn't have to put his left hand back down. Instead he used it to pluck at some loose skin on the back of his neck as the tension built and built. On stage a giant shrieking girl almost made him lose his painfully achieved position.

"…the sacrifice that must attend every meeting of the Elders…" the commanding voice was saying. Ever so slowly, Arnold began to bring his left hand down on the back of Kayleigh's seat. She turned to face him and he jumped back as if stung.

"Hey Arnold, don't this bother you?"

"What?" Arnold was so sure Kayleigh was going to slap his face that it took him a few seconds to register what she had actually said. "Doesn't what bother me?"

"This stuff about the Elders of Zion," she said, gesturing at the stage, which was covered in a sinister mist through which floated shadowy three-meter-high letters spelling out THE ELDERS and below that, in smaller letters, "Starts April 20 in Selected Theaters."

"Oh, that?" Arnold made a face and waved his hand—his right hand—as if flicking away a fly. "Nah, it doesn't bother me."

"But it's about Jewish people."

"Not really. I mean, it's got nothing to do with us, with anything real. That's what my Dad says." He smiled. "Unless you think I've got a black coat and hat and like to lurk in alleys. Boogah boogah!"

Kayleigh chuckled. "Okay, Arnold, it's just that—"

A chorus of shushing arose all around them. The movie was starting. Cheers erupted as a giant Captain Adams strolled out into the control room of his rocket, with a giant Donny Schmitz ("Brad") on his heels.

"He's so cute, isn't he?" Kayleigh squealed, snuggling closer to him when he put his arm around her shoulders. Mission accomplished! He was dizzy with this triumph, but now he had a new mission: getting his first kiss. He chose his moment carefully, waiting till the villain Izzy Goldstein walked in on Brad and Janey, brandishing a zap gun and an evil grin over a Fu Manchu beard. This made Kayleigh raise her hands to cover her face and lean toward Arnold. She was rubbing against him!

He could feel the pressure of her body against his in the dark... he was so glad it was dark... he tightened his grip on her shoulder, straining to give her a reassuring hug just like Donny Schmitz had just done to what's-her-name. All the blood rushed to his head and, with a lurch, he leaned forward to give her a kiss. His lips landed on her cheekbone, missing her right eye by less than a centimeter. Never mind, it didn't matter, she had snuggled up close to him, and she was staying snuggled!

On the stage the bearded, hook-nosed villain was cackling as he tied Brad and Janey up with a steel cable, back to back against a steel pillar in the ship's engine room.

"You see those numbers over there?" he said, pointing at a red, digital display that was counting backwards from 100. "When they reach zero, the engines on the *Intrepid* are going to overheat! And then it's ka-blooey, bye-bye Brad and Janey!"

He laughed maniacally as he dragged the unconscious Captain Adams toward the escape pod, shut the airlock and took off with a bang that seemed to shake the theater as well as the engine room where his helpless prisoners stood trapped.

"I can't look!" Kayleigh cried, pressing her hands against her eyes as Brad struggled to free himself from the steel cable and Janey told him to hurry, hurry, the countdown had already reached 59.

"Will you shut up please?" someone yelled from off to Arnold's right.

"Yeah, keep it down!" another voice said, further off in the darkness.

He had to protect Kayleigh! If he hadn't been able to save Hailee from the ruined world, now he was being given another chance to rescue the girl! The darkness and the fact that neither of the voices had been too nearby emboldened him, and he said loudly, "Leave my girlfriend alone! She was just enjoying the movie!"

More voices rose now, ordering them both to shut up. Something hit the back of Arnold's neck. Things might have gotten ugly if not for the fact that, at that moment onstage, Brad burst free of the steel cables and shut down the runaway fusion reaction Izzy Goldstein had started, with two seconds to spare until it went critical. Soaring orchestral music accompanied his quick yet tender freeing of Janey, and she threw herself into his two-meter-long arms with grateful sobs and began the activity that SCOD had deemed unfit for children younger than 16.

How come movie and tri-vee actors know how to kiss so smoothly, so sexily? What's the matter with me?

No sooner had this despairing thought made its way through Arnold's mind than Kayleigh leaned over and whispered in his ear, "I'm not your girlfriend yet, Arnold." Pause. "But thank you anyway."

Arnold withdrew his arm from around Kayleigh's shoulders and sat hunched over with his hands clasped together and shoved between his legs as Brad turned the *Intrepid* around and began pursuing Izzy Goldstein's vessel, the *Pot of Gold*, as it dodged among asteroids on its way to the villain's secret base.

Out of the corner of his eye Arnold could see Kayleigh gripping her armrests as enormous pitted boulders whirled across the stage like so many tumbleweeds, narrowly missing the *Intrepid* too many times to count. Then came one that looked exactly like a huge baked potato, complete with bits of aluminum foil clinging to it, zooming up too fast for Brad to dodge.

Kayleigh screamed and grabbed Arnold's arm as it dinged the *Intrepid* at a shallow angle. Arnold stopped paying attention to the giants Donny Schmitz and Scarlet Fontaine throwing themselves around the stage as Kayleigh buried her face in his chest. Should he try to kiss her again? If not now, when?

But she lifted her head up before he could make up his mind. Brad and Janey were slapping metal patches over the many holes that had been punched in the ship's hull. Arnold considered telling Kayleigh that that was ridiculous, the ship wouldn't leak like a water balloon but explosively decompress if it had that many holes in it, and neither Brad nor

Janey would look so pretty anymore, but he didn't want to freak her out. *Jo would laugh, though*, he thought guiltily.

Three more times during the movie Kayleigh yelled and hid her face against Arnold's chest. Each time he felt a little taller, a little surer of himself.

Next time I'll kiss her again for sure, he vowed, but then Brad rescued his father the captain from Izzy Goldstein's secret base, the villain fled one bare step ahead of them in his damaged ship, and a close-up head shot of Brad and Janey showed them kissing like two Easter Island statues shoved right up against each other. *The lights are gonna come up in a second! It's now or never! But don't lunge this time!* Arnold bent over Kayleigh's seat, cupped her chin in his left hand *(that's why people do it*, he suddenly understood, *so they can find the girl's lips)* and leaned in for the kiss.

She hesitated, started to turn her head, but then stayed still and let him do it. Her lips were cool and moist. She giggled and broke away. "Come on, let's go get ice cream now! My mom meant it about being home at six."

He followed her out of the theater into the almost-spring late afternoon. The salty tang of the sea was in the air as they walked next door to Muller's ice cream parlor, which was popular enough with locals that it opened on the weekends off season. They had to stand in line, and as they waited Arnold thrilled when Kayleigh daringly tucked her hand in his left jacket pocket, entwining her arm with his.

"Did you like the movie?" he asked her.

"It was okay. Maybe next time we can see something romantic."

He couldn't believe what she was saying, and loud enough for people around them to hear! In a town as small as Chincoteague, the news was sure to spread everywhere by the time the sun went down. "You mean with smooching and stuff?" he said.

She smiled and pressed against his side for a moment. "Yeah, but who says 'smooching' anymore?"

"A—a friend of mine," he said. He couldn't exactly tell her about Jo. *I'm supposed to meet her this afternoon... well, there's still plenty of time.* He glanced at his watch, but it had stopped. He always forgot to wind it.

The line inched forward. Kayleigh spotted another girl from their class, someone whose name Arnold couldn't remember, and they chatted about how dreamy Donny Schmitz was and what a washout Scarlet Fontaine was.

"Taylor Fields has more class in her little finger than Scarlet does in that whole skinny body," the other girl said.

"Yeah, but what a whiner," Kayleigh said. Then they talked about what was going to be on next week's algebra test. "I'm not too worried," Kayleigh said, glancing at Arnold, "not now that I've got the Brain from Baltimore to help me!"

Arnold smiled and rolled the sound of that around in his mind for a while. It sure beat "Gross-fart."

Arnold still had a solar and a few loose lunars left after he paid for Kayleigh's sugar cone of chocolate ice cream and his own cone of peach sherbet, which was as orange as the sun that was sinking to the west, out over the causeway. It was still chilly enough that they had the outdoor picnic table to themselves as they ate.

Kayleigh glanced around, then leaned over and said quietly to Arnold, "I hear you and Matt and Jared are in the Resistance."

Arnold tried to model his expression on Captain Adams—noble but aloof. "I can't discuss that," he said.

She nodded seriously. "I think it's a great thing you guys are doing. Everybody in school does too."

A hint of a smile cracked Arnold's aloof, noble face. *Aw, heck.* He let it become a full smile.

Kayleigh's eyes gleamed. "Can I join you guys?" she whispered.

"I'll have to take it up with the other guys in the group. Um, assuming that there actually *is* a group." Though there wasn't really any good reason he could think of for keeping her out, seeing that Jo was in the Resistance, and even Sis was, sort of.

"I hate the Slugs," Kayleigh said suddenly.

Arnold eyed her in surprise. She had never seemed any different from any of the other girls to him, all busy talking about boys and clothes and whose mother let who wear nail polish (he was glad Mrs. Scott let Kayleigh do it). None of them except Alison ever seemed interested in anything that went on beyond Chincoteague, and Alison probably only cared because she was Dad's daughter.

Now he started to wonder if Kayleigh had only agreed to go out with him so that she could get a chance to fight the High Ones. If so, he was all in favor, in theory; but then why did it feel so disappointing?

"Why? What have they done to you?" Arnold asked.

Kayleigh's eyes widened. They were an unusual color, he noticed for the first time: the irises such a dark brown they were almost black. Bitter chocolate.

Her eyes looked left, then right. "How can you ask that?" she hissed. "They're horrible! They've totally ruined the seafood business!"

Mr. Scott, Arnold remembered now, was an out-of-work waterman. There were all kinds of rules you had to follow if you wanted to catch oysters and clams, which were supposed to be to help restore the species to what they had once been and make the bays as healthy as they had been before the English settlers came, but which people snickered quietly were really due to family feeling on the part of the echinodermoids.

"Why doesn't your father take some of those job training classes they offer over at Wallops Island?" Arnold asked.

Kayleigh folded her arms and shook her head, making her curly brown hair bounce around. "You don't get it. The Scotts have lived on the Eastern Shore since 1625. My dad says he won't take a handout offered at the end of a tentacle."

"What about your mom?"

Kayleigh shifted her weight on the bench. "She works in the school district office down in Accomac. That makes my dad even madder. He says a man ought to be able to provide for his own family. Sometimes he yells at her and, you know, pushes her around a bit, especially if he's been drinking."

She looked away from him, clenched her fists, drew in a breath and said, "That wouldn't never happen if not for the High Ones! If it wasn't for those *things* he'd still be out seeding oysters on his own claim, in his own boat, the *Mary Lou*. Instead it got repossessed by a bunch of greedy J—I mean, by a bunch of greedy bankers." Her face colored.

Arnold looked at his hands and tried to think of the right thing to say. Heroes in the movies and on the tri-vee stage never were at a loss for words. And here he was, Mr. Straight-A in English, with his tongue all in knots.

"I'm sorry," was all he could manage.

Kayleigh shrugged. "It ain't your fault. But can't you see, I've got good reasons for being a real, true-born patriot. You'll get me into the Resistance, won't you?" Her eyes were huge and shiny with unshed tears.

He reached across the picnic table and grabbed her hands, which were cold. "I promise I will," he said. His heart sank as he said it, but he forgot all about that when she lunged across the table at him, grabbed his face in both hands and kissed him hard.

This was the kind of stuff the bigger boys talked about in low voices in the locker room, sniggering quietly about how far this or that girl was willing to go. And it was happening to *him*, to the ultimate "come-here," the nerdiest of the nerdballs.

Kayleigh wasn't as beautiful as perfect cheerleader Hailee or even scarred Hailee from the ruined world, but she was *his* now and he gave it everything he had when he kissed her back. The others would *have* to let her in, that was all, just like they had let Jo in when he said she was his cousin from Philadelphia. Arnold would *make* them.

When she pulled away at last and glanced at her watch, which had a pink watchband studded with rhinestones, she let out a little gasp.

"It's five after six! I've got to go, Arnold, sorry!"

And she got up and ran away, disappearing around the corner of the movie theater by the time he got to his feet and saw someone standing on the other side of Main Street in front of the closed tourist trap souvenir shops. Someone standing there staring right at him.

Jo.

24

When Jo saw Arnold looking back at her she bolted, running away up Main Street toward the high school. Arnold ran after her, ignoring the puzzled looks people gave him as he puffed past. Sure enough, as he rounded the corner onto Hallie Whealton Smith Drive he glimpsed Jo slipping through the fire exit.

Luckily, neither Bubba nor Mr. Ramsey seemed to be around. Maybe they were taking a dinner break. So Arnold ran right around the side of the building and followed just a few seconds after Jo.

She was leaning over the counter shouting for Gloria to come, please come quickly. When she heard Arnold she swung around to face him. "You! Get away from me!"

"Jo, what's the matter? Why are you acting so crazy?" Her braid had come undone and swirls of dirty blond hair were in her face, which was wet with tears.

"How could you do it? How? I thought we were friends!"

"We are friends," Arnold said.

"I waited for you for a whole hour. Then I went out to find you and saw you kissing that girl!"

"Okay, I was kissing Kayleigh, but so what? She wants to join the Freedom Fighters of Earth too."

Jo took a step away from him. "Are you kidding me, mate? A girl like that can't fight the Slugs. She'd be too busy worrying her nail polish might get chipped!"

"That's not fair, Jo. You don't even know her. Her father—"

Jo said a very bad swear word about Kayleigh's father. Very bad.

Arnold was completely shocked. If Mrs. Purnell had heard her, she would have been in deep trouble.

"But, Jo," Arnold said, taking a step toward her.

She backed away again. "Keep away from me! As far as I'm concerned, you can fight the Slugs all on your own! I hope they drown you in mucus!"

"I don't get why you're acting like this," Arnold said. He was beginning to tear up. "Didn't you say you wouldn't be my girlfriend?"

"I most certainly did! I wouldn't walk out with you if the Slugs had covered every other boy on Earth in slime."

"Didn't you say no smooching or disgusting stuff?"

"I didn't just mean no smooching or disgusting stuff between us, I meant no smooching or disgusting stuff with *anybody!*"

"But Jo—"

"I thought you were more serious than that, Arnold. I really did." She turned and darted around the counter and into the door that led into the Gray Zone. Again, Arnold followed her, but he tripped on the steps and went sprawling on the hard floor.

He got to his hands and knees, but instead of the familiar windowless corridor he found himself on a darkling plain. Those were the words that popped into his head: *a darkling plain.* It was so dark he could barely see the ground at his feet, a flat, hard surface like a pounded dirt playground. A chilly, dusty breeze blew in his face, so he had to be outside, and yet the air seemed to close in around him.

"Hello?" he called. No one answered, but there was a distant jumble of noise, as if a crowd was far away on the invisible horizon.

A darkling plain. The words came from a poem Mr. Wolff had made the class read. "Over the Beach?" No, it was "Dover Beach." He remembered because Jared had wanted to know how come the poet was so dumb he didn't know Dover, Delaware wasn't even on the water, and Mr. Wolff had explained the poet was thinking of Dover, England, and… and nobody really got the poem, but Arnold remembered it was really depressing. There was a line in it, something about stupid armies fighting.

Could that be the noise he was hearing? People fighting far away? But it seemed to be getting closer. There were distant shouts and screams, explosions and the clang of metal against metal, crunching and ripping and tearing. Arnold started to back away but whichever direction he went, the noise got closer.

"Hello?" he called hoarsely. "Jo? Are you there?" Someone shrieked so close by Arnold almost lost his balance. *That sounded like a girl!* He wanted to run and help if it was Jo, but he wasn't sure what direction the shout had come from, and he couldn't see anything. If he took a step, would the ground still be flat and featureless? Or would he bump into something, or fall off a cliff? What should he do?

When a hand fell on his shoulder Arnold screamed and tried to run. But another hand grabbed his arm.

"Arnold! It's me, Mr. Wolff!"

"Mr. Wolff! Thank God. How did you get here? Where are we? How do we get out?"

"Just follow me, Arnold. Don't worry, I won't let go of your hand." Arnold couldn't see anything but Mr. Wolff's sleeve. He had his usual herringbone sport jacket on. "Try not to listen to any sounds you might hear," the teacher said as they started to walk.

Someone or something made a terrible scream right by Arnold's ear. Voices snarled and there was a wet sound like a knife slicing into a Thanksgiving turkey.

What if Jo's in danger? I can't just leave her! "Mr. Wolff, I ran here after a friend of mine—"

"Just follow me and worry about yourself for now, Arnold," Mr. Wolff said sharply.

Arnold nodded, then realized how stupid that was, when Mr. Wolff wasn't looking at him. He started watching the ground carefully but could see no change as they walked, or rather jogged along. It was all gravel and dust. The terrifying noises continued all around, bellows of rage and fear, shrieks that might have been made by Jo or another girl, voices crying and pleading until they were suddenly cut off.

A roar sounded in Arnold's right ear and he flinched and almost let go of Mr. Wolff's hand, which seemed to be changing in his grip. Instead of skin he felt thick hair, or fur. He began to scream, but couldn't hear himself over a snarl like a furious dog's. The roaring on Arnold's right turned to yelps, and he couldn't help it, he let go of Mr. Wolff's hand, which had turned into a wolf's paw, and fell to his hands and knees, gasping as his forehead hit something that felt like splintery wood.

When he sat up he found that he could see the back door to Gloria's book shop in Gingo Teag. *Except that she always shows up to help me over the dimensional threshold—so what do I do—*

He gasped again as something hit his side hard and the world turned inside out. Staggering to his feet he saw Gloria and Mr. Wolff standing there staring at each other, in the back of the store among the impossible Beatles albums and the unknown books by famous authors.

"You," Mr. Wolff said after a long pause.

"You," said Gloria, her arms folded.

"Um, don't you know each other?" Arnold said. "You do work in the same school. Mr. Wolff, this is—"

Gloria snorted. "'Mr. Wolff,' is it? The name suits you."

"—Gloria, and she—"

"So that's what you're calling yourself now?" Mr. Wolff said. "You always were vain, but this is ridiculous."

"…I guess you do know each other," said Arnold, who was starting to wonder if he'd be safer back on the darkling plain. Or facing Jo's wrath.

Mr. Wolff took his hands from behind his back—his large, hairy hands, Arnold noticed as if for the first time—and began examining the contents of the bookshelves. "Same taste as you always had, I see."

"Oh, and I suppose your shelves are full of military histories? 'Then General Grant attempted to outflank the Confederates.' So dry and analytical! You don't see all the pain and suffering and blood and mangled limbs that way, do you?"

Mr. Wolff turned around and winked at Arnold. "My students do get a good bit of guts 'n glory. Isn't that so, Arnold?"

"He told me about Thomas Jefferson saying the tree of liberty needs to be watered with the blood of patriots," Arnold said. "It's really not so different from how that plant you gave me needs to drink milk, is it?"

"So that's your game now, is it?" Gloria snapped. "Encouraging children to enlist? Teaching them the old lie, that it is sweet and fitting to die for one's country? How about living for it?"

"I only encourage them to think for themselves, and I give them a few plays and poems to help them along. I should think that is something you'd approve of."

Gloria clenched her fists. For a moment Arnold thought she was going to hit Mr. Wolff, even though he was at least thirty centimeters taller and twenty kilos heavier than her.

"You're feeding them war propaganda and making them think they thought it up themselves. That's—that's *dastardly*."

Mr. Wolff smiled. "Ah, but my dear 'Gloria,' aren't you doing the very same thing?" He picked up the Mark Twain book, which Arnold had finished and returned. "*Letters to a Woman Sitting in Darkness*? This book doesn't belong in this world, my dear. You are corrupting the minds of the youth."

Gloria scowled. "Like Socrates, and like you. Have you no sense of decency at long last?"

"No more than any senator or king you admire, my dear."

"Decency is an evil word," Arnold interrupted. Gloria and Mr. Wolff both turned to look at him. He blinked, but said louder, "It's an evil word! The Society for Common Decency stands for the exact opposite of what it says it does."

"That's called hypocrisy, Arnold," Gloria said in a gentler tone. "Pretending to a virtue one doesn't possess. Just because SCOD abuses the word decency doesn't mean that decency isn't a real virtue."

"If we're speaking of hypocrisy, my dear," Mr. Wolff said, "what do you call your actions? You show up uninvited in Arnold's world with your hippie skirts and your books about peace and free love, and you try to plant the seeds of rebellion just as much as I do! Only you think you can water them with milk—" he spat the word "—and not blood! That has never worked, and it never will. Not among humans and not among echinodermoids."

"What about Gandhi? What about Martin Luther King, Jr.?"

"What about them? Dead of assassins' bullets sooner or later, in all the worlds I know of. And more than willing to see their own followers' blood shed while they lived, the better to make their oppressors look bad." Mr. Wolff smiled, showing all his teeth. "I see you have no answer to that one."

"An eye for an eye leaves the whole world blind," Gloria said, quoting Dr. King.

"Is it better to let the echinodermoids put out all the humans' eyes? Because you know that's what they always do in every world where they slime their way to power."

"I know no such thing. I believe in free will."

"So do I. The free will of the oppressed to fight their oppression." Mr. Wolff smiled again. "You and I are really on the same side. Admit it at last."

"Never," Gloria said quietly. "I won't be part of your revolution of blood. What begins in blood always ends in blood. The means you use shape the ends you achieve. I've got shelves full of books from every world that prove this truth—in France, Haiti, Russia, China, Iran, the ONUG—"

"What's the ONUG?" Arnold interrupted.

"One Nation, Under God," Gloria said with a shudder. "You don't want to know, trust me you don't, Arnold."

"It's America in another world," Mr. Wolff explained, "with the 'God' in question bearing a striking resemblance to a certain Huey Long. She's trying to change the subject. To will the ends while being squeamish about the ends isn't virtue. It's hypocrisy. What do you think, Arnold?"

Arnold jumped. "Me? I, I don't know what to think. I just want to go find Jo."

"That's not such a good idea tonight, Arnold," Gloria said.

"On that," Mr. Wolff said drily, "we are agreed."

* * * *

Eleven o'clock at night had come and gone and Jo was still lying face down on her bed, the same position she had flung herself in when she burst in the door five hours ago. There was a timid knock.

"Jo? May I come in?"

"It's your house, Dad," Jo said, her voice muffled by the pillow. Dad always made everything all right for her. But not now. No one could do that now.

She heard his footsteps as he approached her, his feet making the wooden floor squeak in the same spot they always did. She heard him put something down on her bedside chest of drawers with a soft clatter, followed by a light touch on her shoulder.

"I brought you up some dinner," he said. "Mum made your favorite, devilled kidneys."

"That's breakfast food, Dad," Jo said, not turning her head. Mum was a stickler for everything at its proper time.

"She said she'd make an exception tonight." She could hear the little smile in his voice, but it couldn't reach the empty place inside her. He touched her shoulder again. "Want to talk about it?"

"No, Dad."

"It's something to do with that boy Arnold, isn't it?" Jo made no response. "I should like to have words with that little bounder!" Dad said.

Now Jo did smile, a little. "I'm sure you would, Dad. But it's all right. I don't care about him."

"He has made you cry. That's all I need to know."

"I don't care, Dad."

The silence stretched out. "I have to go to bed now, sweetheart. But if you want to talk, you can come wake me up. Mum won't mind, either."

"Thank her for me, Dad. But you can take the food back to the kitchen. I'm not hungry."

A final touch on the shoulder. "A week from now you'll have forgotten all about him, sugar."

No I won't, she thought, listening to his footsteps going away and the door shutting quietly. She waited a minute or two to be sure Mum wouldn't follow him in to try to cheer her up. Then she sat up in bed. Her face felt dried-out and sore, and the devilled kidneys, which Dad had left behind with a glass of milk, were mighty tempting. But she only took a small sip of milk to wet her parched throat.

A clear, cold night like this was also a good time to tune in to the thoughts of Ir'befunzu and her kids. The mama dragon was sleeping, but Ir'gassaphet, the boy who had dropped poor Alison in the ocean, was chattering with his sister Ir'klugg, the "smart one" of the family. What they were "saying" mostly didn't come across in words but in pictures in her mind. She saw bluefish and the oily mess they made when you chomped down on them, which Ir'gassaphet hated and Ir'klugg loved. She saw a puffy white cloud they had raced each other to reach earlier that day, until Mama called them back with their goal still far away.

Hi guys, Jo called.

There was a moment of confusion until they both called back in their brassy green voices, *HI, JO!*

Hey, Ir'gassaphet. Remember when you scooped up that human girl from the beach? It was fun, wasn't it?

There was a long pause. *NO FORGET! MY BEAK'S STILL GROW-ING BACK COZ MAMA MELTED IT!* Ir'befunzu was a good mother, but dragon discipline was notoriously rough.

But what if you had a chance to do it again, without hurting the human too much and without Mama knowing? I mean, Alison made a nice loud splash when she fell in the water, didn't she?

YOU GOING TO GET GASSAPHEE IN BIIIIG TROUBLE, Ir'klugg accused.

No I won't, honest! There's no way Mama will find out. I have a plan...

25

Arnold spent a lot of time in the days that followed thinking about Mr. Wolff's question, but he couldn't decide what he believed. It was clear to him that Palermo Teresa would have sided with Mr. Wolff in his great debate with Gloria. Like everyone except Mr. Wolff, she liked Gloria, but she would have sneered at the idea that you could fight an empire with nothing more than words. Words were necessary, sure—that's why she had built her own printing press—but only to rally "the people" to fight for their freedom.

Gloria and Mr. Wolff both believed in freedom, which they had called "free will"—at least they said they did. But they clearly hated each other, too. That was confusing. If you wanted the same thing, you had to be on the same side, didn't you? Well, maybe not—the League and the Front sure hated each other, even though they both wanted to get rid of the High Ones. Dad had once said that if they'd ever been able to agree between themselves, and stopped hurting innocent people, the High Ones wouldn't have stood a chance.

Gloria and Mr. Wolff were just as bad. Each insisted the other was completely wrong and Arnold shouldn't listen to anything the other one said. But he could see, too, that they were contradicting themselves about "free will."

For Mr. Wolff, the High Ones had no free will—they would sooner or later turn on the human race and try to kill everybody, like they were doing in Parallel Hailee's ruined world. That was just the way they were. For Gloria, any revolution that involved killing people was bound to fail. But that wasn't free will either, that was—whatever the opposite of free will was.

Arnold asked Dad, who said the word he wanted was *determinism*—the idea that everything that happened had to happen that way, as if someone or something had determined it in advance. But that idea just confused Arnold more. If there were all these parallel worlds side by side, so that anything you could imagine happening, and some things you couldn't, had really taken place somewhere, neither free will nor determinism meant anything, did it?

"I'm not a philosopher, Arnold, so I can't answer all these questions for you," Mr. Wolff said after class one day. Everyone else was at lunch, their happy chattering voices drifting in the open windows along with the smell of fresh-cut grass on a cool early spring breeze. Mr. Wolff made a face. "All philosophers do is argue with each other, anyway. You know what I think about Gloria's cowardice, but you have to make up your own mind. We're for freedom, and that means the freedom, and the responsibility, to think for yourself."

Arnold bit his lip to keep the tears back. Why did everything have to be so hard?

"I've got good news, by the way," Mr. Wolff said, lowering his voice and winking slowly. "I've made contact with some friends from out of town about the *extra credit project* we talked about. It's like that other *project* you did with Matt and Jared."

Mr. Wolff had told Arnold they were going to have to start speaking in code if they were talking about "missions" in school, to mislead anyone who might be listening. But he hadn't given him a code book—it seemed the teacher expected him to make it up as he went along.

"The art project, you mean? The, the one that involved Asian culture?"

"Yes, exactly. That was a fantastic job you three did," Mr. Wolff said with another slow wink, and a warm glow spread through Arnold's stomach.

He'd been right in scaring James away, then! If Mr. Wolff thought that was good, he'd surely approve of stealing the ditto machine, too. It obviously wasn't safe to ask his advice about that here and now, so how could he get Mr. Wolff to come talk to him outside of class?

Inspiration came to him so suddenly Arnold couldn't understand why it hadn't occurred to him during all those long weeks when he and Jo and Matt and Jared were trying to come up with a plan. *Well, I wanted Mr. Wolff to be proud of us—proud of me. But I'm really stuck, now that Jo's dropped out.* "I'm so busy with my homework during the week, Mr. Wolff, is there any way you could come talk to me about the new extra credit project at my house this weekend? I have some ideas of my own about it."

Mr. Wolff frowned. "That's great, Arnold, but I think you should wait for my out-of-town friends…" He trailed off as Arnold frantically winked first one eye and then the other. Then he smiled. "I guess I could make an exception this once. But how about tonight instead? Say eight o'clock?"

Arnold told Mr. Wolff his address. Then he ran off to the cafeteria, arriving less than ten minutes before lunch ended. Everyone else was almost done eating, except Gus, who was getting a second helping of apple cobbler and another carton of milk.

"Sorry guys," Arnold panted at Matt and Jared, "I was just talking with Mr. Wolff about, you know, our special project." He tried to wink slowly, like Mr. Wolff had done.

Jared said, "What's the matter with you, spaz? We're not dumbasses, we know what you're talking about."

"Yeah. Well, he's coming by my house at eight o'clock tonight to help us plan that thing, you know, that we're doing for that project."

"I don't think I can make it," Matt said. "My dad expects me to help him wash the car."

"At night?" Arnold said.

"Yeah, and I'm going surf fishing on Assateague with my Uncle Fred," Jared said, turning it into a sneer. "We're catching blind cave fish."

Anger ran through Arnold's guts like electricity. "All right, you guys. I'm going to ask someone who will help. Hey, Gus."

The bigger boy was just sitting back down with his tray. The others stiffened, and Matt gave Arnold the evil eye.

"I need your help for a project," Arnold said to Gus. "It's something really cool I've been working on with Matt and Jared."

"I knew you guys were up to something," Gus said amiably as he swallowed almost half his hamburger in a single bite.

The bell rang, and Arnold looked quickly around the emptying cafeteria. "Can you come by my house at eight o'clock tonight?"

"Sure, no problem." Gus devoured the rest of the hamburger and said around the mouthful of food, "I wondered when you guys were going to let me join the Resistance."

Jared fell off the bench, scattering the remains of his lunch across the floor. Everyone still in the cafeteria slow-clapped and whistled, including a wide-eyed, slack-jawed Matt.

When Arnold caught up with Kayleigh just before last period and asked her to come that night for "a meeting of that group you wanted to join" at his house, she was so thrilled she dropped her books on the floor and hugged him.

"You won't regret letting me join, Arnold!" she said. "I can help out with, well, with everything! I used to be in Girl Scouts, I know lots of great wilderness lore! I can tie knots even better than my big brother Kyle!"

"I don't think we'll need any of that," Arnold said. "And, er, it's not actually my decision whether you can, umm, officially join. I'm not really the head of the group."

"That's okay, Arnold. Just so they give me a chance!"

"I'll ask," Arnold promised. "But what about this big brother? You never mentioned him before."

Her face darkened. "Nobody takes me seriously at home," she said. "All they care about is him. It's all Kyle this, Kyle that. Kyle is on the construction crew at the new Martian settlement in Elysium Planitia. The name of the place is another word for heaven, but actually it's an area of ancient extinct volcanoes with nothing but rust-red rocks and dirt everywhere, and you need to carry an oxygen mask outside just to breathe, so he's always in extreme danger, or anyway Mom and Dad act like he is, like he might die any day. He's out there on a two-year contract. Somehow he finds enough time to talk to Mom and Dad for, like, an hour every night, and they hang on every word. I could come home with all A's on my report card and they'd barely notice." She sighed and smiled. "What I'm trying to say is, thanks for taking me seriously. If I join the Resistance, Mom and Dad will *have* to pay attention to me."

But for a long moment that night it looked like Mr. Wolff wasn't going to let her. His eyes narrowed when Arnold opened the door for him and he saw Kayleigh and Gus in the Grossbards' living room, instead of Matt and Jared.

Arnold's mom was there too. "Hi, I'm Rachel Grossbard," she said, extending her hand.

Mr. Wolff put on a smile. "Gibur Wolff," he said, enfolding Mom's small white hand in his large hairy one. "Your son is a great student, Mrs. Grossbard."

"I know. We're very proud of him," said Mom, ruffling Arnold's hair. His ears burned as everyone chuckled.

"Mo-om! You're embarrassing me!"

"That's the natural function of a teenager's parents, isn't it, Gibur?" she said with a wink. "Well, I'll go do some shopping and leave you in peace. My husband's out playing poker with his friend Bruce, and Alison is doing homework at her friend Shaniqua's house, so you won't have any distractions. I think it's just great you're going the extra mile with Arnold and his friends, Gibur."

"Happy to do it," Mr. Wolff smiled, adding when Mom had shut the back door behind her, "especially considering you two kids aren't in my class *or* our group."

"Kayleigh and Gus are okay, Mr. Wolff," Arnold said, talking loud and fast. "It's Matt and Jared who are a problem. All those two want to do is beat people up."

"We have to do that sometimes, Arnold," Mr. Wolff said, but his eyes were on Gus and Kayleigh. They were both frowning seriously. "You know what you're getting into, all of you?" said Mr. Wolff. "This isn't hide-and-seek. This is a war. You can get hurt."

"I hate the High Ones," Kayleigh growled. "They've ruined my dad's life. I'd like to ruin theirs."

Mr. Wolff stared at her unblinkingly for a long moment, then nodded and said to Gus, "And you, son?"

"My dad owns a tour boat company," the bigger boy said mildly. "He's actually had High Ones go out with him to study the wildlife in the bays. If anything, his business is going to suffer. But I don't think a bunch of starfish from space should be telling us how to run things."

Mr. Wolff held his gaze in turn, then nodded and said, "All right. First order of business is these." He reached into his briefcase and pulled out four copies of a paperback book. Arnold peered at the cover in surprise. It was *For Whom the Bell Tolls*, by Ernest Hemingway. Kayleigh and Gus looked equally puzzled.

"In case anyone walks in on us," Mr. Wolff said impatiently. He turned to Arnold. "All right, son. You said you had an idea for an operation. I like your initiative, but what is it exactly you propose?"

Arnold took a deep breath and told him, watching carefully for any change in the English teacher's expression. His biggest fear was that he'd say it was a dumb idea.

Instead, Mr. Wolff nodded thoughtfully. "It could work. It could actually work," he said, rubbing his stubbly chin. "But who, now, did you say wrote that pamphlet for you?"

Suddenly Arnold couldn't meet his teacher's gaze. "Her name is Teresa," he mumbled. *How am I going to explain that Gloria brought her here from Gingo Teag?*

"May I see what she wrote?"

Arnold gulped as he handed over the typewritten page. Mr. Wolff's forehead creased as he read it. "This doesn't sound like something a high school student would write," he said, "and I don't think there are any Teresas in Chincoteague High at the moment."

"Well, she's not from Chincoteague. She's from Sicily," Arnold said. Mr. Wolff's eyes bored into him. He broke into a cold sweat and began to babble, giving away everything about Jo and Teresa, the strange British America they came from, and the secret entrance to it through Gloria's library. "Though I guess you know about that, I mean, you were there and everything." There was a long pause after he finished. "Well? Aren't you going to say something?"

But it was Gus who said something first. "A whole other world? One where there aren't any High Ones?"

Then it was Kayleigh's turn. "Who's this Teresa and this Jo, again?"

She might have been Arnold's first girlfriend, but thanks to his older sister he knew trouble when he heard it in a girl's voice. "B-but I just told you about them, I—the thing is, the thing is—"

"Yes? What's the thing, Arnold?"

"Well Teresa's, like, old, and Jo said no disgusting snogging when she set up the Freedom Fighters of Earth with me, and Mr. Wolff, what's so funny?"

The English teacher was holding his sides, bellowing. "Oh, that's a good one," he huffed while everyone stared at him. "That's a hot one! That namby-pamby, shrinking violet of a Gloria brings two Valkyries into her nonviolent revolution! Ha!"

"What are Valkyries?" asked Kayleigh, who was still eyeing Arnold distrustfully.

"Tough goddesses," Arnold said, "though Jo and Teresa are really just plain tough."

Kayleigh bunched her fists. "Well I can be just as tough as them! If we're ever going to do anything more than just sit around talking, that is!"

Mr. Wolff stopped laughing and nodded at her. "You're quite right, Kayleigh. Let's get down to brass tacks. It's no problem, using the ditto machine."

"It isn't?" said Arnold. "But Jo and I have been talking it over for weeks and we haven't figured out a way to steal it."

Mr. Wolff slapped him on the knee hard enough to sting. "I'm a teacher, remember, Arnold? I can go in there and use the machine any time I want."

"Oh." Arnold should have been excited, but he felt like an idiot instead. "But don't you have to get Mr. Wright's permission first? And doesn't he stand there and watch you?"

"Nobody watches while a teacher is running off a boring handout, Arnold. In fact Mr. Wright grumbles all the time about the noise and goes to sit in his secretary's office. But just to be safe, I'll run off a real class assignment first for camouflage. So don't worry about me. I'll have the whole thing done by the end of the day tomorrow, and I'll bring them over here in a box tomorrow night. You kids can fold them and stick them under people's doors over the weekend." He glanced at Teresa's text and chuckled a little. "Of course, your friend's work can use a little editing. The language is a bit too flowery for Chincoteague."

"Hey," Gus and Kayleigh said at the same time. They were both "from-heres."

Mr. Wolff held up a placating hand. "I don't mean that the words are too hard for people here to understand. I just mean they'd laugh at some of Teresa's turns of phrase. 'The precious seat of love and art,' indeed. You have to know your audience."

Just then Arnold heard a key turning in the front door. Everybody stiffened, even Mr. Wolff, but it was only Alison. When she saw Mr. Wolff, Gus, and Kayleigh sitting with Arnold, her eyes darted around and she blinked.

Arnold stared back at her. Jo had told him she had made Alison a member of the FFE, but he didn't trust her. "Something you need help with, Sis?"

Mr. Wolff stood up, his back to her. "Good work, kids," he said, "I think you're finally grasping the themes of *For Whom The Bell Tolls*."

"Thanks, Mr. Wolff," said Gus, standing up. "I think I'm really starting to get the importance of ol' Ernest."

"That's really wild, as you kids would say," Mr. Wolff grinned. "All right then, kids. I'll expect outlines on my desk Monday morning."

"You brought your girlfriend and some other guy from your class here for an extra credit English project?" Alison exclaimed. "You're even weirder than I thought, Arnold."

"Ask not for whom the bell tolls," Arnold growled, "it's for you, Sis."

"Listen, turd-breath…"

"Can I talk to you outside for a second, Arnold? Alone?" Kayleigh said.

"Thanks for having me over, Arnold, but I think I'd better be getting home," Gus said, clapping him on the arm. "Good luck with the girls. You're gonna need it," he added in a whisper.

26

In English class the next day, Mr. Wolff handed back a vocabulary quiz. For the word "insidious," Arnold had written the sentence, "The terrorists made <u>insidious</u> plans for attack."

There was a red checkmark beside this, and Mr. Wolff had written, "Bravo, defender of the Cosmic Harmony! The materials for your extra credit project are ready. I will drop them off at your house tonight." He tried to catch Mr. Wolff's eye and give him a wink, but the teacher had his back to him.

Arnold decided to give Matt and Jared one last chance to participate in *Operation Volantini*. But when he got to the lunch table, only Gus and Kayleigh were there. He motioned toward them and they leaned over as he whispered, "Mr. Wolff has got the pamphlets ready for us. Let's meet in the Value-Mart parking lot at midnight Saturday to hand them out."

Gus frowned. "Pardon me, Arnold, but that's sort of dumb. The Value-Mart keeps those bright orange lights on all night. They're so strong you could read your pamphlets by 'em."

"So, what's wrong with that?" Arnold said. "We have to see where we're going, don't we?"

"Yeah, but we don't want anyone to see *us*." Gus bit his lip, trying not to laugh.

Arnold appreciated that Gus was being considerate, but he burned with embarrassment anyway. "All right then, smart guy, where *should* we meet?"

"Easy, Arnold. How about the marsh behind the trailer park?"

"Nobody goes back there! Those guys throw all their trash in the reeds!"

"Exactly."

Kayleigh wrinkled her nose as if she could smell the ruined marsh from here, but when Arnold reluctantly agreed to the idea she went along with him.

"Motion carries unanimously, then," Arnold said.

"Motion?" Jared said, slouching up to the table. "You mean a bowel movement? You crap your pants, Gross-fart?"

"I thought we were beyond all that," Arnold said, clenching his fists under the table.

"I thought we were beyond all that," Jared mimicked. "Fancy-pants little yid, barging in thinking he can boss everyone else around!"

Were the people around them really lowering their voices, or was it just that the blood was roaring in Arnold's ears? "I didn't notice you or Matt coming up with any ideas for *our project*, Jared," Arnold said evenly. "Or doing anything to help. Where is he, anyway?"

"He has lunchtime detention, because someone snitched on him for spray-painting graffiti," Jared said, looking Arnold straight in the eye.

Arnold darted his eyes from side to side, trying to see if the teacher on lunch duty was around. Miss Kelley was known to duck out on it—rumor had it someone had seen her kissing Mr. Wright, though the details were vague. At any rate, there didn't seem to be any sign of her. He could have it out with Jared once and for all.

"Shifty-eyed little Jewboy," Jared was sneering, "I knew all along we couldn't trust—"

Arnold was on his feet trying to gut-punch him before he could finish the sentence. But Jared dodged and the blow glanced off his arm. Breathing heavily, he swung for Arnold's face, and though Arnold turned aside his nose suddenly exploded with pain, and blood began running from it. That just made Arnold madder, and he started whaling away on Jared with both fists. But the blows didn't seem to touch Jared, and he fetched Arnold a punch on the side of the head that left his ears ringing.

Through the hum he could hear all the kids in the cafeteria chanting, "Fight! Fight! Fight!" In a blur of rage Arnold fought back. Fought back for every time since nursery school that some kid had called him a nerd, or a geek, or a weirdo, or a little Jewboy, or a teacher's pet, or a sissy, or a brainiac. He was being shoved backward, he was falling, his head hit the floor and he saw stars, but still he fought, still he clawed at Jared's face and bloodied his nose and screamed, "You're the traitor, you're the snitch, it's you itsyouitsyou" until a fist slammed into his mouth and he tasted more blood, and finally the gym teacher Mr. Lynch was pulling Jared away, and someone else was lifting Arnold to his feet and marching him out the door, it was Mr. Wright and he was shouting he was going to expel him, he wasn't going to let him get away with it this time, and whether he meant Jared or Arnold or both of them, *Arnold didn't care*, because he had fought back for once in life, fought back and Jared's face was all bruised and bleeding and his right eye was swelling up to prove it.

"Hey, Jared," Arnold said, or tried to say. There was something in the way of his tongue. He spat it out on Jared's left sneaker and saw it was a tooth. "Gift for you," he said. "Put it under your pillow, maybe the tooth fairy will bring you some brains."

Jared lunged for him and was pulled away, and Mr. Wright yanked Arnold's arm painfully up behind his back and hurried him on ahead. "That'll be enough out of you, young man," he panted.

Arnold bent his head far enough around to see that the principal was sweating, the armpits of his white collared shirt were drenched, and his cheeks were flushed. Also there was a strange little smudge of scarlet to the left of his mouth, as if *he* was the one who had been in a fistfight. A wild tide was rising from Arnold's gut up to his neck until it flooded his head and he could barely see through the pulsing red glee. *He had fought back. Nothing else mattered.*

Even though Mr. Wright called Dad at work and made him come get him, Arnold was still on top of the world when Mr. Wolff stopped by the house that night with the box full of pamphlets.

"I didn't have time to fold these," he said apologetically as he handed the box to Arnold. "I'm afraid you'll have to do it."

"That's okay," said Arnold.

"This must be some extra-credit project. Mind if I have a look?" said Mom, who was standing behind him in the living room. She was dressed in her fancy work clothes, a crisp white blouse and a dark skirt—she had started working as a paralegal, what she called "a not-very-glorified secretary" to Greg Allen, a criminal defense lawyer in Salisbury, Maryland, eighty kilometers north. The commute took her over an hour each way, the days were unpredictable long, and she came home exhausted, but not too tired to complain about how she spent half her time waiting around the courthouse for some magistrate to grant a writ of habeas corpus, which was lawyer-speak for confirming that the police had a suspect in jail. Under the Bicentennial Constitution they didn't have to do that unless the guy was accused of murder or something almost as bad.

Arnold's heart stopped for a moment at Mom's request, but then he remembered about Mr. Wolff's clever camouflage. "Sure thing, Mom," he said, and handed her a sheet of questions on *For Whom The Bell Tolls*.

"Wow," Mom said as she looked it over. "The Spanish Civil War, huh? Sometimes we forget just how screwed up the world was before the High Ones came."

Mr. Wolff caught Arnold's eye and shook his head slightly. He obviously meant Arnold shouldn't start arguing with Mom, but it was very tempting.

"I'm afraid I have to be running along now, Mrs. Grossbard. Nice seeing you," said the teacher.

Mom waved goodbye absently and handed the fake sheet back to Arnold. "This is good stuff, Arnold. I just wish you'd concentrate on school and not get into fights all the time."

"Turd-breath got in another fight today? So that explains why his face is an even bigger mess than usual," Alison said. She had come straight from the kitchen holding a wooden spoon in her hand. Since Mom had gone back to work, Alison had had to take over the cooking again.

Arnold smirked at her. "You should see the other guy."

"That's enough from both of you," Mom said. "Arnold, I don't understand how you go from fistfights to extra-credit projects, all in the same day."

"That's no extra-credit project, is it?" Alison whispered after Mom took the spoon from her and said she was going to check on the ravioli so they didn't stick.

"None of your business."

Alison grabbed his arm and shook it. "It's those pamphlets, isn't it? You morons are actually serious about this!"

Before he could answer, Mom called from the kitchen, "Good job, Alison! Supper's almost ready!"

"Okay, Mom," Alison called back. "I just want to pay Arnold back for some change he gave me." She dragged him upstairs to her room and shut the door before letting go of his arm. "Well?" she snapped.

"Of course we're serious," Arnold said, rubbing his shoulder. "I thought you were too, until you went and told Dad on me."

Alison's shoulders slumped. "The truth is, I was hoping you weren't serious. That it was all a bunch of big talk between you and those so-called friends of yours. And that you'd think Palermo Teresa's idea was way too much work. But I've got to give you credit: you meant it."

"But why were you hoping we were all talk?" Arnold asked. "So you could make fun of me when nothing happened?"

"No. It's because I'm afraid," Alison said. Arnold stared, expecting Sis to crack up any second, but she didn't smile. "That's why I told Dad—I hoped he or Mom would stop you. But Dad's actually encouraging you! I don't understand it."

"What are you afraid of? That we'll get caught?" Arnold's chest swelled. "No Resistance fighter fears getting caught. We will die with honor to defeat the High Ones!"

"Are you kidding me? You cry like a baby when you get a little paper cut." Arnold scowled and tried to shove Alison out of the way, but she stood her ground. "Sorry. Look, if you're going to do this thing, you'd better let me help you so you don't do anything really dumb."

"Thanks for your confidence in me," Arnold said sarcastically. "If you really wanna help, you can fold them with me after dinner. Unless you've got a date, that is."

Alison glared at him, but nodded her agreement. They both went to his room to get the job done immediately after supper, but not before Alison complained about the revised text of the pamphlet.

"This sounds like a kid wrote it," she said softly as she peered at a purple-printed, pickle-smelling page.

"It was Mr. Wolff, and he's an English teacher, zit-face," Arnold snapped. But he couldn't help seeing what she meant:

```
People of Earth!
    The Day of Revolution is dawning! Stop do-
ing what the Slugs tell you to! Their n-network
melts your brains! But their tyranny is about to
end! So rise up and fight for the human race—if
you know what's good for you!
    We are everywhere, and we will win!
    Human  Defense  League—Freedom  Fighters  of
Earth
```

"Mr. Wolff must have a really low opinion of people's intelligence," Alison said, blocking Arnold's attempt to punch her in the arm. Again, she was probably right—after all, Mr. Wolff wasn't really human—but he would be damned if he'd admit as much.

They sat folding the pamphlets in a freezing silence, though their eyes met once—when they heard Dad, talking softly to Mom down in the living room, say, "At least one good thing has come out of all this— the kids are getting along. It's so nice of Alison to help Arnold with his schoolwork."

"But that fighting," Mom said. "It really worries me, Jerry."

27

The fist fight with Jared really impressed Gus, though. There was solemn respect in his eyes, which were lit from below by a sturdy black flashlight, the kind you could whack someone over the head but good with, as they stood among the two meter high cat-tail reeds on Saturday night.

"It's all anyone can talk about at school, man," Gus said. "Are they really gonna expel you?"

Arnold shrugged. "Beats me. Mr. Wright was talking with my dad for, like, an *hour* in his office with the door shut. There was a lot of yelling. My dad came outta there so mad—I've never seen him so angry, not even when he lost his job back in Baltimore. He said I have to go to the school administration office for a juvie hearing next Friday, and I'm *definitely* suspended till then."

"A juvie hearing, huh?" Gus shook his head. "Good luck with that. My older brother Kevin, he had one of those after he set fire to the trash can in the boy's room, which was only an accident 'cause he was throwing away a lit cigarette, but they didn't let him come back the whole rest of the year. He had to repeat tenth grade."

If that was the worst that could happen to him, Arnold reflected, maybe it wasn't so bad. There would be so many potential recruits for the FFE in juvie, he'd probably come out of it at the head of an army! And repeating a year of school when all the classes were too easy for him anyway would mean he'd have even more free time for the Resistance.

"You have a juvie hearing? Oh, Arnold!" Kayleigh said from behind him. "My dad gave me the belt the one time that happened to me. I couldn't sit down for a week!"

Arnold hoped the darkness had hidden how high he'd jumped. But it was a relief that she'd come. He'd been worried she would chicken out, or her parents wouldn't let her out of the house.

"Okay then, should we start dividing up the streets?" Gus said, shining his flashlight on a town map.

"We have to wait for my sister. She has all the pamphlets. I made her fold them," Arnold lied.

"You didn't 'make me' do anything, twerp." This time there was no hiding the fact that he'd jumped, because he tripped and went down on one knee in the marsh mud. At least he didn't fall flat on his face. "Nice going," she said. "Yeah, I brought all nine hundred of the pamphlets. Should be enough for every house in town."

"I think we should skip the trailer park," Kayleigh said, glancing through the trees. A dog had started barking over there, and three other dogs joined it.

"It's all right. I'll do the trailer park," Arnold said, wishing as he said the words that there was some way to take them back.

"Good idea! I'm sure there are lots of people just itching to join the Resistance there," Alison said.

Are you trying to get me killed, Sis? You always saw the most posters of the High Satrap in the trailer park. THE SILENT MAJORITY, they said. But if he backed out now, he'd look like a sissy.

Gus took charge of dividing up the rest of the island, and Alison handed tied-together stacks of pamphlets to everyone. They might have been newspaper circulars in the darkness, and Alison said that's what everyone should say they were, if anyone asked.

"We folded 'em so they won't see what's really inside till they open it."

"Can I read one first? I don't even know what it says since Mr. Wolff rewrote it," Kayleigh said.

"Me, either," Gus said. He held one up to the light, and after a moment said, "Wow. That's pretty strong."

"Yeah. I sure hope we don't get caught," said Kayleigh. "I'll be in big enough trouble as it is if my parents realize I snuck out."

She shivered and Arnold put an arm around her, causing Alison to roll her eyes. She'd roll them even more if she knew how afraid he really was. It was the word "slugs" that seemed to leap off the page. A "slug," he suddenly remembered, also meant a lead bullet. Would they really just get sent to juvie if they were caught? Or would they be sent to a firing squad?

The death penalty wasn't used much anymore—they didn't need it, when they had SCOD holes—except that they did still shoot terrorists. Which was exactly what they were about to become.

Arnold swallowed hard and looked around at the others. Gus's mouth was clenched tight, and his jaw muscles stood out. Alison's face had gone blank—for once, he couldn't guess what Sis was thinking. Kayleigh's eyes were wide and her hands were shaking, and that was a relief because it gave him something to do. He took her left hand in his right, hoping he could stop his own trembling. Her palm was cold and damp.

"Everybody ready?" he said, looking into her eyes. She nodded, and so did Gus and Alison. "Good. When we're done, everyone just go home. It's too risky to meet out here again."

"Yes sir, commander," Alison said, her voice dripping with sarcasm.

For once, Arnold couldn't think up a snappy answer. He whispered to Kayleigh, "Meet me up on the new fishing pier, the one where the old bridge used to be, tomorrow afternoon?" She nodded silently. He brushed his lips against her cheek and walked quickly away through the trees, trying to outrun his fears. It didn't work. A voice in his head started rambling and wouldn't shut up as he approached the first run-down Airstream parked at the edge of the trailer lot.

It won't ever work it won't even matter no one will read the things they'll just think they're junk mail and throw them away we didn't even put anything in them about how to join up if someone was interested but the only ones who will be will be the cops they'll figure it out from fingerprints we should've worn gloves they'll send dogs after us I hate dogs especially big scary pit bulls like the one in that trailer it'll crash right through the door and rip my throat out better run better run fast no better not run they'll think I'm up to no good which I'm not better just stroll around like I'm enjoying the stinky air back here if they throw me in juvie everyone will pick on me worse than ever they'll beat me up beat me to death I'll never make it out of there

It seemed like every trailer in the first row he walked down had a huge dog inside, barking and snarling and throwing itself against the door. Arnold stopped walking up to the doors to drop the leaflets, instead sticking them hurriedly in the old-fashioned rural mailboxes out by the gravel road and walking away. The second row of trailers was dark and silent, but Arnold stuck to the mailboxes. The quiet gave him a chance to think. He still didn't understand why Jo got so mad when she saw him with Kayleigh, but it made him feel ashamed, like he should make it up to her, somehow, even though he also didn't think he'd done anything wrong. Why was this boy-girl stuff so complicated for him? Everyone else seemed to have it figured out.

"Hey, you! Boy! What are you doing out there?"

Arnold couldn't figure out where the voice was coming from. But he forced himself to breathe easy and not break into a run. "Advertising circulars for the Value-Mart, ma'am!"

"Old Man Hutchins is paying for circulars *and* offering discounts now? That's a good one! You tell him them peaches he got in last week was half-rotten!"

"I will, ma'am! Thank you!" Now he did hurry away, straight out of the trailer park, before that lady could get a good look at the pamphlet, or at him. He wondered if it had really been such a good idea to schedule *Operation Volantini* for Saturday night. Sure, Chincoteague didn't have much of a nightlife—Dad liked to say they rolled up the sidewalks early—but there were bound to be *some* people around, even though the late show at the Island Roxy got out around 11:30, which was an hour ago now.

The rest of his delivery route turned out to be a lot less exciting than the trailer park, especially since Arnold stuck to his method of putting the pamphlets in the sidewalk mailboxes for the houses that had them, which was most of them. It made him much more nervous to have to go up to people's front doors.

He was on his last street and had just started to hope that he'd finish the night without having to talk to anyone else when a police car came around the corner. Arnold shoved the remaining handful of pamphlets in his pockets and forced himself not to run *(they'll probably shoot me if I do)*, although he felt like a cockroach someone was about to step on when the side-mounted spotlight hit him.

The cop rolled down his window, leaned out and yelled, "Hey you! Kid!"

"Who, me?" Arnold said.

"Yeah, you! What are you doing wandering around this time of night?"

"I couldn't sleep." That had to be the stupidest answer ever, but Arnold couldn't think up a better one on the spur of the moment. *I really should have planned for this.*

The car glided slowly up alongside him, and the policeman blinked when he got a good look at Arnold's face. "Where are your parents, kid?"

"They're at home, asleep. I didn't want to wake them just 'cause I can't sleep."

"Such a good boy," the cop said, in a voice like knives. "Get in the car, I'll take you home."

(*run I should run for it if he searches my pockets I'm dead*) The world seemed to waver around Arnold, as if he was climbing the dimensional divide with Gloria. His feet wouldn't obey him.

The cop snorted, got out of the car and grabbed him by the arm. "Come on, kid. Let's go."

(*he's not holding me that hard run I should run*) But the cop was shoving him into the back of the patrol car, and then it was too late. In a daze Arnold watched the darkened houses start to move past the windows. Everything looked so different at night. He didn't think he'd ever been to this neighborhood before. And now he might never see the town again. Arnold thought desperately of escape but of course the back of the police car had no door handles.

He realized the cop had said something to him. "What?"

"What's your address, kid? I ain't running a taxi service here."

"Oh." Arnold told him. The cop made a left and Arnold recognized Maddox Boulevard. Less than five minutes later they pulled up outside the house. Arnold had to wait to be let out, then the cop took his hand and walked him up to the front door as if he was a little kid. His pounding on the door brought no reaction at first. Then he heard Mom saying something, and a muffled groan from Dad. A minute or so later he came down and opened the door, wearing his maroon-colored University of Chicago sweatsuit and looking confused. "Yes?"

"Sir, is this your son?"

Dad turned to look at Arnold, and his eyes went wide. "Yes, of course. Arnold? What are you doing outside this time of night?"

"That's exactly what I wanted to know, sir," said the cop.

Arnold turned and got a good look at him for the first time. The man was young and clean-shaven, with a buzz cut and pale blue eyes. The corners of his mouth were turned slightly down. His upper body was bulky under his blue uniform, and in a flash of hatred Arnold thought that if the cop were a few years younger he would be Matt and Jared's buddy. Fighting against "tyranny" was an abstract, bloodless idea, but if the cop hadn't had a gun Arnold would have liked to bloody his nose for him.

Instead he had to look down as if he was ashamed and mumble, "I was hanging out with some friends earlier and I was just too wound up to go back home and go to sleep, Dad."

The cop looked at him, one eyebrow raised, then turned and said to Dad, "I don't mean to tell you how to run your family, sir, but it's probably best if you give the boy a curfew. My older brother got into all sorts of deviltry before my dad told him he had to be home no later than ten o'clock on Saturday night and eight-thirty on school nights."

"Yes, of course. Good idea. It's just been so hard for us, being new in town and all," Dad said, grabbing Arnold's arm and hauling him inside. Mom was standing by the tri-vee stage, her arms folded over her nightgown, and on the stairs he caught a glimpse of someone's bare feet. Surely it couldn't be—?

Dad was thanking the policeman once again and shutting the door. The bare feet came down the stairs and turned out to be attached to Alison's legs, which were covered in her pink "Barbie" pajamas Arnold always liked to tease her about. But she was smirking as she came all the way down into the living room. She all but stuck her tongue out at him. *You got caught and I didn't, nyah-nyah!*

"Yeah, what 'deviltry' were you up to, Arnold?" she said innocently. "Not corrupting poor innocent Kayleigh, I hope!"

Arnold clenched his fists helplessly as Mom and Dad started in. How could he be so irresponsible, he was on the verge of getting expelled from school as it was, what about his future, blah blah blah.

Alison folded her arms and shook her head slowly back and forth. It was only when she actually said "tsk-tsk" that Dad sent her upstairs. "I don't need your help, young lady!"

"Stupid-head sure needs *some* kinda help," Alison said as she went away.

"Well?" Mom demanded when she was gone. "What do you have to say for yourself?"

"Yeah, what? I can't keep getting these calls at work that you're in trouble, Arnold," Dad said.

"Sorry. It won't happen again," Arnold mumbled, looking at the floor.

"It better not," Mom said. "I don't want you leaving this house at all, for anything, unless it's on fire, until after your disciplinary hearing!"

"But that's *days* away!"

"You should have thought of that before the stunt you just pulled, shouldn't you?" Dad said. Without waiting for an answer, he and Mom stomped up the stairs and slammed their bedroom door. Arnold collapsed on the couch, exhausted, and waited in the darkness until he heard Dad snoring before going upstairs himself.

He walked straight into Alison's room without knocking and whispered, "What's the big idea?"

"Whaddya mean?" she said. She was sitting up in bed reading—obviously she'd been expecting him. "And don't you even knock anymore before bursting in on people?"

"You—you—you better have delivered all your pamphlets!"

"Oh, yes sir, great leader! For your information, all three of us were finished, like, hours ago! What took you so long?"

Arnold sputtered.

"That's about what I thought," Alison said. "It's a shame all the terrorists aren't as dumb as you. If they were, all those kids at the Capitol would still be alive!"

"That wasn't the League! It was those Patriotic Front fascists!"

"As if *you* know anything about it. Or have any idea what a 'fascist' is. Go to bed now, before you get us in real trouble."

When I become a real Resistance leader, the first thing I'm gonna do is move as far away from Sis as possible, Arnold thought as he lay tossing and turning. Even reaching out to touch the waving leaves of Gloria's spider plant didn't give him any relief.

28

Jo had first found the weapon she would use to get revenge on Arnold on a quiet, late summer morning last year, months before she even met him. The weather was cool, with a light drizzle, obviously not a beach day, so Jo had come into Gloria's Gateway Books first thing when it opened and promptly settled herself in her favorite corner with a pile of books.

Of course, she'd been spending all of her free time there anyway ever since Gloria suddenly came to town back in June and opened the bookstore in an old house that had been abandoned and falling apart ever since the widow Collins died. Whenever Jo, Tom or Philadelphia Teresa asked her why she would close up her shop in the British capital of Philadelphia and move to a backwater like Gingo Teag, Gloria would just smile mysteriously.

Having the ability to mind-speak could be a nuisance, especially when a grumpy dragon interrupted you while you were trying to concentrate on some really hard maths in a book called *The Einstein-Penrose Grand Unified Theory: A Beginner's Text*, which claimed to have been published by the Institute for Advanced Studies at Princeton University, which didn't exist in Jo's world.

Still, the maths was really interesting and there was a cute overleaf photo of a young man with his arm around a stooped, grandfatherly figure with a bushy white mustache. Jo almost felt as if she knew them, though she'd never heard of anybody called Albert Einstein or Roger Penrose. Nevertheless, she was conducting a friendly mental discussion with them—*Oh! I see what you blokes are getting at. But I'm not sure your differential equations can give you the result you're after, in which case your "grand unified theory" doesn't really hold water*—

WHAT'S THAT ABOUT HOLDING WATER? a loud green voice said in her mind, dropping a large felled tree, as it were, across the tracks of her train of thought. I'VE BEEN OUT OVER THE OCEAN ALL DAY, DIVING INTO THE WAVES, BUT THE FISH JUST AREN'T RUNNING, AND MY DRAGONETS ARE HUNGRY!

I'm sorry, Ir'befunzu, but could you keep it down a little? I'm trying to concentrate—

YOU TRY TO CONCENTRATE WHEN YOU'VE HAD A DAY LIKE I HAVE! I'VE HAD TO FLY SO FAR, ALL SIX OF MY WINGS ARE ACHING FIT TO FALL OFF!

Wait a minute, what do you mean "all six wings"? I've only ever seen two! Where are the other four?

OH, I FORGOT. YOU HUMANS CAN ONLY SEE THE SET I USE IN YOUR FOUR-DIMENSIONAL WORLD. THERE ARE TWO MORE SETS I USE IN THE HIGHER DIMENSIONS. There was an interesting pause. YOU DO KNOW ABOUT THE HIGHER DIMENSIONS, DON'T YOU?

Of course I do! Gloria takes us through them every time we pass through the Gray Zone on the way to another world. Well, the few times she's taken me anywhere.

WELL, JOLLY GOOD FOR YOU, BUT IF YOU'LL EXCUSE ME I HAVE TO SEE TO THE DRAGONETS BEFORE IR'GASSAPHET SETS FIRE TO THE FOREST AGAIN.

Jo shook her head and pinched the bridge of her nose between her thumb and forefinger, trying to stop the headache she always got if she tried to mindspeak for too long. She didn't think she could concentrate any more on her mates Bertie and Rog, so she put the book down and wandered out into the bookshop's foyer, where a tea kettle was whistling.

Gloria smiled at her. "Like a cuppa, dear?"

"Yes, please, Gloria." Jo watched her fuss about with the little tea-cups and saucers—unlike her Mum, the bookshop owner never seemed to remember where she put anything, though considering the number of dimensions she had to deal in, perhaps that wasn't so surprising. Jo deftly caught a saucer just as it tipped over the edge of the counter and set it firmly back in place.

"Oh, thank you, love," Gloria sighed, doing her best British-American Imperial accent as she put down a teacup filled with mouthwateringly rich and dark liquid. "I don't know what I would have done if that one had gone smash. These are the last two in the set."

"You would have used a saucer from a set that didn't match. That's what you always do."

Like the time she'd absent-mindedly served tea on a commemorative set from the crowning of "Emperor Aaron IV of Mexico," which wasn't an empire in the history Jo had learned in school.

"Right as always, dear." She gave Jo a shy, sly smile. "Have you found the flaw in the Einstein-Penrose GUT yet?"

"How do you know it's flawed—oh, right, higher dimensions. I wanted to ask you about those, actually. Did you know that dragons can move among them as easily as you can?"

"Well, of course, dear," Gloria said, stirring the tea in her own cup and carefully putting the spoon down on the empty air about two inches from the edge of the counter.

She didn't seem to notice it clattering to the floor, but Jo winced. *What if she's that clumsy someday taking me between worlds? She could accidentally put me down in one where the atmosphere is poisonous!*

"How come you never mentioned it before?" Jo asked.

Gloria raised her thin orange eyebrows so far they disappeared under her feathery orange bangs. "It never seemed important. Why, did Ir'befunzu say something?"

"Only that all six of her wings are aching. How come they've got that ability? The natural philosophers say dragons are related to terradracos, right?" (Philadelphia Teresa called terradracos "dinosaurs," which Jo thought was an ugly word.)

"Only as much as you humans are related to those cute little mousy thingies that used to run around between the terradracos' feet." Gloria smiled as if she was personally acquainted with the mousy thingies. Maybe she was.

How old is she? Do I really want to know? Instead Jo asked, "So the terradracos also used to travel the higher dimensions—and went to other worlds?"

"You'd be surprised what some of those chaps could do, but no," Gloria said. "Ir'befunzu's distant ancestors gained the ability the good-old fashioned Darwinian way."

"Through natural selection?" Jo exclaimed. "How could going to higher dimensions help them survive?"

"Her."

"What?"

"Help her survive. There was only one *Quetzelcoatlus* who could do it, and her name was Ya'el."

Jo frowned. "I thought Quetzelcoatl was an Aztec god?"

Gloria beamed at her. "Exactly! That's why they named the largest of the winged terradracos after him. But not only was poor Ya'el the only one who could reach the higher dimensions, but she only found that out *in extremis*, as it were."

"Come again?"

"When she was in danger of her life, dear. When all the Earth was, because the Gray Ones had pushed that space-rock onto a collision course with the planet."

"The space-rock that killed the terradracos was *on purpose?*"

Gloria dropped her cup and saucer. They shattered on the floor as she clapped both hands over her mouth. Her green eyes went round and her face went pale as a cloud.

Jo noticed that her fingernails were painted all different colors. The contrast was jarring. But not as jarring as Gloria's obvious fear.

"I shouldn't have told you that," she whispered. "But it just slipped out, you see?" Jo was horrified to see tears filling Gloria's eyes. "To keep the secret so long…"

Jo touched Gloria's shoulder. "I won't tell anyone. I swear it! Just tell me what happened to Ya'el."

Gloria uncovered her mouth and began poking around, looking for the dustpan and brush she kept under the counter. Jo bent down and handed them to her.

"Thank you, luv," Gloria said, as a little color returned to her face. "I should think it obvious. Ya'el tumbled through the higher dimensions, alone and afraid, until the firestorm had passed. When she found her way back home, there was no home. All her family was dead… but there were fertilized eggs in her egg-sack, and so a race of dimension-spanning *Quetzelcoatli* was born… in this world." She sighed again at the look of disbelief on Jo's face. "I know how very unlikely it seems, my dear, but all life is nothing more than the most fantastic series of miracles. How terrible that some people never realize that."

Remembering, Jo thought, *It'll be a real miracle if I get away with this little prank.* Could you actually lie to someone while mindspeaking? The question had never come up before, but she was about to find out.

Ir'befunzu had been off hunting when Jo walked over to her nest from the ocean beach, where Dad was supervising a small tour group from the Far West of Louisiana who were perfectly happy watching the dragonets through binoculars from a good mile and a half away. Jo was a little disappointed that they were just a timid and ordinary-looking bunch of grown-ups, none of whom wore a ten-gallon hat, carried a six-shooter, or was in any other way recognizable as a *vaquereau* (pronounced "vuh-CARE-oh"), one of the legendary solitary cattle-drovers of the wide Louisiana prairies that were the subject of so many Westerns.

She said *bonjour* to them politely in Creole—Mum would kill her if it got back to her that she'd been rude—tolerated Dad bussing her on the cheek, then set off across the dunes and through the belt of loblolly pine forest to the pond, which was a seething, thrashing mess of green scales when she got there. Her mind and her ears were deafened by the racket a brood of giggling dragonets made, but luckily Ir'gassaphet "heard" her easily enough and came bounding up onto the sand, drenching her with chilly pond water.

ARE WE GOES-ING TO ZEE FLOWER WORLD AGAIN? he asked.

Gloria had never actually said Jo shouldn't visit other worlds with the dragons instead of with her, and so she had, riding Ir'gassaphet with Ir'befunzu's permission. But the dragon mom was strict, so mostly they stuck to the Flower World, where the giant space rock had missed the Earth 65 million years ago, so the terradracos still thrived.

Over there, dragons were honored citizens of a peaceful, sleepy civilization now tens of millions of years old who spent their time on philosophical arguments so subtle no mere mammal could understand them, instead of being freakish monsters who barely clung to existence in a human-dominated world. Even Gloria didn't seem to know the place existed—Ir'befunzu said it was a Double-Dragon-Secret, even more so than the fact that dragons could sail between the various worlds as effort-lessly as they soared through the air.

And best of all, when Jo was soaring with Ir'gassaphet through the void to the Flower World, the horrid Gray Ones and their stinky Gray Zone were no more than shadows in the far distance of the higher dimen-sions. True, you felt as if they were watching you the whole time, and it was creepy… but it didn't matter, not once you got to the Great Dragons' Symposium, the bubbling cauldron of life called Chesapeake Bay back home.

But that wasn't where she wanted to go now. *Not this time, Ir'gassaphet. Remember what we mindspoke about? We're going some-where even more fun!* She sent him a mental picture of Arnold's Earth and how to get there through the higher dimensions. Not only couldn't Tom, either of the Teresas, or even Arnold find their way through higher space; they got sick at the very sight of it. Jo wondered with more than a little pride if her ability might be unique in the whole history of the human race.

But it's a secret, she warned the dragonet. *You can't tell your Mum! Just say when we get back that we went to the Flower World after all.*

She'd sensed hesitation from the dragonet, and hoped that was only because he'd never lied to his mother before, not because he knew deep down he *couldn't* lie to her. Otherwise it would be the end of transdimen-sional adventures with Ir'gassaphet. Adventures boring old Gloria would never let her have. The arguing and pleading Jo had had to do, just to get Gloria to take her to Arnold's Earth!

Well, now she was about to find out the hard way whether you could deceive a dragon. Clutching onto Ir'gassaphet's scales, she felt his mus-cles shudder powerfully, like a bucking *bronceau* times about a million.

Her world fell away and higher space opened up before her eyes, with the other Chincoteagues, the other Earths, swirling in blues and greens and tawny sand colors all around. Her breath caught in her throat at the wonder of it; she barely noticed the swirling, churning spirals of the Gray Zone like giant dust devils in the middle distance. *We could go anywhere*, she thought. *We could go places that make the Flower World look as boring as Mum's vegetable garden. And we will! But first, we're going to pay back that rotter.*

Ir'gassaphet glided smoothly out of the transdimensional void and over the sparking blue waters of Chincoteague Bay with a lowering orange sun over his left (normal-space) wing. Jo told him to bank right, eastward toward Chincoteague Island, and keep a mental ear out for Arnold's thoughts. He'd visited Gingo Teag enough times that the dragonet ought to be able to recognize his "voice," or so Jo hoped.

As they sped along Jo looked down and to the right, marveling at the causeway that connected Chincoteague Island to the mainland in Arnold's world. This miles-long bridge was a Holy Grail Mum had been pursuing for years, all the way to the Parliament in Philadelphia, and here it was just an ordinary fact of life that had been in place for the better part of a century. She watched the strange electric carriages people used here and tut-tutted over the way they drove. Were they really supposed to crash into each other like that, and then leap out and gesture wildly at the sky…? Oh, of course, they were reacting to the appearance of a dragon in the sky. Jo whooped and called out to them gleefully, as the wind whipped her ponytail back and forth around her head.

Ir'gassaphet interrupted her: I HEAR YOUR FWEND.

He's not my friend, Jo snapped. *Where is he?*

HE'S SITTING ON THOSE DEAD TWEES UP AHEAD.

What dead trees? Then she saw what he meant: a wooden fishing pier jutting out into the bay from Chincoteague Island. It was crowded with people, a few of whom had stood up and were pointing at Ir'gassaphet. She was still too far away to make out faces, but there was a boy with his arm around a girl, a boy of about the right size… The girl was on her feet, tugging at the boy's hand. He stood up slowly, as if reluctant, but then his mouth opened in a tiny black O of surprise.

Now, Ir'gassaphet! Grab him before he runs!

The dragonet flapped his wings, kicking up waves that crashed on the pier. The crowd turned and began to run in all directions, their shouts no louder than seagulls' cries from this distance. The boy and girl had turned their backs to the water; he was trying to elbow a way through for them with his right arm while gripping the girl's right hand with his left.

Suddenly the pier flashed directly below. The screams rose to a cacophony as Ir'gassaphet instinctively set fire to a wooden piling right next to the pier. Jo was gladder than ever of her ability to mindspeak with him; her voice would never have carried in all this noise. *Just grab him! Don't hurt anyone else!* Since she was sitting atop the dragonet, she couldn't see if he had succeeded—but then Ir' gassaphet began pitching back and forth, his muscles rolling beneath his thick, scaly skin as he gripped onto a struggling Arnold.

Jo let go her two-handed grip for a moment to pump her fist in the air. *Got him! Ir'gassaphet, swoop low over the water.* He did as she asked, banking left and gliding parallel to the bay shore of Chincoteague, where more and more people were gathering to watch the unbelievable scene. *If the island was a ship, they'd have capsized it by now*, Jo thought, giggling helplessly. But this fun couldn't go on long. Arnold had stopped screaming and was beginning to cry.

"Hey, Arnold, you bounder!" Jo had to scream to be heard over the roaring wind of their passage.

Ir'gassaphet's muscles suddenly stopped squirming around.

"Jo? Is that you?" a muffled voice said.

"Well, it ain't Queen Camilla, you skunk! Can you swim?"

"What?"

"I asked if you could swim, you lowdown, no-good rotter!" If he said no, they'd have to risk flying low enough to drop him in the Wildcat Marsh on the northern end of the island.

"Y-yes!"

All right, Ir'gassaphet, you can drop the rot— Before Jo could finish the thought there was a whining noise near her right ear, like a mosquito. Except they were flying too high for mosquitoes. *What the—*

Ir'gassaphet screamed, both aloud and in his mind, a scream that ripped at the insides of her ears and filled her with terror. It was the loudest noise Jo had ever heard, louder even than the explosion that followed a moment later as the world turned upside down and she blacked out.

When she came to, Jo was choking on salt water that burned her throat. She panicked and started flailing around, trying to reach the surface where she could swim, but something was clamped around her chest. She struggled and scratched at it, trying to pull it away, but she couldn't even see what it was because her eyes stung with salt foam. But she felt herself being pulled upward and a moment later broke the surface and began gasping for breath, still trying to wriggle free of whatever had her trapped.

"Jo?" a voice was calling.

She coughed, trying to clear her throat so she could answer. It was an arm that was holding her up, she could see that now, a person who had hold of her, who had been trying to save her.

"Leggo!" she gasped. "Leggo, I can't swim like this…" The arm loosened and let her go. With enormous relief she saw bright green marsh grass rising from the water only a few yards away. With just a few powerful strokes she had reached it and collapsed coughing in the mud before turning over on her back to thank her rescuer—who was Arnold. She scrambled to her feet with difficulty, her soaked clothes trying to drag her back down. "Get away from me, you bounder!" she growled, clenching her fists when she saw he wasn't listening to her. He wasn't even looking at her. He was twisting his neck around, staring up into the sky over the bay. "What is that?" he whispered.

"You've seen a dragon before, you—" Jo's voice died away, because Ir'gassaphet wasn't up there.

Instead there was an enormous, circular, dark gray cloud churning in the bright blue sky, a voracious vortex blocking the sunlight on the water from the Chincoteague shoreline, the shadow stretching halfway across the bay to the mainland. The cloud was rumbling, but not like thunder, unless a thunderclap could go on and on like a world-swallowing tiger growling.

"Did—did that thing swallow Ir'gassaphet?" Jo asked in a small voice. Arnold just shook his head. A hard wind was blowing in off the water, whipping up small whitecaps and bending the marsh grass flat. "Arnold—I think we'd better run," Jo said, tugging at his sleeve.

He didn't need to be told twice. Together they stumbled through the marsh, trying to reach dry land. Jo willed herself not to look back, not to do anything but run as fast as she could, though her ruined shoes kept sinking in the soft, sulfur-stinking mud until she had no choice but to leave them behind. Once she tripped and fell in a narrow, brackish creek and Arnold reached down to help her up; a minute later she did the same for him. They staggered on toward the town, running from something that was too big to run from. *But don't look back. Or you'll turn into a pillar of salt, like Lot's wife in the Bible.*

They reached a stand of loblolly pine, on the other side of which Jo glimpsed some trailers. She broke into a shambling run and almost collided with Gloria, who stepped out from behind a tall, spindly tree as if she'd been hiding there waiting for her. Jo's knees gave way and she sank down to the soft bed of dried-out pine needles, sobbing with relief. She longed to throw her arms around Gloria's gypsy skirt but was afraid of smearing marsh mud all over it, so instead she rubbed her eyes with her filthy sleeve and looked up—but the words died choking in her throat when she saw Gloria's face. Never had she seen so much anger and disappointment in a grown-up, not even that time Mum found the secret trapdoor she'd made in the floor of the kitchen pantry for eavesdropping.

"Jodie Marybeth Purnell," Gloria said, so softly Jo could barely hear her, "what have you done?"

Jo began to cry again, while Gloria just stood there with her arms folded. Her expression never wavered, but the air around her did, and an orange cat's tail flicked across her sad, angry face.

"G-gloria, you're shape-shifting—"

"Never mind that, my girl," Gloria said harshly. "Whatever were you thinking, using Ir'gassaphet like that, as if he were a tool and not a person just like you? You brought him to a world that knows nothing of dragons, so of course someone shot at him and he took fright!"

"Is he all right?"

"I don't know! And you haven't answered my question."

"I—I was just playing a little joke on Arnold." There was a rustling off to the right. Out of the corner of her eye Jo saw Arnold's face, which might have been a copy of Gloria's except for the lack of a swishing cat tail.

"A joke?" Gloria said, her green eyes wide.

"Well he shouldn't be walking out with that—that strumpet!"

"You may have read enough Shakespeare to learn insults, my dear, but you clearly haven't understood what you've read, or you would know the futility of vengeance, and the terrible damage it causes. You have rare gifts, the ability to mindspeak with dragons and to navigate the higher dimensions with ease, gifts you have abused. I am so very, very disappointed in you."

Jo squeezed her eyes shut. She climbed to her feet, turned and looked at Arnold. "I'm sorry, Arnold. It was an awful thing I did. You could have gotten really badly hurt, and I don't know what I, what I did to Ir'gassaphet. And th-thanks for saving me from drowning."

Arnold stood with his arms folded and said nothing. He wouldn't look at her. Jo supposed she deserved that. She turned to Gloria. "You can take me home now. I shall accept whatever punishment Mum gives me."

Jo saw with horror that Gloria was shedding a cascade of crystalline teardrops that fell from her face and rolled around in the pine needles where they lay glittering like diamonds.

"I wish I could, Jo, but I can't," she said.

"What do you mean, you can't?"

"In his panic, Ir'gassaphet tore a hole in the world and let the Gray Ones out. That vortex you saw… it's the Gray Zone pouring through."

Jo turned, dread in her heart, and looked back toward the bay, but the nightmare storm spiral was gone. "B-but I don't see it!"

"That's because it's expanding outward at the speed of light, Jo. And it's made it quite impossible to travel between the dimensions." Gloria tried without success to flick the cat tail out of her face. It swished back and forth, connected to nothing above her head where a cat's body should have been. "We're both trapped here, Jo."

29

At first Alison thought she was dreaming when someone began pounding on the door in the middle of the night. It had to be one of those stupid dreams where you have to relive something that's already happened to you, with a few details changed around. After all, it had only been three days since that policeman brought Arnold home. She'd never admit it to turd-breath, but she'd been lucky herself, dodging what might have been the same police car by ducking behind a Dumpster, which spooked her enough that she tossed the few pamphlets she was still carrying into it and ran home, slipping in the unlocked back door, changing into pajamas, and pulling the covers up over her head just minutes before that cop came knocking.

It was a trauma, sure enough, so Alison wasn't too surprised to be having a nightmare about it. For a few confused moments, the real knocking was mixed up with dream-fragments, so Donny Schmitz was frowning and telling her to please get the door and tell whoever it was to go away so they could keep making out. Then she came fully awake.

"Open up!" someone was shouting. It was a man's voice, high-pitched and angry, and familiar somehow. "Open up right now in there!"

Jo was sitting bolt upright in the cot Mom and Dad had bought for her. "Who is that?" she whispered, reaching over to pluck at Alison's sleeve.

Alison shook her off and glanced at the luminous green hands of her bedside alarm clock. Two-thirty in the morning. What the hell? She turned on her lamp, got out of her bed and peeked out into the hallway. Dad was already standing there in his University of Chicago sweatsuit, his mouth set in a tight line. Mom was standing right behind him in her nightgown, Arnold was framed in the light of his doorway, his eyes and mouth forming perfect circles, and Jo was panting on the back of Alison's neck.

"Just hold on! I'm coming!" Dad shouted. He turned and lowered his voice. "Everyone stay up here. Rachel, you get on the phone and call the police. If they break in and I can't stop them, hide!" The pounding and yelling started up again.

"No way, Jerry. I'm going with you," Mom whispered, clutching his arm.

He glanced at her, his mouth tightening. "We know who it's got to be, Rachel. And they're coming for me. Don't put yourself at risk."

Mom shook her head, dark, messy hair flying in her face. "I won't let you face them alone, Jerry!"

Alison bit her lip so hard she could taste blood. The town had been a madhouse in the three days since Jo had arrived on dragonback and unleashed whatever that *thing* was in the skies. It had seemed to dissipate, spreading out to cover the whole sky but fading to the lighter gray of an ordinary cloudy day—although without the irregular swirls of real clouds—before fading away entirely and leaving behind a clear, starry spring night.

After the mass stampede away from the bay shore, people had locked themselves in their houses, which made Alison wonder how many people had seen her brother and his friend staggering up to the house through the empty streets in their ruined clothes. Town and state police cars followed close behind them, blaring the unnecessary news of a nighttime curfew.

Sunday the streets were full of soldiers in khaki uniforms escorting at least a dozen different High Ones laden down with some kind of complicated equipment. Jo stayed in Alison's bedroom, pale and trembling, looking like a little girl in clothes that were actually only slightly too big for her.

"I did all this," she said when Alison brought her a bowl of cereal. She tasted the cup of Lipton's tea Alison had made her, made a face and carefully set it down on the bedside table.

Alison shook her head. "I still don't get it. There are rumors that the Bubble Drive isn't working, and flights to the High Ones' Homeworld and other nearby star systems have all been cancelled. How could you have done that—even if you did have a dragon under your command?"

Jo's brown eyes flashed as she looked at her. "Ir'gassaphet is not under my command! He's my friend, and that's the only reason he did what I asked!"

"But I thought he's really a dragonet—a baby dragon. So maybe he wasn't old enough to know any better," Alison said. She was trying to talk gently to the younger girl, but couldn't stop it coming out like an accusation.

Jo stared at her and began to cry. "We were only going to toss stink-breath in the water! We weren't really going to hurt him!"

"'Turd-breath' is the preferred term," Alison said drily, "and I think you got a lot more than you bargained for."

"This must be my fault, too!" Jo whispered now, her eyes twin terrified moons in the darkness as the pounding got louder and the voice threatened to break the door down if it wasn't opened immediately.

"Open up, in the name of decency!" it bellowed.

"No. I don't think it is," Alison whispered, finding Jo's hand and squeezing it as her parents started down the stairs hand in hand. She needed the other girl's touch as much as Jo needed her, because it couldn't be the cosmic disaster Jo had caused that had brought SCOD to their door; no, it had to be that stupid pamphlet. How could she have let Arnold talk her into handing the damn thing out?

Since Arnold and Jo were standing still as statues, Alison darted into her parents' room and made a grab for the phone that hung on the wall. But when she lifted up the receiver, she heard nothing. Silence. She tried hitting the line switch a couple of times, but there was still no dial tone. Then she realized someone had come into the room with her and nearly screamed till she saw it was only Arnold. The front of his pajama pants was wet.

"Open up in the name of decency!" the voice downstairs bawled again. "This is your last warning!"

"The hell I will! Get a warrant!" Dad shouted. At that the pounding started up again, louder than ever, followed a moment later by the sound of wood splintering. Mom yelped.

"You are Gerald Seymour Grossbard?" the voice said.

"Get out of my house!" Dad said. "This is breaking and entering!" Then he shouted in pain. There was a loud thump, and Mom screamed. Arnold grabbed Alison in a tight hug. She could smell his pee.

"You're coming with us, you terrorist!"

Alison twisted out of Arnold's grasp and ran on tiptoes to the top of the stairs, crouching down on the top step so she could see through the bannisters.

"What for? I haven't done anything!" Dad said. To her horror a man so huge he had to bend not to hit his head on the ceiling was putting handcuffs on him, and another man almost as big had Mom pinned against the wall.

"Recognize this?"

Alison almost gasped out loud. A bald man was confronting Dad with a crumpled copy of Arnold's pamphlet. It was Mr. Wright, the principal!

"I didn't write that thing!" Dad said. He should've left it at that, but being Dad, he had to add, "But whoever did write it was within his rights! Freedom of speech—"

"...is the last refuge of a terrorist!" Mr. Wright snarled. He was quoting the Vice-Satrap, of course. A man Dad never had a good word for, even though he had once been governor of Maryland. "Well, let me tell you something, Mr. *Gross*bard." Mr. Wright said their family name like it was a swear word. "This town was mighty generous to you and your two little delinquents, after what you did back in Baltimore. But we don't tolerate terrorists in our midst! You're coming with us!"

And with that, the super-sized gorilla, who was wearing the green uniform of the Decency Shock Troops, dragged Dad out the busted-in door. His buddy shoved Mom, who fell on the floor with a loud thump, and Mr. Wright followed the men out. Alison heard a car door slam, and the squeal of tires. Then everything was quiet again.

In a daze, Alison walked down the stairs. Nobody had had time to turn on a lamp, but a streetlight cast a bright orange glow. She knelt down over her mother, who had made no move to get up and was crying quietly.

"Mom, are you okay?" She was crying too hard to answer, so Alison and Jo, who had tiptoed down the stairs, helped her over to the sofa.

While Jo went to the kitchen to get Mom a glass of water, Alison squatted down and picked up the crumpled-up pamphlet Mr. Wright had dropped. What did they think they'd been playing at, telling people to rise up against tyranny? She'd known all along that Arnold and his little friends had no idea what they were doing, so why had she gone along with them? Why, when there was no other way it could have ended but this? Of course *they* were blaming Dad. They'd probably been keeping tabs on him ever since he first came to town. After all, he was what the Vice-Satrap had once called "a typing transmitter of terrorism, a newspaperman of nihilism."

Now that SCOD had taken Dad away, they might never see him again. SCOD didn't arrest people, it *disappeared* them. Even if Mom could get the lawyer she worked for to help, what was he going to do? Call Pierre LaWayne?

"Hello, Mr. LaWayne? Two of your thugs didn't happen to take away a guy named Gerald Grossbard in the middle of the night, did they? … Well, would you mind checking?"

Alison sank into the easy chair, covered her face and wailed. Through her fingers she could see the ruined front door and the dark, silent houses across the street. Dark and silent. Sure they were. Everybody on the street must have heard the commotion—hell, everyone on the island must have—but they were all hiding in bed with the covers pulled up over their heads, telling themselves it wasn't any of their business.

Suddenly a dark shape moved into her line of vision. She stiffened, wondering if Mr. Wright and his musclemen had come back to clean up the loose ends. But it was only Arnold, shuffling around the living room, staring at the mess SCOD had left behind.

Next thing Alison knew she was standing in front of Arnold, grabbing him by the shoulders and screaming in his face. But quietly, so the neighbors wouldn't hear. "This is your fault, you moron! Your fault! You and your stupid pamphlet got Dad DISAPPEARED! How do you like being a terrorist now? Huh?"

She wanted him to scream back at her. Wanted him to say it was just as much her fault, to lash out with his fists. Because it *was* just as much her fault, and she deserved to be punished. But he just stood there, not saying anything, not reacting when she shook him. She slapped him in the face, but it was like slapping a doll, and she shoved him so hard he went over backwards, his head hitting the floor with a thump.

"That's enough, Alison!" Mom was on her feet, holding the glass Jo had given her. Holding it crooked, so the water dribbled out unnoticed onto the carpet.

"But Mom, you don't know what he did! He—"

"Let's go upstairs, all four of us," Mom interrupted. "I don't want the whole street to hear this. And there are things we have to decide quickly."

As they trudged up the stairs Alison realized she was going to have to tell Mom the whole truth. It was no good trying to pin it all on Arnold; that had never worked before, since she was the older sister and was always expected to be the responsible one. And she had handed out the pamphlets, too. Nobody had twisted her arm.

So as soon as they walked into her parents' bedroom and Jo shut the door behind them, before Mom had even sat down on the bed, Alison blurted out, "Mom, those pamphlets—Arnold and I handed them out and—"

Mom sat down and looked up at Alison with her swollen, tear-filled eyes. "Allie, it's all right. Did you think Dad and I didn't know?" She chuckled softly at the look on Alison's face, chuckles that quickly turned to sobs. "Oh, my darlings. Kids always think they're so much smarter than their parents, but you forget, we were once your age and we also thought we could run rings around our parents. The truth is, kiddos, we're proud of you, that's why we didn't stop you.

"Why so surprised? You know how Dad and I feel about the tinpot dictatorship our beautiful America has become, and the violent men who say they're fighting back by murdering innocent people. We're so proud—so proud…" She started to sob again, and Alison put her arm around her mother's shoulders and handed her a tissue. "—th-that you are fighting back with words, not guns."

Alison wondered if Mom had actually read the pamphlet, but she kept quiet.

Mom dabbed at her eyes and smiled shakily at Alison. Then she turned to Jo, but before she could do more than say her name, the younger girl was stammering, "It's really all my fault, Mrs. G-grossbard. The High Ones and their human flunkies are all over Gingo Teag, I mean Chincoteague, b-because of the hole Ir'gassaphet tore in the sk-sky, a hole that probably k-k-killed him…" Jo was crying now, too.

"Jo, honey, that's not so. I mean, it isn't your fault SCOD took my husband away," Mom said. "They've had it in for him ever since we lived in Baltimore. They were just waiting for an excuse, and now they have one—that pamphlet Arnold and Allie made."

"But that's my fault too. I brought Teresa here, it was her idea," Jo said, rubbing her eyes.

"Jo, that isn't so, and it's not important, anyway. What's important is we need to find another place for you to stay," Mom said. Jo stared at her, wide-eyed, and Mom said, "It's not safe for you here. SCOD or the police could come back any time, and how would we explain who you are?"

"I've told everyone she's my cousin," Arnold said, his voice hoarse.

"But the police will quickly find out that isn't so," Mom said. "And we don't need to attract their attention, that's for sure. It's just dumb luck no one seems to have realized it was you Jo's dragon grabbed." She turned to Alison. "Allie, do you think you could ask your friend Shaniqua if Jo can stay with her family?"

Alison bit her already ragged lip and again tasted blood. *Are we good enough friends for me to ask her a thing like that?* "Well, I guess I can ask her," she said slowly, "but…" Suddenly her hands flew to cover her mouth.

"What is it?" Mom said. "What's wrong, Allie?"

"I just remembered… Shaniqua's Gingo Teag double, Sharon, was visiting here yesterday! I hung out with them at Muller's around lunchtime… they like the same flavor of ice cream, cookies 'n cream…"

"So Sharon is trapped here too because of me!" Jo said, fresh tears spilling down her cheeks.

"Shaniqua and her family are going to have their hands full, then," Mom said. "I wish I had some friends here that I could ask, but I was so sick for so long… Arnold, can you think of anyone? Anyone at all?"

"Only one," said Arnold. "You're not going to like it, Jo."

30

"You can't be serious, Arnold! This girl tried to kill you. *With a dragon.*" Kayleigh stared at Jo, and couldn't seem to tear her eyes away.

The stranded dragon rider was dressed in Alison's clothes, which were a little too big for her, but in Arnold's eyes there didn't seem to be anything so very alien about her. But he supposed that to Kayleigh, being a from-here, anyone from anywhere else was an alien.

"She didn't really mean to hurt me, or you," Arnold said.

"And I'm really sorry," Jo said, reaching out to Kayleigh, who flinched.

"I don't think so, Arnold! I can't ask my parents to have some, some alien girl from another world stay in our house!"

This was too much. "Kayleigh, she's no alien. She's a from-here," Arnold said.

Kayleigh's eyes narrowed. "She doesn't sound like she's from Chincoteague. She doesn't sound like anyone from anyplace real."

Arnold sighed. "I told you, Kay—she's from a parallel world where America is still part of England—where America sort of actually *is* England—just like Teresa. And we've got to help her. She's key to the Resistance."

"And I'd appreciate it if you didn't act like I'm not here," Jo said, shifting the weight of the backpack Mom had packed for her from her right shoulder to her left. It was stuffed with food and water and toiletries and a bunch of Alison's old clothes and God knew what else, and there was a sleeping bag dangling from the bottom of it.

Arnold darted his eyes around the forest trail. The Chincoteague Wildlife Refuge on Assateague Island had seemed the best place to go so they wouldn't be overheard, but when he'd thrown a handful of gravel at Kayleigh's second-floor bedroom window early Sunday afternoon he hadn't even been sure she'd be there or would be willing to come out. But he'd guessed correctly that she'd be back from church by then. Her mother took her to Union Baptist every week, though her father only went sometimes, "if he doesn't get too drunk the night before," as Kayleigh put it bluntly.

Now she was biting her lip. "Arnold, even if I got my mom to say yes, my dad wouldn't never go for it," she said. When she got nervous, her grammar tended to get worse—or as Allie unkindly put it, "she sounds more like a hick."

"But she's got nowhere else to go," Arnold said.

"That ain't my problem, Arnold. I'm sorry," Kayleigh said, folding her arms and turning away.

"This isn't about, uh, I mean, the problem isn't that, umm…"

"That I'm a girl, and his friend?" Jo said helpfully. Arnold made a choking noise. "You don't have to worry, Kay—"

"Only my friends get to call me Kay," Kayleigh snapped.

"—I told him straightaway, long before he started walking out with you, that there wasn't going to be any snogging or disgusting stuff."

"What is 'snogging?' It sounds pretty disgusting, itself," Kayleigh said.

Jo reddened. "Never mind. The point is, he's all yours."

"…if I even want him," Kayleigh said. Arnold gulped as she turned back to face him. "All right, here's an idea for you. My dad used to take my brother fishing on Assateague all the time. The week before Kyle left for Mars last year, my mom made him take me too, and I found out they keep some of their gear hidden under a loose floorboard in an abandoned hunting lodge up near the Maryland line."

Jo frowned. "Hunting lodges? The only building on Assateague Island in my world is the lighthouse. Anything else would just be trampled by the dragons."

"Thanks for reminding me you're the dragon girl. You want a place to hide, or don't you?" Jo looked at Arnold, who looked back at her, and they both shrugged. "Well, we'd better get moving now, then," Kayleigh said. "My mom's going to expect me back home in time for dinner, and it's a bit of a hike."

"I know every inch of this island, all the way up to the Sinepuxent Inlet," Jo snapped. "I've hiked all twenty-five miles of it! I'm not scared of a little walk. And any dummy knows Maryland is on the other side of Chesapeake Bay from Nanticoke."

"There's no such place as Sinepuxent Inlet, and you're the dummy!" Kayleigh said, clenching her fists. "How can you claim to be a from-here when you don't even know Maryland's just a few miles north of here?"

"It doesn't matter!" said Arnold, forcing a laugh as he stepped between the two girls. "Anyway, you're both right. Things are all different over in Jo's world, I told you that, Kay. Jo, this is a great idea, it's very nice of Kayleigh to take us there." When they both glared at him, he laughed again, a little desperately, and said, "C'mon, let's get moving!"

He pushed through the trees toward the beach, turning around to see if they were following him only when he'd emerged from the forest into the hot, dry space behind the dunes. To his relief, they were, though Kayleigh looked really, *really* unhappy about it.

It turned out to be a very long walk even after they got out on the beach and turned left to follow the shoreline north. A *very* long walk. It took the better part of three hours, and Arnold was sure Kayleigh and Jo would have been fighting the whole time if it wasn't such a tiring walk. Well, tiring for him and Kayleigh—Jo soon took the lead and kept calling back to them to catch up. Everyone's sneakers quickly got soaked, because they had to switch from walking over the dry sand, where you sank in with every step, to the firmly packed wet sand beside the ocean on their right—only the tide was coming in, and it was impossible to keep entirely beyond the reach of the waves.

"Kayleigh, are you sure you know where we're going?" Arnold asked when they stopped to take a water break. The sun was climbing high over the ocean, and the day was rapidly warming. Normally he loved the beach, but the long, boring plod and the unchanging scenery of dunes on the left, sea on the right was getting to him.

"It's an old hunting lodge. I'll know it when I see it."

"How? You can't see anything over top of those dunes."

"I know how far it is," Kayleigh snapped.

"Come on, slow-boats!" Jo called from way up the beach.

About half an hour later Kayleigh said they should climb up an extra-tall dune, which rose maybe ten feet above sea level. Their reward was a glimpse of a very unimpressive-looking building in the far distance. Jo had to come running back to meet them.

"You might have warned me," she complained.

"Serves you right for racing on ahead," Kayleigh snapped.

The two girls glared at each other; for a moment, Arnold could have sworn an invisible streak of lightning leapt the gap between them. Then Kayleigh snorted and stomped off over the crest of the dune, the effect ruined by the soft sand her feet kept sinking into. On the other side was a thin screen of pine trees and beyond that, a patch of marshy ground surrounding a grassy hummock where the "lodge" sat.

They made their way over to the sagging wooden structure. Arnold eyed the rusty padlock on the door doubtfully.

Kayleigh nudged him aside and tugged the lock and a good-sized chunk of the door away with a single pull. "Oh well," she said, "we can put this back in place when we leave. Everything here is so broken down no one will notice the difference."

"What am I supposed to do if a park ranger comes inside to check?" Jo said.

"That's your problem, ain't it?" Kayleigh snapped.

"I'm sure it'll only take a day or two for Gloria to figure out a way to get you back home," Arnold said.

"It didn't sound like that to me," Jo said, but she shrugged her backpack off and put it on the floor.

Arnold took a few steps back and looked at the building. It was covered with clapboard siding that had once been white. The windows had all been boarded over with plywood, and up this close the gaping holes in the roof were impossible to miss. Arnold couldn't help wondering what would happen to Jo if it rained. *She'll get wet, I guess.* The inside didn't exactly look waterproof. The biggest hole in the roof was matched by a corresponding pile of broken shingles and rubble heaped high on the floor beneath it, with the sun shining through like a spotlight where tiny motes of dust danced. There was nothing else to see, just a big open space four or five meters long and three wide. If there had once been interior walls they were long gone. The rotten floorboards shrieked with every footstep.

"Looks like what my Aunt Hilda, the real-estate agent, calls 'a fixer-upper,'" Kayleigh said.

Jo bent over, her hands on her knees, and peered at the nearest wall. "Hey, Kayleigh, how old is this place, anyway?"

"Don't know. Why?"

Jo pointed. "Look what someone carved in the wall."

"Musta took a pocketknife," Kayleigh said. But the letters were sharp and neat. "JIM LOVES ANNIE. MAY 1872," it said.

Arnold's mind was on other things. "Are you going to be all right here, Jo?"

"I've stayed overnight at the lighthouse many times," Jo said, but her voice wavered a little.

Never alone, though, I'll bet, thought Arnold.

Kayleigh put a hand on Jo's shoulder. "Don't worry about it none. There aren't any dragons on this island."

"I wasn't worried," Jo said, shaking the other girl's hand off. "I know how to build a fire and everything. And Mrs. Grossbard gave me lots of food and water and bug spray. I'll survive. You two enjoy holding hands and snogging."

In fact they barely even talked on the long walk back. Arnold kept sneaking glances at Kayleigh, wondering if she was jealous or mad at him. She might have at least asked about Arnold's father—everyone in Chincoteague had to know SCOD had taken him away last night. *Maybe she's keeping quiet because she doesn't want to embarrass me, or make me start crying. Not that I would... not in front of her.*

When they got close enough to the beach parking lot to see other people in the distance, Kayleigh stopped walking and said, "Arnold, I'm going to have to keep away from you for a while. My parents made me promise."

He couldn't think of anything to say. He knew he shouldn't be mad at Mr. and Mrs. Scott, since they were only trying to protect Kayleigh, but he couldn't help it. *Cowards, the bunch of them.*

"But we can take turns bringing supplies to Jo," Kayleigh said. "Don't look so startled. I can't take someone way out there and just leave her to live on clams and rainwater. Even if she is a dragon girl."

Arnold nodded reluctantly. "That's a good idea, I guess. Alison will take turns with us too, I think, so we'll each have to go only once every three nights." He paused. "It's really true, what Jo said. She doesn't like me—not like that—and you're the one I like—"

"I know that, Arnold," Kayleigh said. "I'm sorry for being mean to you earlier. I just had to make sure. It's a good thing she's really ugly, with that mousy hair and squashed-in nose. And I *am* sorry about what happened to your Dad. I hope he gets back safe."

She turned to go and Arnold said, "But how will I get hold of you, I mean for the Resistance, and me and Alison taking turns with Jo...?"

"Just leave notes in my locker," she said.

"But I'm still suspended."

She shrugged. "You take stuff to Jo tomorrow night, I'll take her stuff Tuesday, and then Alison can go, okay? I'll call you when my parents are out. Or when my dad drinks enough to *pass* out."

"But what if I miss you," he blurted, and wished he could melt into the sand like the waves.

She smiled. "I'm gonna miss you too, Arnold. Everything will blow over, you'll see. Your dad will come back, you'll be back in school, and Jo will go back to her dragons."

Before he could say anything else stupid, she pecked him on the lips, then turned it into a lingering kiss and ran off. He followed after a few minutes, hoping she was right about things getting back to normal.

31

It was all very well for Arnold to go sneaking off with Jo to meet his girlfriend, the ultimate nerd turning into the ultimate lady's man. Mom was burning up the wires trying to find where Dad had been taken, but at least she was doing something about his disappearance. Alison was left totally to her own devices, which meant she was alone with her guilt and her fear.

The streets were still full of soldiers, police, and strange men in plainclothes who had to be SCOD. This last group had to know where Dad had been taken, but what could Alison do about it? Nothing. She never would have thought she could miss the boring torture of school, but there it was. Anything to take her mind off how powerless she was.

She couldn't even help Shaniqua. Her friend's house was the first place she'd gone, early enough to catch her before her mother dragged her to church.

"Tavon won't go, so Mom is extra strict about making me go," Shaniqua liked to complain. "It sucks being the good girl!"

It wasn't even nine in the morning when Alison rode her bike around the corner into the Thomases' street, but she almost missed them. Mrs. Thomas was already outside, dressed in her good purple skirt and a matching jacket.

"Oh, hello, Allie," she said. "Shaniqua will be out in a second. We're already late to church. I keep telling her how embarrassing it is to walk in right in the middle of the sermon, but does she listen?"

"I'll be right down, Ma!" Shaniqua called from upstairs.

"Don't you go yellin' like a fishwife in front of all the neighbors!" Mrs. Thomas yelled back.

Alison rolled her eyes—they were almost as bad as her family. And just like in her family, it was the mom who insisted on going to religious services while the father slept in. Alison had never said much more than hello to Mr. Thomas, but she suspected if she did he'd sound just like her own dad on the subject, grumbling about "missing sleep for a bunch of religious mumbo-jumbo."

Mrs. Thomas started tapping her foot, while Alison tried hard not to laugh. The fact that she shouldn't be laughing at anything on this of all mornings just made her want to laugh all the harder.

But then Mrs. Thomas looked at her, lowered her voice and whispered, "I'll be prayin' for y'all in church, hear?"

"Ma, did you have to make Allie cry?" Shaniqua asked a few seconds later when she emerged from the house.

"She didn't make me cry," Alison managed between sobs, "I-I'm fine."

Mrs. Thomas looked at the ground as the two girls hugged. "You can come with us if you want," she said, and Alison surprised herself by accepting the invitation. They had barely reached the corner when a friend of Mrs. Thomas's joined them, and as the two women struck up a conversation Alison and Shaniqua deliberately hung back.

"Is Sharon stuck here?" Alison whispered.

"Yeah. Mom told her to stay in my room. With all this trouble in town, it's too risky for her to be out running around."

"So your family knows about her?"

"We tried keeping it a secret, but too many people had seen us together. It was fun while it lasted though, pretending like we were twins, fooling people into mistaking us for each other."

"You never did that to me, did you?"

"Of course not!" Alison thought there might be a twinkle in Shaniqua's eye as she said that, and she changed the subject with suspicious speed. "That don't matter anyhow. Sharon is safe for now. It's you I'm worried about. What happened to your dad?"

Alison told her in a whisper, swiping irritably at the blur that came into her eyes as she talked.

Shaniqua's eyes grew round. "I'm sorry, Allie, really I am," she said.

Alison wondered if what she really meant was, *but you shouldn't have gone looking for trouble.*

Well, she could change the subject too. "Have you seen Gloria?" Alison asked.

Shaniqua shook her head. "Not since she showed up here yesterday and freaked out Sharon and me, saying Sharon was stuck here maybe permanently."

"You could always say she's your cousin or something, if she really has to live with you," Alison said.

"I guess," said Shaniqua.

She didn't sound too happy about it, and Alison had to stop herself saying that it was way better to gain a member of the family than to lose one.

The Thomases' church didn't look any different to Alison than any other church, with its white walls and steeple, but everyone inside was black and she felt like they were all staring at her. The service was weird, too.

Going to synagogue meant being bored out of your wits for two whole hours while the rabbi and cantor droned on in Hebrew and then made a bunch of dull announcements. The services at Island AME weren't quite as long, they were all in English, and they involved a lot of singing and shouting from the pulpit. The pastor sounded angry as he told the congregation they had to be strong with all the trouble in town. There was a lot of mm-hmming and ah-ha'ing when he told them to keep in mind the dignity of the early Christians among the Roman soldiers. Afterwards the congregation filed past and took turns shaking his hand.

When it was her turn the pastor clasped her hand in both of his, looked her in the eye and thanked her for coming, which was more than she expected. She wondered if Mrs. Thomas had asked him to pray for her family, too.

Mrs. Thomas asked her to stay for lunch at their house.

Alison didn't really want to but was afraid of hurting her feelings, so she said yes. It turned out to be just the three of them, plus Sharon, who was wearing Shaniqua's clothes and looked so much like her Alison blinked in confusion.

The Gingo Teag native asked if Jo had managed to fix the damage she'd caused yet, and Alison shook her head. "I don't think she can."

Sharon bit her lip and put her ham sandwich down. "This place is really scary. I just wish I could tell my mum that I'm all right."

"It's scary for us, too. It's not usually this bad here," Mrs. Thomas said apologetically, as if she was responsible.

But Alison was the one who felt guilty, since Jo was Arnold's friend. Wasn't there anything her rotten little brother couldn't mess up? As soon as she could get away Alison thanked everyone and fled.

But she didn't want to go home. What was waiting for her there but a broken front door and Mom's desperation? By contrast, everything seemed calm as she walked around town. A warm sun was shining overhead, and people were chatting with the soldiers, many of whom were local. It might have been the Fourth of July, Empire Day, only without the cookouts and parades.

Whatever the visiting High Ones and human scientists were up to, they weren't anywhere to be seen at the moment. Except for that one creature making its way down Maddox Boulevard as if it owned the place, with a man in jeans and a V-necked green polo shirt strolling alongside it, his hands in his pockets as he talked to the alien.

Alison did a double take as she stepped off into the street to detour around them. The man was Dad's friend, Mr. Nomura!

"Hi, Alison," he said before she could make her escape. "I want you to meet my friend, Sssssssssss-sh'onkelos."

Since "hello, you alien murderer" wasn't prescribed etiquette, and she was wearing jeans rather than a skirt, Alison awkwardly bowed and mumbled the all-purpose, "Greetings, your eminence."

"I am not an eminence, Miss Alison," the High One rumbled, sounding amused. "Neither am I a dominance. I am not even a prominence! Please don't bow to me, I am only a commoner."

"Sorry, your eminence," Alison said, her face heating up.

"Don't apologize either, Miss Alison. If I had any choice, I wouldn't be here."

Alison edged back up onto the sidewalk. "You mean here in Chincoteague? Me either," she said.

"I don't just mean in Chincoteague. I mean anywhere on this cold, dry planet of yours."

Alison stared at the huge, multi-armed creature, its rainbow scales glistening in the afternoon sun. "But we're part of the Cosmic Harmony, just like Homeworld!"

The creature did a weirdly accurate imitation of a human snorting in disgust, making the water bottles it was carrying to breathe with rattle as they knocked against each other. "I can't believe a young human would parrot Imperial propaganda so perfectly! They really have you creatures well trained, don't they?"

"Now, now, Sh'onk, there's no need to be rude," Mr. Nomura grinned. Turning to Alison he added, "Sh'onk has some rather unusual views for a High One."

"I can see that," Alison said, nervously looking around to see if anyone was eavesdropping. People were trained to keep a respectful distance from High Ones, though.

"As to why I'm here on Chincoteague, it's my misfortune to have to pilot our esteemed leaders around in our dinky little atmospheric craft," the alien said.

Alison didn't think she'd ever heard of a High One being sarcastic before. It made her head spin.

Mr. Nomura darted his eyes from side to side, leaned toward Alison and lowered his voice. "I heard what happened to your father, Alison. I think it's terrible, and so does Sh'onk."

Alison blinked. *I am NOT going to start crying in front of a Slug!* "Then why don't you do something about it?" Alison said, not sure if she should be talking to the human or the alien or both of them.

"My dear human, it might seem to the person sitting in darkness that the Empire controls everything that goes on, on this dried-up husk of a planet," Sh'onk said. "But that isn't really so. No, the Imperials merely set the guidelines. They leave it to human quislings to carry them out."

"Keep your voice down!" Alison hissed, while Mr. Nomura grinned even wider. She stared at the creature. "The person sitting in darkness? Have you been reading Mark Twain?"

"Reading him? He is one of my touchstones!" the alien exclaimed. "As is your Mr. Orwell, and your Mr. Camus, and your Mr. Paine… How have you creatures forgotten your glorious heritage of liberty so quickly?"

"Sh'onk, really, let's not cause too much trouble," Mr. Nomura said with a chuckle.

Was it a nervous chuckle? Alison couldn't be sure. And what if this whole thing was a setup, to get the rest of the family in trouble? Had she said too much already?

Better safe than sorry. With a hasty bow, Alison said, "Good seeing you, Mr. Nomura. It was an honor to meet you, your eminence."

"I am not an eminence!" Sssssssssss-sh'onkelos called after Alison as she darted across Maddox Boulevard, heading home.

But just as she was about to turn onto her own street she collided with a skinny man wearing a suit and tie. Alison started to apologize, then stopped and stared at the guy. There was something familiar about him. He was clean-shaven, but his clothes hung loose on him and there were dark circles under his eyes. He smelled strongly of aftershave.

"Mr. Freed?" Alison gasped.

His eyes darted back and forth. The irises were grayish blue and shot through with red veins. Bending toward her—he was about half a head taller—he whispered harshly, "Not so loud!"

"Sorry! You, uh, you look good!"

He barked out a laugh. "I look like an undertaker."

Alison saw what he meant. The suit was black and shiny from wear.

"Why are you—what are you—?" she stammered.

"Walk with me. I'm heading back to the church."

Alison suddenly noticed he was carrying a plastic shopping bag filled with odds and ends from the Five & Ten Lunar Store down the street.

"I heard how the pigs took your father, Alison," he said.

They were walking quickly, almost jogging. If it was Union Baptist he was heading to, it was only a few blocks away. *I ought to be able to hold it together for that long without bawling my eyes out.*

"I was lucky I was crashing at the church when the heat came down," Mr. Freed panted. "Pastor Mills actually takes his Christianity seriously, and he said I could stay hiding in the vestry until things cool down. Of course I had to be out and about during services this morning, so I took the opportunity to change my look." He rubbed his jawline, which had little cuts on it, and grinned wryly. "It's been almost fifty years since my face was naked like this."

Alison couldn't help but smile a little. "You look okay, Mr. Freed."

He lowered his voice still further. "I might as well let you in on a secret. My name isn't really Barry Freed."

"No?"

"No. I'm actually Jeff Wineman." He paused, looking disappointed when Alison didn't say anything. "*The* Jeff Wineman? Of the Chicago Seven? Of course, poor Abbie got all the attention, even when that stupid judge kept getting my name mixed up with our lawyer's."

"What's the Chicago Seven, an old rock band?"

Mr. Freed—or Wineman—sighed. "*Sic transit gloria mundi*," he muttered.

Alison brightened. "You know Gloria?"

"No, that was an expression. It means that mortal fame is fleeting. Who's Gloria?"

"She's an eleven-dimensional cat-woman who takes me and my brother to a parallel world where there are telepathic dragons and bi-planes."

Mr. Wineman sighed again. "I really wish I could take the stuff you kids are on today, but I don't think my heart could handle it. Back in the day all we had was pot and acid."

"It's not a drug hallucination, Mr. Fr—Jeff. Maybe you should talk to her. She could take you someplace where the Sixties never ended."

"What a concept!" the old hippie chuckled.

Alison didn't think she'd ever heard such a sad laugh in her life.

"It's true!" she insisted. "I have a record at home that she gave me—a Beatles reunion album. You can come over and listen to it sometime, if you want." As soon as the words left her mouth, she wished there was some way to take them back. Under the aftershave, there was still a faint whiff of pee.

"Take care of yourself, Alison. My old comrades and I used to yell a lot about fascism... but of course, we didn't have the faintest idea how to fight the real thing, when it came." Mr. Wineman stepped over the white picket fence surrounding the church lawn, darted swiftly into a side door and was gone.

32

Arnold had been kind of looking forward to the "juvie hearing." He'd give those school administrator idiots a piece of his mind, and if they expelled him, so what?

But everything was different since the night SCOD disappeared Dad. Mom had gotten the door replaced first thing Monday morning. The new door was light blond wood, almost white, where the old door had been stained a medium brown.

Every time he passed it, it was a silent reminder of how helpless he'd been when SCOD had come for Dad. And how cowardly, too, when he should have stepped forward and said the pamphlets were his idea, that they should take him and leave Dad and Allie alone. That's what a real hero of the Resistance would have done, instead of hiding upstairs wetting his pants like a little kid.

So now he didn't care what the school administrators did to him. Even the thought of not seeing Kayleigh again didn't seem to make much difference. He climbed listlessly into the car when Mom told him to and slouched his way down the halls of the school administration building in the mainland town of Accomac.

Somehow he'd expected a whole courtroom, with impressive dark wood paneling and a judge sitting up on a dais in black robes, like on the tri-vee stage. But it was just an ordinary office, smaller than Mr. Wright's and without even a window, in which a dumpy gray-haired woman with a tired face was sitting behind a desk.

She stood up with a fake smile and held out her hand to Mom. "I'm Gina Wilkes, the assistant superintendent. It's Mrs. Grossbard, I presume?"

"Yes. My husband is—unavailable, at the moment."

"I see," the lady said in a disapproving tone. "Well, have a seat. You too, Arnold." She gestured at two flimsy-looking wooden chairs. "You've been asked here today because of your son's unacceptable behavior, fighting in school with his classmate Jared Nichols. I presume he has explained this to you."

"Yes, he has, and I have told him that his actions are unacceptable," said Mom. She had remained standing, so Arnold had, too. The school official nodded, but Mom was just getting started. "I told him he should have blackened both of that bully's eyes, not just the one."

The assistant superintendent sat up straight, as if someone had goosed her, and glared. At any other time Arnold would have felt a rush of love for his mother, but nothing could get past the dull ache that had settled in around his heart.

"Mrs. Grossman, I don't know how it is in the big city, but down here we believe in settling our differences non-violently." The lady had a pronounced drawl. *Non-vahh-lently.* "You people may believe in an ah for an ah, a tooth for a tooth, but that's not the way we do things here."

"What do you mean, you people?" Mom said, an edge to her voice.

"Your son has already been suspended once this year, for interfering with school security. In these times, that is no light matter, Mrs. Grossman."

"GROSSBARD," said Mom, but the lady talked over her.

"Ah won't have it said that we haven't given you people every chance. Arnold may return to school tomorrow morning, but if he gets in any more trouble before the end of this school year, we will have no choice but to expel him. Do ah make mahself clear?"

"Perfectly," said Mom, turning to go. "Good day, Miss Wilson."

"WILKES," said the lady.

"Well, that was fun, wasn't it?" said Mom as she started her car. She set it on automatic and let the network take over the driving, a straight shot up U.S. Route 13.

Arnold grunted in response.

Mom gave him a long look. "Arnold, Dad will be home soon. They can't hold so many people for very long." In addition to Dad, the SCOD raid had picked up Paul Tingle, the publisher and editor of the *Chincoteague Lighthouse* (although they hadn't even printed anything about the pamphlet, much to Arnold's disappointment) and a grumpy old waterman named Dean Greene who was always saying stuff about the government.

"You don't know that," Arnold said.

"That's the way it always is," Mom replied. "Something happens that SCOD doesn't like, so they go around and kidnap everyone they don't like in the neighborhood and try to scare the pants off them for a few days, then they let them go. Mr. Allen is already working his contacts, trying to get Dad out."

"Lawyers can't help," Arnold said.

"Well, what do you propose we do instead, Arnold? Find out where Dad is and kidnap him back?"

"It would be a start," said Arnold. But he knew how ridiculous he sounded.

"I meant what I said back there, that you were right to fight back," said Mom. "But you have to know how, and you have to know when. A dumb kid like Jared doesn't need anything more than a punch in his snot-nose." Arnold smiled in spite of himself. "But usually it's more complicated when you're an adult," she added.

"Maybe that's what's wrong with adults," Arnold said. "You've forgotten how to fight back."

They rode in silence the rest of the way home. When the car pulled up in front of the house, Mom said, "I have to go into the office to get some work done the rest of the afternoon. Are you going to be all right here on your own?"

"Unless SCOD disappears me," Arnold said.

Mom's face crumpled, as if she was about to scream, or cry. "That's not funny, Arnold."

"It wasn't meant to be," Arnold said, slamming the car door behind him. He paused at the front door to the house. *Coward*, his mind whispered when he saw the blond wood. He slammed the door behind him, half hoping it would break like the other door had. In the kitchen he made himself a peanut butter and banana sandwich, leaving a big mess on the counter. Stomped into the living room, turned on the tri-vee, and recoiled when he saw the unmistakably resplendent scales of Risssss-erianus, Viceroy of All Earth.

"Most Exalted High Viceroy, Archduke of the Homeworld Risssss-erianus, you do this shriveled worm of an Earthling an undeserved honor by agreeing to this interview," simpered the network anchor, a pudgy man named Rodger Ales.

"It is my duty, my *noblesse oblige* if you will, to correct the irresponsible rumors that antisocial human elements have been repeating since Saturday," boomed the alien.

"You may be Oz, the Great and Powerful," Arnold yelled at the hologram while Ales did some more toadying, "but pull the curtain aside and you're just a slug!"

"As your High Satrap says, let me make one thing perfectly clear," the alien poobah was saying. "There is no malfunction in any ship's Bubble Drive. There is simply a minor cosmic storm under way. It poses no threat whatsoever in normal space, indeed it is well-nigh undetectable here, but it does affect the higher dimensions that lower-order creatures such as yourself are unable to perceive. Therefore, out of an abundance of caution, it has been decided to temporarily suspend creation of bubble universes."

"Which means we are temporarily limited to saucers that travel slower than the speed of light, correct, Your Exalted Highness?" Ales said.

"Your limited understanding serves you adequately in this case, Mr. Ales."

"And when may we expect a resumption of transluminal service to the outer planets and other star systems, and normal rapid intercity service on Earth, O Exalted Highness?"

"When the storm passes, of course, Earthworm Ales. Our sole concern is for the safety and well-being of inferior creatures such as yourself who depend on us for protection."

"Thank you for that fair and balanced statement, your eminence," Ales said. "We now return to our regularly scheduled programming."

The anchor's flabby features dissolved into Jack McInnes's chiseled ones. Just then there was a knock on the door. Arnold decided to ignore it, but it came again, softly but insistently. *Can't be SCOD. They pound like the hammer of doom.* Sighing, Arnold got up to open it. Mr. Wolff was standing on the step.

"I want to make sure you're all caught up by the time you come back to my class tomorrow morning, Arnold," Mr. Wolff said, a bit too loudly. "May I come in?" As soon as Arnold shut the door behind him, the teacher put his arms behind his back and started pacing. He was wearing his usual sport jacket and dark trousers, and he adopted the same lecturing tone he used in class.

"That was excellent work you and the other kids did on the pamphlet, Arnold. Really excellent, and I must commend you and even Gloria for bringing those Valkyries from the other world here to help you. You've obviously learned what I meant you to. The spark of rebellion has been lit! You know, the Hungarian Jewish poet Hannah Szenes, who died fighting the Nazis, wrote a famous poem that says, 'Blessed is the match that is consumed but kindles a flame.'"

"I don't feel very blessed," said Arnold. "SCOD kidnapped my father. They think he wrote the pamphlet."

Mr. Wolff smiled slowly, showing sharp, vulpine teeth. "That was just the beginning, Arnold. I've let *our friends* know that you're ready to do more than just spread the word."

"From the League?" Arnold gasped.

Mr. Wolff put his index finger to his lips. "Let's just call them two gentlemen of my acquaintance."

"What are their names?"

"You don't need to know their names, Arnold. You just need a place and time to meet them."

That was a problem. SCOD and the police were bound to be watching the house very carefully. Arnold didn't think he'd be able to bear it if they *disappeared* Mom, too. And what would happen to him and Alison, then? They couldn't very well move in with Grandma, in the retirement home. Did they have some special juvie prison for kids whose parents were both in SCOD holes? Arnold shivered. He didn't want to find out. But then he remembered—there was the old hunting lodge where Jo was hiding! Not only would that be the perfect place for a secret rendezvous, it would give Jo the chance to join the fight for real, instead of waiting around uselessly until Gloria could figure out a way to get her home.

Arnold quickly explained his idea to Mr. Wolff, who smoothed down the corners of his mustache as he stood thinking a moment.

"I see," the teacher said. "And when are you going there next to bring Jo supplies?"

"Tomorrow afternoon, after school."

"Hmm. I'll have to see if my friends can make it then. It sounds like a good idea to me, though."

Mr. Wolff turned toward the door, but Arnold grabbed his jacket sleeve. "This is going to be real fighting, isn't it? Not some kid thing like carrying messages for the actual fighters?"

Mr. Wolff smiled again. "Don't worry, Arnold. You'll see all the action you can handle. This cosmic disaster your little friend caused? It's a blessing in disguise. The viceroy and all his lackeys are panicking, because they can't get supplies and reinforcements from Homeworld. I mean, just look at that!"

He was pointing at the stage of the tri-vee, which had been chattering away the whole time unheeded. "Superastronauts" had given way to a commercial, one Arnold had never seen before. A balding man was sitting in an office chair in front of a typewriter, looking bored and sad. The camera zoomed in his forehead, and his skull opened up to show a tropical beach where the man lay on a deck chair, grinning from ear to ear as several hot girls in bikinis jostled each other in their haste to bring him drinks and sandwiches.

"Tired of the routine?" a breathless female voice said. "Longing to escape? Outer space may be blocked, but this is the perfect time to explore inner space!" The camera zoomed back out of the balding man's dirty mind to focus on his desktop, where a sleek, gleaming new n-net hub sat. It was much smaller than any of the devices Arnold had ever seen. "The brand-new, in-home nodes of the n-net are available to rent for just 49 solars and 95 lunars a month!"

Arnold's hands flew to his mouth, then his head swelled fit to burst as the implications sunk in. "They're going to give millions of people NINA like Mom had! But why?"

"The Winged-Thinkers think they can calculate their way out of this mess, but they're wrong," said a new voice.

Arnold and Mr. Wolff turned and saw Gloria framed in the open doorway. Her green eyes were ablaze, and for a long moment Arnold forgot everything but that cold fire. She was so old, and not just human old. She looked thirty years old, but she might really be thirty thousand years old, or thirty million.

"What are you doing here, Wolff?"

"Just checking up on the boy, Gloria," Mr. Wolff said, winking at Arnold. "This mess is all your doing, you know. First that spaghetti rebel of yours has him taunt the flying slimeballs—oh, don't get me wrong, I enjoyed every word of it—"

"—which I know you rewrote in your barbaric style," Gloria said.

"—then your dragon-speaking little buddy burns all the bridges between this world and all the others. A fine and glorious setup for a true, Jeffersonian revolution of blood, my pacifistic pal." Mr. Wolff patted Gloria on the shoulder, gave Arnold another wink, and strolled out the door chuckling.

When he was gone and the door shut behind him, Gloria slumped like a deflating balloon. "He's right, Arnold. Every word he said is true. This enormous disaster is my fault."

Being in a position to comfort a grown woman—well, a being who looked like a grown woman, anyway—made Arnold feel very grown-up and powerful. "It's all right, Gloria," he said. "Mr. Wolff is right that something had to force the revolution to happen."

She shuddered. "You sound like Vladimir Lenin," she said. "That kind of thinking can get millions of people killed!"

"But with the Slugs putting the n-net in people's homes, they'll be destroying millions of people's brains!" Arnold exclaimed. "Isn't that the same thing as murder?" He watched incredulously as Gloria actually wrung her hands, something he'd thought was only an expression—with the surreal touch of her orange cat's tail dropping down out of nowhere and interlacing itself with her fingers.

"If we can only let people know what's going on, this terrible plan can be stopped without violence," she said.

"We tried that already. All it got us was my father getting disappeared. And Dean Greene, and poor Paul Tingle at the *Chincoteague Lighthouse*! I'm surprised they didn't grab Barry Freed as well." Arnold shook his head. "No, it has to be this way, and it has to be now, before the Slugs can fix the Bubble Drive."

"They won't be able to do that so easily. And violence only begets violence. If you manage to kill all the Winged-Thinkers in the solar system, you'll bring back all the human nations and armies with their wars—with the Human Defense League and the Patriotic Front around to make things even worse."

Arnold talked loud and fast to drown out the sinking feeling in the pit of his stomach. "I think Mr. Wolff is right about you—you're just afraid. And your idea of nonviolence also leads to people getting hurt and killed! What about my father? What about all the people whose brains are being melted while we sit around and do nothing?"

Gloria bowed her head. "Some of what you say is true, Arnold. But please be careful. Think before you act. Some things can't be taken back after you do them, no matter how sorry you are." She paused. "Do you still have the spider plant I gave you?"

"Of course." Arnold smiled despite himself. "It seems to like milk."

Gloria managed a half-smile. "Keep taking care of it, and it will keep taking care of you."

"I'll do that." Arnold deliberately turned his back on Gloria and turned the tri-vee off. "Goodbye, Gloria. I've got a lot to do to get ready for school tomorrow."

* * * *

Later that afternoon, Jo was dragging driftwood into a heap for a small campfire when she looked up at a long shadow cast by the setting sun. "Oh, hello, Arnold," she said, then shaded her eyes and blinked in surprise at seeing Kayleigh. "What are you doing here?"

"Arnold and I agreed that we'll take turns with Alison, bringing you food and stuff," Kayleigh said. She unslung her backpack and held out a jar and a loaf of bread. "Here. I don't know if you have peanut butter on the Gingo Teag planet, but—"

"Of course we have peanut butter," Jo said, snatching it and the bread from Kayleigh. Her eyes narrowed. "You didn't poison this, did you?"

"Of course not!" Kayleigh said, her mouth twisting. "You're the one who goes around trying to hurt people!"

"I told you, I didn't really mean to hurt Arnold. I was just playing a little joke on him."

"You have some twisted sense of humor! He could have drowned!"

Jo lowered her eyes. "I know that. It was a stupid thing I did. But I think I'm being punished enough for it. I can't go home!"

Kayleigh tossed her backpack on the sand and sat down with a grunt.

Jo squatted next to her and eyed her, wishing she would go away.

Instead, Kayleigh asked, "How did you tell that dragon what to do? I thought they eat people. I mean, if they were real, that is."

"They are real, in my world. And I mindspeak with Ir'gassaphet and the others—"

"You do what?"

"Mindspeak. You call it psychopathy, I think."

Kayleigh covered her mouth and giggled. "I think you mean telepathy. A psychopath is a crazy person. And telepathy ain't real, anyhow. We learned all about that in science class."

Jo could feel annoyance rising in her chest, flowing down her arms and into her fingers, which itched to wrap themselves around Kayleigh's fat neck. But strangling Arnold's girlfriend would probably not be a good move at the moment. So she said patiently, "Maybe you people don't know everything. Mindspeaking *is* really rare among human beings, which was one reason why people didn't understand for such a long time that dragons are just as intelligent as human beings. Maybe more so."

"And they breathe fire and everything?" Kayleigh's voice was scornful.

Definitely they're smarter than some people. "It's not really fire. It's hydrogen peroxide and fatty acid that they mix together in their beaks—"

"They have *beaks*?"

"Do you always interrupt people so much? Crikey, that's rude!" Mum might think that she, Jo, was rude, but if she ever got her hands on this Kayleigh person she would strap her within an inch of her life. Talking quickly to keep Kayleigh from interrupting again, Jo filled her in briefly on dragon biology. "But the best thing about them, something I think I may be the first person ever to discover, is that they can fly between worlds. That's how Ir'gassaphet and I got here."

"But not now. That's why you're trapped here."

"Yeah. I'm not too happy about that."

While she'd been talking to Kayleigh, Jo had managed to get a fire going with a pocketknife and a bit of stone she always carried around. She stared into the flames, lost in thought, and hardly even noticed when the other girl softly said goodbye and walked away into the gathering dusk.

33

When he went back to school on Tuesday, Arnold found himself in what he quickly came to think of as the Alone Zone. Every class he went to, someone was always sitting in what had been his desk, as if they'd expected him never to come back. And they wouldn't get up and move when he asked them to. They acted like they didn't hear him, and he had to make his way to the back of the room. And the people he did know were acting all weird.

Mr. Wolff made everyone read aloud from *Harmonious Literature,* the official textbook, which he had refused to use before and which was full of crashingly boring "patriotic" verse. Obviously he was being extra careful, with SCOD and the Slugs and the army all running around, but knowing that didn't make the time go any faster. He groaned inwardly when Mr. Wolff handed him back his last quiz, on which he'd gotten a C minus, and the teacher had written, "Tonight is no good for our extra credit project. Meet me Thurs."

Three whole days before he could find out if the League would use him for a real mission! After school today, he'd have to hike all the way out to Jo's hiding place with nothing but an extra apple he'd remembered to grab from home at the last second before leaving the house. And without those League agents there to impress her, she'd start lording it over him again. What if, when Kayleigh went to see her last night, they'd started laughing at him behind his back? His ears burned at the thought.

Finally lunchtime came around. Arnold smiled in relief when he saw Gus sitting in his usual spot at the table, but Gus eyed him and said mildly, "Better move along, Arnold."

Arnold's mouth fell open, but Gus had already turned his attention back to his food. When Arnold tried to sit down beside him anyway, Gus put out his arm to block him.

"Don't make me tell you again," he said, and added in a hoarse whisper, "What kind of trouble have you gotten us into?"

Arnold just stood there, his lunch tray loaded down with a toasted cheese sandwich that looked fossilized, bright yellow peach slices in gooey syrup, and a chocolate milk he'd already started drinking. His mind was a blank. Someone bumped into him and flipped his tray up, spilling its contents onto his shirt and the floor.

"Didn't you hear him, Jew-tard?" hissed Jared. "He said, move along!"

Arnold picked up the spilled food, put it in the trash and got back in line, while everybody pretended not to watch.

"Hungry boy, hah?" the lunch lady said loudly as she rang him up.

Someone snickered. He looked around for Kayleigh, but his heart sank when he spotted her sitting with a pack of girls, including her old best friend Madison.

"That witch," she'd called her just last week, when he asked why they didn't hang out anymore. "All she ever did was tell everyone all my secrets and laugh at me behind my back."

Now Kayleigh was sitting right next to Madison, and when they saw him looking their way they bent their heads together and laughed loudly. Arnold's ears burned. Maybe Kayleigh was only pretending, like Mr. Wolff, but it made Arnold feel as if things were right back to where they'd been a year ago.

Actually, they were worse, as he found out when he carried the tray over to the Reject Table. Overbite Jason and Nose-Picking Greg were at their usual places. Only James Park was missing. But when Arnold sat down, the rejects both got up, took their food and shuffled away. What was really amazing, though, was that people made room for them at the other lunch tables. Arnold had the whole of the Formica-topped Siberia to himself for the rest of the period.

It doesn't matter, he told himself, and concentrated on catching up the chapters he had missed in math. Numbers didn't change. It was a relief to forget all his troubles and solve for *x*. Unfortunately he forgot his troubles too well, because when the bell rang and he got up to leave, someone tripped him and sent him flopping belly-first onto the floor. He picked himself up, ignoring the snickers and his sore right leg, and made his way through the stuffy, smelly halls to his locker, which was painted with a blue-eyed swastika.

It really isn't fair, he thought as he scraped at the drying paint with his thumbnail. *I gave up everything for the Resistance!* But maybe that wasn't enough. If Mr. Wolff's "gentlemen" didn't come through, what was he going to do?

He kept brooding about that on the long walk out to Assateague. Luckily it was good weather, a warm, dry evening with a light breeze off the sea. On his way he stopped at a store and bought extra bottled water, energy bars, and sunscreen for Jo, putting the supplies in his backpack.

It was going to be awfully late by the time he got back, but that was all right, Mom knew what he was doing.

He crossed the bridge to Assateague, walking past cyclists and guys trudging back home carrying their fishing gear. It was a couple of kilometers just to reach the beach along a winding blacktop road through the thick, forested waist of Assateague Island, past the turnoffs for the old lighthouse and the Visitor Center, past the cars stopped in clusters so the tourists could get out and take pictures of the wild, potbellied ponies grazing in the marsh. Even this early in the season there were already lots of tourists, and only a few locals heading back the other way into town who eyed Arnold curiously as they passed.

At the beach it was cooler thanks to the breeze off the water, but the afternoon sun shone down bright as a spotlight as he turned left for the long hike north past the dunes. After the first kilometer or so he had the entire broad strip of sand between the dunes and the lapping waves to himself. The sun was low in the sky by the time Arnold made his way over the dunes to the hunting lodge. He had to stop and drain two of his water bottles before he could go on, and his steps were dragging by the time he got there, his sneakers full of sand even though he'd stayed on the damp ground near the waterline as much as possible. To add to the misery of his aching feet the final fifty meters went through salt marsh, and cold, smelly mud oozed into his socks. *I hope Jo appreciates what I'm doing for her!*

When he found her, she was skipping bits of broken clamshell across the calm waters of the bay. She wasn't as happy to see him, or as excited by the news that the League agents were coming, as he'd hoped.

"It seemed like an exciting game, kicking the Slugs off the Earth, when it was your Earth we were freeing," she said. "Now that I have to live here, it's just scary and awful."

"I'm sure Gloria or Mr. Wolff will figure out a way to get you home eventually," Arnold said.

Jo half-smiled. "Maybe. Meanwhile I'm an actual castaway on a desert island, straight out of *Robinson Crusoe*."

"That won't last long. As soon as we get rid of the Slugs and SCOD, my dad will be free and you can come stay with us again."

The shard Jo threw then sank without a trace. "I don't think that would be such a good idea, Arnold," she said, not looking at him. "I'll have to figure something else out, when the time comes. Who knows, maybe I have a twin here, like Sharon has Shaniqua."

"The only Purnells I know of in Chincoteague are black," said Arnold, but he was thinking, *why doesn't she want to live in our house? It would be fun, having another sister.*

"So? That don't make no never mind, as Kay would say. She's all right, Arnold."

Oh. So that's why. She thinks the Scotts will take her in. That'll be... weird.

* * * *

Thursday the weather was almost hot. In English class the air conditioning was broken and Mr. Wolff left the window open, letting in a smell of fresh-cut grass and the pungent scent of the sea.

Arnold sat daydreaming, thinking how much easier it would have been to be a hero back in the days of the American Revolution, when he could have captained a ship raiding the British Navy. Suddenly the redcoats are swarming up the sides, attempting to board and capture the *USS Gloria!* The first mate tosses Commodore Grossbard his saber, and he uses it to singlehandedly hold off half a dozen redcoats! He skewers one right through the chest, and the brute groans and lets go of a screaming Hailee Washington, the great general's daughter, who throws herself sobbing into his arms.

"Quit waving your pencil near my face, you little freak," a voice said. It wasn't Hailee but Madison.

He mumbled apologies while the class chuckled.

Lunch couldn't come soon enough, but when he got to the cafeteria he nearly collided with Kayleigh.

"Watch where you're going, stupid," she said. Loudly, so everyone around would know she had nothing to do with him.

But he knew that wasn't really true, and anyway nothing could spoil his good mood now that has was about to make contact with the League. Gloria might be too much of a wimp to help him out, but Mr. Wolff had come through!

As soon as the final bell of the day rang, Arnold shoved his books in his locker, took his empty backpack and ran. So he wasn't going to do his homework tonight, so what? School wasn't his job anymore. Being a full-time Resistance fighter was.

There'd be plenty of time to catch up, after the Revolution, when the Slugs were all kicked out. Not only would he be a hero then, but nerds like him would be the indispensable heroes of the whole human race. They'd have to study and work extra hard to make sure Earth copied and improved on all the Slugs' weapons and their Bubble Drive, so they could never come back and try to take over again.

To make extra sure, maybe Earth would have to take over Homeworld. Arnold might end up being a viceroy himself!

But seeing Mr. Wolff lurking in the woods just past the entrance booth on Assateague helped bring Arnold back to earth. The teacher was scowling, wearing his usual sport jacket and a tan, broad-brimmed hat against the sun.

When he saw Arnold he beckoned him into the woods and took him on an unmarked trail through the evergreens, skirting the edge of a large manmade pond and wildfowl paradise called Snow Goose Pool. They took care to keep a screen of trees between them and the pondside path, which was crowded with strollers and birdwatchers.

By the time Mr. Wolff cut over and across the dunes to the beach, Arnold was sweating, panting and sore from the scratchy brambles they'd had to climb through, but Mr. Wolff didn't seem winded at all. "Keep up, will you?" was all he would say to Arnold for the rest of the hike to the hunting lodge.

When they got there, Arnold's legs were trembling with exhaustion. He couldn't imagine how he'd ever be able to walk back. He didn't see anyone at first and wondered where Jo was, and if the walk had been for nothing. Then he noticed two or three sets of deep footprints breaking up the bright green marsh grass, leading up to the lodge from the direction of the bay. The chunk of door with the lock in it was missing, and the door itself stood ajar. The inside was shadowed against the light of the setting sun.

"Hello? Jo?" he called, pushing the door further open. Silhouettes shifted in the dimness. When his eyes adjusted he saw two strangers standing in the shadows. He glanced behind him and saw Mr. Wolff standing there with his arms folded, a silhouette himself against the too-bright sky. *Where's Jo? Only one way to find out.* He took a step into the lodge and said, "I'm Arnold. I'm a student at—"

"We know who you are," a deep voice rumbled. "Stop wasting time."

"Sorry. Where's my friend Jo?"

"You mean that little girl who was hanging around here? We told her to scram."

"You did *what?*"

"We don't need no ponytailed little tomboy messing with our plans!"

Mr. Wolff stepped forward and cleared his throat while Arnold stood paralyzed with outrage. "Gentlemen, I know the young lady in question, and believe me, she would be invaluable on any mission you'd care to design."

"Oh yeah? Doing what, knitting socks for our agents?" the heavy voice rumbled.

"She sure scurried away good and proper when we told her to," sneered another voice. This one was fast-talking, higher pitched, with some kind of East Coast big-city accent. Not Baltimore, though. Somewhere further north, maybe Brooklyn.

Arnold drew himself up. "If my friend Jo can't take part, I won't either."

"I understand your reluctance, gentlemen," Mr. Wolff said. "But Jodie Purnell is no flower eater. She may not look it, but she's more of a dragon lady!" He winked at Arnold.

"Fine, have it your way," the guy from Brooklyn snapped.

"Well, where did she go?" Arnold said after a brief pause.

"Toward those dunes over there," the big bruiser said, waving an arm as thick as a normal person's leg further up the beach.

Arnold started running, calling out Jo's name. He found her a few minutes later, crouched down in the barren hollow between two dunes with a small pile of sticks at her feet, as if she planned on building a fire and making camp for the night right there.

"Go away, Arnold," she said when his shadow fell over her.

"Mr. Wolff—he's my English teacher—talked those guys into letting you join."

"Bully for him."

"I thought you wanted to fight the Slugs!"

Jo looked up at him, her eyes huge with unshed tears. "This isn't my world, Arnold. I told you that when you were here two days ago."

"It is now, like it or not. Admit it—you're scared. You said as much then."

Jo was on her feet in a flash. She pushed Arnold with both hands, and he fell over backward into the sand.

"I'm not scared of anything! But I don't trust those bullyboys. And I don't trust you."

There was a silence as Arnold got to his feet, as if the words Jo had just said had punched a hole in the air. He struggled for something to say. "Jo, please. You may not trust me, but you're the only one *I* can trust." He bit his lip while Jo stared at him over folded arms. "I need you. Without you, there's no Freedom Fighters of Earth."

"So I'm going to be your loyal helper?" she shot back.

"No! I don't need a sidekick."

"A sidekick? What's that? You deserve a kick in the arse, you do!"

"I mean, I don't want to boss you around. And I don't want you to boss me around. Can't we just be equals?"

After another moment Jo shook her head. "That's not how it works in armies. Don't you know anything, Arnold?" She took a step toward him, and then another. He backed away in confusion. "Good heavens,

Arnold, don't look so terrified! I'm not going to beat you up. I'm coming back with you."

"Oh," Arnold said, and turned to walk back to the lodge with her. After a few moments he said, "What did you mean, about armies?"

"Only this, Arnold. In armies someone always gives the orders. And it's never people like us." She paused. "It's people like your new friends. We're going to have to be the loyal soldiers."

They walked over the crest of a dune, and Arnold saw Mr. Wolff and the two strangers standing waiting, their long shadows stretching out to the east, pointing back toward the beach. Arnold shivered inwardly and wished there wasn't a rule against holding Jo's hand... even though that might make Kayleigh jealous, if she found out about it.

As soon as they were in earshot, Brooklyn said, in a voice that was probably supposed to be friendly, "That was good work you kids did on that pamphlet, for amateurs."

"Umm, thanks," Arnold said.

"You can thank Teresa. It was her idea," Jo said, in her best South Philadelphia accent.

"Who's Teresa?" Brooklyn said, looking sideways at Mr. Wolff.

"It's not important," the teacher said. "She's solid for the cause, don't worry."

Arnold scuffed around in the sand, knowing he should look these League agents straight in the eye but not wanting to. There was a strange smell in the air, something sharper than the sulfurous marsh mud. It hadn't been there the other day, when he'd brought Jo the apple and the energy bars.

"All right. We're here to give you your first real mission," Brooklyn said to Arnold.

"I used the ditto machine again, to print the message you're going to leave at the scene of the attack," Mr. Wolff said. "Here, take these."

Arnold glanced at the papers he was handed. They looked like school worksheets torn in half, but all they said was:

We are everywhere—Human Defense League.

When he managed to speak, he could barely hear his own voice above the thundering of his heart. "Attack? I'm going to take part in an attack?"

Bruiser spoke up. "You're going to be the attacker, Arnold," he said. "I'll be watching in case you need help."

In case I screw up, you mean. Arnold felt his face burning. *But I won't screw up, I won't!*

"What about me?" Jo asked.

"You?" Bruiser looked her up and down, as if she was a shriveled-up hamburger he might want to eat, but only if he got really, really hungry. "Tell you what, girlie. You can surveil the scene for your boyfriend here and make sure the coast is clear before he mounts the attack."

"He's not my boyfriend!" Jo growled.

Arnold hardly heard her. He had more important things on his mind. "Will I be hurting SCOD?" he asked. "They took my father."

"You'll put the fear of God into SCOD, the High Ones, and the government's lackeys. All of them," Brooklyn said. He paused. "Kid, do you know what a Molotov cocktail is?"

Arnold darted a glance at Jo, who looked blank. "I'm not old enough to drink," he said. Bruiser snorted, and Arnold wondered what he'd said wrong this time.

"No, kid." It sounded like Brooklyn was trying not to smile. *I have to show these guys I'm not a stupid kid!* "A Molotov cocktail is a bottle filled with gasoline or some other flammable liquid, with a rag stuffed in the top. You light it and throw it at the target."

"What's gasoline?" Jo asked.

"I told you having a little tomboy around was only gonna waste time," Bruiser said. "Haven't you ever seen a car before, you bimbo?"

"He means petrol, Jo," Mr. Wolff said hastily.

"The stuff they use in small motors? But that's dangerous!" Jo exclaimed.

"What's the target?" Arnold asked.

"The target? You're going to burn down the town hall," Brooklyn said.

"What? But why the Chincoteague Town Hall?" Arnold exclaimed.

"The town fathers are lackeys of the High Ones, just as much as the White House," Brooklyn said. "Think of it as practice for burning the White House down." He grinned, showing his teeth like Mr. Wolff. "Which we'll be doing soon, the way things are going, with the Slugs cut off from supplies and their home ball o' dirt."

"But—but—somebody could get hurt!" Jo said.

"Don't worry. He can do it at night. No one's there then," Brooklyn said. "This Saturday would be a good time—it's Easter weekend, a lot of folks will be out of town visiting relatives."

"But where do I get a Molotov cocktail from?" Arnold asked.

"You go to a gas station and fill up a gas can," Bruiser said. "Then you pour it into a glass bottle and stuff a rag in the top. Your girlfriend can do it, if you're afraid of getting your hands dirty."

"I AM *NOT* HIS—"

"If you don't have any more questions, we can start your practice," Brooklyn said.

"My practice?"

"Do you have to repeat everything, like a moron?" Bruiser snapped. "Stop wasting everyone's time."

* * * *

The sun was almost on the western horizon as Arnold meekly followed the League agents, who said Mr. Wolff and Jo should wait by the lodge. Bruiser was carrying a red plastic gas can and an empty quart-size glass bottle. Brooklyn had some rags.

"All right. You're going to fill the glass bottle and put a piece of rag in the top," Brooklyn said.

Arnold knelt in the mud and unscrewed the black cap from the gas can. Nothing easier, right? He'd seen vids of riots from the 1960's, and people throwing burning stuff that he now realized must have been Molotov cocktails. But when he picked up the gas can it was heavier than he'd thought, and he spilled some gasoline on his shoes. He waited for Bruiser to laugh at him again, but there was silence except for the wind hissing through the grass. He set the bottle between his feet and poured as carefully as he could.

"Not so full. You need to leave room for the rag," Brooklyn said.

Arnold splashed a little gas out of the bottle into the thick grass, and stuffed a rag in the bottleneck. "Okay, I'm done," he said.

"Great. Now you light it, and throw it," Brooklyn said.

"Throw it at what?"

"At that dead tree," Bruiser said, pointing.

Arnold opened his mouth, but no sound came out. He thought of the gas on his shoes and the bottom of his trousers. What if they caught fire? He'd never even been a Cub Scout, never learned to build a fire, and nobody in his family smoked. But Bruiser was already taking a cigarette lighter out of his pocket and handing it to him. Arnold swallowed, nodded, and tried turning the little wheel. Nothing happened.

"You need to flick it quicker," Bruiser said impatiently.

Arnold tried again and again, but it still wouldn't light. Bruiser grabbed it back, flicked it once and produced a beautiful clear flame like a candle that glowed in the gathering dusk.

"Okay, now you," he said, handing it to Arnold, who swallowed once and, feeling foolish, flicked it one more time.

This time it worked, though he yelped and almost dropped the lighter as it burned his thumb. But he held on somehow, and touched the flame to the rag stopping up the bottle.

"Now throw it!" Brooklyn cried. He backed up a few steps, as did Bruiser.

Arnold's left hand, the one holding the bottle, started shaking, and he needed to bring up his right hand to steady it and give the thing the heave-ho. As it sailed through the air he had a vivid flashback of a softball game in gym class last year, and Matt jeering at him, "You throw like a girl!"

Maybe that was true—but then again, Jo would surely do a better job than he was doing. The bottle barely reached the roots of the dead loblolly pine, even though it was less than five meters away. But it didn't matter, because it burst into bright yellow flames with a loud *whump*. As he watched, fascinated, fire raced up the side of the trunk, and the gray branches and brown needles went up with a hiss. He gulped. *What if it sets fire to the forest?* But the League men had chosen a tree that stood off by itself in a drift of sand. After a few minutes it toppled over and lay quietly burning.

When he walked back over to the lodge with the others, Mr. Wolff greeted him with a smile. "It was a pleasure to burn, eh?"

He looked at the teacher blankly for a moment, then smiled. "That's the first sentence of Ray Bradbury's *Fahrenheit 451*," he said. "Dad made me read it when I was little. He said any book SCOD disapproved of was required reading."

Mr. Wolff clapped him on the back. "I knew from the start you're all right, kid. Well, see you in class."

"Wait, aren't we walking back together?" Arnold said, as the teacher and the two League agents headed off into the marsh, in the opposite direction from Chincoteague.

Mr. Wolff raised a hairy hand in farewell but did not turn around.

"Where are they even going?" Arnold said.

"I think those blokes came in a motorboat," Jo said, reverting to her real accent. "It made the most awful racket. Why is everything so noisy in your world?"

"Beats me." Arnold was suddenly very tired. "Look, I've got school tomorrow. I'd better get back."

"What, and miss this lovely bonfire you started?" Jo gestured at the smoldering tree. "I was just about to roast the hot dogs Kay brought me last night."

So she's Kay now, is she? Arnold felt weirdly jealous. "Are you coming with me on the mission Saturday night?"

Jo sighed, blowing some loose bangs off her forehead. "I suppose I'd best, Arnold. Otherwise you're like as not to burn yourself."

"Thanks for your confidence."

"Well earned, I'm sure."

Arnold started to get to his feet, but stopped in mid-motion when Jo said, "Your Mr. Wolff's another one like Gloria, isn't he?"

"How," Arnold swallowed, straightened up slowly and said, "how did you know?"

"Trust, Arnold, remember? You said I was the only one you could trust. And you didn't even tell me that. Can he take me home?" Suddenly Jo sounded like a little girl.

"He's stuck here, same as you and Gloria. I'm sorry, Jo. Really I am."

She said nothing as she stared through a gap in the dunes at the gaudy scarlet sunset over the bay.

Walking home along the beach through the gathering darkness, Arnold wished he could have said something to make her feel better, but couldn't think what.

34

The night the sirens began was unusually warm for mid-April. Alison would always remember the damp, stifling heat. The air conditioner was broken, and Mom was too busy trying to track Dad down to have it fixed, or maybe she didn't have the money, Alison wasn't sure which. Either way, she didn't dare complain.

Thanks to Gloria, Mom had been about to start a new life, but now she had no life at all but going to work and rushing home to pay bills and make long-distance calls trying to find out what SCOD had done with Dad. There were dark circles under her eyes every morning, and a couple of times during the week she had even dozed off during dinner. But she only smiled sadly when Alison asked what she could do to help.

"Allie, you can't possibly do anything more than you're already doing, fixing all of us breakfast and dinner, taking dinner to Jo on Wednesday, and all while keeping up with your schoolwork."

"Poor Jo, I didn't mind the walk. She was so pathetically grateful. But couldn't I make some of those calls about Dad? Everyone says I sound older on the phone."

Mom pressed her lips together into a thin white line. "It's better you don't get involved," she said.

The worst thing all week had been the strain of having to go to school and pretend like everything was normal. Only Shaniqua treated her any different, and that was unbearable in its own way—the look in her big brown eyes, the look that said we're praying for your dad, made Alison want to burst into tears. Which she didn't dare do because she might get sent to Mr. Wright's office, and if that happened she didn't know if she'd be able to stop herself from ripping his ugly head off.

At the end of the school day she'd stop in the library for a cup of Gloria's cocoa and a few blessed moments of peace browsing her impossible books. Geographies were her favorite. *A Walking Guide to the Phalansteries of North America. Discover Alta California, Tejas, and the Other Lands of Northern Mexico! Plan Your Vacation in the Republic of New England!*

When Alison could finally tear herself away and walk home she was no longer bothered by Mr. Freed, who was really Mr. Wineman. It should have been a relief that he was staying out of sight in that church, which was only sensible, but Alison found she actually missed his crazy rants. Lucky for him he wasn't locked up with Dad in some SCOD dungeon somewhere.

She tried to force her mind away from such thoughts, but they returned to plague her in every quiet moment, and especially when she was lying awake on her sweat-soaked sheets, listening to the whine of the rotating fan as it turned back and forth, back and forth. At moments like that she kept picturing Dad lying on the floor in a gray, concrete basement, convinced that his family had forgotten him.

When the sirens started up Alison didn't pay much attention at first. The noise was unusual for Chincoteague, but she was used to it from back home, her real, lost home in Pikesville. It took shouts and running feet in the street to bring her to the window. But she couldn't see anything except the darkened house across the street. So she started down the stairs, hoping she'd be able to see something through the living room window, when a thump from Arnold's room brought her up short. She knocked on the door.

"Arnold? Are you all right?"

When there was no answer she opened the door a crack and peeked in, just in time to see him pulling the sheets up to his chin. His window was wide open, and the spider plant had been knocked onto its side, where it lay waving its leaves around frantically, like a turtle turned over on its back. There was a faint but sharp stink in the air.

Alison shivered as she closed the door as quietly as possible. She knew better than to ask Arnold where he had been. Last night when he came home late from bringing food to Jo and she'd teased him lightly about having two girlfriends, he'd given her such a murderous glare she'd flinched as if he'd struck her. *What if he really tries to hurt me? Not just a punch on the arm but something serious?* It was better not to find out.

Downstairs, Mom was looking out through the Venetian blinds. She was wearing her pink bathrobe and her hair was even messier than usual.

"What's going on?" Alison asked, joining her at the window.

"A big fire a few blocks away, looks like."

Alison bit her lip. "Most of the houses in this town are wooden. Maybe we'd better go get Arnold, in case the fire spreads."

Mom nodded and went to the foot of the stairs. "Arnold?"

There was a grunt from his room. *He's really faking it. This wasn't his night to go bring food to Jo. Where was he just now?*

"Arnold, I think you'd better get down here. There's a big fire nearby," Mom called.

"Gimme a minute," he called back, his voice muffled. *To change out of pajamas, or into them?*

Mom walked over to the front door. "I think I'd better find out what's going on." She opened the door, admitting a gust of air that stank of smoke.

Alison watched her walk out to the sidewalk, where a small group of neighbors had gathered. After a few seconds she came back, shaking her head.

"What is it?" Alison asked after her mother shut the door. The new door replacing the one that had been useless against SCOD.

"It's the town hall, over on Community Drive," said Mom. "I don't even know where that is. Do you?"

"I think so," Alison said. "We should be all right here. Unless the fire spreads to the whole town."

"What fire?" Arnold said.

They turned to watch him coming down the stairs in his blue striped pajamas. He was rubbing his eyes and yawning widely.

"A fire at the town hall," Mom repeated.

"Yeah? Who cares? Why'd you wake me up for that?"

Another fire engine racing by drowned out Mom's response, if she made one. For lack of anything better to do, Alison headed for the kitchen and started setting out graham crackers and milk for everybody. But her mind was whirling faster than the blades of her fan. *That was gasoline I smelled! Arnold set that fire. But why?* It wasn't that she couldn't understand his hating the town. She hated it too, and wished more than anything that they'd never left Pikesville. But it was a long way from that to arson.

Arnold came into the kitchen, took his plate of crackers and his glass of milk without a word of thanks, and went back upstairs, leaving Alison alone with Mom, who said, "Well, I certainly hope no one was hurt. Thanks for putting out this snack, Allie."

"No problem," Alison said.

"You look worried about something, hon. Want to tell me what it is?"

"N-nothing, Mom. Go back to sleep. I think I'll sit up for a while."

"All right. But you need your sleep too."

As if anyone cares about that, Alison thought at her retreating back. It felt good to be annoyed at someone, even if she knew she was being unreasonable. It took her mind off her fear. But not for very long. Her thoughts went round and round, faster and faster, shading off imperceptibly into a nightmare where she was locked in the unknown basement with Dad, calling and calling for help though she could only whisper.

Through the bars in a ground-level window set high in the wall she could see Arnold's face, staring impassively down at them.

She yelped when the blank sky behind him was replaced by the kitchen walls, but he was actually there, his expression unchanged.

"Fell asleep at the table, Sis?"

"What? Umm, yeah, I must have," she said, sitting up and running her hands through her tangled hair. She must be as much of a mess as Mom had been a few hours ago. "What time is it? I'd better go shower."

"Where's my breakfast?" he yelled after her.

"Get it yourself," she called back from the stairs, and stopped herself from adding "turd-breath" in case it made him mad enough to hurt her.

The merry-go-round of thoughts started up again as Alison rushed to shower and get dressed for school. Arnold had already banged out the door, so she must be *really* late. But that didn't matter. What mattered was why he had set that fire, and even more important, what she should do about it. She knew Arnold was on probation at school. They would definitely expel him for this. But what then? If she could have been certain he would only get sent to juvie, she'd tell on him to Mom right this second. But what if they wouldn't stop at juvie? What if they decided it was terrorism, or what if SCOD got involved? Or both? She couldn't do that to her own brother, no matter how scared she was of him.

That thought stopped her cold, with the shower water running over her and a bar of soap in her hand. She was afraid of him, but she was also afraid *for* him. That was really messed up.

Her dilemma had resolved itself for the moment by the time she came downstairs, because Mom had already left for work. But when she got to school, things were a million times worse.

She'd barely sat down at her desk in homeroom when Mr. Wright (*I wish Arnold had set fire to his house*) came on the loudspeakers and said everyone had to go to the auditorium for an emergency assembly. There was the usual excited hubbub, the usual pushing and shoving. Alison tried to tune out the chatter around her, the rumors flying thick as autumn fog on the marshes. A fireman had been killed. No, two firemen. They'd had to call trucks from down-county, and from Pocomoke, up above the Maryland line. No, that wasn't true, the local firemen had handled the whole thing. The mayor had been working late in his office and had barely gotten out alive. It must've been Ron Reynolds, who lost to him by ten votes in the last election, who had set the fire.

"That's a filthy lie!" said Don Peabody, clenching his fists and scowling at Lee Parker.

"Hey man, that's just what I heard from Tom," said Lee, throwing up his hands. "I didn't mean nothin' against your uncle."

"Where's Tom? I'll kill him," said Don.

Alison was relieved they weren't picking on her this time.

"Time to sit down and shut up!" boomed Mr. Wright, his hands clenched on the podium.

Alison stared at his shiny bald head, wishing she had laser-beam eyes. She pictured his scalp crisping like fried chicken. But the creep really seemed angry, and the auditorium rapidly fell silent.

"That's better," he said, his mouth so close to the microphone a squeal of feedback started up.

Instead of the usual dulled rage she felt every time she passed him in the hallway, Alison had a wild impulse to stand up and scream, "What have you done with my father?" But she stayed glued to her seat.

"I'm sure you've all heard about the fire at the town hall last night," Mr. Wright began. "But what you may not yet know is," he paused dramatically and shouted, "Terror has come to Chincoteague!"

Alison flinched from the noise. So did almost everybody else.

"That's right," Mr. Wright said, "our own little island haven has been attacked! The police found a note at the scene last night, 'claiming responsibility' by the Human Defense League. HA! As if those cowards ever took responsibility for anything!" He paused and leaned so far forward, the podium shifted and for a crazy moment Alison thought it might tip over and fall off the stage with the principal still clinging to it. "They are among you, these traitors," he whispered. "Some of them may be your friends. Some may be members of your family." His amplified heavy breathing sounded like a gale. "I know what you all say about the Society for Common Decency, which I am proud to head the local chapter of."

He seemed to be looking right at Alison. It was all she could do not to leap from her seat and go running from the auditorium.

"You think we're a bunch of old fuddy-duddies. A coven of killjoys."

Oh, no. That's not how I think of you at all.

"Well, now you see why our work is so vital. The spread of these subversive ideas that breed terrorism, it's like the spread of a disease. You have to fight it with antibiotics."

Alison had a sinking feeling she knew what was coming next. And she was right.

From the stage beside him, Mr. Wright produced a large metal box with a thick padlock on it and a thin slot on top. You saw them all the time in big cities, these "Judas boxes" where anyone could leave an anonymous note denouncing anyone else as a traitor. They were as common as mailboxes in Baltimore, and when Alison started middle school back in Pikesville they'd started installing them in the schools there, too.

But not here in Chincoteague. She'd never seen one on the island, which was one of the few things she liked about the place. Now Mr. Wright was going to ruin that, too. He was busy explaining in a just-between-you-and-me tone of voice that he wasn't going to put just the one box outside his office, he was also going to put one in each of the locker rooms "for extra privacy."

Then he went on about how it was everyone's patriotic duty to rat out everyone else. "Because if you don't," he said, and waved his hand. The lights went down and the tri-vee stage lit up with an enormous close-up of someone's red, blistered forearm. Blood oozed from it and a man's voice yelped as a pair of hands began applying lotion and bandaging it up. "That's Jeb Birch, our own cheerleading captain Sydney's father."

Loud sobbing could be heard from the front row, and Alison watched with distant queasiness as several boys converged around her trembling mass of blond curls. Yeah, Sydney was a witch, but she didn't deserve to have her father hurt or to have all those guys swarming all over her like bees on a flower with their fake sympathy.

And Mr. Wright wasn't done yet. "He was the worst injured fire-fighter last night, with third-degree burns all over his arms and chest from a wooden beam that fell on him. He could have been killed if two other firemen hadn't pulled him out just in time. If anyone knows any-thing about who set that fire, it's your duty of common decency not just to your country, not just to the Harmony, but to your friend Sydney to step forward and turn them in, before they hurt someone else."

Alison knew it was just paranoia—wasn't it?—that as Mr. Wright scanned the crowd, his eyes lingered an extra moment on her.

I can't do it, Alison told herself later that day, as she plodded into the lunchroom. *He's my brother. I can't get him in such serious trouble.* But she had to beat down a nagging voice inside her that asked if she would have felt differently if it hadn't been the blond queen bee's father who got hurt, but someone she cared about. *Shut up,* she told her inner voice. *Arnold didn't mean to hurt anyone. He's just upset about Dad's kidnap-ping. Maybe now he's got it out of his system.*

"Hey, Allie," a familiar voice interrupted her thoughts. She looked up and smiled with relief when she saw it was Shaniqua.

"Any news?" her friend asked, lowering her voice when they had sat down facing each other across an empty lunch table.

Alison shook her head. "Mom spends all her time trying to follow leads about where they might have taken my dad. I think she does it at work, too. What'll happen if she loses her job?"

Shaniqua shrugged. "Try not to worry about it."

"As if," Alison said, stabbing at her cherry cobbler with a fork. "What about Sharon? Has your family decided what to do about her?"

"Not yet," Shaniqua said. "We're going to tell people for now she's a cousin on my mom's side. I have an uncle I've never met, my mom's older brother Dave, so it could work. That way she won't have to hide out in my room all the time, which is getting kinda old."

"I thought you two were thick as thieves."

Shaniqua got a faraway look in her eye. "It's funny, she seems like a better version of me. She's even better at school, in her world."

"You do just fine," Alison said.

Shaniqua shrugged. "I guess so, but I could do better if there wasn't always trouble with Tavon around the house. Sharon's big brother Tad doesn't live at home anymore, he's a sailor in the Royal Navy.

"But it's not like Little Miss Smarty Pants could just start going to class with us. My mom says she'd have to get caught up on all kinds of things, so it's better if we wait and see if she still can't go home after the summer. Then maybe she can start as a senior like we are this year, or even as a junior." She scowled. "Would you believe it, Sharon keeps nagging me to look at my homework so she can get a head start if that does happen! I mean, I know she's bored and all, but still."

"Maybe she'll get so good at it, she can do your homework for you. You must have the same handwriting, right?"

Shaniqua shook her head. "Naw, they have really beautiful hand-writing over there, like something out of Victorian times. I wonder why things are so different for them. Maybe it's because they ended slavery thirty years earlier, without a whole civil war like we had."

"And they don't have the Sl—I mean, the High Ones running things."

"Yeah." Shaniqua scratched her head again. "Everything is so different over there, you can't really say what *makes* the difference, can you?"

"I guess not." Alison's mind was drifting back to Arnold. If she wanted to make sure he didn't do anything like he'd just done ever again, she was going to have to talk to him. But that never went well. And if she told Mom, all hell would break loose. She was tempted to ask Shaniqua's advice, but it seemed better not to tell anybody what she suspected. Maybe, just maybe, she was wrong and someone else had set the fire.

"Allie? Hey, Allie?" Shaniqua said, waving her hand in front of her face.

"Huh? Sorry, I guess I was daydreaming."

"I was just saying, I almost forgot to tell you my mom said to invite you and your family over for Easter dinner after church on Sunday afternoon."

"Oh! That's really nice of her." Alison frowned. "But I don't know if we can come. Passover starts the same night this year, and my parents always have a Seder, a whole big dinner thing..." She trailed off and put her head in her hands.

"Hey!" Shaniqua tapped Alison's shoulder. "Hey, it's no big deal. I'm sorry I mentioned it."

"I'm sorry," Alison said, wiping her eyes with a crumpled napkin. "Maybe it would be a good idea, to get us all out of the house. I'll ask my mom." Just then the bell rang, and Alison jumped up with relief.

As she trudged home later that afternoon through streets that were hot and humid and stank faintly of smoke, she started going over in her mind what she could say to Arnold, and how she could say it. She made sure to get his damn peanut-butter-and-banana sandwich ready so he'd be in a good mood, or at least not a bad one, when she talked to him. *I can say I understand how upset he is, that I'm just as upset. That I want to fight the Slugs too, but this isn't the way to do it. Next time someone might get KILLED.*

But four o'clock came and went and there was no Arnold. Alison was so preoccupied she ate his whole disgusting sandwich herself without even realizing it, then wondered where it had gone.

For distraction she turned on the tri-vee and tuned in a rerun of "The Spacefarers." She hadn't seen it, but it hit a little too close to home: Izzy Goldstein had blackmailed a crew member who owed him money into planting a bomb on the *UNSS Intrepid*. Everyone was running around like crazy trying to figure out where it was, when Brad caught the guilty man climbing into the ship's lone escape pod. Donny Schmitz's eyes were pure steel-blue rage as he grabbed the weasel with both hands and started shaking him.

"Where is it?" he shouted. "Where did that little Jew tell you to plant the bomb?"

That little Jew. Finally it hit Alison. Her parents were right, the show was anti-Semitic. In sudden anger she threw the remote control at the tri-vee stage. It bounced off, slicing away half of the traitor's face as he stammered that he hadn't meant to hurt anyone, that that Shylock of a Goldstein made him do it. Alison got up and kicked the stage until there was a pop and something started smoking. *There! Arnold's not the only one who can start a fire!*

She sat back down on the couch and started crying. Only, once she'd started she couldn't stop. She sobbed and sobbed until her eyes, throat, and chest all hurt. Then she sat numbly staring at the empty space where Donny Schmitz had been until she heard Mom's key in the front door lock.

She walked in muttering to herself, then looked up, startled to see Alison just sitting there in the dark. "Allie? What's wrong?" She sniffed the air and wrinkled her nose. "What's that smell?"

"It's the tri-vee." Alison had thought she'd cried out all the tears in her body, but she was wrong. "I think I broke it," she sobbed.

Mom sat beside her on the couch and put her arms around her. "It's okay, Allie, it's okay. We can get it fixed. What's really wrong?"

"I miss Dad!" Alison howled, and put her head on Mom's shoulder. *And Arnold's probably an arsonist. What do you think of that, Mom?*

"I'm sorry I didn't make supper," Alison sniffed several minutes later.

"Allie, it's okay. We'll order in from the House of Siam. Where's Arnold? I'll ask him what he wants."

"No idea. I don't think it's his night to visit Jo." *He's probably burning down half of Accomack County, that's where he is.*

But Mom was also getting used to Arnold's odd comings and goings and didn't say anything else about it. Instead she ordered a chicken dish for herself and Buddha's Delight for Alison. When the food came Alison ate it without tasting anything. Mom was talking, saying something about going to Washington in a couple of weekends to meet with some people who might know where Dad was.

Alison tried to focus. "Wait, why not this weekend?" she asked.

"It's going to take time to round up all the people I need to meet with. Besides, this weekend is Passover, don't you remember?"

"Of course I remember! I told Shaniqua about it, when she invited me to her house for Easter dinner."

"She did? That was nice of her. Why don't you invite her and her parallel-world twin to our Seder, if their dinner ends early enough?"

"Yeah, but … but what's the point of doing all that religious mumbo jumbo when Dad's in a SCOD hole somewhere?"

Mom reached across the table to take Alison's hands, but she yanked them away. "Allie, I understand how you feel, but it's important to keep everything as normal as possible till Dad comes back."

"Why?"

"Why? Because if we let ourselves fall apart, what kind of family will he be coming back to? Besides, you know what Passover's all about."

Alison groaned. "Don't give me all that Hebrew school crap about how God freed our ancestors from slavery in Egypt."

Mom's mouth tightened, and for a second Alison thought she was going to start yelling at her. Instead she lowered her voice, forcing Alison to lean forward to hear her. "What are we suffering from now, but lack of freedom? What are you and Arnold fighting against if not that? And what did they do to punish us? They took away Dad's freedom!"

Alison held up her hands. "All right, all right. You want to have a Seder, we can have a Seder." She pointed a fork at her mother. "But I'm not doing all the cooking, and neither should you! Arnold can help out for once."

"Well, you're right about that," Mom sighed. "But he seems so… distracted, lately. Maybe it's all that walking back and forth for Jo… I wish she could stay here, but it's just not safe for her."

Alison nodded, trying to keep her face blank. That whole thing with Arnold and Jo and Kayleigh was… weird, that was for sure.

"The least we can do is invite her to the Seder," Mom was saying. "And Kayleigh, too, for everything she's done."

That'll be interesting. Why not make it even more interesting? "Isn't there a part of the Seder where we say anyone who is hungry should come and eat?" Alison said.

Mom beamed. "You do remember something from Hebrew school after all!"

"We should invite Mr. Freed—I mean, Mr. Wineman." She explained about her odd encounter with him.

"All right, why not," Mom nodded, and began to giggle a little hysterically. "We're already an outlaw family. The more the merrier!"

"And how about a High One with some unusual views?"

Mom stopped laughing. "What?"

Alison explained about Mr. Nomura and Sh'onk.

Mom stared at her. "I know Bruce is Dad's friend. He's always been nice to me, but this, this is pretty weird. Especially considering that you kids are fighting to kick the Slugs off Earth."

"But he's a *good* Slug, Mom. Maybe meeting him will help Arnold see things a little differently."

"Since when did you care so much what Arnold thinks?"

Since he started expressing his views with gasoline and matches. Alison shrugged, and Mom said she'd see, which probably meant yes. Alison cleaned the table, then took her backpack and went to her room. But she couldn't concentrate on her homework. She ended up lying in bed staring at the ceiling, wishing the dull pounding in her head would go away and that her fan actually cooled something off instead of just making a racket.

Mom knocked once and asked if she was all right and Alison said yes, fine, in a flat voice. She was very grateful Mom didn't ask to come in. Outside it was getting dark, but what good was that? If another day was over it just meant another sleepless night was on its way. But that was the last thought she remembered having before dozing off.

35

"You've invited one of those *things* into our home?" Arnold yelled.

"Calm down, Arnold," Alison said. "Sssssssssss-sh'onkelos isn't like other High Ones. For one thing, he isn't nobility. I think he might surprise you, if you can keep an open mind."

The room seemed to twirl around before Arnold's eyes. Was his own sister a traitor? *Wait, maybe this is an opportunity.* Could he figure out some way of killing this Sh'onk or whatever its name was when it came to the house? Not many things short of high explosives could harm a High One. He became so preoccupied trying to figure out some way of killing Sh'onk without burning down his own house that he almost didn't hear Alison say he'd have to help with the cooking.

"No way," he said.

Alison poked him in the chest. "Why not, oh brave warrior? Scared you'll burn yourself on the stove?"

Arnold poked her back. "I'm very busy in the Resistance, Sis. I don't have time for things like that."

"Oh, of course not, great leader." They were in Arnold's room, and Mom was in her bedroom with the door shut, on the phone with someone who might know where Dad was being held. Still, Alison went over and shut the door, and when she turned back to Arnold her voice was softer and her face was pale.

"I know you set that fire, Arnold."

"Congratulations, Nancy Drew."

Alison took a deep breath and said, "Why did you do it?"

"Why? It was a Resistance mission, that's why!"

"A 'mission' you dreamed up yourself, you crazy firebug!"

"Nuh-uh!"

Alison rubbed her temples as if she had a headache. "Somebody *ordered* you to set these fires, Arnold?"

"Yep! The Revolution has come to Chincoteague!"

"Arnold, this is *insane*. Jeb Birch is still in the hospital with the burns he suffered fighting the fire at the town hall. The fire *you* set."

"He has his job, I have mine. I'll do it again if they tell me to," Arnold said, a little louder than he meant to. He had to make Allie understand.

"But Arnold! Innocent people could get hurt again!"

"No, they won't! We only attack the quisling government's buildings at night, when there's nobody there!"

Alison watched his face. "You're crossing your fingers, you little liar!"

"Am not!"

"Are too!" She grabbed his right hand from behind his back. The fingers were indeed crossed. "You could have killed Mr. Birch!"

He flinched, but then he lifted his chin. "I'm not sorry I did it. I'm proud!"

"Arnold, you have to cut it out before you kill someone!"

"Anyone who's working for the Slugs is just as slimy as they are!" He paused and shook his finger in her face. "You're just upset that I wouldn't trust you with the secret. But you went and told on me to Dad, don't think I've forgotten. I can't trust you."

Alison glared at Arnold. "You're changing the subject. Don't you even care that you'll get caught?"

"So what if I do?" He lifted his chin again, but it trembled slightly. "I'll be a martyr to the cause! Maybe they'll put me in the same cell as Dad. Maybe they'll send us to the firing squad together!"

Alison's face got even paler. "Don't talk like that, Arnold! Dad is coming home!"

"Dad is coming home!" Arnold mimicked. "You and Mom can keep fooling yourselves. I'm going to be getting revenge!" He grabbed her arm and squeezed hard. "You'd better keep quiet about what you know, Sis. There's no room in the Resistance for rats."

"Are you *threatening* me, Arnold?"

He smiled slowly. "Not me. I would never do anything to hurt you. But the other League members might."

Alison gasped, turned, and fled the room.

Well, she won't ask me to cook for the Seder again.

* * * *

Mom told Arnold he should invite both Kayleigh and Jo to the Seder, but the next day in school, as he mulled it over, he thought he'd better have a bigger, stronger ally on his side than a couple of girls, as scary as Jo could be when she was mad. So he sauntered over to the bullies' table at lunchtime, as bold as you please (it helped that both Matt and Jared had lunchtime detention) and asked Gus if he'd like to come to a Seder.

Gus looked at him as if he was a filthy wad of gum he'd just scraped off his shoe. "Are you talking to me, you little terrorist?" he said loudly, and growled under his breath, "Not here in front of everybody, numb-skull! Meet me in the boys' room during fifth period study hall."

Arnold scurried away to the Reject Table, watching glumly as the rejects stood up and took their trays elsewhere. He could see Kayleigh across the cafeteria, gossiping with Madison and the rest of that brat pack just like old times, but he knew if he dared approach her she'd cut him even deader than Gus had. So he ripped a piece of paper out of his notebook and scrawled a note to slip into her locker, asking her to sneak over to his house Sunday evening for "a vital intelligence mission for the Resistance." Jo he could talk to later, on his regular supply run.

Gus was apologetic when he talked to Arnold in the boys' room, once he'd checked under the stall doors to make sure they were alone. "My dad says I have to be real careful not to be seen around you. They were starting to pull some of the state police and FBI out, but now—" He broke off and stared at Arnold. "It was you who set that fire, wasn't it?"

Arnold shrugged and tried to look casual. "It was no big deal. Just something the League told me to do."

Gus shook his head. "I don't know, Arnold. I don't think that's something I want to get involved with."

He's as big a sissy as Gloria, Arnold thought in surprise. *Better not say it to him, though. I like my head unbroken.* "You don't have to get involved in it," he said quickly. "I'm just asking you to come to my house Sunday night—"

"—I've got to go to Easter dinner with my family—"

"—*after* your Easter dinner, for an intelligence mission."

"I don't know, Arnold. It'll be pretty hard for me to sneak over to your home without anyone noticing me. Besides, what kind of intelligence mission can you be having in your house?"

"We're having all this company over—it's for a Jewish religious thing called a Passover Seder." He tried to say it quickly, so it would slip past Gus's notice, and casually, like it was no big deal, in case he did notice. As a result, the words came out in a mumbling rush.

"What was that? Better make it fast, the bell's about to ring," said Gus.

"It's a Jewish holiday called Passover," Arnold said, paused dramatically, and added: "And we're having a Slug to dinner."

Gus rubbed his chin. "Interesting customs you have," he said, "but I think I'll eat at home first."

The bell rang before Arnold could ask if he was joking.

* * * *

Jo was more enthusiastic when he asked her. "Yes, of course I'll come," she said, before Arnold could even finish explaining. He couldn't stop a huge grin from spreading over his face, but Jo scowled at him. "Don't flatter yourself, Arnold. I'd do anything not to be a castaway, even if it's only for a few hours. It's so boring here."

Arnold started guiltily. "I never thought of that. I should bring you some books. You can take some back with you from our house."

"That's really nice of you, Arnold," Jo said.

She was talking around a mouth full of three-bean salad Alison had made for her, so he wasn't sure if she was being sarcastic or not. He thought she had it pretty good out here, not having to go to school, being waited on hand and foot, and toasting marshmallows over a campfire every night, as she was doing now. He'd been inside the lodge with her once or twice and had seen the cozy little nest she'd set up for herself with the sleeping bag and a little popup tent Mom had dug up for her somewhere for when it rained, which luckily for her it hadn't yet. Alison had brought her the tent and a bunch more old clothes on one of her nights, and of course she'd made a really big deal to Arnold of what a martyr that made her.

"Maybe I'd better bring you a flashlight so you have something to read by," Arnold said.

"You mean a torch? Don't bother, Kay already brought me a couple, and some extra batteries too."

"Kay," again, Arnold thought. *They're becoming, like, best friends. How can I compete?* "What kind of books would you like?" he asked.

"Anything on Slug maths and natural philosophy," Jo said at once.

"You mean their science? But I thought we're fighting against all that!"

Jo rolled her eyes. "Sometimes you sound just like my big brother, Tom. Anything French he hates like poison, just because it's French. Their natural philosophy is more advanced than anything humans in either of our worlds have, so why wouldn't you want to learn about it?"

Arnold was silent. Jo was right, as usual. "So, you don't mind coming to our house for a Seder?" he said after a pause.

"I already said it'll be great! I'm really looking forward to meeting a Slug in person, and I've never been to a Passover meal before."

"So it's two alien things at once, is that it?"

Jo jerked away the stick with the toasted marshmallows she'd been offering him. "Why do you have to make everything negative, Arnold?"

"I didn't mean anything," he mumbled. "I just hope you don't mind going to a Jewish thing, that's all."

"Why would I? There aren't any Jewish families in Gingo Teag, but we learned all about Jewish customs in our religion class last year. A rabbi came from Baltimore to talk to us. It was really interesting. No one in my class said anything bad about Jews."

"Well, here everybody hates us," Arnold blurted.

"What? That's terrible! There's hardly any hatred of Jews in my world, except in *l'Empire's* Eastern provinces—what you call Russia. It's like something out of the Middle Ages."

"So are some of our customs," Arnold muttered.

"You shouldn't talk like that." Jo touched Arnold's hand briefly, quickly drawing away. "I'm sure it'll be a great time. And we get to meet a High One! Wizard!"

* * * *

It *was* pretty cool having so many people over for the Seder. The Grossbards' Passover table had never been so crowded before, not even when they lived in Pikesville and Grandpa was still alive. Even Grandma was coming, having taken the saucer down from Baltimore. Since they had to leave so much extra space on one side for the High One the seating arrangements were pretty tight, even with the card tables Mom made Arnold bring in from the garage and set up at either end.

"I don't understand how that *thing's* even going to fit in the doorway," Arnold said, trying to keep the quaver out of his voice. *Maybe it will realize that too and just turn around and go, and I won't have to try and kill it.*

There weren't as many deadly weapons around as Arnold would have liked. The knives at the place settings were all butter knives. Dad never brought out the carving knife for the roast turkey until the bird was ready to serve, and Arnold was sure Mom would do the same.

Everyone sat around fidgeting while Mom ran back and forth with plates of this and that—Arnold had reluctantly agreed to make the *charoset*, a dish of chopped apples and walnuts mixed with wine that was supposed to be a remembrance of the mortar the Israelite slaves had used to build the pyramids in Egypt, though Arnold was only able to tolerate the chopping and grinding job by imagining it was a Slug tentacle he was mangling.

I can't believe Mom agreed to this, after what they did to Dad! Arnold was brooding so intently as he sat down between Kayleigh and Jo that he jumped and banged his knee when Alison tapped him on the shoulder.

"Can I talk to you upstairs for a minute?"

"Umm, but isn't it good manners for me to sit here with my guests?" Arnold said, producing a fake grin as he threw one arm around Kayleigh's shoulders and the other around Jo's. They both pushed him away, so he reluctantly followed Sis up into her room.

As soon as she had shut the door behind them she grabbed his left ear and pinched, hard.

"Ow! What's that for?"

"Don't do anything stupid when Sssssssssss-sh'onkelos gets here, turd-breath!"

"What are you talking about? Leggo my ear!"

"Don't play innocent with me. You've got the same look in your eyes that you always have before you do something really rotten to me. What do you think you're going to do, stab him to death with the carving knife?"

"Of course not! Cut it out already, that really hurts!"

Alison let go, and as Arnold rubbed his ear she said, "Look, if it helps, you can pretend you're gathering intelligence for your little make-believe army, but don't do anything that'll get us all disappeared."

"You said yourself they don't do that to kids!"

"How do you know *what* they'll do to someone who actually succeeds in harming a High One? That hasn't happened in thirty years, and back then they lynched the guy who did it before the cops could even arrest him! And now everyone's on edge thanks to that pamphlet and the Bubble Drive not working. They'll tear you limb from limb."

Arnold bit his lip. He hated to admit it, but Sis had a point. "All right. I'll just gather intelligence."

She studied his face carefully, nodded and turned to go, but yelped in surprise when Arnold punched her in the arm. "What was that for?"

"That crack about the Freedom Fighters of Earth. If we're a joke, you're part of it!"

"Don't remind me," Alison grumbled. "The only reason why I'm going along with it is to keep you and Jo out of trouble."

"Everything all right?" Mom said as Alison and Arnold came down the stairs.

"Just great," Arnold started to say, but his mouth suddenly went dry, because the front door was open, and Sssssssssss-sh'onkelos was oozing through.

There was really no other verb that could describe the way the High One was fitting itself through the door frame. You wouldn't think that would be possible, what with all the armor plating, but its arms were all bunched up like a bundle of cables and the alien was wiggling its way in with no apparent trouble.

Arnold was reminded of a nature film he'd seen once about an octopus. *Any second now it's going to hit me in the face with a blast of ink. Which would be ironic for a pamphleteer.*

Instead it emerged into the living room and flowed out into its full size and shape, like a balloon animal being blown up. Though no one would dare make a balloon animal in the shape of a High One, unless he really, *really* wanted to be disappeared.

"Hello," it said, sounding like a pleasant middle-aged guy. "Thank you for inviting me into your home."

"We are honored to have you in our home, your eminence," Mom said and made an honest-to-God curtsey in her good blue holiday skirt. Everyone followed suit, Arnold included.

True, he wanted to kill all the invaders, and preferably nuke Homeworld until it glowed like a watch dial, but he'd only come to that opinion recently, whereas he'd been trained in Xeno-Etiquette since kindergarten. So he came all the way down the stairs and went automatically into the ritual for Obeisance to a High One (Rank Not Specified).

"I am most deeply honored to make your acquaintance, your eminence," he said, bowing until his head almost touched the floor.

"And this lowly being is blessed to be in your presence once again," said Alison, bowing too.

Girls were supposed to curtsey like Mom just had, but nothing would make Sis wear a skirt. Arnold suppressed a smirk at having gotten the jump on her, even if it was at brown-nosing a High One.

"Please don't do that," the thing said, as Kayleigh, Gus, Shaniqua, and Sharon all hastened into the living room to pay their respects. Only Jo and Grandma remained seated, Jo with her mouth open and Grandma with hers firmly shut in a stubborn line.

"I hold no noble rank," the alien said, waving several of its tentacles around. Could the alien actually be *embarrassed*?

"Well, it *is* an honor to have you in my home," Mom said after an awkward pause.

"Sh'onk is actually a regular guy," said Mr. Nomura, appearing behind the creature. He was dressed in chinos and a yellow polo shirt with an alligator over the pocket.

Arnold hadn't noticed him till now, he was so busy making a fool of himself. *Some Resistance fighter I am!*

"You really call yourself Sh'onk?" Arnold asked.

The High One waved around the smallest of his tentacles, in a gesture that was somehow disarming. "I know it's easier for English speakers to pronounce. And I don't approve of the airs my brood-fellows put on. Please just act as you normally would."

Kayleigh giggled nervously. Everyone sat down, except of course for Sh'onk.

"Oh dear, I am afraid I am taking up far too much room at your table," he said.

"Don't worry about it. It's a pleasure to host such an honored guest," Mom said.

"Oh, please stop saying that word!" Sh'onk said.

"What word?" Mom asked.

"Honor! I know my brood-fellows are obsessed with it. And yet they are utterly without it."

All the humans looked at each other, except for Mr. Nomura, who was looking down and smiling slightly, as if he found something humorous in his place setting.

"Yes, well, maybe we can discuss politics later," Mom said, her voice quavering.

"Everything smells delicious, Mrs. Grossbard," Jo said. "Let's eat!"

"We don't serve the meal until much later," Mom explained. "There's the whole Haggadah to get through first!"

"I was hoping you'd forget," Arnold grumbled.

"What's the Haggadah?" Sh'onk asked.

"It's this book," Mom said, holding up a slim paperback. There was one at each place setting. "It has the story of the Exodus—our ancestors' escape from slavery in Egypt—and many prayers, and other things besides."

"And if you do the whole thing, everybody is liable to starve to death before they get to eat," Alison said.

Shaniqua and Sharon both put their hands over their mouths and stifled giggles.

"Allie! Set a good example for our guests!" Mom said.

"I am actually quite curious about your customs. I have never been inside a private human home before," Sh'onk said.

Just then there was a knock on the door. Arnold looked at Jo, who looked at Alison, who shook her head silently. *It can't be SCOD! Not again, not now!*

Mom stood up.

If he'd been sitting next to her Arnold would have grabbed her by the arm and begged her not to answer the door, even though it would have meant making a scene in front of everybody. As it was, he could only watch helplessly as she squeezed herself out, muttering apologies, walked over to the door and opened it as if nothing was wrong.

For a long, frozen moment Arnold didn't recognize the guy in the black suit standing in the doorway, his eyes round as coins as he stared at Sh'onk. It was only when he spoke that Arnold recognized the voice: it was Mr. Freed, somehow clean shaven and all dressed up and gasping, "It-it can't be... that thing..."

Suddenly he pushed past Mom and lunged at Sh'onk, yelling, "Take that suit off! Take that stupid rubber suit off, you fakers!" He grabbed at one of the Slug's tentacles, pinched and pulled—and was suddenly flying backward across the living room, where he crashed into the easy chair and lay groaning on the floor.

"Oh dear! I do apologize," Sh'onk said, waving his tentacles around, "it was pure reflex, I had no control..."

Everyone sat stunned except Grandma, who got up and fussed over Mr. Freed as he sat on the floor rubbing his head and moaning.

Mom went into the kitchen, got an ice bag and gave it to Mr. Freed, helping him to his feet and then into an empty folding chair at the end of the card table.

"This is a dream. It has to be a dream," he mumbled. "I haven't been to a Seder in, what, fifty years, and then one of those things…"

"It's all right, Mr. Wineman," Alison said, getting up and offering a glass of water to the old hippie. "You're not dreaming, and Sh'onk, here, is just as much against the establishing as you!"

"Against the what?" he said, as Arnold said, "Who's Mr. Wineman?"

"His real name is Jeff Wineman," Alison explained to Arnold, and to the hippie, "Isn't that what you were all against in the Sixties? The establishing? I wrote all about it in my history paper!"

"*O tempora, o mores!*" Mr. Freed, or Mr. Wineman, said.

"'Oh the times, oh the manners!' Cicero," said Sh'onk with satisfaction. "I enjoy your classical writers very much, sir! Those Romans, so like my own people in their pompous arrogance!"

While Mr. Wineman gaped at Sh'onk, Mom said smoothly, "And that's a great introduction to our Seder ritual, which dates back to Roman times. Arnold, would you start us off by asking the Four Questions?"

"But Mom, that's for the baby at the table."

"You are the youngest person here who knows Hebrew," Mom pointed out.

The trouble was, he didn't really. He'd forgotten most of what he'd had to learn for his Bar Mitzvah, so it was a real struggle to read those four short sentences.

Alison smirked at his embarrassment, until Mr. Wineman jumped in and chanted the traditional Hebrew questions smoothly, though his voice cracked on the high notes.

Mom read them in English, and Sh'onk suddenly said, "Those are very good questions. Why do you observe these customs? And why do you tell this story over and over again, every year?"

"Well, the Haggadah says it's our duty to retell it, to remind ourselves that we were slaves in Egypt," Mom said.

"Oh, I understand very well about ancestral duties," said Sh'onk. There was a weird buzzing undertone to his speech that hadn't been there before. "My people's lives consist of one ancestral duty after another, from the time you are barely a larva. Heaven help you if you overlook your duty! But I still don't understand the purpose of retelling this story now."

"But I just told you," Mom said, crinkling up her forehead. "We tell this story because once we were slaves, but now we are free."

"But that's just it," Sh'onk said. "You are *not* free." The silence that followed was so heavy it was a wonder the house didn't collapse under its weight.

Arnold shot a glance at Jo, who was staring at Sh'onk.

"I thought all you Winged-Thinkers wanted to conquer the Earth forever," she said.

There was a clatter as Kayleigh suddenly fell out of her folding chair, and Arnold helped her up.

"I never heard a human call us that before! That is a much better translation of our true name," Sh'onk said. "As for wanting to conquer, I'd happily turn the whole cold, dry planet back over to you primitives if I had anything to say about it."

"I think," Mom said, and cleared her throat, "I think maybe we should eat now. I have a whole meal ready, but we start with matzah, the unleavened bread our ancestors ate when they were leaving Egypt because they had no time to wait for their dough to rise. It tastes just like a cracker."

"A cracker made of cardboard," Alison said. "I can't stand it."

"I'll try anything," Gus said happily. "Pass me some of that matzah stuff." Mom handed him a whole slice about the size of a piece of notebook paper, and he broke off a bit and chewed thoughtfully. "Hmm, Alison, I have to disagree with you about the taste," he said.

"Really? You actually like it?"

"Sure. It reminds me of when I was in kindergarten and I ate some dried paste once."

Everyone laughed, even Mom, and a grinning Gus handed another piece of matzah to Kayleigh.

"I think I'll pass," she said. "I'm not feeling that well."

Arnold glanced at her and did a double-take. Her face was paler than the matzah, which was made of white flour.

Arnold leaned toward her. "Are you all right?"

"Fine! I'll be fine. But, uh, I just remembered, I promised to help my mom clean up the yard so we can plant our vegetable garden. May I be excused?"

"But I was just about to start serving the soup. It's got matzah balls in it," Mom said.

Kayleigh's eyes widened. Arnold wondered why she was acting so weird.

"N-no thanks, Mrs. Grossbard. I'll eat at home. Sorry!" She stood up so quickly she made everyone's dishes rattle. "Sorry!" she said again, pushing past Arnold and stumbling toward the door.

Arnold got up and followed her outside. "Kayleigh, what's wrong?"

"Nothing, Arnold," Kayleigh said, her eyes darting back toward the house.

"It's that Slug, isn't it?" he said in a low voice. "I hate that it's here in my house too! But we can gather a lot of intelligence for the Resistance just by talking to it. Maybe we can get it to reveal how to blow saucers up!"

"It's not that, Arnold," Kayleigh said, bouncing up and down on the balls of her feet. "Can I go now, please?"

"I don't get it. You were fine until Mom started serving the meal. What happened?"

"It's the matzah," she said, and clamped her right hand over her mouth, her eyes round.

"The matzah? If you don't like it, don't eat it. You won't be offending my mother's cooking. It comes out of a box."

"Yeah, and who knows what *they* put in it?"

"They who?"

"The Elders of Zion!" Arnold goggled at Kayleigh. "Oh come on, Arnold, don't look at me like that!" she said in a hoarse whisper. "Everybody knows what goes into matzah!" She leaned closer and said, "Blood!"

For a long moment Arnold had no idea what she was talking about. Then he remembered Hebrew school back in Pikesville, and he closed his eyes. "Oh Kayleigh, that's not true! That was some crazy stuff people made up in the Middle Ages about Jews. It's like how they used to burn old ladies alive for being witches. Who told you such a stupid thing?"

Opening his eyes, Arnold saw Kayleigh's face was all twisted up, like she was mad and embarrassed and queasy at the same time.

"My dad," she said. "If he knew I went to your house for Passover he'd beat me within an inch of my life. I told him I was going to after-school homework club."

Arnold clenched his fists at his sides. "Where'd he hear that old lie? At church?"

"Naw, like I said, he ain't much of a churchgoer."

Alison is right, Kayleigh does sound like a hick when she gets upset.

"It's from Duke Davis's tri-vee program. Dad watches it every Sunday, even when he's hungover."

"Kayleigh, I." Arnold stopped. He couldn't think of what to say to her. "It's—it's just so silly." *Lame! Think of something to say that isn't lame!* "You know me and my family. We don't eat blood." He giggled helplessly. "Alison doesn't even eat meat! Didn't you see the tofu burger Mom made her to eat instead of the turkey?"

"I, I know it's probably stupid, Arnold. I'm sorry. Please tell your family I'm sorry." And she turned and fled.

Too late, it came to Arnold what he should have said: *There's a thing from outer space sitting in my dining room, a monster the whole human race has to band together to fight, and all you can do is repeat some dumb old prejudice people came up with?*

Arnold slunk back into the house, his ears burning. *If anyone asks me if everything is all right, I might go up in flames!*

Mom looked at him and opened her mouth, then shut it and looked away. Even Alison seemed intensely interested in the soup rather than in what had just happened.

It wasn't her own soup she was fascinated by, though; it was the way Sh'onk was eating his. Which, granted, was pretty interesting. He wasn't using his spoon. Instead, the golden liquid was disappearing between two mandibles to the accompaniment of loud slurping noises, while first one of the dumplings and then the other flew up in the air like ping-pong balls, almost touching the ceiling before they disappeared into some hidden orifice.

"Delicious, Rachel!" the thing said warmly.

"Oh, good," Mom said, "I, uh, I didn't know whether you'd be able to eat our food."

"Oh, I can eat anything, as long as it doesn't have ginger it," Sh'onk said. "I'm allergic. Makes me act like I'm drunk. I start making these weird cooing noises like an Earth bird called the turtledove. You wouldn't want to hear that."

He forced a chuckle, just like a human being would have, and Arnold was amazed all over again. *Can this guy be for real?*

If he wasn't, he was putting on a heck of an act. While Mom and Alison ran back and forth serving everyone soup, turkey, and Arnold's favorite, a sweet-potato-and-carrot stew called *tzimmes*, Sh'onk told them all that he'd never wanted to come to Earth, but he'd been drafted, and if he'd refused, not only would he have been executed—which he claimed not to care about, "not even a jellyblob's worth"—but his entire brood would have been dishonored, "and I couldn't do that to my mother." Worse luck, though, he'd been ordered to fly human prisoners, supposedly big-time terrorists, to the interrogation center on the far side of the Moon and return them, "or what's left of them," back to Earth. Everyone stopped eating and stared.

"What do you mean," Alison said carefully, "what's left of them?"

"Well, we hook them up to a more intensive version of the n-net to get at all their memories. The result is instant, total Network-Induced Neuronal Atrophy."

Mom staggered to her feet, grabbed her napkin and held it to her mouth as she rushed into the kitchen. Alison got up and followed her.

"It turns the subjects into—what's the slang term?—drooling vegetables." The alien sounded angry. "And then they make *me* cart them back to Earth."

"I think I have to go home now," Gus said. "Thanks for everything, Mrs. Grossbard," he called into the kitchen, where retching sounds could be heard. He squeezed past Arnold and practically ran to the door.

"I'll tell you what really dries me up, though," Sh'onk said, as if everyone left at the table wasn't shifting around, eyeing one another, "and that's the way Risssss-erianus and all his toadies keep saying how wonderfully well we've got things under control."

"Are you talking about the Archduke of the Homeworld? The Exalted High Viceroy?" Shaniqua asked, her eyes wide.

"No, I'm talking about the guy who cleans the toilets in my saucer. Of course I'm talking about the Archduke!" The buzz was back in his voice. "Let *him* come see what a suspect looks like once our interrogators are done. Let him *smell* it. Let him help clean out my saucer when they soil themselves. You can't get the stink out, I say!"

"I don't think anyone wants any dessert, Mrs. Grossbard," Jo said.

Arnold didn't feel sick, though. He felt furious. How could this *thing* sit here and confess to them what it had done? What did it expect them to do, forgive it?

"How can I go back home and fertilize a clutch of eggs my fiancé Jusssssssss'tinia has deposited in our special spot on the sea floor just for me, as if nothing has happened? You'd like her," Sh'onk added absently, "she has the most beautiful rainbow scales, and thirteen, count 'em, thirteen arms. Are you all right, Rachel?"

"Fine," Mom said faintly.

She had returned to her seat, but her face was an unhealthy, cheesy color that reminded Arnold of when she had been sick with NINA and enraged him even more.

"I tell you, it was about the happiest day of my life, except for Jusssssssss'tinia accepting my tentacle in marriage, when they transferred me to civilian saucer piloting here on Earth. But it'll be a happier day yet when they let me go home! I hate this stinking, dried-up husk of a planet—no offense—and I think we High Ones have no business being here, even if we need the human mental power in the n-network to create the bubble universes for our interstellar flights. If it was up to me, we'd pull out of here tomorrow and let you humans run your own affairs."

"But we learned in school we were ruining the environment and were on the verge of a nuclear war before the Arrival," Shaniqua said. "What if you guys suddenly left, and there were wars all over the place again, like in the bad old days?"

What was Alison's dumb friend saying? Human beings had to be free of alien domination, that was all there was to it. *We'd get along just fine without them. And even if not, at least the people torturing and killing each other would be human, not monsters!*

"Maybe, but it would be on your oxygen-breathing heads. Er, I hope I got the expression correct," Sh'onk said.

"You did very well," Mom said, carefully patting a tentacle and picking up a book. "Well, who's up for finishing the Seder?"

"I mean, even with your primitive wars, you humans had a certain unspoiled innocence before we Winged-Thinkers arrived and brought the corruptions of civilization with us," Sh'onk said, completely ignoring Mom. "I see from your wrinkled faces and white hair that two of you are old enough to remember the time before we ruined you. Am I wrong?"

"Your tact may leave something to be desired," Grandma said drily, "but things were different back then, that's for sure. Am I right, Mr.… I didn't catch your name?"

"Wineman. Jeff Wineman."

Grandma did the most violent double-take Arnold had ever seen.

"Not *the* Jeffrey Wineman? Of the Chicago Seven?"

"That's me," the old hippie said, blushing. "Were you in Chicago too, Mrs. Grossbard?"

"I'm Rachel's mother, Lila Leventhal," Grandma said. "No, I was only seventeen and my parents wouldn't let me go, so I watched the whole thing instead. I thought you were so cute, the way you called that cop a fascist pig on national TV!"

"Abbie was the star of the show, as usual," Mr. Wineman said.

"I don't agree! Wasn't it your idea to hold the un-birthday party for President Johnson?"

"No, that was him and Jerry Rubin. It was my idea to have the cake spurt fake blood, though."

"Was that some quaint religious ritual?" Sh'onk asked.

Grandma and Mr. Wineman looked at each other and burst out laughing. "You could call it that, I guess," Mr. Wineman said, wiping his eyes. "In a way, we were pretty innocent, running around calling the American government fascists because of racism and the Vietnam War. We thought the House Un-American Activities Committee was the worst thing that ever was... but no one had even dreamed of SCOD and disappearances, back then."

Grandma stopped laughing, and a pall fell over the table. Mom got up and went into the kitchen again.

"That was our fault too. We shouldn't have interfered with your society," Sh'onk said.

Suddenly Arnold had had enough. He pushed back his chair, got to his feet and pointed his finger at Sh'onk, hardly trembling at all. "No one else here has the guts to say it, so I will. You're just as bad as the rest of the Slugs. Worse, maybe, 'cause you knew what you were doing was wrong, and you did it anyway! Do you think you can come here, into our home, a week after SCOD disappeared my father and just say you're *sorry?* Sorry doesn't do it, slimebag!"

Jo was plucking at Arnold's sleeve, but he ignored her. In the kitchen, Mom burst into loud sobs.

"Do you hear that?" Alison cried, jumping to her feet. "How upset you've made Mom? I hope you're satisfied!"

"Oh, I'm very satisfied!" Arnold said. "As satisfied as all of you are, to eat dinner with this alien murderer! Don't bother sending me to my room, I'm going there myself!"

He stormed up the stairs without even glancing back to see how far he'd succeeded in ruining the Seder. Slamming the door so hard he thought he could hear bits of plaster sifting down from the ceiling, he threw himself full length on the bed and buried his face in his pillow, wishing with all his might that Sh'onk would lose his temper, come up after him and rip him to shreds. *That way I could die a hero and not have to worry about all this other stuff.*

It was a long, long time before he cried enough silent, enraged tears to tire himself out and remembered about the spider plant, which was waving its leaves at him, casting its calming spell.

* * * *

When he woke it was completely dark outside. He could tell by the quiet that most of the Seder guests had left, though he wasn't surprised to hear Jo and Alison talking quietly in the next bedroom; Mom had said Jo couldn't walk home in the dark and would have to stay overnight. He could also hear Grandma clearly in the kitchen directly below his room; the heat register carried her voice.

"You're going to need help here, Rachel," she was saying. "I can see you have your hands full with the kids. Believe me, I know how teenagers are. As soon as I get Jeff settled in my place, I'm coming back here to stay."

Jeff? Oh, she means Mr. Freed. Does Grandma LIKE him? Eww, old people!

"I appreciate that, Mom," Mom said, "but it's not safe—" There was a knock on the front door.

Let it be SCOD, let them take me away. I don't care.

"I'll get it!" Alison called from the next room. He heard her footsteps going down the stairs, the front door swinging open, then a muffled exclamation. Arnold put his pillow over his head. Whoever it was, he didn't want to know. But a few seconds later someone was pounding on his door. "Arnold! Open up!" Alison yelled.

Arnold took the pillow off his head long enough to yell, "Go away!" But it was too late, Alison had already barged in. He stared at her, speechless with fury.

"Get your butt downstairs! It's Kayleigh!"

He found her sitting on the couch sobbing, with Mom on her right and Jo on her left. Grandma bustled in from the kitchen with an ice bag and a wad of paper towels, because Kayeligh had a black eye, and blood was dripping from her nose in a steady stream.

Arnold sank into the easy chair, staring and staring. A real hero, like the pretend Sir Arnold, would have known what to do instinctively, but he felt utterly helpless as Kayleigh told what had happened to her, in between crying, hiccupping, gasping for breath, apologizing over and over, and trying to stop her nose from bleeding.

She'd tried to sneak back into her house after fleeing the Seder, but her father had been drunk, "a mean drunk, meanest I've ever seen him, and he was layin' for me." He grabbed her by the shoulders, shook her and demanded to know where she'd been. She tried out her pre-prepared story that she'd been studying with Madison after homework club, but her dad slapped her face hard and shouted that he'd already called the Marburys and he knew she was lying.

When her mom tried to calm him down he grabbed her by the arm, twisted it until she screamed and shoved her out of the room. Then he grabbed Kayleigh, shook her again and demanded the truth. She told him, and he called her a lot of bad names, names she couldn't repeat, and said if she was going to run around with blood-sucking Jews and terrorists she wasn't no daughter of his, not like his son Kyle, a red-blooded American hero he could be proud of.

And then he threw her out of the house—literally, Arnold saw, and closed his eyes on dizzy sickness: her right sleeve was torn and her forearm bloody from where she had landed on the sidewalk.

"I ain't," Kayleigh said, and shook and sobbed. Grandma gave her a glass of water, which she gulped, choked on, finally got down. "I haven't," she said, and shook and sobbed some more. "Got… no place… to go!"

36

Before, Jo had thought she would go crazy from having no one to talk to all day. Even Arnold bringing her care packages of books from his father's secret library and Gloria's more-than-universal trove didn't help as much as she'd hoped. (And he had complained about it into the bargain: "I hope you appreciate that I had to put up with her scolding to get these for you," he'd said about his trip to the school library, and when she asked what Gloria had said, he said, "Well, nothing, but she gave me a LOOK!")

If Jo could have known for sure that she'd be out here for only a week or two, or even a month or two, the whole thing might have been a holiday. Instead she couldn't help brooding when reading *Letters to a Woman Sitting in Darkness* that the American authorities would give her the "water cure" or worse when they caught her. And if they didn't catch her, she'd have to find some way of living in this strange and frightening world. Moving in with Arnold's family was impossible, just impossible, even if he hadn't been involved with that Kayleigh girl.

And now that Kayleigh was stranded out here too, a shipwrecked refugee just like her, Jo thought she might prefer loneliness. Arnold's girlfriend was just so annoying, and you couldn't even get mad at her because of the terrible things that had happened to her. You couldn't forget for a moment that Kayleigh was effectively an orphan, like Oliver Twist in nineteenth-century Philadelphia in the Charles Dickens novel Jo had read three times when she was little. The huge black bruise around her right eye had faded to blue, then a ghastly green, and finally to a kind of snot yellow, and her nose looked a little crooked, as if it had been broken. *Broken by her own father.*

Jo admitted to herself that she couldn't even imagine what that must feel like—not when her own father was so kind and sweet and gentle and funny (and she'd better not dwell on that too much, or she'd have to run away somewhere and bawl her eyes out so she didn't end up crying in front of poor Kayleigh).

Kayleigh's mother must be useless if she couldn't even stop her dad from throwing her out, not like Jo's Mum, who was really strict and not at all hesitant to take Jo (or Tom when he was younger) over her knee for a spanking when they deserved it. But then she'd almost always forget about the offense afterwards, and Jo had lots of happy memories of Mum teaching her songs by her parents' old Liverpool chum Paul McCartney, or baking cookies with her for the Town Council meetings, or sailing with Dad and Tom in Dragon Cove, and *if she didn't cut it out right this instant she was going to be a big blubbery mess, thank you very much!*

The real trouble was, she had nothing to talk about with Kayleigh. It wasn't a matter of all the different stuff they had in this world, like cars instead of electric carriages and telephones instead of voicegrams.

No, the problem was that Kayleigh liked to sit around gossiping about blokes and who was walking out with whom, the same kind of talk most of the girls back in Gingo Teag loved but Jo never took part in. It didn't seem to matter to Kayleigh that Jo didn't know any of the people she was talking about (well, she did know a few of their "doubles," like Madeline Marbury in Gingo Teag, who was a star at track-and-field and popular with the boys).

For her part, Kayleigh couldn't understand high-level maths and questions like how and why the different worlds floated in a kind of higher dimensional sea, and she wasn't very interested in them, either. But she seemed kind and she liked to laugh, even though at the moment she had precious little to laugh about; Jo could see why Arnold liked her although even before her nose was broken she had only been average looking.

The only question Jo really wished she could talk about with Kayleigh was how she did it, getting a boy to like her (NOT that Jo wanted to steal Arnold from her, thank you very much—she was welcome to the bounder). But Jo would never, never, never in a million years humiliate herself by bringing up the subject.

After a while Kayleigh got the message from Jo's grunts and uh-huhs and left her alone to wander the beach and the woods, usually on the thin excuse of collecting firewood, which Arnold's girlfriend couldn't be bothered doing. Jo would stare up at the innocent blue sky, trying to discern the impenetrable curtain of the Gray Zone behind it that was blocking her from going home. But she couldn't see anything, not without a dragon or Gloria to help her over the dimensional barrier.

She drew equations in the sand, smiling a little when she remembered the ancient Greek mathematician Archimedes had done the same thing, and let the incoming tide wash them away.

When she saw Arnold coming she'd walk the other way and let Kayleigh have him to herself. Though she wasn't avoiding him just so she didn't have to see him mashing lips with Kayleigh and feeling her up; seeing him also reminded Jo of the night she'd helped him with his "mission" to burn down the Town Hall, and she wasn't at all sure how she felt about *that*. At the time it had been fun and exciting and scary all at once; the thought that Mum would have been beside herself, would have insisted that Dad thrash her for such a serious offense, only gave the adventure the wild tang of the forbidden, because *they were so far away they'd never even find about it!*

But it was frustrating, crouching in the dark with a battery-powered torch and a jerrycan full of petrol, while Arnold was the one who got to light the bottle and throw it so the silent building lit up in a shower of bright sparks and flame, and then it was scary all over again having to dash all alone through the siren-haunted streets and backyards and over the bridge to the darkened wilderness of Assateague, only to trudge the miles back to the lodge alone along the faintly moonlit shore.

She thought of Matthew Arnold's "Nantucket Beach:"

> *... But now I only hear*
> *Its melancholy, long, withdrawing roar,*
> *Retreating, to the breath*
> *Of the night-wind, down the vast edges drear*
> *And naked shingles of the world.*

A feeling that was replaced by horror the next night, when Alison told her about the injured fireman and asked her whether Arnold had had anything to do with it, and all she could do was look away and change the subject.

She told Arnold the next night that she would never do that again, not for a million pounds she wouldn't, but soon she started to dread Alison's visits almost as much as Arnold's, because the older girl kept asking her and Kayleigh for advice on dealing with him and neither of them knew what to say.

"I'm worried he'll really hurt someone," Alison said a few days after the Seder. "He keeps setting those fires… Last night it was the Park Service booths, you know, the ones the cars have to stop at when they drive onto Assateague Island. It's true there was nobody there, but what if someone had gotten hurt trying to put out the fire? I almost wish he'd get caught."

"Don't say that!" Kayleigh yelled, her knuckles white as she clenched her fists.

"Don't worry, I won't tell on him," Alison said with a grimace. "But can't you two try to talk sense into him, to make him see that what he's doing is wrong and won't help anything?"

"I hope he burns down the whole damn town!" Kayleigh shouted. When Jo and Alison looked at her, she said, "Well, I hope he does! You think everybody doesn't know what my dad's been doing to my mom and me ever since he lost his job and Kyle left for Mars? But we ain't big, famous pioneer heroes like him, so nobody gives a—" An expression of shock came over her face at the word that flew out of her mouth then, and she fled into the forest.

Later, after Alison went home, Kayleigh told Jo that when Kyle got too big for their father to "whup" he had started to protect Mom, and her, too. "But then he went away and left us all alone."

Jo looked intently into the campfire, poking it expertly with a stick to get the flames to rise higher. She heard Kayleigh snort, mutter to herself, and rustle away into the bushes somewhere.

The next morning Jo's heart leapt when she was walking on the beach and saw Gloria come walking along the sand. It had to be her, with that long red hair blowing in the wind and those long skirts and crazy boots. *She must have figured out a way past the Gray Zone!* But when she came near enough for Jo to see her face, her heart sank.

"I wanted to make sure you and Kayleigh are all right out here," Gloria said.

"Sure we are, for castaways."

"I'm sorry about that, Jo," Gloria said, in a tone that said *but it's not my fault*. "I've even been talking to Gibur, who wants to get out of here just as badly as you and me. But so far, we're all trapped."

Don't cry. Just don't, Jo ordered herself. "Well, we're fine, Kay and me. We sit around the campfire singing songs every night. I've taught her French and Loo-siana Creole, and next week I'm gonna teach her calculus!"

"Skip the sarcasm, Jo. You might try being kind to her. Her father—"

"I know about her father!" Jo shouted. "At least she has a chance of seeing him again!"

Gloria waited for her to calm down before unslinging a backpack she was carrying. "I brought you some books."

"Oh, goody, more books," Jo mumbled, but her hands were already reaching in of their own accord. *My First Years Pioneering in Israel*, by someone named Franz Kafka. *The Count of Monte Cristo*, by Alexandre Dumas. "I've read this one," she complained.

"I don't think you have," Gloria said, brushing some drifting sand off the cover, which said in full, *The Further Adventures of the Count of Monte Cristo and his Wonderful Rocketship*, by Alexandre Dumas and Jules Verne.

"It's not in French, is it? My French has been going to pot, being stranded with these savages."

Gloria stood up. "I ought not to give it to you, if you're going to be such a snob!"

"I'm sorry, Gloria. I just can't stand—"

"Being with me," said Kayleigh, who had walked up quietly. Jo jumped, and Arnold's girlfriend made a close-lipped smile. "Oh, I know what you think of me, Jo. That I'm some sort of bimbo."

"I don't know what that is."

"Yes, you do. I could let it go when I thought you were just jealous over Arnold. But I ain't stupid, just 'cause I'm no Einstein and I sometimes say 'ain't.' I can tell when someone's got no respect. At least I'm at home in this world, not a weirdo alien freak like you!"

"Kayleigh, that isn't fair," Jo heard Gloria saying. She couldn't see her face because she'd turned to look out at the waves.

"Who asked you, carrot-top!"

"Kayleigh, I'm…"

"I know who you are, 'cause Arnold told me! You brought Jo here and that Teresa chick who wrote that pamphlet. You made all that trouble for us, and now Jo's stuck here, and you just hide behind your books like it ain't got nothin' to do with you!"

Jo waited for Gloria to say something quietly devastating, something that would reduce Kayleigh to a sobbing, pitiful wreck. She could at least explain that she'd been hard at work, desperately trying to figure out a way to beat the Gray Ones so that travel between the worlds would become possible again, the High Ones' Bubble Drive would work, and everything would go back to normal.

Instead she said, "You're right, Kayleigh. I made terrible mistakes when I came here. I thought working things out more fairly between human beings and the Winged-Thinkers would be a lot easier."

Jo turned around, her arms folded tightly over her chest. "But it hasn't worked out so well, has it, Gloria?"

Gloria's eyes were huge and green, each one a brimming ocean in miniature. "No, it hasn't."

"Has Arnold told you how half the people in town now have n-net nodes in their homes?" Kayleigh demanded.

Gloria started. "No, he hasn't!"

"That's 'cause he ain't talking to you, is he?" Kayleigh said. When Gloria was silent, Kayleigh added, "I don't see as how I blame him. You can't try to help one side in a war while yelling about peace, peace, peace all the time."

"It doesn't have to be a war," Gloria said. "It must not become one."

"You're too late," said a new voice, and everyone turned.

It was Arnold.

37

Alison woke with a start, certain she'd just heard something thump. Outside the window it was pitch black and her alarm clock said it was one in the morning. Just like she had the night before, she got out of bed, tiptoed down the hall and peeked in Arnold's bedroom.

She could see his lumpy form under the sheets and the window wide open, but did that mean he'd just sneaked in or that he'd opened the window hours ago in hopes of a breeze? There was no way to be sure, but there were also no sirens. So she went downstairs, fixed herself a plate of graham crackers and a glass of milk, and went back to bed, her ears straining for shouts, the crackle of flames, the inhuman wailing and blast of fire engines. But there was nothing but the distant cry of seagulls, and eventually she fell asleep.

In the morning everything seemed to be back to normal. Arnold lay in bed grunting when she told him it was time to get up, so she went downstairs and got Mom to go get him. By the time he came downstairs, rubbing his eyes with the sides of his fists like a little boy, she already had everybody's breakfast on the table. It seemed absurd that he could be a threat to anybody, in his untied shoes and raggedy T-shirt.

School was just the normal drag that day. Shaniqua stopped by and chatted at lunch like old times, the weather had cooled off a bit, and there were no sirens that night. But she knew it was just a matter of time until Arnold started up again. In fact, he was probably deliberately biding his time to throw the police off. She was afraid to ask him, talking to Jo and Gloria was useless because they had no more idea what to do than she did, and Kayleigh was openly cheering him on.

"Somebody has to do something before the Slugs turn all our brains to mush," Kayleigh said as she, Jo, and Alison sat munching franks and beans one warm night at the beginning of May.

"Not everybody has one of the new home n-net nodes," Alison pointed out.

"Oh, yeah?" said Kayleigh. "What about your friends?"

"Shaniqua's family doesn't have one."

What Alison didn't say was that Tavon was pressuring his parents to get one, saying it would help him concentrate on his community college studies.

"Mom is afraid of making him angry, so I think he's gonna get his way," Shaniqua had said. "But he ain't gonna use it for studying. He's gonna use it to hit on girls all over the planet."

"And your other friends?" Kayleigh persisted.

Alison couldn't very well tell her she didn't have any other friends, so she snapped, "What difference does it make? Burning down buildings here in Chincoteague isn't going to stop people from getting n-nodes in their homes! You'd have to break into every house in town…" She broke off, not wanting Kayleigh to give Arnold any more ideas. Instead she turned to Jo and said, "Jo, tell her!"

"What do you want my opinion for?" Jo said, not looking at either of the other girls. "I'm just some snobby weirdo alien freak!"

Alison sighed. "That doesn't help anything either, Jo. We do have to fight against the High Ones, we just need some other way of doing it."

"What way would you suggest, Allie?" Kayleigh retorted. "We're just a bunch of kids. We're not soldiers with fancy uniforms and weapons to protect us. Fighting dirty is the only way we can fight!"

Arnold would no doubt make the same argument, if he would even speak to her. She longed more than ever to talk to Mom, to tell her what Arnold was doing in the hope she could somehow get him to stop before he killed someone, got hurt or killed himself, or got arrested or disappeared by SCOD.

But she couldn't burden Mom with one more problem, when Mom was barely holding it together running back and forth to her job and spending every free moment there and at home on the phone trying to track Dad down. There seemed to be no escape.

* * * *

The same night Alison was having her useless talk with Kayleigh and Jo, Arnold burned down the Fish and Wildlife office at the end of Main Street, where the watermen all got their licenses.

The next night he came back from aiding his "damsels in distress," as he thought of Kayleigh and Jo, burning with the thought that everything they were suffering was the Slugs' fault, relishing the fact that he was on his way to his next attack on the invaders. If not for them, Kayleigh's father would be a waterman like his father and grandfather before him, and Kyle would still be living at home so even if Mr. Scott did lose his temper, his son would be there to stop him taking it out on Kayleigh or her mom. As for Jo, she had to hide out on Assateague because it wasn't safe for her in his house, which it would be if SCOD hadn't kidnapped Dad.

Arnold hadn't said a word to Mr. Wolff outside of class in days, and he hadn't seen the League agents at all since the night they taught him about Molotov cocktails, but he could tell by the look in the teacher's large, dark eyes and from hints in the glowing remarks on his papers that he approved of everything he was doing.

Gloria didn't, but who cared about her? "You're a hypocritical, phony goody-two-shoes," he had told her to her face that evening out on the beach, relishing the hurt in her emerald eyes. Who needed her old books, or her spider plant, now languishing with droopy leaves on his windowsill? Now was the time to fight!

As he skirted the pounding waves—there was a brisk offshore wind blowing sand and salt foam into his eyes—he brooded about Alison. What was his sister's problem? *She just doesn't want me having my moment of glory, that must be it*, Arnold decided.

True, he'd been upset himself when those firemen were hurt at the town hall. But that was weeks ago, already. He'd had time to get over it, and Mr. Wolff had helped him. God knew it hadn't been easy.

The morning after that first strike on the enemy, when everyone filed back into Miss Kelley's history class from Mr. Wright's horrible all-school assembly, he'd heard Hailee say, "Those filthy terrorists! What'd they want to attack our town hall for?" There was a murmur of agreement.

Arnold had stared at her. *Your double in the ruined world would understand. She'd be the first to cheer me on!*

But he felt sick, thinking of Mr. Birch getting burned. When Arnold had burned his right thumb the first time he'd tried to use the cigarette lighter, it had hurt so bad he'd had to dunk it in the sea on the long, dark walk home from the lodge. And that was just the tip of his thumb! What would it feel like to have that pain all over your body?

He kept brooding over that as history class ended and English class began, until he had to raise his hand. "Mr. Wolff, may I be excused? I'm not feeling well."

"Of course," Mr. Wolff said. "We're all upset today. Does anyone else need a minute?"

As Arnold stood up and headed for the classroom door, nausea rose in his guts. It was like the time he had stomach flu in fourth grade and was out of school for a week. He stumbled down the hall faster and faster, trying not to picture Mr. Birch's burned skin. Trying not to feel what he felt, but his own arms and chest were starting to itch something fierce.

He barely made it into a toilet stall before he threw up, spattering soggy flecks of corn flakes and orange juice all over and around the toilet. He clutched the porcelain of the tank, his head down, and retched a few more times until his stomach was empty.

After making a half-hearted attempt to clean up the mess with toilet paper, he flushed and went to the sink, groaning when he saw how much had gotten on his shirt and pants. He headed for the door but reeled back in surprise at the sight of Mr. Wolff walking in.

"I came to check on you," the teacher said. "I'm sorry you're not feeling well."

The bell rang for lunch, and the hallway outside filled with the roar of students heading to the cafeteria. Two giggling seventh graders ran in, brushing past Mr. Wolff with barely an apology. He didn't even notice, he was so busy staring at Arnold.

"I think I need to go home," Arnold said.

The teacher nodded. "I think that would be a good idea. Want a ride? I'm not on lunch duty today."

"Thanks, it's just a few blocks."

"Yeah, but you really don't look so good." Mr. Wolff winked his left eye slowly.

"Uhh, sure, that would be great, I guess." Arnold followed Mr. Wolff out into the parking lot. His car was a battered old brownish Ford, with large patches of rust on the doors and around the wheel wells. As he backed out and turned left, Arnold said, "But that's not the way to my house."

"I'm taking the long way, Arnold."

"Sorry about the smell."

"Don't worry about it. I keep my car dirty on purpose." He grinned his wolfish grin. "Makes the cops less eager to search it when they pull me over."

Arnold watched in amazement as Mr. Wolff kept turning the steering wheel. "Isn't your car connected to the network?"

"Nope. That's why I get pulled over so much. But it's worth it not to be under the Slugs' computer control."

"Mr. Wolff, look, I'm sorry but I can't do any more missions." Arnold swallowed. His throat was sore from throwing up. "I, I guess I'm still too much of a kid."

"Oh, bull. It's perfectly normal to have an attack of nerves the first time out. You did great."

"Thanks, b-but I can't stop thinking about Mr. Birch and the other firemen."

"You did your job, and he did his. There's nothing to be upset about."

"But what if someone had gotten hurt even worse?" He couldn't bear to say "if someone had gotten killed," but that didn't stop him thinking it.

"Who? It was the middle of the night." Mr. Wolff slapped Arnold's knee with his hairy hand. "I understand how you feel, Arnold. You're a good kid. But you have to understand, this is a war. People get hurt in wars. People get killed. Even innocent bystanders, sometimes."

"I know that," Arnold said in a small voice.

"Any human who gets hurt in the struggle, it's completely the Slugs' fault, right? If they hadn't invaded and taken over our world, none of this would be happening."

"That's true, but—"

"I know this is hard, Arnold. But I also know you're made of tough stuff." He pulled to a stop in front of the Grossbards' house and turned an intense stare on him.

Arnold shivered despite himself.

"Arnold, we know what happened to your father," the teacher said abruptly.

Arnold sat up straight. "You do?"

"He's being held captive in a SCOD hole in West Virginia."

It was all Arnold could do not to grab Mr. Wolff by the lapels of his crisp white shirt. "Then we have to rescue him! And the other prisoners too, of course."

Mr. Wolff shook his head. "I'm sorry, Arnold. The place is too well guarded. And I have to be honest with you, his chances of ever making it out alive are not good."

Arnold started to cry. "There must be something we can do!"

Mr. Wolff took hold of Arnold's trembling hands. "There is, Arnold, and you're doing it. Every mission you complete successfully is another blow against the Slugs and their helpers in SCOD. But you have to be strong. Strong enough to overcome your own inner weakness."

Arnold swallowed. His throat still hurt. "Yes, sir. I understand."

"Good man." He took a wadded-up napkin from his pocket, scribbled something, and handed it to Arnold. "These are your next three missions. Flush it down the toilet as soon as you've read and memorized it. The night after you finish the last one, come out and meet me and the other two League gentlemen again at the lodge where Kayleigh and Jo are hiding. You still have the flyers I gave you?"

Arnold nodded. He'd hidden them under a pile of dirty underwear in his room. Even the FBI or SCOD might hesitate before looking there.

"Great. Leave some at the scene of each attack. Oh, and you might want to wear this," he added, handing Arnold a black ski mask. "Any questions?"

Arnold's mind was racing, but he couldn't think of anything intelligent to ask, so he shook his head.

"Good. Good luck, soldier. See you in class tomorrow."

* * * *

Arnold soon discovered that Ray Bradbury and Mr. Wolff were both right: it was a pleasure to burn. And so easy, too! He only had to fill up a gas can at the Shell station on Main Street—he made a point of telling the clerk on duty, who was barely any older than Alison, that he needed to fill his family's lawnmower, as if the guy cared.

There was more than enough in the gas can, even with spills, to fill up six quart-size glass Coke bottles, which he did in the garage, stopping up each bottle with a piece of a torn-up tie-dyed T-shirt he'd always hated anyway. He hid them in a large box full of winter clothing and took two out on each mission.

He scouted out the targets Mr. Wolff had written down for him on a long walk around town after school let out. The toll booths on Assateague Island were the furthest from his house, but also the least risky because no one would be there after dark. The Fish and Wildlife office was located by a small wharf, but who cared if somebody's boat got damaged? They could always buy another.

The building on Maddox Boulevard with the SCOD headquarters gave him pause, because there were houses on both sides, as well as behind it on Pension Street. But when he peered in the windows of the houses on Maddox they looked vacant, with the furniture neatly lined up along spic-and-span carpets. Must be summer rentals for tourists, then. And he convinced himself that the house on Pension was too far away to be in any danger.

He longed to burn down SCOD headquarters first, but decided he'd better attack the targets in the order Mr. Wolff had written them down. The booths were the most dramatic, flaring up with a roar amid the silent, dark forest to either side. But the Fish and Wildlife place had been fun to watch, too, as the flames cast dancing reflections on the bay. In his black ski mask he felt invincible, an anonymous superhero saving the Earth single-handed. Arnold-Man!

I'm doing this for Kayleigh, he reminded himself now, on Thursday night, as he walked quickly along the empty streets through an unseasonably chilly wind. He'd had some time alone with her earlier tonight inside the half-ruined lodge, and when he told her what he was on his way to do her eyes lit up and she let him put his hands up under her shirt. *I'm doing it for Jo too, though she doesn't seem to realize it—otherwise why would she fink out on me like that?* He shook off the thought, warming himself on the memory of the rapid beating of Kayleigh's heart under her bare skin.

As Arnold approached the center of town he began to see more people around than he was comfortable with. Maddox Boulevard was the main drag, and even this late there were cars driving up and down it.

Arnold waited in the shadows behind a Dumpster for a break in the traffic, and when it came he was in such a hurry that his first missile exploded harmlessly in the parking lot of the target building, and the flames were blown out by the wind. He put all his strength into throwing the second one through a ground-floor window. There was all kinds of junk in there, and for a horrifying instant he thought he saw a human silhouette amid the leaping flames. But he couldn't stay to be sure there wasn't anyone there, there were shouts from the boulevard and running feet approaching, so he had to take off through people's backyards, his heart pounding and sweat pouring down his face into his eyes, stinging them so he could barely see. Luckily home loomed up ahead of him, and within less than a minute he was safe in bed.

By the next morning, a Friday, Chincoteague was in chaos. *I did this,* Arnold thought in slow wonder as he walked to school. Every block boasted a county sheriff or state police patrol car. There were FBI agents in business suits and ties out talking to every grown-up in sight.

LEAGUE ARSONIST STRIKES AGAIN, screamed the headline in the *Chincoteague Lighthouse,* over a front-page photo of the smoking ruins of the office building from last night. The story was by none other than the editor, Paul Tingle, who had apparently talked his way out of the SCOD hole.

He must have betrayed someone for them to let him go. Maybe I should burn down the paper too, even without orders!

He wasn't feeling so brave by the time he got to school. *It's just as well that was the last one, I'd get caught for sure next time,* Arnold thought as he bent over naked in the boys' changing room in front of Bubba and some gum-popping security guard they'd brought in from the state penitentiary further down the peninsula, as if with two guards checking him out, they might find the arsonist hiding in his butt. Yeah, it was unpleasant being probed even more intensely than usual, but they were treating everyone else the same way, and he hoped it would make all the kids mad enough to join the Resistance.

But that wasn't how it was going out in the hallway. "When they catch this guy, I hope they hang him," Madison was saying to Hailee as they passed by. "The Tilghmans got out by the skin of their teeth last night."

Arnold did a double take. "What happened?" he asked.

Madison turned and sneered at him. "Out of the loop as usual, nerd-face? The terrorists burned down the Norfolk Building, but the wind spread the flames and the Tilghmans' house burned down too."

"Mary Tilghman's in my little sister's class," Hailee added, "I heard they had to airlift her to the hospital in Salisbury. Smoke inhalation."

"That's—that's terrible," Arnold muttered, wondering if he was going to be sick again.

Hailee nodded and said, "The terrorists had better hope when they're caught the cops get them out of town, or we'll have a real old-fashioned lynching here."

Arnold shuddered inwardly and tried to tell himself again that the other Hailee would have understood. But it still hurt to hear her talk that way. Before he could stop his imagination he saw himself standing on top of a chair on Main Street surrounded by an angry mob. Hailee put a noose around his neck and Gus kicked the chair out from under him while Matt and Jared stood sneering.

He tried to shake off the vision. It helped that in English class Mr. Wolff was handing back last week's vocab quiz, where he'd written in red across the top, "Good work, Arnold, but be sure to get that assignment we talked about to me by tonight." There were two red slashes under the word "tonight." Arnold looked up, willing to risk everything for a wink from Mr. Wolff, but the teacher's back was turned.

The day crawled by with agonizing slowness. Lunch was repulsive gray Salisbury steak, mashed potatoes that tasted like wet sawdust, and mushy, too-bright green peas that didn't taste like anything at all. Gym was a dodge ball game where Arnold was tripped twice before Jared slammed him in the head with that evil, hard red rubber playground ball. The teacher said that was a foul and Arnold wasn't out, which gave Jared a chance to whack the ball right into Arnold's stomach. The next period was study hall, and Miss Kelley, who was proctoring, took the opportunity to hand back last week's quiz on the Bicentennial Constitution. Arnold's had a big red F on it.

As if he cared, when he knew everything he had to know about the government: that it was the enemy. He held onto that thought so tightly it was a wonder he didn't strangle it, trying to block out the mental image of freckle-faced Mary Tilghman lying in a hospital bed with tubes hooked up to her arms. When the bell rang Arnold slipped out a fire exit, figuring he might as well skip last-period math and get a head start walking to the League meeting.

A passing shower had cleared and cooled the air, and Arnold drank it in with relief. The bridge to Assateague was crowded with people fishing, and on the far side two rangers in Smokey the Bear hats were sitting on folding chairs fanning themselves near the burned-out wreckage of the toll booths.

One of them eyed Arnold curiously as he passed. "Shouldn't you still be in school, kid?"

Arnold's heart sped up. "They let us out early," he said, hoping he sounded casual. "Everyone was so upset about the Tilghmans."

The ranger stared at him for a moment, the top of his face shaded by his broad-brimmed hat, then shrugged. Arnold let out a breath, shouldered his backpack, and strolled past, absently kicking a waterlogged, burned plank as he passed.

He started to worry as he hiked that he'd left too early and no one would be there to meet him at the site of the lodge, but in fact Mr. Wolff and his two unnamed companions were waiting for him. The guy with the Brooklyn accent was lying propped up on one elbow in the sand as Arnold came over the dunes, but he got to his feet and stood with the other two men, silently watching Arnold approach.

Kayleigh was standing in the doorway of the lodge. When she saw him coming she squealed and started to run toward him, stopping in her tracks when Mr. Wolff held a warning hand up. As Arnold drew closer, all three men brought their right hands up to their foreheads and saluted.

Startled and confused, Arnold stopped walking and clumsily saluted them back.

"Brother Grossbard, congratulations," Brooklyn said. "You have been inducted into the Human Defense League as a full member. We don't normally admit anyone under eighteen, but you have distinguished yourself in four operations, in conditions of increasing danger." He stepped forward and pinned something to Arnold's T-shirt. It was a button depicting the Earth as seen from space, all swirls of white cloud over blue seas and brown continents, with a red-white-and-blue ribbon attached at the bottom.

"Unfortunately you won't be able to wear that to school," Mr. Wolff said, and Arnold shot him a glance.

Do you think I'm an idiot?

Then Bruiser stepped forward, holding another beribboned button. "Arnold, four missions completed successfully is four more than a lot of our members can boast," he said. "The Regional Executive has decided to name you a Hero of Earth, Second Class." The button was the same image of Earth, but the ribbon was made of a soft, shiny gold cloth.

Arnold's chest swelled as the pin joined its twin on his shirt. A little more and he might float away into the sky like a balloon.

The big guy stepped back, and all three men saluted Arnold again. He returned the salute, trying to hold his hand steady this time. Mr. Wolff gestured to Kayleigh and she ran up to Arnold, threw her arms around his neck and kissed him.

He kissed her back hungrily, forgetting everything else for a moment, until one of the men cleared his throat noisily and Arnold drew away, blushing.

"Well, what's my next mission?" he asked. "I don't think I could get away with another arson."

"No, Brother Grossbard, you're right, that tactic has run its course," Mr. Wolff—Brother Wolff—agreed. "That was the reason we called you out here today—my friends are going to give you your next, most important mission. It's so vital that it is top secret—neither I nor anyone else can be allowed to hear about it." He turned and smiled at Kayleigh, showing all his teeth.

"But why can't I take part?" Kayleigh said.

Stop whining, Arnold commanded her silently.

"Kayleigh, Arnold is the experienced operative," Mr. Wolff said. "Now come with me. I'd like to talk to you about your paragraph structure."

"My what? But I haven't even been in class in weeks!"

"That is no matter, a true student never stops learning," Mr. Wolff said, striding up and grabbing Kayleigh's hand. "By the way, where is Jo?"

"Off skulking in the woods somewhere. Stop pulling so hard, Mr. Wolff, you're hurting me!" Kayleigh said as he dragged her away.

Brooklyn and Bruiser watched over folded arms. Both of them were smiling slightly. "All right, brother," Brooklyn said when Mr. Wolff and Kayleigh disappeared over the top of a dune, "come with us."

Arnold joined them inside the lodge. It was so dim he had trouble seeing their faces, which somehow frightened him. He scolded himself for being a sissy. What did he have to be afraid of from his allies?

"In a way all your missions have been preparation for this next mission," Brooklyn said. "We had to make sure you could keep your nerve and do what you had to."

Arnold's heart sped up. Obviously the League agent was thinking of how he had overcome his doubts.

"You have been selected for the honor of mounting an attack that marks a new phase in our war of liberation," Brooklyn continued.

Arnold smiled tentatively. "What is it?"

Bruiser now spoke up. "You're going to blow up the Wallops Island Fusion Plant… tomorrow morning."

Arnold stopped smiling. "What?"

"Don't worry, you don't have to use a Molotov cocktail," Brooklyn said. "We'll give you instructions on which levers to pull and buttons to press to start a runaway reaction. You won't believe how easy it is to sneak in, by the way—you have a head start since your Dad worked there and you must have visited him in his office, right?"

"I've only been there a few times, and never in the actual plant," Arnold said. His brain felt flash-frozen, his lips numb. Mr. Nomura's humorous face floated before his eyes. "What about all the people who work there? Won't they be killed?"

"That can't be helped. It's a war, like we said after you burned down the Town Hall, remember? Besides, they took the risk, working with alien machines."

"But it's not just the people who work there," Arnold said slowly. He was trying to remember what he'd learned in history class about the hydrogen bombs they used to have during the Cold War, which were also fusion-powered. "All the people at the Interplanetary Saucer Base will be killed too, won't they?"

"Oh, don't worry about that," Brooklyn said smoothly. "We've checked the schedules, and there are no flights tomorrow until about two o'clock. This is your chance to help save the world. Be a hero, Arnold."

Arnold closed his eyes, seeing the ruined world with its unburied skeletons lying scattered in the streets. "I'll try," he whispered. "I just don't know if I can do it."

"Of course you can. You're already a Hero of Earth, Second Class," Brooklyn said. "When this operation is over, you'll be one of a handful of volunteers—we can't tell you how many, but you're not alone—to be remembered as a Hero of Earth, Supreme Class. People will be writing songs about you a thousand years from now."

Remembered as. That means I'm going to die, too. The thought should have terrified Arnold, but in a weird way it made things better. If he was giving up his own life, maybe it was okay that he was taking other people's lives, too. And it was all for the good of the whole human race.

"People will be chanting your name as they drive out the last of the Slugs and their collaborators," Bruiser said.

Arnold tried to imagine it. Kayleigh throwing herself into the coffin with him, crying that she didn't want to live without him. Hailee, real-world Hailee, leaning over the coffin in her cheerleader outfit, tears streaming down her face as she said his name over and over again. Alison would probably kill herself when she remembered how mean she'd been to him. Jo would never stop crying, and if she ever got home she'd make everybody in her world remember his name, too. Huge crowds would be chanting "Ar-nold, Gross-bard, Ar-nold Gross-bard..." If Dad was still alive, SCOD would have to let him go. And nobody would ever be able to say again that Jews like him were secretly helping the Slugs.

He opened his eyes, drew a deep breath. Brooklyn and Bruiser watched him intently. "Can I have a day to think about it?"

"You're wondering if you are brave enough to do it. Of course you are, Arnold," Brooklyn said patiently. He pulled a sheet of notepaper and an old fishing map out of his shirt pocket, and Bruiser broke out a flashlight. "Look here. You get to the plant by wading through the salt marsh. There are a lot of people out clamming on the weekends this time of year, so nobody will give you a second look if you wear shorts and a T-shirt and carry a bucket."

"But there are always kids out there with their parents. Won't they be killed, too?"

Bruiser leaned toward Arnold and jabbed a finger at him. "If we let the Slugs win, all the little kids on Earth are going to be brain-damaged slaves. Or dead. A few have to be sacrificed to save everybody." When Arnold said nothing the League agent turned back to his map and pointed to a dotted line drawn in ink. "This is where the fence runs. But over here, it crosses a gut—a tidal creek. You can easily duck under it by holding your breath for just a few seconds. On the other side, hidden in some reeds, you'll find a white plastic shopping bag with a change of clothes. You enter the plant itself over here, there's a cargo door leading to a warehouse. The security is really, really sloppy. I mean, the guards are stupider than the ones in your school."

Arnold smiled faintly, thinking of Bubba. Brooklyn patted him on the shoulder and produced another piece of paper. "This is the inside of the plant. You have to go down one level from where you come in, down a staircase on the left side of the warehouse. When you come out you'll see a red control panel that looks something like this—" a blurry black-and-white snapshot— "and you just have to find this button, here, flip up that lever, there, and turn this switch, over on the side here, to the right as far as it will go. And that's it."

"And what do I do then?"

"Well, whatever you want to, I guess. I mean, you'll have less than fifteen minutes until the magnetic containment field fails, and then BOOM!"

Arnold jumped and Bruiser chuckled drily, sounding like a gravel crusher. Brooklyn handed Arnold the map and papers and put the photo back in his pocket. "I'll meet you behind the Island Roxy at eight o'clock tomorrow morning—they're not open that early, nobody will be around—and we'll go over your instructions. Don't be late."

"I'll meet you there," Arnold promised, thinking, *and maybe I'll tell you I can't do it.* But it made him ashamed to be such a coward, even in his secret thoughts. *I've got to do this for everybody—for Kayleigh, for Mom and Dad, even for Jo and Alison.* So he thanked the League agents and saluted. They solemnly returned the salute.

Arnold walked out of the lodge and began following the footprints Mr. Wolff and Kayleigh had left in the sand. Out of the corner of his eye he could see Brooklyn and Bruiser walking swiftly through the marsh, doubtless making for their speedboat. He suppressed a flash of resentment at having to walk home—at least this way he'd get to tell Kayleigh all about it.

When he spotted her, though, she was still with Mr. Wolff, whose eyes narrowed when he saw Arnold coming. He shook his head slightly, and Arnold understood: *Don't say too much.*

"Well? Did they tell you about the new mission? Can I come with you?" Kayleigh blurted when he got close enough to hear her.

"Yes, I have a new mission, but no, you can't come with me, Kayleigh. It's... its too dangerous." He paused at the look of hurt on her face. "I might get killed," he added. *That must be what the Brooklyn guy meant, surely. That there's a <u>risk</u> I might get killed. But surely I can run fast enough to get away from ground zero before the plant blows up—?*

Kayleigh's hands flew to her mouth. When she lowered them her eyes were brimming with tears. "Please let me help you, Arnold. You don't have to do it alone."

"Sometimes a man has to go it alone," Arnold said, feeling incredibly noble and secretly ridiculous at the same time. "What they need me to do—"

Mr. Wolff cleared his throat noisily. "Arnold! That's enough. Neither of us needs to know the details. Why don't you walk back with me. My car's in the beach parking lot, I can give you a ride home the last couple of miles."

"I—I think I need to be alone with Kayleigh for a while, Mr. Wolff," Arnold heard himself say. *Did I really just say no to my teacher and commander? To an eleven-dimensional being? What if he gets mad?*

Mr. Wolff recoiled, but then he smiled with all his teeth. "Okay, Arnold. Sure. Just promise me you won't break mission security."

"I promise, Mr. Wolff."

"And Kayleigh, I need you to give your word you won't try to make Arnold tell you what he needs to do."

"Yes sir, Mr. Wolff. I promise."

"All right then, kids. Enjoy yourselves." Mr. Wolff gave them a slow wink, which should have been embarrassing and creepy, but Arnold was past caring about things like that. The teacher turned his back and walked quickly away.

As he dwindled to a dot down the beach Arnold took Kayleigh's hand, his heart hammering, and began walking with her back to the lodge. *Will she go all the way? She has to go all the way, I'm risking my life tomorrow.*

Arnold didn't exactly know what "going all the way" meant—SCOD had made sure that health class didn't get into details, and while Dad kept mumbling that he had to have "the talk" with Arnold, he was somehow always too busy. Still, he knew it had something to do with taking off all your clothes, and he figured that Kayleigh, being a girl, would know the rest.

So as soon as they walked into the lodge, he shut the busted door behind them, pulled Kayleigh down beside him on the floor, and began kissing her hard and fumbling with the buttons of her shirt.

She was kissing him back and tugging the tucked-in bottom of his shirt out of his pants when an all-too-familiar voice said right in Arnold's ear, "What do you have to blow up a bunch of flowers for? Doesn't sound very heroic to me!"

38

Arnold leaped backward from Kayleigh as if she'd suddenly given him a high-voltage electric shock. As she turned aside and began buttoning up her shirt, Arnold turned on Jo, struggling mightily to control an impulse to punch her in the face. *But then I'd be as bad as Kayleigh's father.* He settled for shouting at her. "What the hell are you talking about?"

"Those guys want you to blow up a purple flower? They must be crazier than I thought! My mum used to grow those fuchsia plants. The purple flowers are really pretty."

Kayleigh spun around, her eyes bulging. Her shirt was buttoned up wrong. "Arnold, they want you to destroy the fusion plant at Wallops Island? That's what the mission is?"

Arnold glared at Jo. "You were eavesdropping, you—you traitor!"

"Sticks and stones, Arnold. I still don't see the point of exploding a bunch of flowers."

Kayleigh eyed Jo and suddenly burst into hysterical laughter. She laughed so hard she lost her balance and rocked back on her elbows, gasping for breath. "You call me a dumb-dumb!" she finally managed to say. "How can you confuse a nuclear reactor with a bunch of flowers?"

"A reactor? You mean that big building over at Wallops Island?" Jo said. "Arnold called it a 'nuclear reactor' when he showed it to me, not a fuchsia plant. It's not even purple!" She glared at Arnold as if her looking stupid was his fault.

"Not fuchsia, *fusion*," Arnold said. "It fuses hydrogen atoms together to produce energy, using the Slugs' technology." He raised his chin. "My job is to destroy it. That'll kill a lot of the Slugs and their helpers, and remind people just how dangerous alien technology is, so they'll stop using the n-net."

Kayleigh stopped laughing and sat back up. "But how are you going to do that, Arnold, without getting killed yourself?"

"They gave me directions," Arnold said. "I'm not allowed to tell you. I shouldn't even be telling you this much, except that Jo, here, is a lousy eavesdropping snitch!"

"That's a really big building, Arnold," Jo said slowly. "Blowing it up would probably kill everyone inside. My world doesn't have atomic power, but I know from reading the books in Gloria's shop that interfering with an atomic reaction would be really dangerous... it would produce an enormous explosion. Wasn't atomic power first used in your world to make powerful bombs?"

Kayleigh nodded vigorously. "The High Ones... I mean the Slugs... must've been scared of those bombs. That's why one of the first things they did when they took over was to destroy all of them." She clenched her fists. "If we still had them, we could fight back! Of course they wanted to take them away from us!"

But Jo was looking at Arnold, not Kayleigh. "How about it, Arnold? Sabotaging the plant isn't just going to kill everyone inside the building, is it?"

Cold sweat prickled on Arnold's forehead, and suddenly he found he couldn't look at Jo, or at Kayleigh, either. So he was gazing at the dust motes swimming in the orange evening sun that streamed down through the hole in the roof when he said, "No, that's true. It's going to destroy all of Wallops Island, too. I'll have to get far away, fast, to have a chance of surviving." *That Brooklyn guy didn't seem to think I can.*

"We have to get an old car, one that isn't hooked into the network, to drive him out of there. A getaway car!" Kayleigh exclaimed, and smacked her right fist into her left palm. "My dad has one... but I haven't got the key and it's up on blocks anyway."

"You're kind of missing the point, Kay," Jo said. "What about all the other people who are going to get killed when the plant explodes?"

"It's a Saturday. There won't be that many people at work," Arnold said.

"And what about the saucer airfield you showed me? People just flying to other cities? Don't you care about them?"

"The League guy said they checked and there aren't any saucer flights tomorrow morning."

"You have an answer for everything, don't you, Arnold?" Jo leaned toward Arnold, grabbed his chin and turned his head until he couldn't avoid looking at her. "But the causeway also passes by there. And there are always people out doing stuff in the marsh and the bay... boats that will capsize when the shock wave swamps them. Whatever way you look at it, you're going to kill innocent people."

Kayleigh grabbed Jo's arm and pulled her hand off of Arnold's face. "It's a war, Jo. People die in wars. Innocent people, too. You may not care because it's not your world at stake—"

"—it *is* my world, now—" Jo interrupted.

"—and anyway, doesn't your precious Dragon-British Empire kill people in wars?"

"That's not the point! This isn't a war Arnold is planning, it's a terrorist attack!"

"That's just words," Kayleigh sneered. "What difference does it make whether a man in a fishing boat gets killed by the shock wave from the fusion plant blowing up, or by a cannon from one of your warships?"

As Jo spluttered, Arnold said, "I have to do it, Jo. It's easy for you to judge, when all you've got in your world is friendly dragons." He took a breath. "And since when did you get so squeamish, anyway? I don't remember you having any attack of conscience the night we burned down the town hall. You were having fun, don't deny it!"

"I don't deny it," Jo said. "I'm ashamed of it. I've had to live with it ever since, thinking how Jeb Birch got hurt and, and, might have got killed!"

"Oh yeah?" Arnold snapped. "No wonder you've been avoiding me. Well, the Slugs don't mind killing people one bit. I know for a fact they're just biding their time before they kill us all!"

"What? How do you know that?" Jo said. Even Kayleigh was staring at him.

Arnold swallowed. *Now I've put my foot in it. I'll have to tell them.* He took a deep breath and ran a shaky hand through his hair. "I've been to another world—a *third* world, not yours, Jo. It wasn't Gloria who took me, though…" He explained about Mr. Wolff, and the ruined world, and the other Hailee. He didn't necessarily expect to change Jo's mind, but he thought at least she'd understand his dilemma.

But all she did was clap her right hand over her eyes and shake her head slowly back and forth. "Oh, Arnold…"

"And they're going to do the same thing to us! It's just a matter of time!"

Kayleigh was glaring at him. "What's all this about Hailee?"

"It's not the real Hailee, I mean, not the one we go to school with, and I never saw her after that one time, and I didn't *do* anything with her anyway…" *How did I go from being a nerd the girls all laughed at to having too many girls in my life?*

"Save it for another time, you two," said Jo. "The point is, Arnold… you don't really know what happened to that world Mr. Wolff took you to."

"Huh? Of course I do! People rebelled against the High Ones, and the lousy Slugs killed almost everybody in the whole world!"

"Really? Is that what the other Hailee told you? How old was she when it happened?"

"Little. Like, six, I think."

"Huh. How do you even know it was the High Ones? How do you know it wasn't some other aliens?"

"*Other* aliens? But that's ridiculous…" He stopped and frowned. Had the other Hailee called the things hunting her clan High Ones, or Slugs? He couldn't remember. He thought she might have just called them aliens. Or "them." *Mr. Wolff wouldn't have lied to me, would he?*

Unfortunately it was all too easy to imagine how he would justify such a lie. "You needed a kick in the pants to find your courage, Arnold. All's fair in love and war."

"And how do you know the League guys aren't lying to you?" Jo said. "Or do you just trust everything they tell you?"

To drown out the sinking feeling in his gut Arnold raised his voice. "It doesn't matter anyway, it's still a war, it's us against the Slugs, and in a war people get killed, like Kayleigh said! If some kids get killed now it's to save many more kids later! There are people whose brains are melting right now because of their n-network!"

The more Arnold doubted, the louder he shouted.

"That's horrible, Arnold," said Jo. "And what happened to your father is horrible. And what happened to you, Kay, is awful too, and maybe it is the Slugs' fault in a way. But you still can't just go around killing people. And it isn't the same thing, deliberately doing something you *know* is going to kill innocent people and fighting in a war where innocent people get killed by mistake."

"I think it probably *is* the same, if you're the one getting killed," said Kayleigh. "Anyway, we don't have an army. The Slugs took that all away from us, and besides, we're only teenagers. We have to fight back however we can. I just want Arnold to survive, that's all. I don't care about anyone who's stupid enough to be hanging out near a Slug base on a Saturday morning."

"Arnold, you have to see it's wrong!" Jo cried.

Arnold clutched his head in both hands. He couldn't see that clearly at all. Jo was right, but Kayleigh was also right. How could he decide? If he asked Mom, she'd be horrified, but mainly at the thought that *he* might get killed.

Gloria said one thing, Mr. Wolff said another. The Bible said not to kill, but it also talked about wars God had commanded people to fight. Other books gave you all kinds of answers. And he had to decide *now*, tonight. Without thinking about it he was staggering to his feet and heading out the door into the sunset.

"What are you going to do, Arnold?" Jo called after him.

Kayleigh shoved her aside. "You have to fight, Arnold!"

The walk home seemed endless, the thoughts in his head chasing themselves around and around in circles as he plodded through the gathering dark. Whatever he did, he would be doing something wrong and hurting a lot of people. If he did what the League wanted him to, he'd kill a lot of people in the fusion plant and the Interplanetary Base. If he didn't, and their operation failed, he would be a traitor to the cause and might be dooming the whole human race. What was the right answer?

What if there wasn't one?

When he got home it was very late. Alison was sitting on the couch reading a book—Arnold was annoyed to see it was *Letters to a Woman Sitting in Darkness.* Had she been talking to Gloria on the sly, tattling on him? But picking a fight with Sis now, on what might be the last night of his life, seemed really petty.

So he sat down beside her with a grunt. She didn't look up. After a minute he asked, "Where's Mom?"

"She had to go to Washington for the weekend to meet with some people who can help her find Dad. She told you that this morning. Don't you listen?"

Arnold's heart sank, though there was no way he would have discussed his dilemma with her. She'd freak out and lock him in his room. Still, he was disappointed she wasn't here. She might have suggested they do something fun as a family, which would have been nice.

As tired as he was from the long walk, he didn't think he'd be able to sleep. And Alison wasn't going to do anything to help him chase the ragged thoughts away. He sighed and picked up the remote control, forgetting for a moment that the tri-vee stage was broken. When it didn't turn on he threw the remote on the floor.

Alison didn't look up at the clattering.

"Hey, Sis."

No response. He waved his hand between her face and the book.

Without looking up, she said, "What is it, turd-breath?"

You won't be calling me that after tomorrow. "Why did you wreck our tri-vee? I mean, it's pretty thoughtless to go around breaking things other people want to use."

Alison stared at him and burst out laughing.

Arnold didn't see what was so funny. He flounced upstairs, slamming the bedroom door behind him. He could still hear Allie laughing, high-pitched, frantic giggles interrupted by hiccups. *What a moron.*

Then he forgot about her, because there was no need to turn on the light. The spider plant cast a green glow bright enough to read by, except that the motion of the leaves made it flicker like a strobe. They were whirling so fast they blurred to near-invisibility. Arnold tiptoed toward the window and stretched his right hand out cautiously. He had to snatch it back when it was still a good fifteen centimeters away. That thing was *hot*. He lay down on his stomach on his bed, propped his chin up on the headboard and watched the alien plant's motion.

When he blinked, morning light was coming in the window. *What happened? Did I fall asleep?* His eyes darted to the clock. It was already after seven. He was supposed to be meeting the Brooklyn guy in less than an hour.

The thought should have filled him with panic, but he felt strangely calm, because he knew what the answer was—or at least, what *his* answer would be. His eyes strayed to the spider plant, whose leaves were twisting slowly, hypnotically in the sunlight. Perhaps it had done something to him last night, something that helped clear his mind of the fear and rage and confusion that wouldn't let him see what his heart knew was true.

"No. I can't do it," he said aloud. "I won't. Never in a million years." No matter how terrible the things the Slugs and their human helpers were doing, there were some things you couldn't do to fight them… or you became no better than them.

The clear calm in Arnold's mind stayed with him as he dressed, went down to the kitchen and made himself a huge breakfast. He'd gone to bed without dinner the night before, after all, and the hunger he felt wouldn't be denied, as he devoured most of a loaf of white bread with a small jar of peanut butter and all the bananas in the house, washing it down with an almost full half-gallon bottle of milk. He was just finishing his third apple (Macintosh, his favorite) when Alison wandered into the kitchen yawning.

Her eyes widened when she saw Arnold had put all the banana peels, apple cores, empty wrappers and containers in the trash and stacked the dishes neatly in the sink.

"I'll wash my dishes as soon as I get back, Allie," he promised. "It shouldn't be long." It was ten minutes to eight.

"Wait, where are you going so early on a Saturday morning? Arnold?"

He shut the door carefully behind him and headed for Main Street.

As he walked, his calm slowly drained away and he began to cry quietly. Some Hero of Earth, Second Class. He felt like a Fool, First Class. How could he have let some guys he had never met before talk him into such an unimaginable crime? At the same time, he was so relieved at his decision that his feet felt floppy as he walked.

As he turned into the alley in back of the movie theater, Arnold saw Brooklyn sitting in Mr. Wolff's beat-up old Ford. Bruiser was not with him. Arnold sighed with a rush of relief.

But someone else was sitting in the passenger seat beside him … a girl. Jo.

"Jo? What are you doing here? Why…" Arnold's voice died away when he saw how wide her eyes were, how taut the skin around them was, and most of all, what Brooklyn was cradling casually in his lap.

39

"Good morning, Brother Grossbard. Ready for your final instructions?" Brooklyn said.

What have you done to Kayleigh? Arnold wanted to know. But he dared not ask. "I can't do it, Mister—Brother," Arnold heard himself say. "I'm not a murderer. I won't kill innocent people, even if it would hurt the High Ones."

Brooklyn nodded thoughtfully. Before Arnold could react, he picked up the gun in his lap, which had a long metal tube attached to its muzzle, pointed it down and to his right, and pulled the trigger. There was a muffled bang.

Jo's whole body jerked and her eyes went even wider. Brooklyn clamped his free hand over her mouth to stifle her screams and shoved the gun in Arnold's face when he started to dive in to help her.

"You have one hour to do what I told you," Brooklyn said. "One hour, Brother Grossbard, or I'll blow your little girlfriend's brains out. If the plant doesn't explode in one hour, or if I see police coming, I will shoot your girl in the head."

"Arnold, don't," Jo managed to say, through Brooklyn's hand. He turned the gun around and hit her on the head with the butt. It made a flat, dull sound, and she collapsed stunned against the far door. At her feet was a spreading pool of impossibly bright red blood.

Brooklyn pushed a button on the dashboard. There was an electronic beeping, then the amplified sound of a phone ringing.

Arnold stared in disbelief. "You have a phone in your CAR?" On the tri-vee stage only spies and other Very Important People had car-phones.

"Hello?" a man's voice said. It sounded like Bruiser.

"Plan B," said Brooklyn.

"Right." There was a shifting and scraping noise. Muffled voices in the background. Then Arnold's blood froze, because Alison was calling his name.

"I'm here," he said numbly.

"These men broke in—they—OW!"

Bruiser got back on the line. "Plan B, then."

"B, right," said Brooklyn. "One hour. Set your watch."

"Yes, brother," said Bruiser. There was a click.

As Arnold was opening his mouth to speak, Brooklyn took off in a squeal of tires. Too late, Arnold realized he should have made a grab for the gun when the thug had been distracted dialing. But that would have left Alison in danger. What could he do now?

Only one thing. He turned and began walking in the direction the car had gone. The service station on Main Street sold buckets and clam rakes. He could probably even hitch a ride with someone heading out to the Wallops Island marshes.

And it was just as easy as that. Too easy.

* * * *

Arnold kept hoping someone would stop him, but why should they? He grabbed a plastic bucket and a clam rake, handed the guy behind the counter a couple of crumpled solars, and turned around to see Gus standing beside an older, slightly paunchy, gray-haired version of himself.

Gus sounded happy enough as he greeted Arnold. "This is my dad," he said.

Arnold shook his hand limply. "Pleased to meet you, sir."

"Gus is always talking about you," Mr. Benedict said.

Arnold shot a sidelong glance at Gus, wondering if that was true. Father and son were wearing high black wading boots with jeans tucked into them, along with T-shirts and ball caps, and they reeked of mosquito repellent. *The mosquitoes will eat me alive. But what difference does it make?*

"I don't think I've ever seen you out clamming before," Mr. Benedict said. He peered at Arnold. "Are you all right, kid?"

Arnold forced a grin. "Never better! And it's such a nice day, I figured why not give clamming a try?" His voice sounded completely false in his own ears. Surely they'd notice something was wrong.

But Mr. Benedict smiled and clapped him on the shoulder. "Want to make a day of it with us?"

"Well—"

"Not too good for us, are you, Arnold?" Gus was smiling, but there was a knife in his voice, as sharp as the ones you opened clams with.

Arnold stared at him. *You're the one who stopped talking to me!*

"Of, of course not," Arnold stammered. "It's, it's just that I'm supposed to be meeting someone out in the Wallops marshes."

Mr. Benedict frowned. "Wallops? Who but tourists goes clamming there? We're gonna drive down Route 13 and park over opposite Cedar Island."

That's kilometers away from here. You don't know how glad I am to hear that. "Yeah, but I really have to meet this person over by Wallops," said Arnold.

"Who?" said Gus.

Arnold opened his mouth with no clear idea what was going to come out of it.

Mr. Benedict was elbowing Gus. "It's obviously a girl," he stage whispered. Gus looked at his father, then at Arnold, then back again, saying nothing. Arnold shut his mouth.

"Wow!" Mr. Benedict shook his head. "You kids sure get around these days. When I was your age I barely knew what girls were. You want a ride anyway, Arnold?"

"Sure," Arnold said. He could swear he could hear his watch ticking.

They walked out to Mr. Benedict's pickup truck. "Afraid you'll have to ride in the back, Arnold," he said. "Gus, you want to keep him company till we drop him off?"

Gus frowned, then shrugged. "I guess so."

They sat down facing each other, legs splayed out. Gus eyed Arnold's feet. "You're going wading in those old tennis shoes?"

Arnold struggled to answer. He was distracted, watching the shops of Main Street pass by, peering desperately down Poplar Street to see if he could glimpse his own house. "No boots," he finally mumbled.

"Your feet are gonna hurt something awful. If you can even get around in those things."

Arnold said nothing as the car turned left and headed out onto the causeway.

The drive seemed to take forever. Arnold kept looking at his watch. Forty minutes to go. But then Gus's dad slowed and pulled over to the shoulder.

He leaned out his window and craned his neck around to face Arnold. "This close enough?"

Arnold tried to remember the map. Creeks that were sharp blue lines on it were muddy snakes half-hidden in the marsh grass out here. But that wide one over there seemed to loop back on itself like the one he had to look for. *An oxbow bend,* that was what it was called. It had been on an English test last year. *See how much learning your vocab words helps you in life?* He nodded and said, "This looks like the right place."

"Sure you won't come out with us to Cedar Island? My wife made more than enough food to feed all three of us."

"Nah, that's okay," Arnold heard himself say.

Gus's dad stepped out, opened the tailgate, and helped Arnold out. "Sure you've got everything you need?" he asked. "All I see is that bucket and rake."

"I'll be okay," Arnold said, shaking hands with his free hand. *I'm sorry I never got to know you, Mr. Benedict.* He couldn't afford the luxury of watching the truck as it pulled out in a spray of gravel and headed onto the mainland. *The gut's right over there, behind those bushes, isn't it?*

But before he'd taken ten steps off the highway Arnold was lost. Reeds taller than he was whipped at his bare arms, stinging him, and mosquitoes whined in his ears. He ignored the discomfort and pressed on. *Walk straight ahead or you'll end up going in circles.* Fifteen more paces and he was rewarded with a low *sploosh.* First one foot, then the other went into the mud halfway up his calf. When he tried to pick his left foot up the mud neatly sucked off his shoe. Walking on one shoe seemed pointless, so he took off his right shoe and threw it away, hoping the League agents had included shoes in the package of clothes waiting for him on the inner side of the fence.

The fence around the fusion plant. Where was it? Even if he did have the right gut, he could be following it the wrong way. He could see nothing but the bobbing heads of the cattails a good two or three feet above his own head. There was no fence in sight, and while he could hear traffic shushing by on the causeway he couldn't work out in which direction it lay. There was nothing to be done but hope he had chosen the right way, as he walked along the creek bed, probably doubling back on his tracks over and over thanks to the winding path it took.

He looked at his watch but it seemed to have stopped, so he took that off and threw it away, too, even though it had been a Bar Mitzvah gift from Mom. *What does it matter? It's not like she'll ever see me again and ask what I did with it.* He tried to slam his mind shut on the end of that thought. Never mind what was going to happen to *him*, never mind what was going to happen to a bunch of plant workers he didn't know (*and the people at the Interplanetary Base too, don't forget about them,* his conscience whispered, or rather roared in his inner ear), he was saving Jo and Alison, and maybe Kayleigh too.

And for all he knew the League agents were right and he'd be helping touch off the Revolution that would save people's brains from being melted by the n-net and rid the Earth of the Slugs and their helpers forever (*and not end up with the human race being hunted to extinction,* his conscience snarled).

There's nothing else I can do, he snarled back, *I have no choice, they've taken my choice away from me. Do you want them to kill Jo and*

Alison, to splatter their brains all over the walls? Well, do you? And his conscience fell silent.

So he pushed on, and after a turn around another oxbow bend he saw an ordinary-looking chain-link fence straight ahead of him, its bottom barely clearing the surface of the water. *Well, the Brooklyn guy said I'd have to dive.* He waded up to the fence, pinched his nose and ducked.

The gut was less than two feet deep, and sharp metal raked across his back as he crawled, a three-legged crab burrowing through the mud. He had a moment's panic when he tried to surface too soon and the fence caught at the bottom of his pants leg. To come all this way only to drown in the mud… but he managed to free himself with his clumsy thrashing, and only snorted a little bit of mud up his nose.

He dragged himself onto what passed for dry land and lay on his back in some crushed reeds until the coughing and choking passed. Then he stood up shakily, wondering how in the world he was supposed to find the white plastic shopping bag he'd been told to look for and, after that, the fusion plant.

A few more steps gave him his answer, because the cattail reeds ended in some sort of thick grass that was only waist high, causing him to duck instinctively so no one would see him.

Hey, look over there, it's the Creature from the Black Lagoon! He choked back a hysterical giggle and looked around until he spotted a flash of white a few meters away. Slogging over to it, he found two Value-Mart shopping bags stuffed with towels, clothes, and shoes. A third bag contained two one-quart bottles of water, a bar of soap, and a washcloth. Those guys had thought of everything.

A few minutes later Arnold looked almost presentable in a clean T-shirt, jeans, and sneakers. In the jeans pocket he found a saucer ticket in his name for a flight from Annapolis to Wallops that had landed at six o'clock in the morning. *Nice. So I can say I wandered off from the Interplanetary Base and got lost, if anyone stops me.*

The curved outer wall of the fusion plant was less than a hundred meters away, with the blocky rectangle of the office building where Dad and Mr. Nomura worked visible in the distance behind it.

Maybe Mr. Nomura is there now. Dad always kids him about what a workaholic he is. Arnold pushed the thought away started walking quickly toward the plant. Not running; nothing suspicious. Just a kid looking for his family—where could Mom and Dad have gone off to?

He wondered if he'd have to walk all the way around the building to find the loading dock, but he spotted it right away as he came to the edge of the marsh grass, which stopped abruptly along a ruler-straight border of neatly trimmed green lawn.

He crouched down and studied the concrete platform intently. It was several meters long and perhaps ten feet deep, with a metal warehouse gate partly rolled up on its far side. A tractor trailer was backed up to the edge of the dock, its back door open, but there was no one unloading it. In fact, there was nobody walking around back there at all.

Can it really be this easy? A corner of Arnold's mind was so terrified he was dimly amazed he hadn't wet his borrowed pants. But mostly he was numb. *Just do it and get it done. It'll all be over soon, one way or the other.* So he stood up and crossed the lawn as if he had every right to be there. No one challenged him as he hopped up onto the lip of the platform.

A few cardboard boxes were scattered around the open tractor-trailer when Arnold glanced in, but nobody was doing anything about them. The warehouse, which was bigger than the high school gym, echoed with his footsteps. An engine noise started up on the far side, making Arnold jump and look around wildly. It was a forklift, rolling away down an aisle between high-stacked rows of wooden crates. The blocky shapes on the sides of the driver's head had to be earphones.

Arnold let out his breath and looked for the stairwell on the left. There, through that door. Inside, the walls were painted piss-yellow and there were gray anti-slip strips on the edge of each step, just like at school. *Safety first.* Down half a floor, turn around, down another half floor, push the crash bar and wait for whooping alarms to go off and guards to come running from every direction.

But nothing happened. The basement he'd come out in was a maze of narrow foot-paths between hulking machinery that hummed like ten thousand refrigerators. Again, there was no one around, but where was the red control panel from Brooklyn's black-and-white snapshot?

There, on that wall. Find the button, flip up the lever, turn the switch on the side to the right as far as it goes. A red light started blinking in the upper right corner of the panel, but there was no change in the pitch of the humming all around him and no audible alarm.

Now what? It doesn't matter, I guess. He had fifteen minutes till that magnetic containment field failed. And then what would happen? *Probably it'll be like a hydrogen bomb going off. And I'm at ground zero. I'll never feel a thing.*

He knew now he'd been fooling himself about being able to run far enough, fast enough. He was actually glad, though—glad he wouldn't survive to face the guilt for the rest of his life for all of the people who were about to die because of what he'd just done.

Right now he felt nothing. No sadness and no guilt, just a faint hope the League agents would let Jo and Alison go. Though what kind of chance would his sister have, once everyone learned that her brother was the biggest terrorist in history?

Maybe Gloria would somehow find a way to take her to Jo's world. Yeah, she and Mom could move there when Jo went home to Gingo Teag. That would be nice. Arnold wished he could join them.

In the meantime, he realized he didn't want the last thing he saw to be that control panel. At least he could go back outside, feel the wind on his face, look at the water reflecting the sun.

He ran back up the stairs. Pushed the crash bar on the door to the warehouse and found himself back where he had started, but this time the forklift was headed straight for him. Luckily the driver was looking down at his instrument panel. Arnold darted out of the way and out the open gate, waiting for a shout, for running footsteps. But there was nothing.

Suddenly he was seized with a hopeless desire to run, to get as far away from ground zero as he could. He dashed across the lawn, making for the green marsh grass, and then he did hear someone call out. Calling his name. *Calling my name?*

He looked up and saw Mr. Nomura looking right at him from the other side of the chain-link fence. There was a nature trail back there, he remembered suddenly. A year ago his seventh-grade class had gone on a field trip through the marsh for biology class. Matt had gotten in big trouble when Mrs. Simmons caught him grabbing a baby blue crab out of the muddy water. Everyone knew you couldn't treat a close relative of Earth's protectors that way.

One of those protectors was standing beside Mr. Nomura now, in all his ten-foot, tentacled splendor. "Hello, Arnold!" he boomed. "What brings you out here on this fine day?"

Arnold broke into a stumbling, shambling run, bawling at the top of his lungs, "I didn't want to do it! They made me sabotage the plant! That guy shot Jo in the foot and said he'd kill her and they kidnapped Alison and—"

"What are you talking about, Arnold?" Mr. Nomura said as Arnold collapsed, sobbing, against the fence.

Sh'onk had pulled out a small boxy chunk of black metal, and for a moment Arnold thought it was a weapon and he was about to be turned into gas. But the High One was speaking into it in a frantic series of clicks and hisses, and Arnold realized it had to be a radio.

Suddenly Mr. Nomura understood. Arnold could see it in his dark eyes, which were suddenly surrounded by bloodshot whites. He grabbed the fence with both hands and shook it as if it was the bars of a cage he was trying to escape. Arnold had never seen him angry before, and the change was terrifying.

"You stupid kid!" he hissed, while the alien clicked and hissed, clicked and hissed, and waved its tentacles around. "Sh'onk can't save us! No one can! If you sabotaged the magnetic containment field, we're all going to die! Nothing can stop the laws of physics. You have just killed us all, and everyone for fifty kilometers around!"

40

Those men are back to kill us after all, Alison thought, as the pounding and yelling continued downstairs. But the pain in her arms and back was so intense she hardly noticed the new discomfort.

She was trapped in the attic, spread eagled and handcuffed by both wrists to a steel pipe that carried water from their rooftop solar heater. All around were Dad's heaps of musty old books. There was no light except a few stray bars of sunlight that came through a boarded-up window. In the corner Jo lay unconscious in a pool of blood.

She may already be dead, Alison thought. *Less work for those goons.*

She had gone back to bed after Arnold left the house and was starting to drift off when she heard someone knock on the back door. Thinking Mom might have come home early, she made her way back downstairs and opened the door. Two men she'd never seen before burst in, shoved her against a wall and started yelling and waving guns around. She had gone limp with fear, thinking they must be SCOD scum come to disappear her like they had done to Dad. It was only after the smaller guy left and the big bruiser stuck a gun to her head and put her on the phone with Arnold that she realized they must be from the League. And that was even worse, because there was no chance anyone would ever figure out who had kidnapped her or why.

She'd tried reasoning with them, telling them she was on their side and wanted to get rid of the Slugs and their helpers as much as they did, while thinking she'd rather the Slugs got rid of these guys first. Anyway it hadn't done any good.

"Just keep quiet and don't give us any trouble," the smaller thug said before he left. "Your job is to help us convince your brother to do what he already agreed to do. After that, we don't care."

Whatever they wanted Arnold to do must be really bad, since he hadn't seen any problem with burning down half of Chincoteague. They must actually want him to kill someone. She thought of pleading with them that he was only a kid, but what was the use? If they didn't have any qualms about burglary and kidnapping, they weren't going to listen to reason.

After hanging up the phone the big goon made her unlock the attic and wouldn't listen when she asked him not to handcuff her. "I won't move, mister, honest. I know you guys have guns."

"Shut up," he said, and hit her across the mouth so hard she tasted blood. He squeezed her breasts hard once she couldn't resist and she nearly blacked out from the pain. But that soon faded to a dull ache, and it was her back and arms that were in torment soon after the goon clomped back down the stairs, locking the trap door behind him.

The pipe she was handcuffed to was less than four feet above the floor, so she had to bend over and half-squat, on top of which her arms soon began to ache, the handcuffs started rubbing her wrists raw, and her spine turned into a red-hot cable writhing in her back. At first she had fantasies of breaking the pipe the thug had handcuffed her to, but a few hard tugs were enough to show her that her wrists would break first. After that she limited herself to finding the least uncomfortable position she could, but even that was impossible. If she stretched her legs out in front of her the pain in her arms became unbearable, but if she squatted her legs soon filled with pins and needles.

It wasn't long before she heard the back door open again, and the smaller thug's nasal New York accent grated on her ears. Less than a minute later the big guy returned holding Jo under one arm.

She was struggling weakly although he had both her arms pinned, and for a moment Alison felt ashamed at not having fought back herself. Then she got mad.

"Is this how you guys fight alien invasion? By kidnapping little girls?" Then she saw the red trail Jo was leaving behind her and began to scream.

Without a word, the goon walked over and punched her in the head so hard everything got dim and far away. Even through the haze she heard a loud thump. When her vision cleared Jo was lying on her side in a corner, her arms cuffed behind her back, and the goon was striding past her, though he paused and copped another feel that made Alison's head swim with pain and disgust.

"Come on, Frank, stop messing around!" the other creep called from downstairs. "We got less 'n forty minutes to get out of here!"

The big bruiser pulled away, winked, and started down the stairs.

"Wait, please unlock these handcuffs!" Alison begged. "You've gotta let me help Jo or she'll bleed to death!" Even in the dim light she could see something terrible had happened to Jo's foot.

"Oh, I wouldn't worry about that," the bruiser said. Only his head was still visible through the trap door opening. He was leering. "When your dopey little brother finishes doing his job, everyone on this jerkwater island is gonna be dead anyway."

A moment later the trap door slammed back into place and there was a metallic snap as the bruiser put the padlock back in place. Alison waited until she heard him clomp down the stairs to the living room and the back door slam behind him before softly calling Jo's name. The younger girl stirred and groaned as a car's tires screeched in the driveway.

"Jo, are you all right?" Alison said.

"The shorter one shot me in the foot," she said faintly.

Alison said a string of bad words, which made her feel better for a split second, as if she could really do anything to save herself and Jo. The younger girl's watery eyes were starting to close again. Alison said, "Jo, what did he mean about everyone on the island dying?"

"The fuchsia plant," Jo gasped.

"What?"

"Fuchsia… really pretty, purple and white-hot… atoms, big, big boom…"

Understanding broke over Alison as if a lightning bolt had struck right in front of her, and she began to shout and struggle against the handcuffs, stopping only when her throat hurt and her wrists were bleeding. Then she sobbed until her eyes hurt.

When the pounding and yelling started downstairs she thought the thugs had come back to kill her and Jo. Even the thought that the big bruiser might rape her before she died wasn't enough to make her call out again. *I won't give them the satisfaction. But I will give them a fight!*

There was a noise of breaking glass downstairs. Sounded like the kitchen. Then footsteps on the stairs, a voice calling out. A girl's voice. "Alison? Mrs. Grossbard?"

Alison's head whipped up. "Kayleigh! Kayleigh, I'm here in the attic! Jo's here too, she's been shot!"

There was a metallic clank as Kayleigh tried the padlock. She said a bad word.

"There are some tools under the bed in my parents' room!" Alison shouted.

A minute later there was another clank, followed by a loud crack, and Kayleigh was clambering up the attic stairs. She gasped when she saw first Alison, then Jo. Without a word she hurried over, knelt down, rolled Jo onto her back, and placed two fingers against her neck.

"Is she dead?" Alison's eyes filled with tears, but Kayleigh shook her head, took off her shirt, and wrapped it tightly around the wound in Jo's foot. "That oughtta hold while I go call for help. Then I'll come back and maintain direct pressure on it till the ambulance gets here."

"Where did you learn—?" Alison asked.

"Girl Scout first aid class. Where's your phone?"

"My parents have one in their bedroom. But Kayleigh, we have to stop Arnold! He's going to blow up the fusion plant!"

Kayleigh shook her head. "If he had done it, we'd be dead already. Something else must have happened. Just hang on, I'll get help." And she vanished down the stairs.

41

"You don't have to do this, you know," said Dad. "If you back out now and just accept the award from the High Satrap, no one would blame you."

Arnold shook his head, trying to clear the dizziness the past several days' crazy events had left him with. "I do have to do it, Dad. After all the terrible things I did—hurting Jeb Birch, burning down all those buildings, and then what I did at the plant—"

"Not only didn't you do anything wrong, you saved the town! Why do you think you're being honored?" Dad exclaimed. Ever since he'd suddenly reappeared at the front door three nights after Arnold's final mission, just when all the FBI and police and media frenzy had begun to die down, Dad's eyes had held a peculiar dark intensity. But now they blazed with a dark light that made Arnold think of black holes in space.

"I'm not a hero, Dad. I'm the opposite of a hero." Arnold's eyes welled up and threatened to spill over. "And I wish you and everyone else didn't insist on being here. I don't want to put you in danger again!"

"I can't speak for everyone else, but being here is *my* choice," said Dad. "You've had to face too much on your own. You don't have to do that now."

Arnold glanced over at Alison, who smiled faintly. Ever since her rescue she'd been acting kind of spaced out. *That's also my fault,* he thought.

Jo rolled herself closer in Mom's old wheelchair and said softly, "Don't worry, Arnold! I'd like to see them try to manhandle you. I'll give them a kick they'll never forget!" She grinned and pointed at the enormous cast on her left foot.

Dad said quietly that the real protection Jo could offer was that they wouldn't dare do anything to a girl in a wheelchair, not with the tri-vee cameras rolling, but all Arnold could think about was that her injury was his fault, too.

How could he have had anything to do with those gangsters, even if they did say they wanted to fight the High Ones? He'd felt nothing but relief when he heard they'd been killed in a gunfight with the Coast Guard after trying to make their escape on their motorboat.

At least I know Mom's safe, Arnold thought.

She had gone to Baltimore and taken Grandma and Mr. Wineman somewhere out of town in case everything went very, very wrong. But not before Mr. Wineman called and said, choking on tears, that Arnold was a hero for "sticking it to the man," whatever that meant. Another unjustified compliment that weighed on Arnold's conscience.

Gloria stepped out from behind the library counter, flanked by Mr. Wolff on her right and Sh'onk on her left. She was wearing an eye-hurting collection of bright silks, but her left shoulder was bare except for a startling fall of intricately braided red hair.

Maybe the bad guys will be so busy staring they'll be distracted at the crucial moment, Arnold thought, smothering a giggle.

"We're here with you too, Arnold," she said. "Whatever happens, we'll stand by you. My hairy friend Wolff, too—even if he does look a little sheepish."

"For that pun alone, you old witch, you ought to be burned at the stake," Mr. Wolff groaned. She patted his hand and pinched his cheek.

"I've been in touch with others who think like me, Arnold," Sh'onk said. "They'll be watching, and when the moment comes they'll do whatever they can to make sure you stay on the air."

An unsmiling man in a gray suit and dark sunglasses popped his head in through the emergency exit. "Are you ready now, Mr. Grossbard? The High Satrap is waiting for you."

Arnold did a double take when he realized the guy meant him, not his father. He swallowed once. "Yes sir," he said, and started forward.

Of all the chaotic thoughts running through his mind, the foremost was the question of whether Kayleigh would be waiting on the platform that had been set up behind the high school. He hadn't seen her since leaving her behind at the old hunting lodge on Assateague Island, six days ago now. When he glimpsed her sitting beside her father, staring straight ahead, her arms folded over her crisp white Sunday-morning-go-to-church blouse, he went limp with relief.

For a moment he saw nothing else—not the crowd of Very Important People on the platform, not the tri-vee technicians and makeup people, and certainly not the huge crowd that was jammed into the schoolyard, spilling out into the road, halfway around the corner to Main Street, waiting to see the biggest thing that had happened in Chincoteague since the Civil War.

Arnold didn't care about any of that. He only had eyes for Kayleigh. *How come I didn't realize before I'm in love with her?*

He kept asking to talk to her, even while the FBI and police and everyone else kept hollering questions in his face, and even in all the excitement of Dad coming home, but by the time he found out what had happened it was too late: Kayleigh's mom had taken the car and left Kayleigh's dad the night he kicked Kayleigh out, and no one knew where Mrs. Scott was when Kayleigh was found and instantly called a hero for rescuing Jo and Alison (*which was justified, in her case*), and Mr. Scott had come to the police station for a tearful (on his side) reunion with his poor daughter whom he forgave in front of everyone for running away… and she hadn't shown up in school for either of the two days Arnold himself had been back, and now here she was, sitting beside her smug-looking father.

And he was as helpless to save her as he had been to save parallel-world Hailee, or to help Jo return home. *Yeah, some hero I am. What a joke.*

"They're only making a big deal out of me because of Peach Bottom and Diablo Canyon," Arnold had said to Gloria yesterday afternoon.

It was a dismal, rainy afternoon. The whole country, the whole world was mourning for all the people who had been killed in New York and California on Saturday, when the League attacked nine other fusion power plants at the same time as Wallops Island. Seven of the other would-be saboteurs had been stopped before they could get into the plants. All were teenagers.

And far from touching off a revolution against the High Ones, all they had done was make people angry and afraid. Pierre LaWayne had been on tri-vee Wednesday, boasting that twice as many people now wanted to join SCOD as already were members.

Gloria had been sitting staring out at the rain, her chin propped in her hand. She hugged Arnold as he cried. "No one else tried to undo what they'd done, Arnold. No one else regretted it. That does make you a hero," she said.

"What kind of hero almost kills thousands of people? If I hadn't happened to run into Sh'onk and Mr. Nomura, I would have been one of the biggest mass murderers in history." A thought struck him, and his hand went up to his mouth. "That was a *yellow-wood*, wasn't it?" he whispered. "Somewhere very nearby, the path turned the other way, and I—"

"You were only there because those men threatened to kill Jo and Alison, Arnold," Gloria said quickly. "You had made your mind up that what they'd asked you to do was wrong. Intentions have to count for something."

"But the night before, I wasn't sure *what* I was going to do. I thought killing all those people might be okay if it helped rid the Earth of the High Ones. I thought—"

Gloria put her hands on his shoulders. Those green, green eyes bored into his. "It's true, you had that thought. You had that desire to kill, to avenge your father and Kayleigh and because you think the Winged-Thinkers are just *gross*. And you'll have to live with that, with the evil spirit that you have in your heart, as every human being does. But you also knew that that desire was wrong. You refused to go through with it. There's no yellow-wood about that. Not about the things that matter, the things of the heart. Only about the accidents and serendipities of the world."

Arnold didn't know what *serendipity* was, but he did know what he had done. What he was guilty of. "I *did* go through with it," he insisted. A memory he'd been trying to bury burst to the surface of his mind, and he covered his face with his hands. "Mr. Nomura said when I changed my mind and ran to warn him, it was already too late. The explosion must actually have happened—only somehow you reversed it. You cheated."

Gloria pulled Arnold's hands away from his face, forcing him to look at her. She smiled a little. "I knew you'd figure that part out. But you don't know the whole story. Your 'spider plant' is much more than it seems. It is the visible aspect of a *chessed*, a creature of lovingkindness, and Arnold, I didn't give it to you. It insisted that it belonged with you. It is a being much more powerful, and much more wise, than me." She was crying silently, perfectly spherical crystalline tears spilling from her eyes.

Arnold wanted to hug her, to give her comfort, but he didn't have the right.

She continued, "And one of its powers, by no means the greatest, was to generate an Asimov field."

"An Asimov field? Like Isaac Asimov?"

"Yes, like the great Isaac Asimov and his novel, *The Gods Themselves*. Have you read it?"

"No."

"Well, the *chessed* can create bridges between worlds that make my own tunnels look like the fragile sand castles they are. I can't reach worlds where the laws of physics, the rules of the game, are different than they are here. But it can. It can even get around the huge Gray Zone that Jo's dragonet accidentally created."

"Mr. Nomura said that the explosion couldn't be stopped, because of the laws of physics."

"But those laws aren't as inflexible as they seem. The *chessed* tapped a world where the strong nuclear force, the power that holds atomic nuclei together, is just a little bit weaker than it is here. And it brought just enough of that world to Wallops Island to soften the nuclear fusion reaction so that the weakened magnetic containment field could still keep it in." Gloria smiled through her tears. "It was a delicate thing, far beyond my powers. A little more of that other world's rules, and all the atomic nuclei on this planet—in this entire arm of the Milky Way—would fly apart. Which would be very inconvenient. But—" she squeezed his shoulders—"it wouldn't have worked, it could never have worked, if you hadn't given the warning in time. What you did *mattered*, Arnold. What you did at that moment made all the difference—not just for Chincoteague, but perhaps for the entire world. People are right to call you a hero."

Now Arnold was crying again. "If the world depends on what I do, we're all sunk. It's a good thing there is an infinity of worlds—in some of them, the screw-up named Arnold Grossbard was never born."

Gloria squeezed Arnold's hands. "That's despair talking, and self-pity. Anyway, you're wrong—there is not an infinity of worlds, not in the way you mean. And what happens in one world affects the others, which is only one reason why it matters so much what choices we make. There was a Hasidic sage once, Rabbi Simcha Bunim of Przysucha, in Poland, who taught that every person should live life as if he carried two pieces of paper with him always—one that says, 'The world was created for me,' and the other saying, 'I am but dust and ashes.' Try to remember that, Arnold. Both parts."

Arnold wrinkled his forehead. "But that's a contradiction."

Gloria sighed. "You four-dimensional beings are so limited. I wish I could make you understand. Instead, all I can tell you is you must be strong—Kayleigh and Jo and Alison and your parents and everyone else are going to need you again before long."

Everyone is relying on me. There had to be someone better to say what had to be said. Namely, any other human being on the face of the Earth. But it was Arnold who was being praised for saving the town, Arnold who was being clapped on the back and his hand pressed by the High Satrap, who looked like a wax museum statue of himself, Arnold in whose face the tri-vee lights were shining, Arnold standing in front of a microphone that would bring his voice to millions of people across the United Satrapy and maybe billions around a conquered world full of brain-damaged n-net users… a world that might be about to start a new war worse than anything that had gone before. Arnold squeezed his eyes shut for a moment against the lights and saw afterimages of the rubble and skeletons in the other Hailee's world. So he had a choice… but it was no choice, not if he wanted to be able to live with himself afterward.

"Thank you, most exalted High Satrap," Arnold began.

The High Satrap ducked his chin down into his dark blue suit jacket, and a grin broke out across his stubbled face. "Aww, shucks, Arnold, you can call me just plain Mr. President."

Arnold almost gulped at the honor. "Th-thank you, Mr. President. I hope what I did shows everyone that blowing things up is no good." The High Satrap patted his back again. "That hate only causes more hate, whether you hate the Winged-Thinkers or a Jew like me."

People in the crowd began murmuring. The High Satrap smiled even wider and combined another pat on the back with a little shove.

Oh, no you don't, Arnold thought, and braced his feet.

"Hate and violence are not the way to fight back, even though the n-net causes NINA in everyone who uses it."

The man in the dark sunglasses made a grab for Arnold, but Sh'onk knocked him off the platform. There were shouts and scuffles breaking out around the tri-vee cameras.

"Let the boy speak!" someone yelled.

"Even though the Winged-Thinkers stole our mental power to make the Bubble Drive work, they also did a lot for us. They're just as *human* as we are," Arnold said loudly.

Glass shattered, one or two of the lights went out, and someone screamed. The High Satrap had vanished.

Arnold wondered if his voice was reaching anyone but the people right in front of him. Over the growing roar of the crowd, he cried, "To the person sitting in darkness, we must bring light, not fire!" The micro phone toppled over, someone grabbed Arnold by the neck and he fell over backward in a scrum of hands and feet and kicking shoes. But instead of being knocked out as he expected, he heard a snarl and screams of terror. He sat up just in time to see a gray blur with white fangs chasing several men in dark suits and sunglasses. The crowd boiled away.

"Where are they all going?" Arnold wondered aloud, watching them head out on Hallie Whealton Smith Drive toward Main Street. There was nothing out there but a park and a marina with a chain-link fence around it. Then he spotted a little figure in blue frantically shaking a gate in the fence until it gave way and the figure made a flying leap onto a police boat that was already pulling away from the dock.

"Looks like the President got away by breaking into the water gate," Gloria said. For some reason this caused her to break into peals of laughter.

Arnold looked around. Besides Gloria, Dad, Alison, and Jo in her wheelchair, there was no one left on the platform. He stiffened. *Where was Kayleigh?*

While everyone else looked at each other Arnold jumped off the platform and took off in the direction of Kayleigh's home, his heart hammering in his chest. Far behind him he could hear Jo shouting at him to wait, she couldn't keep up in this damn wheelchair, but there was no time. He ran up to the white picket fence around the yard just in time to see the front door slam shut on a struggle. There were shouts and sobs, followed by a sickening thump from inside. Arnold jumped the fence and was at the door in seconds, only to find it locked.

He pounded on it with his fists, and nearly tripped when it swung open and he found himself staring at a double-barreled shotgun. "I ain't gonna tell you but once, go away and never come back, you filthy terrorist kike," Kayleigh's father growled, adding several swear words. The gun barrels wobbled.

He's drunk, Arnold realized. *He couldn't face the tri-vee cameras and the High Satrap and everyone sober.*

"Mr. Scott," Arnold began. There was a bang inside the house, and Arnold glimpsed Kayleigh darting out the back door.

Kayleigh's father swung around, fumbling the shotgun, which fell to the floor and went off with a deafening roar. He lunged for it, touched the hot barrel, dropped it with a curse and ran after his daughter, closely followed by Arnold.

Kayleigh's dad was gaining on her, shouting that he was going to kill her for being a terrorist slut, and Arnold was falling behind as they ran back toward the high school.

Out of the corner of his eye Arnold glimpsed huge shapes lumbering toward the island along the causeway over the marsh, and an enormous circular shadow passed over him as he ran for all he was worth. It wasn't good enough; he had always come in dead last at the fifty-meter dash at school, and even if he could reach Kayleigh before her father did, they were both going to die—they were all going to die—in a few moments, when the Slugs' counterattack reached Chincoteague and turned it into an exact copy of the one where Arnold had met the other Hailee. Nevertheless he kept running. It was the only thing left to do.

Arnold didn't actually hear the loudest noise ever to have struck Chincoteague Island. One moment he was running and the next he was flat on his back, staring up at the sky.

Enormous green shapes were pouring out of a jagged, fiery hole the size of a thundercloud, swooping and diving and flapping wings bigger than those of the jet airplanes he had seen once on a school trip to the Smithsonian Air and Space Museum in Washington. The downdrafts from those wings kicked up gales that slammed into the small fleet of saucers that had been heading toward the island, tossing them like fall leaves into each other.

One tumbled out of the sky like a dropped Frisbee, hitting the lead tank on the causeway edge-on. The tank teetered for a moment before falling into the bay with what must have been a tremendous splash, swamping the police boat the High Satrap had fled to. The tank behind it braked too late, and within seconds the causeway was blocked by a wall of twisted metal three stories high.

Where Arnold lay, dust and sand and leaves blew every which way. He shouted but couldn't hear his own wordless cry as a dragon the size of his house settled slowly to the ground in front of him. It didn't much resemble Assateague Ashley, having a long thin snout like an alligator's and four legs thicker than tree trunks, but Arnold barely glanced at it, because his eyes, like everyone else's, were riveted on what the dragon was carrying on its back. Or rather, *who* it was carrying.

Mrs. Vivian Purnell stepped daintily onto the grass, took a clothes brush out of her shiny black handbag, and cleaned off her mid-calf-length black skirt. Nodding satisfaction, she dropped the brush back in her bag and strode over to where an out-of-breath Jo was struggling to her feet using the toppled-over wheelchair as leverage. When she spoke it sounded like she was talking underwater, and Arnold realized his eardrums must have ruptured.

"Young lady," she said to Jo, "you are in very big trouble!"

"I'm sorry, Mum," Jo said, and began to cry.

"We can discuss your punishment when you get back home. Even this herd of dragons from the Flower World, whose leader was most fortunately able to speak the King's English when they paid a visit to our world last week, can only hold open the interdimensional hole they have blasted for a few minutes, thanks to the damage you did."

"Drove," said Gloria, who had already clambered onto the dragon's back.

"Excuse me, Gloria?" Mrs. Purnell said.

"A group of dragons is a drove, not a herd. I thought you read all of the *Wrinkle in Time* books after Jo finished them, so you should know that."

Mrs. Purnell blinked. "I would appreciate it if you did not correct me in front of my child, Gloria. It is the most appalling bad manners."

Before Gloria could apologize, a large gray wolf bounded into the schoolyard, blurring as it went until it turned into Mr. Wolff, who leaped nimbly up behind Gloria, grabbing her around the waist.

Gloria half-turned, raising an eyebrow. "Need a lift, Gibur?"

"Don't mind if I do, m'dear. Don't half mind," he grinned.

"Well, everything is in order then, I see," Mrs. Purnell said, yanking Jo's arm. "Come on then, you miscreant."

"But Mum, I haven't even said goodbye to everyone!"

"No time," Mrs. Purnell said tightly, "the hole is going to close!" She turned to face Arnold, Alison, and Dad. "I do thank you for taking care of my fool of a daughter. Now I am afraid we must—"

An ear-splitting shriek broke the air. Arnold clapped his hands over his ears, groaning at the pain, as Kayleigh dashed past, screaming, "Take me with you! Please, I beg you!"

Her father was right behind her, charging like a bull with his head down, screaming curses and threats.

Mrs. Purnell calmly let go of Jo's hand, took a half step back, and, with a single roundhouse punch, knocked Mr. Scott out cold. "You can take the girl out of the Liverpool docks," she said, primly rubbing her knuckles. "And who are you, my dear girl?"

"Kayleigh saved my life, Mum!" Jo said.

"I suppose you must join us, then," said Mrs. Purnell, helping both girls up onto the dragon's back.

"Wait—I want to come too!" Arnold cried, clambering to his feet.

But Dad and Alison grabbed hold of his arms as Jo mouthed "sorry" at him and Kayleigh smiled sadly, a smile that would always haunt Arnold's dreams. Gloria and Mr. Wolff waved as the dragon flapped its wings once, twice, and rose up into the air, spiraling higher and higher with its kin until it vanished into the rapidly shrinking hole in the sky.

42

A blinding white light like a flashbulb lit up the night sky, followed a few seconds louder by a loud bang. Arnold flinched and looked away. Faint cheering followed, but Arnold turned his gaze on the ocean waves, focusing so fiercely on the breakers they began to blur. He didn't want to watch the rest of the fireworks across the water on Chincoteague, no matter how many or how colorful they were. After all, he'd snuck out here to Assateague on purpose to get away from the celebrations.

He was almost sure of having the whole wildlife refuge to himself tonight, as the biggest Fourth of July party in many, many years drew people to Chincoteague from kilometers around. Even the absence of the guest of honor, the Hero of the Second American Revolution, wouldn't put much of a damper on things, he was sure.

And to think that three months ago, he had been the lowliest, most despised student at Chincoteague High! "Hero," Arnold said aloud to a breaker that crashed at his feet in a storm of twinkling foam. "Arnold Grossbard, Hero."

The only thing he liked about the sound of those words was how easily they were erased by the ocean's roar. There was nowhere else he could go to escape from his own unjustified fame. Even leaving the planet wouldn't help, not with the biggest settlement on Mars being renamed Arnoldsburg, and the recently repaired mothership of the Winged-Thinkers' fleet newly rededicated as the Arnold Samuel Grossbard Center for Interspecies Cooperation (Sssssssssss-sh'onkelos, Chairbeing).

Chincoteague, of course, was the worst of all; he still couldn't believe he'd managed to talk the town council out of renaming the island after him. There had been nothing he could do to stop them from setting up memorials, complete with bronze plaques, at the site of each building he'd burned down, not once they'd found out he'd done it. *Can't they understand the horror and shame I feel, every time I have to walk past one of those markers?*

When Jeb Birch solemnly put out his scarred hand and shook Arnold's at that ceremony back in June, Arnold had just had to take it and not burst into tears or go down on his knees and beg forgiveness the way he'd wanted to. And that was worse punishment than anything SCOD could have done to him if they'd caught him just weeks before.

The only mercy was that school had been cancelled for the rest of the year, or he would have had to put up with being a bigger idol *than the entire football team put together*. When he'd happened to pass by Hailee on Main Street, she'd winked at him, Bill Cherricks be damned. He could have her as his girlfriend. Or Taylor Fields, or Scarlet Fontaine, or any girl on the face of the planet.

But he didn't want them, he wanted Kayleigh, the one girl who was forever beyond his reach. If Gloria had been around, she could have told him that he was suffering from that well-known paradox of the human heart, wanting only what it can't have, while scorning that which is in its grasp; but she wasn't there to pose her impossible riddles and be disappointed in him.

Nor would Arnold ever again have to put up with Jo's bossiness. All he had left of her was the pocket watch she'd given him to spy on the saucers, which she'd told him once was a gift from her dead grandmother that her mother would be appalled to learn she'd given away.

He took it out of his pocket now and stared at its glimmering hands in the gathering darkness, thinking about time and all the worlds and all the links between them that only Jo could have explained to him.

He was all alone. Even Alison wasn't around anymore to call him turd-breath and stupid-head; she had cashed in on her fame by starting class at Olympian University three months early, along with her friends the "Thomas twins" (and Sharon's stranding in this world also weighed on his conscience, even though Shaniqua had cheated a little to help her get into the most famous college in the solar system).

"At least we won't have to live in Arnoldsburg," he had overheard Sis telling Mom, and he hadn't blamed her one bit.

As for his parents, it was as though the disbanded and banned SCOD had kidnapped them and put worshipful lookalikes in their place. He could stay out all night and they wouldn't say a word. If he decided to go out with Hailee, he could probably hang out with her in his room, *with the door closed*, and they'd never disturb him.

All his wildest dreams had come true, but they were worthless because when he looked at the orange sun setting behind the fusion plant at Wallops Island, he saw it turn to blinding white, saw Chincoteague Bay turn to steam in an instant as the homes, forests, and marshes of Chincoteague and Assateague burned to ash and blew away, taking thousands of lives in an instant… all because of a choice that he had made, a choice he could never take back.

"Intentions have to count for something," Gloria had said, but what had his intentions really been, before the *chessed* soothed him to sleep the night before the "mission?" The *chessed* must have worked on his mind, tipping the balance toward refusal… so he didn't even deserve the credit for his own change of heart. And then the *chessed* had intervened again to stop the worst from happening, but now it had vanished, leaving an empty flowerpot behind.

He had nothing that could take away his guilt, or wipe out the knowledge that he'd been ready to commit murder on an unimaginable scale. In a book about the invention of the atomic bomb that he'd found in Gloria's abandoned library, he learned that at the moment of the first nuclear explosion in New Mexico in July 1945, the physicist J. Robert Oppenheimer had recalled a Hindu scripture: "Now I am become death, destroyer of worlds." He couldn't get away from that, or around it, or under it or over it. And he didn't see how he could live with it.

It was now full dark over the ocean, and the wind off the water was chilly after the warmth of the day. Arnold turned away with a shiver, hugging his bare arms as he shuffled up the deserted beach toward the dunes. Maybe he'd see if he could find Hailee walking around town after the fireworks. He could pretend he was with Kayleigh—their names rhymed, after all—and make believe he was really the hero everyone kept insisting he was, and not a murderer-in-all-but-fact who deserved to die.

As he reached the crest of the dunes and started down the far side into the darkness, he was thinking that he might bring Hailee out here if he could find her, that walking with the girl of his childish daydreams in the quiet of the nighttime island might somehow soothe his spirit for an hour. "If she deserves to be with a killer," he murmured aloud.

"EEEEEEE-ITH-ILLL-RRRRR!" screeched a voice like a rusty hinge.

Arnold stopped dead in his tracks. Something big was moving, flopping around in the sand a few yards to the left. He fumbled a flashlight out of his pocket and clicked it on.

"No way!" he breathed after a stunned moment.

Broken bits of shell littered the sand around… something… as big as a medium-sized dog. It didn't look like Assateague Ashley, and it didn't look like the creature Mrs. Purnell had ridden bareback. It might have been a cross between a giant iguana and a pelican, with an exuberant purple coxcomb, giant glowing red eyes, and a green pouch under its lower jaw that looked big enough to hold a bag of groceries. The creature opened its mouth to reveal a double ring of razor sharp teeth. "Noooo-aaaaaaaaaay!" it mimicked.

Arnold turned the flashlight aside so as not to hurt the dragon's eyes. "Are you intelligent? Do you understand me?"

"AAAAAAAAND-EEEE!"

Arnold thought for a moment, then took a partly crumbled granola bar out of his pocket and offered it to the creature. Its tongue shot out of its mouth, nimbly curled around the granola bar, stuck to Arnold's palm for a moment, then retracted. Arnold could see the morsel bouncing around inside the pouch.

"I'll call you Andy," he decided. It seemed like a good start.

* * * *

Less than ten meters seaward, as three-dimensional space is measured, but quite a considerable distance away along an n-dimensional axis, Kayleigh sat alone, staring at the breakers spreading out along the coral atoll. Although it was nighttime, the water glowed green with bioluminescent creatures, lighting up the beach as bright as midday. Shaggy palm-like trees taller than the loblolly pines back home cast dancing shadows on the water. The jungle at her back was alive with strange noises, most of which were drowned out by the surging tide. That was just fine with Kayleigh.

Whenever she needed to be alone, she asked Jo to ask Ir'gassaphet to take her to the Flower World. The fact that she wasn't telepathic and couldn't communicate with him was just fine with her, when she was in one of those moods that nothing could help but to be the only human being in an endless rain forest full of enormous scaly creatures.

Six weeks had passed since she'd made that choice she could never take back, and the first bloom of excitement at living in the strange new world of Gingo Teag was starting to wear off. She had her own room at the Purnells', Jo's big brother Tom's old room, with a cozy bed and a view of the bay.

Mum Purnell was really strict—she would never let Kayleigh get away with the kind of sneaking around she had done with Arnold back in Chincoteague—but she bought Kayleigh the nicest new clothes and did her hair and cooked her favorite breakfast of bacon and eggs over easy with her legendary tea, though she grumbled that that was a "breakfast fit for barbarians."

Dad Purnell and Jo took her over to Assateague Island practically every day, where the boring old beach and marsh became something new and magical thanks to Ir'befunzu and her giant family. Sometimes Jo had them do private air shows just for her.

Luckily school was out for the summer, so Kayleigh didn't have to adjust to that right away, though Mum Purnell drilled her every day on "proper," which was to say Britishy, spelling and grammar. That wouldn't be the hardest part when she had to start class again, though.

No, the hardest, strangest thing would be having to make friends all over again with people she had known all her life, but who weren't the same people at all, like Madeline Marbury, who gave her a puzzled smile and gently pushed her away when she ran into her on Main Street and tried to give her a teary bear hug. Kayleigh was going to miss the old Maddy, though she could be awfully mean sometimes.

She missed Arnold a lot, too, but she was also relieved to be away from him—they'd done some really bad things when they were together, things she didn't want to think about. She missed Mom so much it hurt, and there was a hole in her heart at the thought that she'd never even be able to talk to Kyle on the phone again. She missed her dad, too.

That was messed up, but there was no getting away from it. She missed *everything* about home, even the strip searches at school. Well, maybe not those. There was no way of knowing what was going on back home, whether what Arnold had done had made any real difference, whether he and everyone else were safe or not.

"If only there was some way of finding out," Kayleigh sighed.

A creature that might have been a distant descendant of a stegosaurus, except that its armor-plates were delicately filigreed works of art, poked its streamlined head out of the jungle canopy behind her and said mildly, "It seems likely to me, begging your pardon, Miss Kayleigh, that your troubles stem from an inadequate philosophical perspective on your situation. Didn't one of the greatest of your primate poets write, 'there is nothing either good or bad, but thinking makes it so?'"

Kayleigh put her head in her hands and groaned. *Oh no, why did I have to talk to myself out loud?*

"Idealissssm, Idrasssssian?" said a creature that might have been a ten-meter-long boa constrictor—if a boa constrictor was bright scarlet and had twenty pairs of legs, nightmare fangs, and a razor back. "You ought not to teasssse a poor, ssssslow warmblood with ssssuch consssssepts."

"Not so, Ts-sssarianusss," the sorta-stegosaurus replied in the same mild tones, "for I was not discussing the broader ontological nature of reality with the poor, confused primate, but merely her apprehension of such—"

Kayleigh took her hands off her face and clapped them over her ears. "Will you reptiles please SHUT UP with the philosophy, already? Or at least chatter in your own language?"

"But it would be intolerably rude not to include a fellow sapient in our conversation," Idrasian said, in shocked tones.

I know Iddie's only trying to be nice, but these guys have manners so delicate, they make Mum Purnell look like a slavering cavewoman. "It's all right! I give you permission not to speak in English! I need to be alone with my thoughts!" Kayleigh cried.

Then she really cried, cried real tears until her throat and chest ached. There was a light touch on her shoulder, and she whirled around to see Jo leaning on a stick, her weight on her good leg. "It's getting awfully late. Ready to go home now, Kayleigh?" she asked softly.

Kayleigh dabbed her eyes with her sleeve and nodded. "Let's go, Sis."

ACKNOWLEDGEMENTS
AND NOTES

I wish to thank my son Daniel for suggesting the character of Mr. Wolff, and for an important discussion of the philosophical implications of parallel worlds for the concept of free will; Carla Coupe, my editor at Wildside Books, for tireless and invaluable effort polishing the manuscript; the D.C. Speculative Fiction Writers' Group, for workshopping Chapter 1; and my wife Jackie, for her inexhaustible love and patient support, advice, and help.

I have taken certain liberties with literature and history. Mark Twain never wrote a novel about the brutal American war against those Filipinos who were foolish enough to think our rhetoric about liberty in what Secretary of State John Hay called our "splendid little war" against Spain was meant to apply to *them*, though Twain's essay "To the Person Sitting in Darkness" condemned this and other horrors of the twilight of Western imperialism. I also must beg pardon of the shades of Charles Dickens, whose *Oliver Twist* is set in London rather than Philadelphia and whose novel *The Mystery of Edwin Drood* remained unfinished at his death; of Matthew Arnold, who was inspired to write his deeply depressing poem on the beach at Dover, not Nantucket; of Alexandre Dumas *père* and Jules Verne, who never coauthored a novel (more's the pity); of Franz Kafka, who never made it to Israel despite his early interest in Zionism; and of course of the Beatles, who never came together again.

www.ingramcontent.com/pod-product-compliance
Lightning Source LLC
Chambersburg PA
CBHW020211260626
47156CB00002B/324